That Summer in Malta

To Roberta,

With Best Wishes,

From *John ...*

September 2010.

That Summer in Malta

John V Lloyd

That Summer in Malta

Spiderwize
3 The Causeway
Kennoway
Kingdom of Fife
KY8 5JU
Scotland UK

www.spiderwize.com

This is a work of fiction. Names, characters and incidents are products of the author's imagination. Any resemblance to persons living or dead is entirely coincidental.

ISBN: 978-1-907294-74-7

Acknowledgements

A special "Thank You" to my friend, Catherine MacDonald, for the long hours she spent typing immaculately and her patience as chapters were endlessly redrafted. She managed to decipher my handwriting which, had she handed it to a pharmacy, could have been mistaken for a prescription!

I am particularly indebted to another friend, retired English teacher Tom Lee, who sacrificed so much free time in amending grammar and punctuation and, without whom, I would never have known what a transferred epithet was!

Thank you also to the Publishing Company, Spiderwize, for their kindness and expertise, Bob Kirk, Jim Cannon, Brian Devlin, Richard Lloyd, Brian Reynolds, Bob Savage, Bill Williamson, Margot and David MacDonald, Martin Scerri in St Julians Malta, Desmond Lloyd, Gerry and Anne Marie Harran in Bridlington, First Choice holiday reps in the 1990s at St George's Park Hotel in St Julian's Malta, especially Marie Louise, Belford Travel Dalgety Bay, DDS staff at Ninewells Hospital Dundee for the peace to write the book, St Patrick's Church in Sliema, Ramona McAuliffe at the Sunflower hotel Qawra, for help with the Maltese words, Tony Leszczuk for help with the Polish words, Linda Gerletti,similarly, for help with the Italian words,Dalgety Bay library, Dunfermline Athletic FC and Tigne Primary School in Sliema, Malta. HMRC in Edinburgh, SKY TV in Dunfermline, and the China Ruby Restaurant in Dalgety Bay.

The Author

John V Lloyd grew up on the Island of Malta, when it was a British naval base, prior to Malta's independence, and attended A C S Tigne Primary School in Sliema. He has been there many times since and one suspects he was never happier than when taking a party of tourists around the Maltese islands. He knows the small island nation, its language, religion, culture, history, geography, sport, humour, politics, food and drink, climate, little idiosyncrasies, etc., and his affection for the country and its people permeates this book. Former Foreign Secretary, and novelist himself, Douglas Hurd, once remarked that one should only write about a topic you know and that is, clearly, the case here. Having co-authored Scottish Football Today (1987) and Scottish Football Today 2 (1989), he wrote the Scottish best-seller The Giant That Awoke (1990), later serialised in The Sunday Mail, and Simply The Best (1996). Born in Dunfermline, John is an avid Pars supporter. He takes an annual break in Yorkshire. It is no surprise then that, of the main characters, David is a Dunfermline Athletic fan while Sarah and Jenny hail from Bridlington. A graduate of the Universities of Stirling and Aberdeen, John taught for many years and his telling of a good story derives from that. He has a prolific output as a freelance writer. With a grown up family in Dalgety Bay he is a close neighbour of the former Prime Minister, Mr Gordon Brown, and author Iain Banks. John is now completing the fantasy novel, Carol At Christmas, due out next year.

Chapter 1

Is the Blue Lagoon blue or green, bluey green or greeny blue? David put down his note pad and looked up to the clear blue sky for inspiration. But not for long. It was a sweltering hot day and even with his photo chromic lenses, the blinding Maltese light soon had him blinking and looking back at the clear turquoise water. It's turquoise, he decided, wrote it down and sucked his pen thoughtfully. It was still a week till the first tour party arrived for '18-130 Tours' and he would hand his first group his tourist itinerary and whet their appetite for their week ahead. He watched as a handful of holiday makers enjoyed lunch on the deck of the red hulled pleasure boat, Captain Morgan, tied up about 100 metres away. Two or three of the youngsters were swimming with rubber rings and lilos and keeping an eye out for the jellyfish which, from time to time, made an unwelcome appearance in peak summer to the little island of Comino. Two little motor boats selling ice creams and the other Coke, 7-Up, Pepsi, Fanta and the local drink Kini, manoeuvred between them.

David repositioned his large red towel over his legs. He was not going to be caught out by the sunburn or sunstroke which had dogged him in his first year as a courier all of 8 years ago when he left University in Stirling. He began to unwrap his ham sandwiches and flicked off the sand and a few ants which usually accompanied a picnic on a Maltese beach. He repositioned his ludicrous red "I love Malta" hat to protect his exposed neck and reluctantly pulled down his sleeves. It was after 1pm and approaching the hottest point of the afternoon. Gingerly, he walked a few paces to where his 7-Up can was cooling in the water, where the sand met the sea. The flip-flops were little protection against the jagged rocks beneath. He picked up the can, ran it along his face, then opened it and drank it in a few gulps. He sat back down, finished his sandwich and picked up 'The Times of Malta'.

Suddenly there was an almighty splash and a cry of "Oops sorry!" David folded the sodden paper and watched as a blonde long-legged young lady attired in a blue bikini stopped her doggy paddle, stood up, seemed visibly surprised the water only came up to her waist and then removed the snorkel whose blue colour exactly matched her bikini, and added "I just didn't see you. In fact, without my specs I can't see a lot, actually!"

"Dr No circa 1962," muttered an intrigued David under his breath.

The girl, who looked about twenty, shook her hair and looked around the rocks.

"Have you lost something?" David asked helpfully.

"I thought I was sitting on this side of the lagoon," she replied "but maybe not. I am always forgetting where I leave things. Somewhere I've got my towel, purse, suntan lotion, sun bloc and above all my clothes and specs. I am so short sighted, you see".

"Here," said David patting an unusually flat piece of rock. "Have a seat. You can use my spare towel and get dried". David handed her it and put his other one across his swimming trunks to disguise the obvious pleasure he had in meeting her. "I am David". He held out his hand.

"I'm Jenny. Pleased I am sure." She sat down, dried her back and grimaced as she rubbed her visibly sore back with its red skin peeling off.

"You've a lot to learn about not staying out in the heat of the summer sun I think," David added. "Mad dogs and Englishmen and all that".

Jenny gave a blank look. "What does your Dr know?"

"My Dr is back home in Scotland. How do you mean?" David asked.

"You said your Dr knows as I walked up the rocks."

"No, oh I see, no. It's an old James Bond film. Ursula Andress walked up the beach in a bikini looking sensational and you, well, walked up a beach," he enlarged rather shyly.

"Looking sensational?" the girl quizzed him.

"Maybe." beamed David. Good looking girls were not usually so easy to speak to he reckoned. "How short sighted are you?" he enquired.

"Well I can't see my stuff lying on the rocks on the other side of the lagoon," she explained.

"Too far away?" David proffered.

"No, bloody red boat in the way," she laughed.

David laughed too. This was going well. "Did I tell you about the heavy polar bear in the Antarctic?"

"No," the girl replied quizzically.

"Well it broke the ice," David beamed.

"Do you have many corny jokes?" Jenny asked putting the towel down.

"Oh I could bore you all evening," David suggested. And would too, given the opportunity, he thought. "Now point to where you reckon your stuff is and I'll go and get it. You're lucky there are so few folk around if your purse is there."

David passed her his towel, undid his shirt and dived in with a large splash. He could, of course, have simply waded out but here was a chance to impress. He was already quite bronzed after four weeks on the island and hoped she would admire his physique such as it was. The Blue Lagoon is not exactly large and it didn't take David long to locate her stuff just a few metres away on the other side of the inlet. The meal had finished on the Captain Morgan and many of the tourists had taken to the clear turquoise water too. David carefully walked back along the rocky foreshore avoiding lizards as he went. It was mid afternoon and even his new sunspecs struggled to cope with the glare.

"Do you want a lager? Only one Maltese pound," the man on the drinks boat shouted up to him, almost despairingly as so few tourists were there to buy some and those on the Captain Morgan, of course, had their own supply.

"I'll take two," David shouted back. "I'll nip across and get my wallet. Oh, and there's no such thing as Maltese pounds."

The man smiled knowingly.

David speeded up, in so far as you can on jagged rocks.

"You didn't take long," said Jenny. She took her sun bloc out of her bag, took out her specs, seemed to think better of it and put on her sunspecs instead.

"I'm off to get you some Hop Leaf lager," David announced, picking up his wallet. "It's time you immersed yourself in some local culture!"

"Is it cold?"

"Will be. These motor boats carry fridges and ice boxes." The bronzed weather-beaten man had two bottles ready and took their caps off.

"Are you not a tourist?" he asked.

"No, I live in St Julian's. I come here every summer," David explained. "So I know the Maltese pound trick."

The man continued unabashed. "Where do you work?"

"The 18-130 club"

"Danny's lot?" he frowned.

David saw his expression. He rubbed a cold bottle on his face. Some lager fell on his hand and he licked it up. "You know Danny?"

"Everyone in Malta knows Danny. He's got his fingers in every pie. So he's in the travel trade now?"

"Yes I'm a holiday rep."

"You speak Maltese?"

"Some, enough"

"Good luck!" the man smiled.

"Hurry up with that drink!" Jenny called.

David laid out his towel, drank in one go and then took his suntan lotion out. "Have you just arrived in Malta?" he asked.

"Yeh, yesterday."

"With family?"

"No."

"Friends?"

"No."

David paused, "Boyfriend?"

"Nope"

"Hard to imagine you haven't got one," he added gallantly. This is going so well he decided.

"I'd one back in Yorkshire but I'm here three months so we ended it."

"Three months, are you dead rich or what?"

"No I got myself a job."

"Doing what?"

"Trainee holiday rep."

David sat up. "You're not the new trainee with 18-130, are you?"

"How on earth did you guess that?" she asked, intrigued.

"Danny said I'd a new trainee to meet. Gosh, what does my horoscope say about today? It must be kismet."

"I don't kiss folk the first time I meet anyone," Jenny pointed out putting a white peak cap on.

"No it's kismet, it's fate," David answered knowledgeably. So she doesn't kiss anyone at first. He lay quietly for a few moments deciding what to infer. "Okay, so you must have met Danny?"

"Yes, a few weeks ago in London. I saw an ad in the 'Telegraph Travel' page for a travel rep and I wanted to see the world, so here I am."

David did wonder what her qualifications would be, but given all the reps Danny had ever employed were young and good looking and invariably useless, and lasted about two weeks as a travel rep before working in one of his bars or nightclubs, he didn't have to speculate too long. "Do you speak any languages?"

"Yes, French, German and Italian," Jenny replied.

"Well, Italian will help," he assured her. "Do you know Malta at all?"

"No."

"Do you know the Med?"

"No."

"Have you read up about either?"

There was a long pause and Jenny's face had got redder despite the sunburn already there. "Do you know Italian, Jenny?"

Jenny turned away.

"Do you?"

"Ok, no. I lied, I lied to Danny."

"Did you say you'd been abroad or a holiday rep before?"

"Yes"

"And have you?"

"No"

"Oh Jenny." David tried to stifle a grin.

"Why are you laughing?" Jenny asked.

"Look, what job have you had?"

"I worked in Thorvik Woollies as a shop assistant."

"Thorvik?"

"It's a village near Bridlington. It has more incest than any other town in England, our paper says. It's twinned with itself."

David laughed.

"Ok I made that up" Jenny admitted.

"I'd guessed," David assured her.

"I was trying to get you off the topic of how useless and unprepared I am."

"Not at all," said David. "I can instantly see why Danny chose you."

"Enthusiasm?" she suggested.

"That as well," David agreed.

"Can you put suntan lotion on my back?" she asked. Jenny lay face down and undid her bra.

A siren sounded on the Captain Morgan and the ship sailed serenely out of the lagoon.

"Oh shit!" said David, "It's two hours till the next one. I was so busy chatting to you, you nut. Don't worry I'll just do a text and arrange a boat back" he said rubbing her back. I am not complaining, not complaining at all he thought!

"What's Danny like?"

"Arthur Daley."

"Who is Arthur Daley then, does he work for the same company?"

David was starting to feel distinctly old at all of 30!

"I've heard of Christian Dailly" she suggested.

"A newspaper?" David wondered.

"A footballer," she explained and made a face.

"I know. I do know football. I support Dunfermline. Anyway, no, he's a wheeler dealer. He has the travel company, a couple of bars, a nightclub, ten-pin bowling alley, two buses, speedboat, and that's just what I know after six years."

"Sounds impressive, how did he get so rich?"

"About 40 years ago, he met Carmen and she had exactly what Danny wanted."

"Looks, charm, personality?" Jenny suggested.

"A lot of liri!" David answered. "You'll soon learn he's quite an influential person on the island."

"Must be worth knowing," Jenny said, watching a couple of fish swimming in one of the rock pools. The two little drinks boats spluttered into action and accelerated away. "Are we alone now on Comino?" she asked, just a little apprehensively.

"Yes and no," said David as he beckoned her down to the water's edge to pick up two more 7-Up cans. "There's a Swiss-owned hotel on the other side of the island beside the one really good sandy beach. The locals can't use it."

"So the Swiss family are robbing some," Jenny replied instantly.

"You are clever with words," David replied as he opened his last two soft drink cans. "Have you seen the world at all, Jenny?"

"Well I got to London and apart from that Leeds, Sheffield, York, Whitby, Scarborough and Bridlington where I come from."

"You told me Thorvik."

"That was my joke, remember?"

"Oh the team are going to like you. Hey, are you staying in our apartments at St George's Bay?"

"I moved in yesterday, are you there too?" Jenny asked.

This is going better than I imagined, David reckoned. "Yes there's me, and Mark who is gay, and Laura this week."

"How do you mean this week?" Jenny asked.

"Forget it. I shouldn't have said this week."

"But you did." Jenny looked worried, even if her sunspecs obscured her face.

"I mean, well," David hesitated, "some don't have a long shelf life, put it that way."

Jenny didn't look much the wiser really.

"When did you actually get in, yesterday?" he asked.

"At an ungodly hour, Air Malta flew us into Luqa airport at six am. I was zonked."

"You pronounce it Luha," David explained. "In Maltese, you don't pronounce the Q."

"So if I stand for a bus I wait in a hoo," Jenny suggested.

"Hey that's clever. I'll use that one," David chuckled. "I will teach you Maltese though."

"Is it difficult?"

"A lot of it is Arabic like suq is a market, and marsa a harbour, but there are easier words which are also Italian like grazzi and skuzi. It's a pity you don't know Italian, actually."

"You say 'actually' a lot, don't you?" Jenny remarked.

David nodded "We all use particular words a lot and you'll find your tourists will either point it out or mimic you, so watch out."

"So I've to meet Mark and Laura, is that it?"

"No, there's a lovely middle aged lady called Theresa Thinn, who acts as a rep if you have a larger number of elderly people on the trip, because she'll take them to look at churches and architecture."

"Sounds riveting," said Jenny, who had thrown a crust of bread from David's sandwiches at an army of ants who were now carrying it along the rocks.

"You don't mind creepy crawlies do you?" David asked, now adopting the role of Malta expert.

"I don't mind these ants and lizards," Jenny replied, fanning her face with the 'Times of Malta'. "What else is there?"

"Cockroaches can be pretty revolting actually."

"There, you said it again!"

"What?"

"Actually!"

David ignored the interruption like any good teacher. "And you may want to consider a mosquito net and spray."

"If I don't get some food soon I'll be eating creepy crawlies like in 'I'm a celebrity get me out of here'!" she moaned.

"When did you eat last?"

"Since I arrived," Jenny contributed, "I've only had a Big Mac meal at that McDonalds in St Julian's. I've little money till I get my first week's pay and I wasn't sure where to go to buy food."

"Heavens, St Julian's is the food capital of Malta. It's a rich area, you see, a suburb of Sliema, the largest English-speaking town. The people there are so well off, folk in Malta call them Tal Pepe or poseurs. Anyway St Julian's has all the foreign restaurants like Italian, French, Indian and Chinese. There are also loads of fast food restaurants. Well you found McDonalds, and like in Spain you can get your usual egg and chips, pie chips and beans and so on."

"I'll learn a lot with you around," she said flatteringly.

Suddenly Jenny stood up and picked up her bag. "And now I am going to get my bikini off. Please turn round David."

"There's no one else here," David replied.

"You're here," she insisted.

David grinned and looked at a Maltese fishing boat passing the island.

"Why do these boats all have eyes at the front?" she asked.

"The boats are called luzzus and, by tradition the eyes ward off evil spirits," he explained.

Jenny gritted her teeth as her blouse and short yellow skirt made contact with her sunburn. "Okay, you can turn round now!"

"Do you want to join me for your evening meal?" David asked. He held his breath. Go on say yes, he hoped and crossed his fingers behind his back.

"That would be lovely. I'm so glad to have met someone nice already," she said.

Nice, he thought.

"I was so bored in that little apartment yesterday evening but now I've Mark, Laura, Danny, Carmen and who else?"

"Theresa"

"Theresa to meet, sounds fun."

The couple picked up their belongings and walked along the craggy rocks down to the little sandy beach. David didn't lose the opportunity to hold her hand but, as she reached the sand, she pointedly let it go.

"I don't see another pleasure boat coming in," she pointed out.

"You're going back in style just wait and watch."

Barely five minutes had elapsed till they heard the sound of a speed boat approaching. It was a light blue colour and the helmsman steered it in such a way it caused a spray which had David and Jenny scurrying up the beach.

"Alright, alright, Tony, stop showing off!" David implored.

Tony brought the boat to a stop. The bronzed middle-aged cap-wearing and almost toothless Maltese grinned broadly.

"Good afternoon Miss," he said and doffed his cap. "Sabiha!" Tony said to David.

"This looks fun!" Jenny exclaimed sitting in the backseat with her bag and towels on her lap and kicking off her flip-flops.

"St Julian's, please, Tony, and don't spare the horsepower!"

Jenny stood up, fell back in her seat, regained her balance and held her hand out to Tony.

"Pleased to meet you I am sure. I'm Jenny Waring."

Tony slowed down, turned round, then withdrew his oil-stained hand. "Skuzi, I am sorry, miss. My hand is dirty, you understand. Danny's boat."

The expression 'Danny's boat' meant a lot to those who knew him but Jenny looked surprised.

"I am Tony Feruggia. I drive Danny's motor boat, run his coach, work in his bar and nightclub. Danny, he good man, I pray for him."

"I am impressed," Jenny said. "You do a lot for him."

"Danny gets me fallen women. I happy," Tony added.

"Come again?" said Jenny incredulously.

"Tony drives women to Valletta hospital when they fall and sprain an ankle or break a wrist at his nightclub," David interjected. "It's on three floors and has a winding spiral metal staircase which is quite a challenge if you are drunk." David enlarged on the theme. He gave Tony a look. David leaned back on the back seat as the boat roared south towards Malta.

"This is cool," Jenny said.

"It's a roasting hot day and it's not even June till next week," David corrected her.

"No, I mean this whole thing is wicked. I am like, wow! What's that large island behind us?"

"You'll have to know all these things before we get our first passengers in seven days," David remarked. "That's Gozo. It is greener and hillier than Malta. Malta has no grass."

"Danny can get you grass" Tony offered, waving at the passing Gozo ferry.

"Isn't Gozo where the Ghostbusters came from?" Jenny asked.

"I wouldn't know," said David who'd taken his floppy hat off as it was in danger of ending up in the Med!

Half an hour later, the boat sped into little St George's Bay and within a few metres of the small apartment block Danny owned. David put a note into Tony's hand, and then held Jenny's arm as she stepped into the water and waded ashore. "Sahah!" Tony shouted and waved as he pulled away.

As they passed reception at the St George's apartments, David enjoyed the cold feel of the marble floor beneath his feet. "Any messages?" he asked a young dark-haired Maltese girl at the desk.

"Le," she replied.

"Right, let's go up to the second floor and you show me which room is yours," David told her.

The block was on two floors. Downstairs there was the reception area, large lounge, games room, a small bar, launderette, a small swimming pool and a store. Upstairs there were a dozen bedrooms. As Jenny and David walked along the corridor the smell of fresh paint battled the smell of the sea outside.

"You will find Malta has the most remarkable smells," David said authoritatively as Jenny stopped at room eight, put down her bag, took off the sunspecs and fumbled for her key.

"This is mine!"

As they entered, David instinctively felt for the fan switch and the three blades on the roof swung into welcome action sending some writing paper on the single bed on the left falling to the marble floor.

The girl kicked off her flip-flops and picked them up. "I was so bored last night I was writing home already," she explained. "I'd make you a coffee, I brought it with me, but I've no milk."

"I'll show you where the store is downstairs shortly. Now come and I'll explain the view from your window," he said opening up the Venetian blind. He blinked as the early evening sunlight streamed into the little narrow room.

"Did I get the smallest room because I am the new recruit?" Jenny asked.

"All the rooms are identical," David explained. "Danny wanted as many folk in his apartments as he could fit in. Next door you've got my room, then Mark, then Laura in that order."

"What about the other rooms?" Jenny asked.

"The receptionists take two of them, Tony whom you've met, Steven the other boatman cum coach driver cum bartender, plus Danny's friends and family on holiday from the UK. Anyway, you've got your wardrobe, desk, chair, bed, TV, radio, fan and small fridge and the bathroom and shower are at the end of the corridor."

Jenny's attention had been drawn to a horse and cab clip-clopping along the narrow road which separated the apartment block from the small sandy beach where kids hired a pedallo.

"That's a karozzin, they are really old. Now the huge hotel complex on the right is St George's Park complex and on the left the new five-star one, where Man Utd and the Italian world cup squad stay."

"Wow," said Jenny. "I must meet them".

"Now I'll nip into my room, get cleaned up and then we can go grab a bite to eat at St Julian's," he said.

I wonder how long it will take Jenny to realise Mark is anything but gay and she gets off with some footballer at a local nightclub, he pondered.

Half an hour later, Jenny met him in the foyer. She had a pink low cut top, short light blue skirt, bare midriff and pink sandals. She was gazing out at the large garden at the back with its palm trees, goldfish pond, garden seats, cactus and even a sundial. "The smell of vegetation and the sea and the sound of locusts are amazing," she said. "You don't get it in Scarborough."

"Hardly," David concurred. "Okay let's walk along the road and we'll be at Danny's small restaurant in a matter of minutes." And Mark won't be there. He's at his bar at the bowling alley at this time of day, David conspired.

"You know it's after 6pm just, yet it is so dark," Jenny marvelled. "As I sat in my room last night, I didn't really notice. Oh listen to those locusts, amazing."

They walked past a series of small restaurants and bars and a couple of nightclubs and the bowling alley where David looked anxiously about for Mark and then entered the restaurant which displayed 'Danny's' in a neon sign.

"What a menu!" Jenny smiled. "Let's see, egg and chips; fish and chips; pie and chips; sausage, egg and chips; bacon and chips - you know, I think I've got the drift."

They walked down three steps into a cool little dining room with a bar and six tables on each of which an HP sauce bottle was prominently displayed. The table cloths didn't look very clean and, as Jenny sat down, she removed a laden ashtray. "I am tempted to ask if I can have a meal without chips but I won't bother," Jenny decided.

She was aware that a middle-aged man dressed in a bartender's uniform which struggled to cover his beer belly, but strangely wearing a chef's hat, had entered the room.

"Ah, David, welcome, welcome. I am so glad you return. I told you the food poisoning wasn't bad at Danny's!"

David's heart sank. Steven's sense of humour was an acquired taste. "And who is your beautiful lady?"

"I'm Jenny Waring," she replied.

"Well I'm Steven, I work here." He took her hand and kissed it.

"I'd guessed that," Jenny replied.

David kept looking nervously out of the restaurant window, partially covered by a lace curtain, in case Mark appeared but, so far, there was no sign.

"Tell her you've had no food poisoning," David implored.

"Yes tifla sabiha!" he replied. "It was a joke. I know David well. He nice man. I joke."

Jenny didn't look too reassured but picked up the small rectangular menu which had leaned on the sauce bottle. "I'll have chips with ...."

"How about fenek?" Steven suggested.

"Which is?"

"Rabbit"

"No. What's lampuki, is it lamb?"

"It's fish," David pointed out.

"Give me egg and chips. It's like being at school dinners," Jenny said with a sigh.

"We'll have two lagers," David said as Steven crashed through the swing door back to the kitchen.

"Smash crash!" echoed David.

"Have you got onomatopoeia?" Jenny asked, her hand hiding a smile.

"No, it cleared up with the ointment," David rapidly replied.

"What happens if you need a doctor for real here?" Jenny asked seriously.

"There's one at the huge St Julian's complex."

"Have you ever seen him?"

"I saw him in a local bar last week. He said, David, I've not seen you in ages. I said, I know, Dr Misfud, I've been ill."

David had hit the target. Jenny's face lit up. "Okay, what was wrong?" she asked.

"A bad dose of onomatopoeia," David got in quickly. "I could play this game for ages. We'll get on great on our guided tours."

"If it's you and me," Jenny pointed out. "What if it is Mark and me and Laura and you?" she inquired.

That's what I fear, David thought. "We'll find out at tomorrow's team talk" he suggested glumly.

"I'd be glad if it's you. You're fun" Jenny added, unsolicited.

"Here come your egg and chips," David announced, suddenly perking up no end. "Have you noticed the photos on the wall at the back of the bar?" he asked, stealthily cleaning a fork on his khaki shorts.

"Gosh!" said Jenny. "There's Danny and the Queen, Danny and Tony Blair, Danny and Mother Theresa and …….."

"Yasser Arafat, the Pope, Britney Spears, Bill Clinton, President Gorbachev, Elton John, Richard Branson and the Maltese PM," Steven added, cleaning a tumbler.

"What a man!" Jenny exclaimed in awe.

"Don't for heaven's sake tell him, but if you look carefully it's all done by trick photography in Steven's photo lab," David explained.

"You'd me going there for a moment," Jenny conceded.

"Of course Danny own my lab, he good man," Steven pointed out.

"Does he have his fingers in every pie?" Jenny asked.

"No need food poisoning, not here," said Steven looking suddenly more serious.

Jenny gathered her thoughts. "Where are Laura, Mark, Theresa, etc, this evening?" Jenny asked, suddenly changing the subject.

"Mark is on the bar at the Karaoke. Laura is helping at the nightclub; Danny has her doing the snooker tables. Theresa is a teacher and only helps us part time so she'll be at home in Sliena marking homework."

"Do you want an ice cream?" Steven asked.

"Chocolate," said David.

"Strawberry," said Jenny.

"Straight away," said Steven, then, "David, I must tell you about my spare tyre"

"Don't be ashamed," said Jenny helpfully "Put an apron over it and I am sure no one will notice, I didn't."

There was a pause. "Tifla, I meant on Danny's luxury coach. It's punctured." He went through the revolving door to the kitchen.

"Oops! I did it again."

"Thank you, Britney," David chuckled.

By 9 pm, Jenny and David had reached the coffee and After Eight mints. A family and a couple sat at two other tables. Outside, a fair number of people were making their way to the nightclub and karaoke bars.

Suddenly, David's worst nightmare materialised. The door swung open and into the restaurant came a handsome dark-haired sun-tanned young man, who looked about twenty-two, with a light blue open shirt, St Christopher medallion and light blue trousers, blue sandals and perfect teeth which glinted like a toothpaste advert.

"Hi David. Hi Darling!" He strode up to the bar, patted Steven heartily on the back and put his arm round his shoulder. "Who's the bird?" he asked.

"She's Waring," Steven replied.

"I wouldn't say that," Mark added with a hearty laugh.

"He means her name," David explained. "May I introduce Jenny Waring, my new assistant courier," David said.

"Pleased to meet you, I am looking forward to working with you," Jenny added innocently."

"Yes we are all tireless," said Mark, pulling up a seat.

"That's what I meant when I offended Steven accidentally," Jenny explained.

Mark threw David a quizzical look.

"Don't go there," David warned.

"Whose team are you on?" Mark asked.

"It'll be Jenny and me, Laura and you," David butted in determinedly.

"I thought Danny would tell us tomorrow," Mark said helpfully, "so it could be you and me after all. Can I have a drink, Darling?" Mark walked back to the bar.

"He's rather open about it, don't you think? And Steven is so much older," she whispered, holding a napkin to her mouth. If she looked carefully at the photos she would notice they were stamped "Darling's photo lab, Sliema", David knew, and mentally made a note to keep her away from the bar. He knew it would be difficult to keep up the white lie about Mark but this had truly been a godsend!

Jenny finished her coffee. "Why don't we head up to the karaoke bar where Mark works or to Danny's nightclub and meet Laura? They sound cool," Jenny suggested. She rummaged in a pink purse for some change but David put up his hand.

"It's my treat and, in any case, we get a discount and you've to get paid yet."

"Where are you two off to now?" Mark asked returning with a glass of wine.

"I'll show Jenny the nightclub."

"And then we'll call in at your karaoke," Jenny added.

It may not have been the tourist season yet but the street was busy that Thursday evening with young Maltese couples. The buildings seemed to shake with the noise from the nightclubs and discos. "I can hear the locusts and smell the palm trees and the sea," said Jenny, hardly able to disguise the excitement in her voice. "Which is Danny's club then, David?"

David took her hand as they weaved their way through the traffic jam where every car, many of them very old, seemed to hoot its horn - but all were gridlocked. Some contained suntanned young men carrying large football flags who hung out the windows and shouted at Jenny.

"Don't be ashamed," David advised.

"I wasn't!" Jenny reassured him. 'Struth! She's lapping it up, David realised, a little disheartened.

Suddenly, having passed Danny's Ten-pin bowling club, they came to the nightclub.

"It's the Gemini," David said, pointing.

A group of dark-haired teenagers were all lined up in a well disciplined crocodile. David flashed a pass at the steward and ushered Jenny in.

The nightclub was on three floors. On the crowded first floor a bar was doing a lot of business. Up a metal spiral staircase on the second floor, hundreds were dancing under a huge disco light. At the side of the long narrow room was another bar.

Up the staircase Jenny and David leapt, two at a time. "On this top floor a few folk dance but there are also snooker tables. Here we'll find Laura Bakewell - as in tart."

Jenny looked surprised. Beside one of the snooker tables stood a tall brown-haired girl who looked about 23 or 24. She too had a bare midriff, low cut white top which showed off an ample bosom, a short white skirt and laced up boots. She seemed to be deliberately standing under one of the roof fans.

"Hello Laura, come and meet Jenny!" David roared above the din.

"Lenny who?"

"Not Lenny, here - Jenny!"

Jenny moved to shake her hand but Laura held up her hand, smiled and said, "Hi! I am exhausted. I've been on the game all week," she said, nodding at the snooker table.

"You would be" said Jenny sympathetically.

"Would you like sex on the beach, you two?" David asked with a grin.

"I'll have a vodka and orange," Jenny replied.

"Not with you," Laura said

"Then make it an advocaat snowball."

"Thanks, David. Do you get discount for drinks too?" Jenny asked.

"Of course," David replied. "This is our new recruit, Laura."

"Oh you poor soul, Penny," Laura smiled.

"Jenny"

"Sorry Jenny," Laura corrected herself. "It's the din."

"I can't hear you," Jenny leaned forward.

"She says it's the din," David shouted. "I'm going to take Jenny to Mark's Karaoke bar. We'll see you tomorrow at Danny's introduction."

Laura returned to chalking a cue. David and Jenny had their drinks and headed back down the staircase. David was well aware that many of the young men were admiring Jenny. Again he held her hand, though she let go at the foot of the stairs.

"The karaoke bar is next door," David said.

As they entered, Mark was at the bar watching Italian football on a wide plasma screen. There were only a few tourists in the bar and, although Tom Jones' "Delilah" blared out and the words appeared on screens above a small stage, no one was actually singing. David bought a couple of drinks and then Steven, minus his chef's hat and apron, came in and joined them.

"Is that you finished?" David asked.

"Yes, 10 pm. That's it. Danny said to come here and get two loose women."

"Toulouse women," he suddenly interrupted. "Danny has some French tourists coming to Steven's restaurant later," he explained.

"If you say so," Steven said having his lager.

"Danny just said they were cheap."

"He said they were chic," David, increasingly agitated, added, and kicked his shin under the table.

"If you say so," Steven replied, rather bemused.

"Can I do a song?" Jenny asked "I am having such a good time. Can I do Unchained Melody?"

"Hey Mark, can she do Unchained Melody?" Steven shouted.

"No problem, Darling!" Mark shouted back. He flicked a switch.

Jenny took the mike at the stage and sang to an audience of seven.

"She's good, your lady. You fancy her, yes?" Steven asked.

"I only met her a few hours ago on Comino," David pointed out, mouthing the words on the screen. "But how long will she be here? Heaven knows what she'll make of Danny, and few girls stay more than a week or two when the other jobs here offer so much more and better hours. Yes, she really does seem nice. Yes I do fancy her but no doubt Mark does too – the double of Tom Cruise and the bain of my life!" he laughed.

Jenny accepted the muted applause, bowed and returned to her seat.

"What did you make of Laura then?" David asked.

"I could hardly have a conversation in that racket but she seems nice. You all do," she replied.

I am off to a good start, David decided. "Look, it's getting late. I'll walk you back to your apartment," he suggested.

"Buena sera," Steven said.

"Night night," Mark mouthed above the din from the bar.

Even at 10.30 pm the heat hit them as they left the air conditioned bar and went out into the busy street, narrowly missing a motor scooter wending its way past the queue of cars.

"I love the sights and sounds and smells, it's all so different," she exclaimed as she held his hand.

She took my hand that time. David's heart leapt. "Yes it's a bit different from Yorkshire!" he agreed. They walked beside St George's Bay as the waves splashed off the pedallos all lined up for the morning's hire. The sound of folk music and dancing wafted out of the downstairs lounge at the apartment block. "Shall we look in?" David asked.

A Maltese folk dance troupe of eight dressed in traditional costumes were entertaining a handful of elderly tourists at the bar.

"Hello David, all set for tomorrow?" A lady of about 60 left the bar, put down her glass of port and gave him a hug.

"And are you Waring? I'm Miss Thinn. Theresa Thinn."

"I'm Waring, Thinn. Sorry, I'm Jenny, Miss Thinn. Call me Jenny." She stumbled and looked embarrassed.

"Danny said he had a new girl starting. You'll love it. Don't let Mark chat you up."

"He won't. I mean it's not likely in the circumstances, is it?" Jenny said innocently.

David screwed his face up anxiously. Theresa frowned quizzically. "Join me for a drink." The proper schoolmarm commanded rather than suggested. "What would you like, Waring?"

"Just light clothes in this heat. Oh sorry, I see what you mean."

David couldn't believe how nervous Jenny had become. "I'd like sex on the beach," she stammered.

"But not with Mark!" Theresa said provocatively.

"I'll have a lager," David replied. He beckoned Jenny to sit on an armchair as the Troupe completed their act and passed a hat around. He put a 5 LM note into the hat.

"That was generous!" Jenny gasped.

"No it wasn't. It's Danny's bar, apartments and folk troupe. The tourists follow suit and Danny pays me back. Never fails! Look, remember Tony and the boat? He's the lead dancer."

Tony gave them a wave as the Troupe counted their collection and headed out into the night. Judging by their facial expressions it wasn't that wonderful. Theresa returned with the drinks.

"I thought you'd be at home doing homework, Theresa," David said, making conversation.

"I've got it all done and I've put up some posters and maps and the projector for Danny's talk in the morning. I couldn't find a modern map of Europe so I've brought one of my school history ones. It won't matter too much. Danny won't even notice! What I haven't got is a large map of the island, but we can find one in the morning. Are you looking forward to joining us, young lady?" Theresa asked more pleasantly.

"I can't wait!" Jenny said. "David's told me all about Danny and the team and I am looking forward to working happy with you all."

"Happily – it's an adverb," Theresa corrected her.

Jenny looked blank.

"An adverb adds to a verb." David, out of Theresa immediate line or vision, winked and Jenny smothered a grin.

"Have you worked with Danny long?" Jenny enquired.

"Oh yes. It supplements my meagre teacher income. We go back a long way, even went to the same primary school in Sliema in the 1950s. We both have one Maltese and one English parent and even they knew each other."

"He sounds a real character according to Tony, Steven, Mark, Laura and David. Oh, did I get all those names right?"

"You did," David confirmed.

"He is, as you'll find out tomorrow," Theresa replied. "Right it's time I was home. Sahah!" Theresa got up, put on a shawl and headed out of the reception.

"I'd a teacher at school like her. She gave me the willies," Jenny pointed out, emptying her glass.

"Time for bed," said David. David walked her along to her room. "Get a good night's sleep. You've a busy day ahead," he said.

"Thanks for such a nice welcome" Jenny smiled. "Good night."

David sat on his single bed and enjoyed a coffee. His window was open and a welcome breeze blew in from the seafront. The parp of an occasional car horn could be heard in the street outside. He glanced up at his pin board where he had blue-tacked photos of all the precious teams. He'd met some very attractive girls as reps but, somehow, Jenny seemed different. It had been a lovely few hours since the chance meeting at Comino. Certainly she seemed a nice person and good-looking but he felt an unusual desire to protect her and look after her as she had this unusual air of vulnerability. I must get to know her better, he decided, and fend off Mark as usual! He switched off the bed head light and turned in. He lay thinking about her till he dozed off.

The bright sunshine always filled the room from the early hours and David got himself up at 7.30 am, washed and shaved. There were already a few tourists taking a dip in the warm blue Mediterranean at St George's bay. I'll have breakfast and go and get Jenny, he thought. He nipped down to the kitchen, passing the reception and had some toast and coffee and some orange juice. Then, quite excitedly, he went up to her room.

He thumped the door. No reply. Either she was already up or a heavy sleeper. The latter would not be good news for a prospective holiday rep. Suddenly he felt a tap on his shoulder.

"Bonju," Jenny said. She was already fully dressed in the same clothes as the night before but with her hair washed, smelling gorgeous from her perfume or deodorant and with suntan lotion fully applied. Her sunspecs were on top of her head.

"Eh, bonju. You've learned a Maltese word I see," David said admiringly.

"Yeh, Maria at reception told me. David, how do I get some food and will you tell me where to find the launderette?"

"Simple, it's behind the kitchen. We'll go and get you some toast now."

Half an hour later they both sat on the wall overlooking the bay. "This is paradise on earth" Jenny said, now with her sunspecs on. "Hey do I have to see Theresa today? She scares the pants off me with her grey hair, half rimmed specs and her manner, and she's so old," Jenny said, stressing the last two words.

"She'll call in but it will be Mark, Laura, Danny and me mainly," David replied waving a mosquito away from his face. "How's your sunburn now?"

"Not as bad. I must wrap up more." Drat! David thought.

At 9 am, David and Jenny sat in a small conference room. A handful of seats were placed in front of a screen beside a desk. Both Jenny and David had to shade their eyes as the glare of the sun reflected off the white screen and dazzled them. On a trolley to the right sat a coffee urn and a plate of biscuits. David looked incredulously at the 19th century map hanging on the wall beside the desk.

At 9 am on the dot Mark and Laura arrived together. Like David, Mark had his khaki shirt and shorts and a red "18-130 holidays" badge beside a Maltese cross. Laura wore the same though the badge, held on by studs, seemed destined to detach due to her heaving bosom.

"Where's the gaffer?" Mark asked, pouring two coffees.

"He's a busy man is Danny," said David. "He'll have been up at the crack of dawn wheeling and dealing, you know what he's like!" Suddenly David noticed an ugly large cockroach climbing up the old map. It dallied in Northern Italy before picking up speed and entering Switzerland. The fan on the roof made the map flap from time to time and the cockroach had slithered into Eastern Europe when Mark took off a flip-flop and splattered it all over the Balkans with a crunching sound. Mark sat down again.

"Revolting-looking thing," Laura said.

"Mark or the cockroach?" David pondered.

At that moment the diesel clack-clack of Danny's car could be heard. A door slammed. Then in came the man himself.

"Ah bonju, bonju, kif innt. Hello, how are you all?" Danny beamed as he entered carrying a pile of brochures and badges.

"Here's Arthur Daley," David leaned towards Jenny and whispered.

Danny was about 5'10", wore a straw hat to protect his bald head in the sun, sucked on a Churchill cigar, had the same khaki shorts as the two young men but wore a white top with a map of the island in red and the sign "I love Malta". He kicked off his brown sandals on the marble floor.

"Ah, you must be Jenny." He shook her hand and in doing so dropped a couple of brochures. "You really fulfilled all my criteria."

And I wonder just what they were, David pondered.

"Welcome, welcome, a new wonderful season lies in wait." began Danny enthusiastically. "Last season was okay. This year will be even better. With Theresa an expert in Phoenician and Carthaginian civilisations and with you young folk on board we can entice new life, examine old civilisations......."

"And boldly go where no man has gone before?" Mark suggested.

Danny gave him a look. "Right, let us look at Theresa's map. Just imagine how your tourists will feel after their long flight over, let's see, Prussia or the Habsburg empire," he began.

"In a time warp presumably," David considered.

"Where's Prussia?" Laura asked.

"Where's the map of Malta?" Danny asked, a little flustered and fanning his face. He took his straw hat off.

"He looks like a boiled egg," Jenny whispered.

"What?" asked Danny.

"I've got a sunburned leg," Jenny quickly replied.

"You've got a map on your top," David pointed out helpfully.

"Okay I'll use that," Danny said reluctantly. "Now see this place," he pointed to his chest.

"It says Bugger ba!" Jenny exclaimed.

"Bugibba," David corrected her.

"Take your group there on day one. I've got a deal on their underwater safari. They will see two wrecks ......"

"Are Carmen and you there then?" Mark shouted out.

"Shut up and pay attention!" Danny said more seriously. "And my ice cream van will be parked at the jetty with Steven so guide folk towards it."

"Do you have hundreds and thousands?" Laura asked.

"The last time I answered that I'd to pay more tax," he groaned.

"I meant chocolate pieces....oh, it doesn't matter," she gave up.

"Then they go to the beach at Mellieha and Popeye's village. Tony and Steven will be dressed up as the main characters."

David and Mark started taking notes on a pad.

"On day two take them to the Blue Grotto and Tony will take them out in the boat. Mark and David, stand casually in front of the government sign which displays the official prices, as usual."

"Do we charge less?" Laura asked innocently.

"Don't be daft," said Mark.

"After that, see the Stonehenge at Hagar Qim."

"It's a load of old stones," Mark enlarged.

"My dad went to see them in concert," Laura added.

"Struth!" Danny sighed.

"On Sunday get them to Valletta market – you know my stalls – then to my ice cream parlour and Tony will have his boat all set at Grand Harbour. You know, girls, I survived the bombing there in World War 2."

"You were aged three," David laughed.

"But I digress," said Danny undaunted. "On Monday, take them to Ta Qali glass factory, Mdina the silent city, Mosta Dome and end up at Golden Bay. On Wednesday they'll be in Gozo all day and get them to my lace making factory, my stalls at the market and my small restaurant in Xlendi. On Tuesday they've the cruise to the Blue Lagoon at Comino and on Thursday take them to my souvenir shop and café in Sliema before they head home. Pick one night for fireworks. Tony and Steven are organising nougat sellers, the hot dog stall and are doing a deal with a brass band. Now let's all have a break and coffee and biscuits."

"How am I going to learn all this if we start in a week?" Jenny asked tugging at David's arm.

"I'll go through it with you but I'll always be with you and we'll have a full dress rehearsal before Friday."

"It's so good that you speak all those languages and have been a holiday rep elsewhere, was it Greece you said?" Danny asked pleasantly.

"Lesbos, I imagine," came a cynical voice behind them. Theresa had entered the room with the promised, if belated, map.

"Alpha Centauri," Jenny replied flustered.

"Aya Nappa, you said," David quickly corrected her.

"Wherever, you'll be brilliant," Danny assured her. "You'll learn a lot from David."

"Isn't she ever with me?" Mark asked. "I checked my horoscope and you are a Gemini. You should be with a Virgo."

"I've not been a Virgo in a while," Laura said, chomping through a chocolate biscuit. "Mark should know. I was a Virgo and then ...."

"David and Jenny are Libra and Aquarius," Danny pointed out.

"What utter superstitious nonsense," Theresa groaned. "You old goat!"

"How did you know I am Aries?" he asked. Theresa looked up to heaven.

"Now if you take your coffee and biscuits to your seats, we've Tony and Steven joining us and I've something to tell you."

Danny waited a few minutes for the two men to arrive, then continued. "I want us to have a new corporation image."

"Corporate," Theresa corrected him.

"Whatever," Danny added firmly. "And a new logo. I want us to be called, 'Say Go Tours'."

There was a pause. "As in pudding?" Mark asked.

"Saga will sue us," Theresa pointed out alarmingly.

Danny ignored them. "And the logo will be a bird"

"Oh no! Not a vulture," Theresa groaned.

"No a young female in a bikini with a Maltese cross background depicting a modern image yet traditional travel values."

"You don't get many birds in Malta," Mark told Jenny.

"Ain't I enough for you?" Laura pleaded.

"I mean the winged feathery kind," Mark elaborated.

David shifted uncomfortably in his seat. He felt like saying, you've got one girl, keep off mine even if, as yet, Jenny wasn't strictly his.

"What do you think?" Danny demanded to know. "I've got the badges to replace the silly '18-130 Club' ones. Just press them on. You'll get your uniform in a few days, Jenny. Now, I also want you all to have discount vouchers for my buses, boats, bars, nightclub, karaoke, market stalls, lace making factory and so on."

Everyone got what appeared to be a roll of tickets.

"Well that is it. You collect your passengers on Thursday at 11 pm at Luqa airport. Jenny, you have a dress rehearsal on Tuesday. Theresa will give you all the books to read and you'll have David with you on your trips. As usual, remember where all the toilets are on each of your itineraries. Ensure you have your daily list of tourists, phone numbers for hotels, hospital, doctor, police and so on. Well, that's it, any questions?"

The meeting ended and David led Jenny out to Reception. They blinked, then looked down involuntarily as the bright sun's glare reflected off Malta's familiar white sandstone.

"Oh let's see his car," Jenny whooped as she spied Danny's beige BMW in the street outside.

"Wow! Look at it. Walnut dashboard, beige leather seats, even cool blinds on the back windows. I do like the 'I love Malta' sticker on them too."

"Right" said David, watching anxiously for Mark coming out. "Let's walk into St Julian's and get a couple of milkshakes."

An hour later they drained their long glasses and watched some fishermen mending their nets in the harbour below the café.

"He must be doing so well to have a car like that" Jenny said.

"He exploits peasants like us" David replied.

"Can I ask an indelicate question?" Jenny asked "What do we actually get paid?"

"Peanuts," said David without hesitation. "You get your room, vouchers for meals in his restaurants and cafes and a batch of discount vouchers for the touristy things which you'd appreciate more than us as we've seen them all too often, but in cash you get about 65 LM."

"Which is?"

"About £100. Mind you, at the end of the week you can make as much again as a thank you from your tourists in tips plus you'll get a backhander from the owners of ice cream, cafes, etc., whom we direct our merry band to."

"I thought Danny said to use his establishments?" Jenny asked innocently.

"You'll learn," David stressed. "Right, let's start seeing the island. We'll jump on a bus and go to the capital, Valletta."

As the orange and yellow gaily coloured ancient single decker bus chugged its way along Sliema seafront and Jenny marvelled at the yachting marina, she came out with the comment David dreaded. "It's such a shame Mark is gay. What a waste. And such an older partner too. He's so fanciable. Laura seemed all over him too, wasting her time really."

David's heart sank. "Well, you saw what he's like with Steven. They are pretty well inseparable," he lied. Only in so far as Steven drove the coach, David well knew.

"How come you know Malta so well, David? How many years have you been doing it?"

David felt like saying he'd not been 'doing it' at all, but Jenny seemed the best prospect in ages. He gallantly resisted the temptation. "Well I lived here for four years as a kid as my Dad worked in the naval dockyard and so I picked up enough of the language to get by. I'd many summer holidays and once I got my degree at Stirling specialising in European Medieval History I did a Masters in the Siege of Malta and rep work seemed a logical next step."

"And what did you do in the winter?" Jenny asked.

"Some years I stay and do odd jobs for Danny – you know, painting boats, working in his bars etc. Other years, I go home and work in a call centre in Edinburgh. Now look out the window. These amazing fortifications around the harbour were built by the knights of St John to ward off the Turks in the 16th century."

"I've seen them at a Leeds Utd home match with their stretchers," Jenny replied.

David looked incredulous. "You haven't told me much about you yet," David pointed out expectantly. "Now this is Malta's main Valletta bus station. Welcome to the capital."

He helped her off the bus and directed her to the cheese pie stall whose smell had greeted them, combating that of diesel fuel off the bus.

"What are these?" Jenny asked.

"These are pastizzi or Maltese cheese pies. They are served warm with flaky pastry and cottage cheese inside. You can't come to the island and not eat these," he stressed.

They walked through the arches to Republic Street with its many quaint small shops through a throng of people: school children in uniform, a handful of tourists, lawyers sweating in wigs and gowns from the local courts of justice, monks and priests in their similarly warm cassocks, market traders, and flower sellers and so on.

"You were going to tell me about yourself," David reminded her as Jenny stopped to put some more suntan lotion on and looked at a shop selling Mdina glass.

"Well my Dad's something in the city"

"What, a stockbroker in London, banker perhaps?"

No unemployed in Leeds mainly or drives a taxi!" Jenny grinned "We rarely see him. He walked out when I was ten. So sad, he left my sis and me. She's my identical twin. It drives me mad when I'm home. Even folk who know us can't tell Sarah from me. She's at Uni in Sheffield now doing a degree in sport. She's got all the brains!" Jenny groaned.

"I wouldn't say that, actually," David said gallantly as he led her past the Parliament building and on to an ice cream shop. "What's your Mum do?"

"She's in Durham prison."

"Oh no." said David "I'm sorry. What's her sentence and why?"

"She's a prison warden," said Jenny clearly enjoying a predictable reaction she'd encountered many times before. "She does get out now and again."

The couple sat on the pavement desperately trying to eat their ices before they melted down their tops.

"Would it have mattered if Mum was in prison?" Jenny asked.

She's testing me, David thought. "Not at all, actually," he lied unconvincingly. She had me worried there for a moment, David knew darn well. He walked her up to the upper Barracca gardens, the fortifications over looking the impressive Grand Harbour.

"You know, I promise you'll be fascinated by the story of the siege of Malta and the story of de La Vallette, the Grand Master after whom the capital is named. When the knights of St John ran out of cannon balls they used Turkish prisoner's heads to fire at the enemy galleys."

"Wow, that's gross!" Jenny declared, rubbing more suntan lotion on and sitting on one of the park benches.

"Then there's the World War 2 story of fortress Malta, the blitz by the Italians and Germans, the defence by Faith, Hope and Charity, the ancient Gloucester gladiators, the arrival of a desperately needed tanker called Ohio and how crucial it was that the convoys got through."

"Do I have to know all this?" pleaded Jenny with concern in her voice.

"Just a few general comments. Theresa takes the older tourists on the specific historical tours but you'll need to throw in some general comments when you bring them to Valletta. A guide does the harbour cruise too. Theresa will give you some notes. It's important you get to know where you are, prices for trips, don't lose your group, get them fed, taken to a toilet, sort out any hotel problems and generally earn your generous tips."

"What about days off?"

"Well, every day we finish about mid-afternoon, though Wednesday is firework night and you meet them off a plane on Thursday night and take them back so you're ok for free time. Laura works on the snooker tables, Mark at the karaoke and I do some painting and electrical work. Didn't you smell the apartments?"

The young couple retraced their steps along Republic Street to the bus station. Jenny admired the Triton fountain, the centre piece of the impressive circular bus stance.

"It's lit up at night," David pointed out.

"If I get a few drinks in me, so am I!" the young girl laughed.

Encouraging, David reckoned.

"I am nervous about my dress rehearsal on Tuesday," she admitted as the old bus chugged out of Valletta belching exhaust fumes.

"You'll be great," David reassured her. "Mark, Tony, Steven, Theresa, Carmen, Danny, Laura and I will hang on to your every word!"

"Yeh, but they all know Malta," she replied.

"You'll have to get reading your notes over a long cool drink," said David "And I'll buy you it. I'll help a lot. I am at your command."

As he bowed Jenny poked his chest. "Don't be daft," she laughed. "You aren't a Knight of St John, you know."

"Do you know I'll never make love on a St John's stretcher ever again," he laughed.

"I just got carried away," Jenny grimaced.

I am making progress, David assured himself.

Once back at the apartments, both David and Jenny had a siesta in their respective bedrooms. David enjoyed a cold bottle of Frisk lager he had in the fridge beside his bed. He gazed up at the photos of all the holiday reps he had worked beside in the last six years. Not one had the impact of this young lady; so friendly, outgoing, funny, enthusiastic .... There was a knock at the door.

"Come in, Jenny!" he called.

In fact it was Laura wearing a light blue swimsuit and a towel over her head.

"How are you getting on with Jenny then?" she asked. "Oh give us a beer too"

"She's great," David replied. "So keen to learn."

"Has Theresa given her the boring history books yet?" Laura asked sitting on the floor and taking the cap off the bottle. She looked one long legged stunner but was already Mark's latest conquest as David well knew and that meant hands off!

"Later today. Hey, why don't we have a drink at the ten-pin tonight? It'll let Jenny get to know you."

"Mark and I are finished by 9 pm, so good idea," Laura said. "You know, she'll soon realise that the money's crap and she'll end up doing bar work at the nightclub like me, or karaoke like Mark," she enlarged. "What do you know about her?"

"Twenty, comes from Yorkshire, no Dad, Mum is in prison, one sis."

"And she's gorgeous," Laura laughed.

"I can't say I've noticed," David fibbed, looking out at the bay.

Laura joined him. She hadn't picked up on the prison remark.

"Does she know how two of these rooms are used at night?" Laura asked.

"I won't tell her yet, though on day one Steven and Tony almost let it slip."

"My God!" Laura muttered.

"We'll be there tonight. Should be a laugh," David said. Pity Mark is always there, he reckoned.

At 9 pm on the dot, Mark, wearing his bar tender's uniform and Laura, dressed with the usual low cut top, bare midriff and hot pants showing off her long legs to maximum effect, entered the bar at the bowling alley. Jenny had finally discovered the launderette and wore light blue slacks and a similar low cut yellow top. Could be some subconscious competition, David reckoned.

"Do you two fancy a game?" he shouted above the din. The two couples selected their bowling balls, put the score page up in to the TV screen above and Mark got the cold lagers in.

"She's a babe, isn't she?" Mark whispered to David as Jenny stooped for the first throw and promptly sent every skittle over. She bowls me over, David thought but he didn't say as he gestured he couldn't hear!

As the evening wore on, Jenny and Laura got increasingly tipsy, laughed a lot, and sat deep in conversation.

"It's so unfair you've got her as your assistant," Mark moaned as the game ended and they moved to the bar.

"Look, you've got Laura," David reminded him.

"How's she getting on with the reading?"

"She's got the books from Theresa this teatime," David confirmed, "but she'll learn most on the job as we all do."

"Yeh and I bet you'd love to be on the job," Mark said cheekily. "Hey does she know how two of the rooms are used?"

"No," David replied firmly. "There's no need to."

"I hear her Mum's in prison."

"Yeh, Mark, a sad story. But there were probably good reasons why she strangled her hubby with her bare hands. She's in for years."

"My God!" Mark gulped. He turned round and looked across at the two girls. Jenny had her arms around Laura's neck.

Mark picked up his glass and nipped across with a little anxiety. "You two alright?" he enquired.

"I am showing Laura a judo throw I learned in my self defence class," Jenny explained.

David had to extinguish a smile. Perfect, just perfect, he said under his breath.

"Where's Steven tonight?" Jenny asked innocently.

"Oh, you're asking me?" Mark replied. "He was down in the cellar as Danny's beer delivery had arrived an hour ago. I caught him bending over. He's got that bad back too."

Jenny nodded. Then she leaned over and whispered in David's ear "He's so blatant, it's astonishing. I feel sorry for Laura. Someone should tell her."

"It's not our place," David confirmed.

"What are you two whispering about?" Laura insisted.

"I'm saying we'll have plaice for tomorrow's lunch," David lied.

"Are you keen on fish, Jenny?" Laura asked politely.

"Not particularly," said Jenny, mystified.

Mark and David had another game. Laura and Jenny were propped up at the bar. Eventually at 11 pm all four staggered into the street. Laura and Jenny were arm in arm and in the crowded street both fell twice. As they negotiated around cars Mark and David were left behind. Laughing and giggling, they staggered into Theresa on her way back from a film. Theresa tutted, looked up to heaven, made the sign of the cross and turned away.

Having said their "Goodnights", Jenny and David flopped into the rather threadbare armchairs in the apartment foyer. David went over to the hot drinks machine.

"A coffee will sober us up," he announced authoritatively.

Suddenly an elderly gentleman with silvery hair and moustache, metal specs and pin-striped suit meandered across to Jenny. "Ah my dear. How much do you charge?"

"Well I am new to it but it depends on the day and how many extras you want and on a Wednesday night I can promise fireworks," Jenny replied helpfully.

Oh my God! David groaned quietly.

"I'll come back then," the old gent confirmed as he headed into the night.

"I must learn up the trips and the different prices for items," Jenny said.

David handed her the paper cup. She is too good to be true, he figured.

Chapter 2

Thump, thump. David woke up with a start.

What idiot was banging his door in the middle of the night for God's sake?

Thump, thump, it continued.

"Alright, alright, I hear you!" he groaned and rolled out of bed, the duvet padding his fall.

"Aargh!" He collided with his coffee mug from the night before as it dampened the floor. David fumbled for his specs, then his keys. He couldn't find his specs. The keys were on the bedside cabinet. He always felt dirty when he was unwashed and never liked people seeing him in that state. He put on his silk dressing gown. He opened his blinds partially and squinted in the glare. He opened the door.

Even without his specs he could make out Jenny wearing a pink dressing gown and no bra, bare legged with something on her head. "Only me!" she beamed.

"Jenny, it must be two in the morning. Are the apartments on fire?"

"Do you want these?" she asked picking up the specs from his desk.

"What's that on your head?" he asked as he gestured to sit on the bed.

"My walkman, I'm playing Westlife."

David picked up the mug and focussed on the stunning blonde. I hate not being washed and shaved, he thought as he glanced at the long mirror which he'd bought personally in Valletta market.

Jenny saw the glance. "I wish I had a mirror like that," she said. "Mind you, I'd end up staring at myself all day probably."

"You've no need, you look just great," said David grabbing the opportunity to make the pass. I am sure she blushed, David considered.

"Look I'll make you a coffee and be back in a minute." David nipped into the communal bathroom, washed, went mad on deodorant, made two coffees in the kitchen and dashed back.

Jenny had pulled up the blinds, opened the window and the peal of Sunday bells rent the air.

"What time is it?"

"Just after 9 am," said Jenny.

"No one gets up before noon," he groaned.

"I was hoping you'd take me to church," Jenny explained.

"Church?" Now that wasn't what I expected, David reckoned.

"Can you find me one?"

"Listen to those bells. This is Malta, doh."

"Thank you Homer," Jenny grinned. "You're saying there's a lot?"

"There's 365 – one for every day of the year," David said in his best rep voice. "Look, I'll get shaved and I'll take you to the English-speaking one in Sliema called St Patrick's. We'll see Theresa."

The bus journey to the Navarino flats bus stop in Sliema did not take long, which was a good thing as Jenny was not yet accustomed to being on an ancient bus with limited suspension!Being a bit early for mass,David took her down to see where the sea had beaten the foreshore into golden gullies and craters,and man had added more regular shapes and allowed the sea to fill them to make safe pools.A short rusted iron ladder,bolted to the rocks,allowed local bathers to clamber into the sea.The surface was tricky and allowed David an excuse to briefly hold her hand.

Two hours later, Theresa looked very surprised to see David walking out of the church. "I never put you down for a church goer" she remarked as she made the sign of the cross with holy water. David tried to follow suit.

"It's the right hand, you wally." Jenny poked him in the ribs.

Theresa looked up to heaven and tutted.

"I'll be honest. Jenny was keen to come" he confessed.

"What did you think of Father de Silva's sermon?" she queried.

David looked blank. He had spent the sermon reading a list on the wall beside him of films the RC church said not to go to in Malta that week and there were now at least two he'd made a mental note to attend.

"Really good," said Jenny like a teacher's pet. "All about the challenge of loving your enemy" she elaborated.

"A lesson there for Mark and you," Theresa winked and began chatting to a nun at the entrance.

David and Jenny walked back to the bus stop.

"Okay" he said "The punishment for calling me a wally is to be tickled," he announced.

"Don't you dare," Jenny implored. "I am so ticklish!" She ran towards the bus stop with the young man in hot pursuit till her flip flop fell off. "That flipping flip flop always flaps" she moaned.

"That is alliteration," said David, showing off. He waited till it was back on then tickled her tummy.

"Stop, stop, that's enough!" she chuckled.

They both stopped. I want to kiss her, David thought. Will I? Her sunspecs are hiding her reaction.

He left it.

The bus arrived. I am sure that was my chance, he regretted as the bus pulled away.

"What are your plans today?" Jenny asked.

"I am painting the boat down at the beach. And you?"

"No choice," said Jenny. "I'll sit on the beach and get thoroughly prepared for Tuesday's dress rehearsal. Laura says she'll look along and tell me about Sliema's clothes shops and where to get my hair done. Oh, and I want you to tell me how I can phone my Mum at weekend cheap rate."

"We can do that this afternoon," David promised. "There's only a one hour time difference."

"She'll be so proud when I tell her I found a church," Jenny said significantly. You are a bit of a paradox, Jenny, David inferred.

David was not long painting the upturned boat on St George's Bay sand when Jenny reappeared complete with lilo to lie on and wearing a light blue bikini.

"Have you got your suntan lotion? Don't stay uncovered too long!" he commanded. Oh my God. Did I really say that? he asked himself.

Jenny put a large beach towel over her arms and lay on her side. "What does the gang do for entertainment?" she asked enthusiastically.

"We're talking of a barbecue tomorrow evening up at Golden Bay. They're always good fun. We go for a swim in the dark and come back to sausages, bacon, egg and beans."

"Doesn't sand get in the food?" Jenny groaned.

"It's half the fun. And you've got lager to wash it down."

"Who cooks it?"

"Steven, of course. He's a chef after all, and he gets us the ingredients."

"Right," said Jenny, fumbling in her pink handbag. "Come and see my photos."

David rested his paint brush on the boat and didn't need any prompting to lie on the warm sand beside her.

"Here, you can use my towel to lie on. I've got my lilo. Now that's my Mum in her uniform. The baldy geek is my Dad. And that's Sarah."

David gasped in disbelief. "I thought that was you," he blurted out as he looked at the blonde girl eating candy floss at a fishing harbour.

"Nope, that's Sarah soon to be BA, in Bridlington, and probably casting her net for a bloke. She's a bloody haemophiliac."

"I think you mean nymphomaniac!" David suggested.

"She can be a little bleeder," Jenny parried.

So it was a gag, David inferred. Touché.

Suddenly, David put the towel over her and tickled her over it so as not to hurt. Jenny rolled off the lilo briefly becoming topless in the process. She readjusted her bikini top and had gone bright red. "I'm sorry. I didn't mean to ……."

"It's okay" she assured him. Her embarrassment suggested it wasn't.

Two hours later, after some milkshakes, and David painting and Jenny reading Theresa's notes, he took her up to the international phone booths and sat outside in the shade of a palm tree. She was on the phone for a good 20 minutes.

As they headed back to the bay Jenny told him, "My Mum's over the moon. She had to take my Dad to the court in Scarborough over ownership of their two-year-old car and she won the case as she made the repayments. Well now she's got a budget of about £500 more than she ever anticipated. Dad was sickened but he didn't have a leg to stand on. She was telling me Sarah's got a job in a legal office in Hull, and Mum's met some murderers in Durham. She mixes in the best company, eh? Whenever she's home she has a few stories."

They were just heading down the steps to the sands when a karozzin pulled up and Mark and Laura jumped out, both carrying towels and swimsuits. Mark quickly threw off the khaki uniform and ran in to the welcoming warm Med.

"Right, I'll tell you about the Armando's Hideaway hairdresser in St Julian's and my fave clothes shops in Sliema," Laura said.

Jenny, however, was distracted admiring Mark's bronzed six pack and his strong swimming.

David nodded his head resignedly. Sooner or later Mark would make his move and what chance did he have then? He'd never met anyone like Jenny, even after knowing her all of four days. He would have to make his move and stop being nervous about it. Perhaps the barbecue would present an opportunity?

Laura, Jenny and David all roared at Mark as he ran up the beach spraying them with water. He sat down with Laura on one side and Jenny on the other towelling himself.

Chancer, David thought.

"Are we having a barbecue tomorrow night then?" David inquired.

"Oh yes, let's" said Jenny excitedly.

"It's all arranged," Mark confirmed, opening a 7 Up. "Steven's got the food, Tony's getting drink and Danny will drive us and Carmen and Theresa in his mini-bus. It'll be great to have a real chat with you and hear all about you, Jenny," Mark said provocatively. Or, at least, provocatively as far as David was concerned.

"And I want to get to know you too," Jenny replied.

Here we bloody go again. David gritted his teeth. Laura too looked noticeably concerned.

"You'll be glad Steven's coming," said Jenny innocently.

Mark looked surprised. "Well it does get cooler beside the sea and he's guaranteed to warm me up," Mark added. "I love his sausages."

"Will I get us some filled baguettes?" Laura asked.

"Not on top of all that fried food, surely," Jenny remarked.

"No I meant now, from that van along the beach."

Half an hour later, all four were enjoying chicken or tuna fillings and lying in the shade of the boat.

"I am dying to hear all about you, Jenny," Mark returned to the theme as he cleaned his mouth with the towel, "but David told me about the killing, you know, your Mum ….."

"Well, she didn't expect to get as much as she did," Jenny acknowledged. "She wasn't sure how the court would go."

"Well, she wouldn't," Mark sympathised.

What are they on about? David sat incredulous.

"Was your Dad choked?" Mark went on.

"Oh definitely, there's no question."

I just don't believe this; David had to hide a smug grin.

"How long will your Mum stay in prison?" Mark asked.

"I'd reckon as much as fifteen years, its nice of you to ask. She's great when I see her at the weekend for a story. She's among murderers, rapists, those who've got done for serious assault – oh and the laughs we have!"

Laura gripped Jenny's hand. "How are the conditions there?" she asked.

"Not bad at all, she's made good friends and meals and fitness facilities sound pretty good. She wouldn't want a prison anywhere else."

"I wouldn't tell Danny the story though," Laura suggested.

"Right," said Jenny. "I must get back to reading all these notes. On Tuesday, at the dress rehearsal, which of the day tours is it?"

"I think we'll do the one where we go to Valletta, since you've seen it and read about the siege, and then on to Marsaxlokk fishing harbour and Ghar Dalam prehistoric cave," David suggested. "We can talk about it at the barbecue tomorrow too."

Jenny spent virtually all Monday reading in her room and playing her walkman. David got the boat completed. His heart leapt when Jenny shouted down from the room overlooking the bay or came down for a cold drink or baguette.

By 6 pm David had showered, shaved, had plenty of deodorant and aftershave on and wore his khaki uniform as Danny had requested. As they stood outside the apartments Jenny looked sensational, he thought, wearing hers for the first time.

Laura and Mark soon joined them.

"You know this silly badge does look like it's saying 'SAGO Tours'," Laura moaned. "Only up close can you make out it says SAY GO!"

Danny's mini bus pulled up driven by Tony. You couldn't make out the colour. It was already pitch black.

"Jenny, you look radiant," said Danny gallantly holding out his hand as she climbed on. "And you too, Laura."

"And me?" Mark asked.

"Shut up!" Danny groaned. "Jenny, I want you to meet my dearest, mia bella donna, Carmen."

Carmen had jet black hair with some grey streaks, was dressed entirely in black and was doing some embroidery on the front seat. "Bueno sera," she said, graciously extending her hand.

Jenny almost kissed it instinctively rather than shook it. She sat down beside David who had been concerned she would sit with Mark.

"She hasn't got that much English," Danny explained.

"Nor have you, you old geyser," Theresa pointed out, climbing on.

Tony revved up once Steven had finished loading the food and drink at the rear. Tony took the coastal route through St Andrew's, St Paul's Bay, Mellieha, and up to Golden Bay.

"This is Malta's best sandy beach," David explained.

"Not that I can see a damn thing," Jenny laughed.

From time to time, the headlights lit up a farm with melons and pumpkins piled up outside, or a water wheel, cactus or a palm tree beside the coast road. "I used to wonder if Malta drove on the left or the right," Jenny explained.

"Tony drives in the shade," Danny replied.

"Is he serious?" Jenny whispered.

"I'm Tony Schumacher!" Tony shouted back.

"Idiot!" retorted Theresa, deep in a book.

Every time the mini bus with its dodgy suspension hit a bump or pot hole there was the sound of bottles crashing about in Steven's crates at the back. Eventually, Tony pulled up in a deserted car park overlooking a large beach with a large hotel clinging precariously to the cliff on the right.

"This is it," David announced. He made a point of taking Jenny's hand as she alighted.

There was no breeze. The smell of sea, and sand and the vegetation mingled with that of suntan lotion. The sound of locusts was everywhere. Jenny avoided a lizard scurrying towards her and seeing the steep steps kept holding the young man's hand.

Suits me, he smiled to himself.

Once at the beach, Steven erected the barbeque beside a wind break which was rather redundant in the clammy conditions. It was similarly ironic that Danny went off to gather wood for a small fire. Theresa and Carmen flopped into deck chairs and the four young ones put down lilos and lay on them. Tony was blasting out a Queen CD still in the mini bus.

"Oh let's go for a swim in the dark," Jenny volunteered. She took off the uniform and dashed down to the sea in her bikini. "I've never swum in the sea in the dark!"

"I wouldn't imagine you would!" David agreed.

"Not in Brid; a bit cold!"

David slid under the water, came up and hummed the Jaws theme until Jenny splashed him.

"Okay. I give up!" he shouted.

The two swam side by side but not too far from the shore. David knew about the deceptive currents off Malta and how it can suddenly become very deep. Then they ploughed through the small waves. Jenny slipped momentarily again and David grabbed her hand. He wanted to give her a hug or a kiss. The moment had gone.

As they walked back to the barbecue, the enticing smell of sausages, beans, egg, tomatoes, toast, etc., wafted towards them. Danny was poking at the fire.

"Once the water boils, I'll make some coffee," he said.

"We could have brought thermos flasks," Theresa pointed out.

"Where is your sense of adventure? Were you never in the Guides?" Danny asked.

"I was in the Scouts," said Mark. "We used to rub two cubs together to make a fire."

Jenny, still getting dried, was the only one to laugh.

I bet she'd laugh at anything Mark said, David considered.

"Grub up gang!" Steven roared. Tony came down from the bus. "The coffee is ready too. I told you I could make it easy in a pan."

"You could make it easily in a pan," Theresa corrected him.

"So why did you say I couldn't?" Danny complained, missing the point.

"Is Theresa always so bloody superior?" Jenny whispered to David.

"Always, she's a teacher of the old school," David explained. "By the way Carmen's a nice old dear but her mind wanders a bit now and she's stone deaf"

"Alzheimer's?"

"Probably the result of being married to Danny for 40 years, no I don't know."

As Jenny got to the front of the queue, Mark fussed over her, making sure she had every item on her plate and, noticeably, left Laura to fend for herself.

"Make sure she gets enough toast, darling," Mark demanded.

"There's only one slice each and, anyway, I think Danny has burnt them on his blasted fire," Steven admitted.

"Eat up, eat up," said Danny, pouring the last of the coffee. "I want us to have a sing song and I'll tell a ghost story."

"He always does," David told Jenny as they got back to their lilos. "He's a creature of habit."

Jenny put her walkman on. "Tell me when he does his story," she asked, licking her plate. Soon, Jenny's head was rocking in time with Westlife.

"Doesn't it worry you her Mum is a murderess?" Mark asked.

"She seems a lovely, enthusiastic person," said David. "It's not her fault after all."

"Good for you," Laura remarked supportively. "I am really looking forward to our girlie trip to the clothes shops, CD stores and hairdresser. She seems so nice and I know she's put so much work into planning her dress rehearsal tomorrow. It's great having a girl on my team again when the alternative is Hinge and Bracket over there," she said controversially.

"Just watch if you are snogging her and she puts her arms around you, that's all I am saying," Mark laughed.

"Don't be daft," said David, still astonished that he'd fallen for the story hook, line and sinker.

"What are you playing on your walkman, Tony?" Laura asked.

Tony took his ear piece off. "Queen, always Queen."

"I love 70s stuff," David concurred. "Give me Bee Gees anytime. What about you, Laura?"

"Oh Abba, I saw Mamma Mia in London. It was wicked!"

"And you, Danny?"

"Bing Crosby, now there was a star," he reminisced.

"We're talking 70s," Mark groaned. "Keep up."

"I can't remember who there was."

"Nor would you need to," Theresa put her oar in firmly. "Vera Lynn, now she was a real singer unlike these overpaid tuneless stars."

"I like Wings," said Steven, chewing on a chicken leg.

"Queen for me too," Mark agreed. "What about you Jenny? I've just said I'm a Queen man."

Jenny looked incredulous.

"We're talking 70s music," David explained hurriedly.

"Oh T Rex, Abba, Wings, I loved the sounds of that period. My Mum played all those records," she added gathering her thoughts.

"Yeah your Mum was on the run and now she's banned" said Mark in a stage whisper. "Banned and on the run – don't you get it?"

Jenny had her headset back on.

"Look it's time for my ghost story," Danny announced. "We've all cleared up. Tony and Jenny pay attention!"

Steven and Tony sat down on an old tree trunk near the fire. "There's a great atmosphere for a ghost story," David told Jenny. "Look at the flickering fire reflecting off Carmen's wrinkled face. The poor soul is so deaf she won't be able to hear the story."

"She'll have heard it a hundred times," Mark calculated. "This story happened when I was a young reporter on the Times of Malta, young, intrepid, enthusiastic, conscientious."

"Sounds like a biased story!" Mark suggested.

"An unlikely one so far," Theresa agreed.

"Well," Danny continued quite undaunted, "there was talk of an old church that was haunted down by the water of Bugibba which was just a village at the time so I went along with my notebook, tape recorder, camera, and so on. Villagers had seen strange lights at night and heard footsteps and a door slamming when no one was there. Well, I met this pleasant old priest called Father Bugeja and he showed me around the church and I spent the night there. The wind howled. Owls hooted. Waves lashed against the shore on a dark cold winter's night. The tape recorder didn't pick anything up. I froze all night and stayed awake nervously and then, in the morning, a young curate called Father Borg opened the oak door and let me out. I remember I expected the door to be open early but it was after 9 am when the curate appeared. It was when I interviewed him that I the awful truth dawned. Father Bugeja had been the ghost! He'd been dead over 20 years."

"Scary eh?" Mark exclaimed.

"And does Malta have owls?" Theresa asked. "Not that I am doubting the authenticity of your story," she added in her usual patronising tone.

"Why can't she just enjoy the story?" Jenny asked quietly.

"Time for a song," Danny proclaimed. David never knew the words of songs apart from Christmas carols and football songs and usually when Danny led the singing David sang the first two lines and then hummed.

"You put your right foot in, your left foot out ......" Theresa began.

"Struth!" said David.

"Don't moan," said Jenny, tugging his arm. "The meal and swim were great. Let the oldies have their fun."

Three quarters of an hour later Danny had done "White Christmas" by Bing Crosby and "My Way" by Frank Sinatra when Tony suggested heading back to the mini bus. He and Steven picked up the barbecue equipment.

"It was nice of you to come, Ariadne," Carmen said, picking up her deckchair.

"Just say yes," David advised Jenny.

"Yes. Who's Ariadne?"

"Her daughter. She lives in London." As they walked up the steep steps, David, carrying the lilos, reminded Jenny, "A big day tomorrow. You'll be great, you know."

Jenny grabbed his hand. She does seem to like me, he reckoned. "Don't forget I'll be there. You'd never be left on your own in the first summer and you've got a clipboard with bullet points to remind you of each day's highlights," he added encouragingly.

As they got dropped off at reception, Mark, Laura, Jenny and David waved off the mini bus.

"I am not staying up," Jenny said. "Just get me a coffee from the machine please."

Mark and Laura headed up stairs. Maria at reception smiled and asked, "Are you Jenny, miss?"

Jenny nodded.

"That old gent wants to know if you have decided your charges yet."

"I'll give him a brochure," Jenny said helpfully.

"Girls here don't normally go to such lengths," Maria replied, clearly surprised.

"We offer a professional service," Jenny assured her. "We're in a competitive business. We can't be seen to lie down on the job."

Maria gave David a look.

It was Tuesday at 9 am.

Jenny nervously synchronised her watch for the fourth time with David's. Both had their khaki uniforms on and had clipboards under their arms. David was enjoying watching the pedaloes being prepared by Maria.

Jenny looked out to sea but kept mouthing her script like an actress. "What are the extras we give the tourists?" she asked.

"Well, you've seen Danny's discount tickets but we also have a map, Malta flag, a silly hat with "Say Go! Tours" on it, bus routes, bank details and so on."

At that moment a light blue coach appeared.

"There they are. Now, where are Mark and Laura?"

They appeared as if on cue, not in uniform, but acting the part of tourists. Laura had on a red sleeveless top with "I love Malta" blazoned on her ample bosom and matching shorts. Mark had gone for the ludicrous American tourist bit with maroon shorts, loud jacket, striped shirt, sunspecs, straw hat and camera. He also brandished a toy cigar! David mentally marked it down as post traumatic dress disorder.

Tony pulled up and the four clambered on. The left hand front seat was empty for them. Danny, sitting opposite with Carmen, handed Jenny the microphone. Mark and Laura sat at the back, Steven and Theresa in different seats somewhere in the middle.

They were about to pull away when the eccentric old gent in sports jacket, flannels, freshly polished shoes, bowtie and white shirt appeared.

"Good morning Captain. What can I do for you?" Danny asked leaning out.

"Damn nice day for a trip Danny. Thought I would join you," he said doffing his hat to Carmen. "Room for one more?" He perused the 53 seat coach with its eight passengers and one driver.

"It's only a rehearsal," Jenny spluttered but the old boy was on and sitting behind her.

"Nice filly you have here," he said.

"She's our new holiday rep," Danny pointed out.

"That too by Jove," he replied and fell back in his seat as Tony hit the accelerator.

"Stupid old buffer," David whispered.

The coach headed out of St George's and St Julian's and on to the main road.

"Welcome on board this Saygo tours coach," Jenny began apprehensively.

"There's a gap between say and go, I think you'll find," Theresa said helpfully in her loud irritating voice.

"I hope you enjoyed your flight last night into Luqa airport ……"

"Well done, well pronounced," David whispered encouragingly.

"And that you've settled into your St Julian's hotel. Remember if there are any problems at the hotel don't hesitate to tell your friendly rep."

"Struth, don't say that, we'll get inundated," Danny moaned. "Tell them to complain to the hotel."

"On your left you can see Malta's water polo facilities," Jenny kept checking her clipboard. "Now we're entering Sliema the largest town on the island and the main English speaking one. Oh there's Marks and Spencers, Littlewoods and Woollies. I didn't know they were here!" she whooped.

"Back to the script," David suggested, nudging her arm.

"We now come to Tig Nee sea front."

"Teenay, pronounce it Teenay," David whispered.

"Named after a Scoutmaster"

"Grandmaster," said David. "Okay, don't get me flustered."

"I need a pee," said Laura heading down the coach. "Where can we stop?"

"We've only been away ten minutes," Jenny complained.

"I'm acting," Laura pointed out. "You see, I am eighty."

"Well I am 84 and I need it too," the Captain added. "All this talk of waterworks – don't worry I know where to go."

Everyone got off, glad to welcome cooler air. David and Jenny stood beside the Captain Morgan cruise boat preparing to sail to Comino. The Captain had gone on board.

"Was he a naval Captain?" Jenny asked.

"RAF I believe. He got shot down twice over Malta fighting the Germans but parachuted to safety. He was a bit of a war hero in his day. Sad case now though. His wife's long gone."

Danny and Carmen joined them.

"He's gone on that large ship," Jenny informed them.

"I thought you said only for a pee," Carmen said.

"Yes, on that ship!" Danny shouted.

Soon they were back on their way. "Those warships on the left beyond the yachting marina are what comprises Malta's navy," Jenny continued from the next page of the clipboard. "They are used to stop drug smuggling and being shallow they come in with a pilot."

"A pirate?" asked an incredulous Carmen.

"She said pilot my dear," Danny explained.

"Now we're approaching Valletta, I think." Jenny checked her notes. "Yes, Valletta, Malta's capital."

"Well done!" David enthused.

"Named after de la Vallette, the grandmaster of the knights of St John, who defeated the Turks in the 16th century led by, led by"

"Sulaiman," David said.

"Yes, Sulaiman. We'll stop at this bus station and we'll walk up to the Grand Harbour, the largest in the Med, and see the forts from this period."

"Is it the fort that counts?" Mark roared from the back seat.

"Shut up!" said David. Mark pretended to photograph everything in sight.

"Come back quick by 12 noon," Jenny implored.

"Quickly," said Theresa. "It's a bloody adverb."

Jenny muttered under her breath. Tony got the bus parked in the gap where the Sunday market was held. Jenny held up a board saying "SAY GO TOURS" and they followed her through the narrow medieval streets.

As David walked up the street to the upper Barracca Gardens, he stopped to look in the "Ship shop" with its metal warships and model kits. He looked around, shading his eyes from the glare. Laura and Mark had disappeared into Boots. Tony and Steven had nipped into a pub. Theresa was choosing a fan in a gift shop watched by Danny and Carmen.

Where was Jenny? He looked up the crowded street. Jenny was still heading up the hill with only the Captain in tow. She seemed oblivious to having lost her party. Then suddenly the truth dawned. She still had her mike on!

"You'll know Grand Harbour from a Second World War viewpoint," said Jenny pleasantly. "I hear you had to ejaculate twice."

"Well more than twice my dear, but one doesn't want to boast!"

David groaned. A huge laugh went up. There were times you just wished Maltese didn't have perfect English. David began to run up weaving his way though shoppers and tourists.

"I've written down my list of extras you asked for," she continued.

Oh my God, David mouthed and sped up.

"Damn decent of you," the Captain replied.

"And I'll come round to you on Wednesday evening and give you one."

"I'd like to tell you about my peccadilloes too," the old boy rambled on "But keep it between ourselves."

"Oh, Maria will help you there," said Jenny as the laughter increased. "She charges £5 an hour but stops for a siesta. At night she ties them up."

"Well you would," the Captain replied.

David almost threw himself at the microphone as he reached her. Every passer by was smiling, pointing at her or shouting some interesting phrases.

"Get it off!" David roared.

"Now, now old boy. You're a bit forward," the Captain asserted.

"Your bloody mike's still on. I am sorry. Your mike is on, pet."

"But what's wrong?" she asked innocently. He led her away from the throng. The old man shrugged and went into a tobacconist's.

"The whole street could hear you, Jenny," David told her. "Be more careful in future."

"You called me pet."

"Did I?"

"You did."

"Well, I was caught up in the emotion," he explained. "Come on." He took her hand and entered the gardens. They had a good ten minutes sitting on a bench before the rest joined them.

"Come and see the view, darling," Mark suggested.

"What an aspect," Theresa affirmed.

"What's an aspect?" Tony asked.

"It's what you get when you bend over in a chicken run," Danny suggested.

"This view brings back hellish memories," the Captain said, lighting his pipe. "All the bangs night after night."

"Oh, the terrible bombing?" Jenny asked.

"All those nights in the Gut brothel with dodgy females, I'll bet," Danny whispered to David.

"Yes my dear," the old man said, "the bombing."

"Well, at this point you would take them down to the boat and David does a half hour spiel. Tony drives the boat. You may get some tourists who only want to go around the shops so just get to know the main shops, museums, Parliament, PM's residence, the Hollywood film water tank where they make so many films and above all, the toilets," Danny explained. "You'll be great, my dear."

They all wended their way back down the hill. Suddenly David remembered there was one particular shop he wanted to point out to Jenny. She was standing outside a Gozo lace shop with her microphone and lead in her hand and with Laura pointing out some delicate handkerchiefs to her.

"There's something I want you to see," he said, taking the empty hand. "It's this Catholic bookshop across the road. You'll find it of interest."

There were, indeed, many books in the window along with an assortment of statues, bibles, rosaries, sacred pictures and the like.

"I must tell my Mum I have seen this," Jenny murmured. "She'd be, like, wow!"

"Look at this amazing colour print above the books," said David.

She looked up to see an enormous picture of an old man on his death bed surrounded by his praying family on their knees. Above him the clouds had opened to show him being welcomed in sheer joy by God and his angels.

"It is absolutely wonderful. It reminds me of the film "Ghost," said Jenny. "I wonder what it would cost."

"They'd never sell it," David pointed out. "Do you know, they say it's been there for 40 years and more."

"I wonder why," Jenny said.

"Your choice of film "Ghost" is remarkably apt," said David. "I hope you're not of a nervous disposition for what I am about to show you," David went on, knowing she'd be curious.

"How do you mean?" Jenny asked tentatively.

"Come with me to the side window."

Jenny followed him around to a much smaller window again with more books on display.

"Look up," he implored.

Again there was the same picture of the old man on his death bed surrounded by his loving family praying but, looking up, as the clouds parted, it was Satan and his angels who were descending from hell to collect the terrified soul.

Jenny stood in shocked silence. The clip-clop of a passing karozzin was the only sound. "That is gross. Oh my God!" she gasped and put her head in David's chest. "Get me away from it" she demanded.

"I didn't mean to actually frighten you" David said, concerned, "I do apologise." He took her hand and walked towards the bus station. All the gang were buying cheese pies at the pastizzi stall.

"Right we're all here," said Danny, glancing at his watch. "Back on board. Are you all set, Jenny?"

The bus moved off.

"Now," said Jenny, collecting her thoughts and checking her clipboard notes and with the mike around her neck, "we're off to Ghar

Dalam prehistoric cave where we will see stalagmites and stalactites. I can never tell the difference," she admitted.

"Always remember, tights come down, my dear," the Captain suggested from behind.

"And many bones of prehistoric animals which must have terrified Stone Age man living in his cave."

"Dinosaurs didn't live at the same time as people," Theresa interrupted. "It's not the Flintstones."

Jenny made a face only David could see.

"But people and mammoths lived happy together," Jenny fired back.

"Happily! It's an adverb," Theresa said and David mouthed.

"What about Tarxien?" Danny asked.

Jenny looked stunned and shuffled her notes.

"Oh there's a film set of Tarzen and Jane we're going to see," she added, clearly guessing.

"No, Tarxien are more prehistoric temples. You're getting confused with the Popeye's village film set where the Robin Williams film was made," Danny explained. "You're doing so well. Keep it up."

Jenny wasn't so convinced. The bus pulled up at Ghar Dalam.

"They have their own guide who was on BBC 2 one night in a historical documentary," David said "But come on, the cave is fascinating and cold and dark. Let's get out of this sun."

Mark and Laura joined them as they marvelled at the thousands of bones lying in the cave. Jenny watched Mark and Laura walking hand and hand holding the ropes carefully. "I reckon Mark is bilingual" Jenny decided.

"Well I know he has some Italian; oh, I see what you mean." The penny dropped. He could never decide if Jenny was teasing all of them with wordplay or not. She looked dead pan even in the poor light, so he made no comment.

As they emerged into the bright sunlight, Danny and the Captain were enjoying a cigar and pipe respectively at the entrance. Carmen had gone for a pee. Theresa was debating with the official guide the age of the bones. Tony played his walkman in the bus.

Steven had dived into the local bar. He emerged with a jar of honey for Mark. "Thanks darling, it is really sweet," Mark said graciously.

"I reckon Steven sees Laura as a threat," Jenny deduced. The coach moved on to Marsaxlokk.

"This is the largest fishing harbour in Malta," Jenny said confidently. "It is not set up for the tourists."

"Well researched," Danny congratulated her.

"There is a market to go and see with Maltese lace and knitted bags. And you'll see the church overlooking the harbour has two clocks. In Malta one is always wrong to fool the devil."

"You have been doing your homework," David observed.

"Oh no!"

"What?" asked David.

"Saying the Devil has reminded me of that awful picture. I wish you'd never shown me it David, sorry."

"I feel so bad about it too," the young man acknowledged.

The group enjoyed their coffee stop and sat in shade under the huge parasols.

"Stanley Matthews lived here once," the Captain told Jenny.

"Who?" she asked.

"A famous footballer," Danny explained "The tourists like little titbits like that, especially the older ones. You can add that Presidents Bush and Gorbachev anchored off shore here for a summit a decade ago."

"Beside little Malta, gosh!" said Jenny incredulously.

"Yes, I'll use that too," Danny sat back and smiled a contented smile.

"You'll soon have a fund of stories" David assured her.

"Are you coming to the shops once we get back?" Laura enquired.

"You betcha," Jenny beamed. "Then when I've got some money I'll know where to go."

"It was nice of you to come, Ariadne," Carmen said.

"Just say yes," Danny suggested.

David waited till the heat of the afternoon subsided and completed his siesta back at the apartments. He put on his red floppy hat and his new sunspecs and headed back down to reception carrying his paint pot.

"Excuse me, David," Maria at reception called to him. "Doesn't your new young lady realise how two of these rooms are used at night by Danny?" David nodded.

"I think she should. Heaven knows what some man may say to her."

David took the point and headed back to the sand. Mark was already sprawled out on the lilo playing a small radio and enjoying a 7 UP. "I told the girls not to go into Sliema in the heat of the day but they wouldn't be told," he said

"They were desperate for some retail therapy!"

"Mad dogs and Englishmen," David agreed.

"She's a real babe, your Jenny," Mark said.

He's looking for my reaction David inferred.

"Well you are hogging her, David, old chum. Anyway I am not making a move."

"How so?"

"Well she seems lovely, but all this talk of her Mum in prison and murdering her Dad and socialising with all the worst criminals. Nope, I don't fancy it. And she seems unfazed by it all."

David splattered some paint in his direction which Mark avoided by rolling off the lilo. David went back to his painting. Mark had seduced so many females that David fancied, this was truly a breakthrough!

"I thought you were daft about Laura?" he asked provocatively.

"Yeh, she's gorgeous, don't get me wrong, but only here for the season and you never know what may appear off the next flight!"

"Yeah, we've our first planeload tomorrow night. We've what, forty or so in total, so that'll be two medium sized groups. I hope we get some Americans or Germans. Their tips were great last year! Have you got the list of names and their hotels?"

"Yeh, Danny left them at reception for us."

"Let's make sure we don't lose any this time, eh." And with that, Mark dashed off down the warm sand and ploughed into the water with a number of sunbathing females admiring his six pack.

So, you've no interest in Jenny eh? Life gets better and better!

An hour and a half later, Laura and Jenny appeared in a taxi beside the bay.

"Wow! What an experience that was," Laura said.

"Yeh, he over took three abreast. I think we'll stick to buses."

"What have you got then?" asked Mark.

"And don't get it near the paint," David reminded them.

They both took out half a dozen tops. "They're so cheap and colourful," Laura said, holding them across her front.

"That's cos they're so flimsy," Mark suggested.

"I am not complaining though," Laura took a pretend swipe at him. "When are you on at the karaoke?"

"6pm," said Mark.

"Same for me at my snooker tables," Laura confirmed.

"We'll call in later," Jenny said. She said 'we'. David smiled to himself.

"Last night of freedom," David reminded them. "We've a long night tomorrow. Let's hope the hotel knows they're coming."

"Surely they must know," said Jenny with alarm.

"Depends. Danny has so much on," said Mark from experience.

"More than we've got with these!" Jenny laughed and headed back to her apartment.

Tony, Steven, Jenny and David sat having a drink at the Karaoke bar, having had a game of 10-pin at Danny's bowling alley.

"We're all set for tomorrow. I've checked both bus engines, Danny's told us the routes he wants us to do and when the breaks are, and you travel reps have all the names," Tony said.

"Where can we go wrong?" Steven asked with sarcasm in his voice.

"Do things go wrong?" Jenny asked innocently still mouthing her script for the following day.

"You'll be alright," said David reassuringly. "The planes get in at 2210 and 2220; we'll check who's going to the Metro hotel and St Julian's hotel, get them on the two buses and Bob's your uncle."

"Who's Bob?" Tony asked.

"It's a silly English expression," Jenny informed him against the background of a strike.

"One thing you'll find," said David, speaking from experience, "is that as the summer goes on, the tour parties change, but essentially you meet the same people because they are stereotypes."

"I am not with you," said Jenny, puzzled.

"Well, first of all there'll be an old person who pees a lot, has umpteen medical ailments and who'll need taken to the Dr, that's stereotype A. Then there'll be an old person who has been here twenty times before and knows the island better than you do. That's stereotype B. Then there's C, an intelligent person who hasn't been here before but will quiz you about what they've read. Then D is all the families with young kids. A few will be horrors, but parents say they are cute. Then there's the E group who are teens and twenties who are here to find the nightlife. Finally, Group F are the lonely single types, and G are Gay."

"What if you are lonely but also know the island well?" Steven asked.

"Then you are an F in B," David replied rapidly.

"You two have done that gag before, haven't you?" Jenny demanded to know.

"Yes they have," Tony confirmed, "on each new recruit they have."

Mark and Laura suddenly appeared, advocaat snowballs in hand.

"Do you want a snowball, Jenny?" Laura asked.

"I'm as pure as snow, did anyone tell you?" Laura chuckled.

"True, but you tend to drift," Mark added till he got a well-aimed nudge in the ribs from Laura.

"Have you told Jenny our tourist types?" Mark asked David.

"Yeh, I've done my annual gag" David confirmed. And got in before you did, he reckoned.

Steven and Tony headed off for a game of skittles. The Queen anthem Bohemian Rhapsody came on and the young crowd waved their arms in the air. Mark had put his arm around Laura so David followed suit with Jenny. He was relieved she didn't push him away.

"There's something I haven't asked you," Jenny said. "Your surname, what is it?"

"I'm Bond, David Bond."

"You're kidding!" Jenny gasped.

"No I really am"

"He's licensed to thrill," Mark pointed out.

"Pity you aren't!" Laura grinned.

David liked the reaction his announcement had got. "We must go one evening to the Dragonera Casino," David said.

"Then you've had your chips, Jenny," Laura said.

"Not with Mr Bond," stressed David in his best Edinburgh dialect. "I can take on Blofeld and Oddjob."

"Never get those names muddled," Mark suggested.

"You'll love the casino, seriously," David reassured Jenny. "And you'll see Danny there for sure. Now let's discuss tomorrow's plans."

"Tomorrow never dies," said Mark, capturing the mood.

The following evening at the back of 9pm came soon enough. Mark, Laura, David and Jenny stood at the balcony at Luqa airport watching for the plane lights which would herald the arrival of the first tour party. There was a strong smell of gasoline and below them on the tarmac a Lufthansa jet prepared for take off.

"Hey, you've got goose bumps, are you cold?" Laura asked.

"No I'm just dead nervous," said Jenny rubbing her arms.

"I kept saying it gets cold at night here," David added. He bent down, rummaged in his holdall, found a slipover and put it on her.

"That's better." she said relieved.

David headed off to the bathroom and splashed his face in the cold water. He knew all too well how tourists could keep you up late at night if they encountered problems at the hotel and he was determined to remain alert. He took a while to brush his hair and then sprayed on more deodorant. Would he dare put his arm around her again? he pondered.

"That's our first one now!" Mark shouted at the door. "I can see its lights. Bang on time for once!"

David dashed out and did put his arm around Jenny. "This is it," he confirmed.

There was a roar as the jet hit the runway and slammed on its brakes. A little yellow vehicle, with "Follow me" displayed on the back rushed out to meet it.

"Air Malta wishes to announce the arrival of KM102 from London Gatwick," the tannoy sprang into action.

"That's it from London, England," he told Jenny.

"Why not just say, London?" she asked.

"It could be London, Canada," David explained.

"He's from Scotland," Mark added.

"In the old days," David reminisced, "the roar of aircraft here as they landed was truly incredible because the runway was short and large aircraft used to slam on the brakes as they landed, but nowadays – and you can tell your party this – it is the largest runway in the Med."

Jenny pretended to take a note on her clipboard but, in fact, the top was still on the biro.

She's starting to look tired, David reckoned.

"Time we got down to the Arrivals gate," said Laura heading for the steps.

The four headed down the stairs two at a time. On either side of these were large illuminated signs advertising hotels, tourist attractions, cruises, taxis and the like. Mark got on his mobile to inform Tony and Steven the first plane had landed. Jenny stood mouthing her welcome then held up a large card saying "SAY GO TOURS".

"You're off your mark," said Mark. "Customs takes a while here."

"I'll get us an orange juice," Laura offered and headed off to the drinks machine.

"I just wish they'd come through the doors and we could get started," Jenny said, highlighting her anxiety.

"In a week or two, you'll be glad of the break," was Mark's opinion.

"It'll be a laugh putting them into your categories," Jenny added, managing a nervous smile.

Laura's return with the frozen orange juice was a welcome diversion.

"There they're coming now," Mark announced.

"Hold your board up," David commanded. He smiled when he saw how high she held it up.

"We're Mr and Mrs Blackwell," said an elderly Yorkshire man as he approached them smiling. "Are you SAY GO TOURS?"

"Yes I am, we are" said Jenny shyly.

"We'll just wait here watching for our luggage on that carousel. See, nowt to it," he told his elderly wife. "Our first trip abroad, you know, and we're both 80," he said proudly.

"Well done," said Jenny. "I reckon Group A," she whispered.

"But do they pee?" David asked.

"We'll soon find out," Mark added.

"Are you SAY GO TOURS? I'm Charley. Lead us to the action, mate," demanded a blonde female about 19 with two similar companions. "We're here to get drunk and laid. Men are like carpets. Lay them right and you can walk all over them."

"Bloody hell!" Jenny said under her breath, then "Yes, just wait here madam and watch for your case on that carousel."

"Group E," conjectured Jenny.

"No question," Mark confirmed.

"Tenth time on this bloody island and customs is still slow. Do they think I'm a bloody terrorist?" asked an old gent in a cloth cap. "If it weren't for me they'd be run by Germans."

"He's Group B, no doubt at all," Jenny winked. "I've got the hang of this now."

Mark and Laura were checking their clipboards and ushering their Group to one side.

"That's our Edinburgh flight in too!" Mark shouted.

"Watch out for kilts," David said to Jenny.

Jenny had marked group D to families of three and four, and suggested that two young men, Julian and Tim, could be Group G till Tim felt her bum in passing.

"Do you have a bisexual group?" Jenny asked.

You do know that word you perisher, David realised. "Right have you got all your team?"

"Yep," Jenny nodded.

"Moi aussi," Mark confirmed. "Look I've got fewer teens and twenties," he pointed out. "Let's balance up our groups."

David agreed. "Yeh, I've got more Group E. Jenny, can you give me Charley and the two E's?"

"Yes, no problem," Jenny said marking her register.

"Skuzi, madam, will you please come with me?" A young suntanned uniformed customs official took Jenny's arm.

David turned his face to stifle a grin.

"What on earth is wrong?" the young girl replied, red as a beetroot.

"Please, you come with me, yes?"

"That's my boss" Jenny pointed out.

"Then, you come too."

David shrugged his shoulders and followed along behind once he'd given his clipboard to Mark. The young man took them into a Spartan little room with a desk, three chairs, a clock, a filing cabinet and a computer. On the desk was a lamp which he pointed in Jenny's face. Although it was not particularly bright it reminded you of a SWW film on a Sunday afternoon on BBC 2 where the German office interrogates a prisoner. The room was clearly sound proofed. Only the fan above their head broke the awkward silence.

"Name?"

"I'm Jenny Waring"

"Why are you in Malta?" "I'm a courier."

"That's what I feared but, at least, you are honest," the customs man said. "It'll mean a shorter sentence"

"A shorter sentence!" Jenny gasped.

"You were passing Es and charley, were you not?" the customs man said firmly.

"Yes, no, it's a nickname."

"Yes, madam, we know it's coke."

"It was people, not drinks," Jenny stammered.

"Are you under twenty-one?" he asked.

"Yes"

"I may need to contact your parents." Jenny looked at her feet. "Where's your Mum?"

"Prison," said Jenny.

"Oh dear!" the young man sighed, taking notes.

Jenny was on the verge of tears.

David suddenly felt this had gone far enough and he winked at the Maltese.

"Ok, I will turn to your boss. Are you a ~~holidayrep~~ counter?"

"Yes"

"Do you have a police record?"

"Just, walking on the moon"

There was a long pause. Jenny suddenly looked up. "Hey, what is this?" she demanded to know.

"Silence," the customs man said firmly. "What is your name?"

"Bond, David Bond"

"I see, Meester Bond, if I can make that clock tock, so will you!" The young customs man could not sustain it any longer and laughed and laughed. David joined him.

Jenny, red-faced, thumped David with both fists, play fighting. "Okay, what's going on?" she roared. "Enough!"

"I am Marco Venturi" the customs man replied and shook, then kissed, her hand.

"I've been friends of David since he came here six years ago. I help Steven at the karaoke, do odd jobs for Danny and sing, dance and play the guitar at the weekly entertainment night. Danny gets me girls."

"To help him with his folk dancing," David quickly interrupted.

Marco, undaunted, continued with a broad smile. "And maybe, since you are a tifla sabiha, you will grant me a date sometime?"

"Not after what you've just done to me," Jenny quickly retorted, dried her eyes and headed out with her clipboard.

"I think she got the joke," David said. "I think."

David clambered up the steps onto the bus. Mark had ensured David's twenty were on the correct coach. Tony looked like a nodding dog as he played his walkman at the wheel. She's got a face like fizz, David instantly recognised as he sat beside her in the coach.

"Ey opp! Are thee off at last?" the old Yorkshire man enquired.

"We are," nodded David, picking up the mike. "We're on our way to the St Julian's hotel……." he glanced at Jenny but she turned away and looked into the darkness of the night, the glass reflecting a sad face.

Half an hour later, Tony pulled up outside the hotel. Jenny and Tony handed the twenty tourists their cases. David went into the hotel. I'd better apologise, he'd decided.

Jenny and Tony led the flock like sheepdogs up to reception. The young ones, like Charley and her two friends, threw off their sandals and enjoyed the cool marble floor.

"Eh, don't be long. It's past my bedtime," Mr Blackwell announced loudly.

"Speak for yourself, Grandad!" Charley retorted, sitting on her case. "It's only midnight, I want to party!"

"Tim and I want to get to bed," Julian added impatiently glaring at Charley.

"Right poofter!" Charley said to her mates.

Jenny, at last, smiled.

The manager appeared at the desk. "Cavetta," he said and handed the Blackwells a key.

"Do we ever get to bed?" implored Jenny. "Sorry, I'll rephrase that." She smiled. "I'm zonked."

"I reckon we are safe to go," said David, his eyes starting to burn.

Charley and the other two blonde clones reappeared at the desk.

"Any problems?" David asked and muttered 'you babes' under his breath.

"We're off to hit the nightlife," she replied.

"A lot shuts down around 2 am here," said David. "Don't get too disappointed!"

"Cor, it ain't Ibiza, is it?" she moaned.

"Why not get to bed and be fresh in the morning?" he suggested.

"Is that an offer?" she flirted.

"Buona sera," David replied.

The three girls headed off into the night. David was sure he'd spotted a hint of concern on Jenny's face at Charley's question but his attention was taken by the arrival of Julian.

"There's a creepy-crawly in my bed," he moaned.

"Oh dear," said David sympathetically.

"It's probably Tim!" Jenny whispered.

The manager rejoined them. "That old man called Winston......."

"The one in the cap?" David asked.

"Yes, he's just told me I'm the most incompetent manager here in twenty years. We only opened eight years ago!" The manager headed off muttering "Bloody English" in a stage whisper.

"That rules me out," David said as he and Jenny got on Tony's bus and headed back to the apartments. He took a deep breath. "Look, Jenny. I want to apologise for what Marco and I did tonight. It was meant to be a bit of a laugh, that was all."

"You've done it before, I take it?" Jenny asked "I was like wow, what's going on here? I was well frightened. You both had me going. Okay I forgive you – this time," she stressed ominously.

David nodded. He just wanted his bed.

At 8 am, his khaki uniform neatly ironed, washed and shaved with extra deodorant and aftershave on, David joined Jenny, Mark and Laura for a breakfast of orange juice, toast, cornflakes and a continental roll.

"We'll have Theresa today," David began. "We've got a few oldies on the trip."

"Where are you doing today?" Mark asked.

"We need to get off to a good start otherwise they'll see the notices for our competitors in the hotel foyer so we're taking them to the under water safari at Bugibba, then, after a snack lunch and to keep the oldies happy, I thought Mosta Dome. They'll be back before it gets too stifling hot."

"I read up on Mosta. It sounds fascinating," Jenny gushed. "Oh, I've sent my first postcards home," she added.

"Where are you folk off to today?" came, a familiar voice from the door. "And is Theresa going? A damn fine woman!" the Captain declared.

David turned round. "And so grammatically correct. We're doing Mosta and Bugibba."

"Suits me, damn all else to do. Are the fillies coming?"

"Jenny is with us."

"And we're girls," Jenny stressed.

Suddenly the two light blue coaches drew up.

"The bloody air conditioning's on the blink," Tony moaned, opening the door.

Mark and Laura headed off with Steven. "I got a letter from Sarah yesterday" Jenny said.

"Your clone" David laughed.

"She's not my clone. We're quite different personalities and she's got brains, I told you," Jenny protested.

The coach pulled away back to the St Julian's hotel.

"There's blasted warm air coming through the air vents," David moaned. "And it'll be a roasting day too."

"I've told Danny," Tony said, "that my coach was full of hot air and he said he'd heard your talks before. I don't think he's too concerned," he shrugged.

"I wish you and I really had clones," David continued light heartedly.

"Why so?" asked Jenny, intrigued.

"We could lie on the beach at Golden Bay or Melieha and our clones could do the tours."

"I don't think it will really happen with humans," she went on.

"You could have a baby who was a clone of yourself," David suggested.

"What about Ethics?" Jenny asked.

"You could still live in Yorkshire," the Captain quipped.

The two young people made a face as the coach reached the hotel. It didn't take long to count 20. Charley and her two blonde companions were dressed for the beach. Winston had summer attire but the cloth cap was still in evidence. Mr and Mrs Blackwell carried a medical box, Julian and Tim wore pink.

Theresa was waiting too. "Come along, come along," she instructed. "It's 9.07 already. We should be on the road."

"She's so wonderfully domineering," the Captain stated admiringly.

Jenny checked the names and they headed up the barren coast road past cactus, palm trees, rocky beaches and scrub land.

"You'll notice," said David, taking the mike, "there are very few birds on Malta not even the Maltese falcon!"

"What about us?" Charley roared from the back of the coach where all 3 girls were strewn, sandals off, across the back seat.

"Let the man talk!" demanded Winston.

"Go for it," Charley called back.

"You see those huts on the hill. Bird shooting is a popular hobby here, although it's now illegal."

"We're now passing Malta's water park," said Jenny taking a turn of the mike.

"Well done," whispered David. "You see, it's easy."

Winston and the Captain sat discussing the war. David could see Julian and Tim holding hands in Tony's wing mirror.

"It's getting awful hot," Mr Blackwell stated.

"Awfully hot," Theresa corrected him.

"That's what I said," Mr Blackwell protested.

"It's a hot day," Jenny agreed.

"The air conditioning, more like. My wife is on medication, too."

"Group A," David ventured. Soon the coach pulled into St Paul's Bay. "If you look now on your right you can see the bronze statue of John F Kennedy."

"That's some bust," said the Captain peering at Jenny.

"It's on the right," Jenny repeated, red-faced.

The bus moved on to the sea front at Bugibba and the undersea vessel was already at the quayside.

"This is cool!" Charley shouted. "Come on, girls."

A little five-year-old girl headed after them. Theresa put her foot out. "Wait for your Mum," she smiled.

"Yes miss, but they said, come on girls."

David and Jenny checked numbers and tickets and walked along the quayside.

"Come on Meester Bond," Jenny laughed. "You'll soon be at the bottom of the sea!"

"Are there any sharks?" Charley asked as she stood at the gangway.

"Only Danny," David whispered. "No, no sharks."

"Wicked," said Charley, relieved.

With all twenty of the party seated on the top deck in a welcome slight breeze, David and Jenny relaxed, knowing the actual trip had a professional guide. About a dozen other elderly tourists from a different party sat next to them. Winston and the Captain sidled up to David.

"Germans," Winston murmured.

"Don't mention the war!" David said quietly back.

The red and white Captain Morgan glass-bottomed boat headed out into St Paul's Bay. The blue Mediterranean was like a mill pond.

"This is where St Paul was shipwrecked in Malta on St Paul's island in 61 AD," said the professional guide. "The area is picture skew."

"For heaven's sake, it is picturesque," Theresa moaned, "Honestly, these half wits read from a card and you can just tell they haven't prepared beforehand."

The Captain came across with a tray of cokes. "I got talking to the Germans. Some only knew Malta from 30,000 feet!"

"You didn't discuss the war?" David enquired apprehensively.

"They're all over 80 and they wanted to," the Captain protested. "One or two had bombed Grand Harbour. I told them about how a Messerschmidt came out of the sun at 2 o'clock and I had a wizard prang."

"It's amazing how you actually remember the exact time of day and even the weather after all these years," Jenny remarked.

The Captain gave a look of incredulity and returned to the Germans. Soon it was time to take their turn below decks and, cokes in hand, they looked out in awe as hundreds of fish were fed and they had an excellent view of the two submerged wrecks.

"You know, I am still pinching myself that I am here at all," Jenny said. "It's a bit different from a summer in Woollies in Bridlington after all. I can't wait till I tell Mum all that has been happening. It might stop Sarah from dominating all the discussion although that will depend on where she ends up on holidays. She even gets a better summer job than me; it was a lawyer's office last summer."

Is this a conversation or thinking out loud? David pondered.

"I am surprised these two naval vessels sank at St Paul's Bay and so close to the shore," said Winston.

"Don't tell anyone, but they got towed here," David informed him. David and Jenny went back up the vertical steps to the top deck and got two cool glasses of 7Up on the way back. It had been so cool below deck and both rapidly put their sunspecs back on.

"Get the ice cream van discount tickets out," David commanded, "and once they've done that and found a toilet we can get them to Danny's Restaurant in the main square and I'll show you some of the cheaper souvenir shops."

As they walked back along the seafront it seemed natural that David should take Jenny's hand. They showed the tourists the shops with their Maltese lace, fans, tea towels, flags, tops, kiss-me-quick hats, models of Maltese boats and knights of St John, calendars and so on.

"I am making a mental note and once I am paid I'll have some real fun next week," Jenny smiled as she shook a Grand Harbour snow shaker.

"As if Valletta ever got snow," Theresa sniffed.

"They did in 1947," the Captain interrupted.

"I'll incorporate that in my tour talk," David confirmed.

"Is that how you do it?" Jenny enquired.

"Yes, I've six years of anecdotes and little stories," David said. Well, actually 8, David knew well, but that made him 30 and 28 did sound much younger.

"12 noon," Theresa announced "Time for Mosta."

Forty minutes later, the coach parked outside the most beautiful church in Malta.

"This is the third largest unsupported dome in the world," David told the group.

"A bit like Hull City," Jenny suggested.

"It's got a dome?"

"No, unsupported!"

As they entered the church many of the tourists gasped at the beauty of the paintings. Charley and her two companions headed off to a bar opposite.

"In the Second World War a bomb fell through the roof of the church and landed during a mass without exploding," David elaborated. "It is now in the sacristy and you can see it!"

"A miracle," said Theresa.

"A fluke," Jenny suggested.

"Get your arms covered," Theresa commanded and Jenny grimaced as she put on her cardigan. "And cover your head, child."

Jenny rummaged in her bag. She found a "19" magazine and put it over her head.

"Oh Heavens!" Theresa groaned. She took out a scarf and gave it to her.

David handed over his party to a priest guide and took Jenny outside into the blinding sunshine.

"I hope you'll show us the nightclubs tonight," Charley demanded as they entered the bar and ordered cool lagers.

"Of course we will, but don't stay up too late when we've the Blue Grotto and Hagar Qim tomorrow," he suggested.

"Is this your bird?" Charley asked, exhaling a cigarette as if Jenny wasn't there.

"She's a close friend," David replied in the best traditions of any TV celebrity. I wish she was my bird, he'd already decided.

"I'm a holiday rep," Jenny replied emphatically.

Chapter 3

It was 8 pm. David sat, fanning his face, on the wall over looking St Georges Bay. He was waiting for Jenny and then planned to take the young ones up to the bars, nightclubs, karaoke bars and restaurants which "SAY GO TOURS" recommended or, in other words, the ones Danny owned. Theresa was already up at the St Julian's hotel where she planned to give a talk to the older and more cultured contingent on the siege of Malta.

As the local church bells struck 8 pm, Jenny meandered out sans clipboard. She had her yellow mini skirt, bare midriff, low cut pink top and a pair of laced up sandals. She held David's hand as a car roared down the narrow street and they headed up the hill to the hotel.

"You haven't told me much about yourself yet," Jenny pointed out. "What's your family like, for example?"

"Dad's in Rosyth Dockyard, Mum's a housewife, brother in the Navy, sister in the Navy."

"So you're a naval family," Jenny said.

"Yeh, we're all this height," said David gesturing at his belly button.

Jenny walked slightly ahead and peered at some cactus and prickly pear at the side of the narrow lane leading up to St Julian's. The lights from the 5 Star Corinthia Hotel on the opposite side of the bay reflected off the sea. David had a good hard look at Jenny's legs. He'd always been a leg man. If you were a male you either went for the face, breasts or legs. David admired legs and Jenny's surely went all the way up to her neck.

They were almost at the hotel. Jenny skipped over a lizard going about its business. She took a deep breath. "Can I ask a favour my old mate?" she asked.

"Anything" David replied, though not enjoying the old mate comment.

"I'm almost out of money. Can you let me have 10 lira?" she asked nervously.

"Liri," he corrected her.

"Oh don't get like that schoolmarm," she implored.

"Of course," David assured her taking out his wallet. "But the good news is you'll get a pay packet from Danny in the morning."

"Then I'll quickly pay you back," she reassured him.

Charley and about 9 girls and Tim and Julian waited patiently at the entrance.

"Hurry up, you're wasting good snogging time!" Charley shouted.

All the girls were dressed to kill and all had thigh high skirts on. The smell of perfume and deodorant hit you at 30 paces and David had to stifle a smile at the deodorant of the young men too.

"Ok. I'll take you up to the disco where you'll see Laura at the karaoke and Mark at the restaurant and bar where Steven works and Tony is at the 10 pin this evening.

"What about the nightclubs?" Charley asked as they moved at some speed towards St Julian's centre.

"I've got discount tickets for APEX," David announced.

"Okay," the girls shouted back above the din of the street.

The street indeed appeared to shake with the beat of loud music as they wended their way among gridlocked cars, all of which seemed to hoot their horns to no discernible effect.

Having left the girls at APEX, and the boys at the restaurant, Jenny and David made their way to the disco. Laura, as usual, was at the snooker tables. She beamed and mouthed "Hello" against the racket. Hundreds of young people were dancing on all three levels while queues seemed endless at the bar.

"Tell me what you want and you won't have to wait," she kindly volunteered.

David had his lager and Jenny, a vodka and coke.

"You'll enjoy yourself tonight," Laura roared at Jenny.

"How so?" she enquired.

"Some Italian players are here and they're all fit."

Just great, David muttered into his glass. Laura sat tapping the table in unison with the pop songs, all the time watching the snooker tables she was in charge of. Then Laura and Jenny got deep in conversation, with Laura putting her hand up to Jenny's ear to make herself heard. Now and again both would throw their heads back and roar with laughter.

Suddenly, four bronzed young Gods in all black stylish tracksuits and an Italian flag on the breast pocket came up the metal spiral staircase.

In an instant the music stopped and the DJ came on. "Ladies and Gentleman. Tonight in our disco I am pleased to announce the arrival of four of the Italian World Cup squad."

Laura grabbed Jenny's hand, raced on to the disco floor, put down their handbags and began to dance in such a way her bottom nudged the first of the Italians. Suddenly 2 of the studs were dancing with Laura and Jenny. David felt totally marginalized. He sat guarding their glasses and playing with a beer mat and looked forlornly at a full length mirror beside the bar where the girls titivated themselves before venturing on to the dance floor. How the hell could he hope to compete with this lot? He'd always failed in the past. The music became a slow number. The two Italians both put their hands behind the girls' bottoms and pressed them up close. David sat trying so hard to look nonchalant and, from time to time, threw Jenny a smile though, frankly, she didn't appear to be noticing.

Suddenly at the top of the spiral staircase, a red-faced Danny, looking totally out of place given all the dancers were in their teens and twenties, appeared. He pushed his way across the disco floor, spoke in Laura's ear and she returned rapidly to the snooker tables. The two young Italians shrugged and simply carried on dancing with the next two girls patiently queuing up. Jenny returned to her seat and finished her glass in one go.

"I was just starting to enjoy that," she moaned.

"Don't look at me," said Danny, waving to the bar for a drink. "Laura is here to work, not dance."

"Yes, but when would I ever get to dance with World Cup International footballers?" she complained.

"Look," said Danny, furtively looking around him, "you didn't then."

"I just did," Jenny assured him, "just there."

"No, you didn't, love," Danny said adamantly. "There are Italian World Cup Players on the island in a five star hotel at Grand Harbour in Valletta, but they aren't here my dear."

"So who are those guys in the neat tracksuits?" Jenny asked incredulously.

"Well, actually they are Marco's water polo playing mates. They simply put Italia badges on top of their black tracksuits! We've done the scam before. Last week they were French rugby stars," he elaborated as if in excuse.

Danny headed off to the bar.

"Don't be too down," David said sympathetically. "You've still got me."

Jenny made the sort of face which suggested that wasn't too much of a consolation really. It didn't reassure David.

Suddenly, Charley and her two friends ran up the winding spiral staircase two at a time.

"Everyone says that there are Italian World Cup stars here," Charley asked, her head spinning like a top.

"Over there," David pointed.

"You are as bad as old Danny," Jenny said.

"Look, they are having a good time. Why spoil it?" David asked "That's our aim after all, a week's happiness away from the drudgery of life at home."

"Somehow I doubt those three have a boring existence," said Jenny who was enviously watching the fact the two young men had blatantly ditched their dancing partners and latched on to them.

Suddenly Charley returned. "Hey, how do you say, you're really good looking?" she asked. "Be quick!"

"Inti sabiha!" David shouted above the din.

Danny returned. "My friend, they are Italian not Maltese."

"I forgot," David apologised.

"Don't worry, young lady, Jenny is fluent in Italian," Danny suggested kindly.

Jenny looked momentarily anxious and whispered in Charley's ear. She beamed and headed back to the Italians.

"What did you say?" David asked quietly as Danny chatted to Laura.

"I said just say it in Maltese, they'll know it. In Italian it's harder to remember."

The reverse is true, David knew.

Within minutes Charley returned. "He laughed at me. He said sabiha means a good looking girl or, if said to a man, it means poof!"

"Oh shit, that's right," David said and put an embarrassed hand to his mouth. "Sabih is good lookin' to a guy" he corrected himself.

"No harm done," she grinned, "cos he asked for my phone number."

"Sabiha is what I would say to..." he hesitated, "....Jenny" he added as nonchalantly as he could mutter.

"Well you would," Charley confirmed and the three girls returned to the dance floor. Jenny gave him a look, wow what sort of look was that? David decided to analyse. He watched Charley and her two friends dancing. All three were undoubtedly stunning, but one sandwich short of a picnic. He looked across at Laura flirting with everyone at her snooker tables. How much nicer Jenny was than any of them: good-looking and bright and funny, but was she at all interested in him? There had been one or two of the girls he fancied over the years but, while one or two called him a friend, that was all. Mark had much more success. For that matter so did Marco. He had taken to saying he was twenty-eight not thirty. Thirty sounded far too old.

Suddenly lights flashed, steam came up, and a cage descended from the ceiling. Inside, Laura, now clad only in a tiny bikini, gyrated to the loud pop music. Danny looked on approvingly.

Charley and the two girls returned to the table. "Hey I fancy that. How do you get that job?" Charley asked.

"Ask a guy called Danny sometime," David suggested.

At that moment the two young men in tracksuits took the hands of the three girls and led them away down the spiral staircase. Above them Laura whisked off her bikini top and the lights went out.

It was getting late, and again Jenny seemed quite content that David should take her hand and lead her through the cars and mopeds back along the narrow road bordered by cactus, down to the apartments at St George's Bay.

"You know, when I eventually leave here, I won't just remember all that I have seen, I'll think back to the smell of cactus and palm trees, the sounds of locusts and the clip-clop of that karozzin passing my apartment," she reflected, "and Malta being pitch dark at 6 pm."

As they got into the foyer, David selected two tomato soups at the hot drinks machine. The Captain emerged from the bar and made a beeline for Jenny.

"Do you really have a list of extras?" he asked.

"I can offer you a map" she suggested.

He looked quite incredulous and headed off to his room.

At 8 am, David smiled when he saw the delight on Jenny's face as she noticed Danny's pay envelope on the breakfast table held down by a tumbler of orange juice.

"That what you were waiting for?" David nodded.

"You bet!"

"We've yet to do our retail therapy," said Laura as she came into the room drying her hair.

"I'm all set now," Jenny confirmed.

"Charley and pals intend to meet us at Golden Bay and will miss out the Glass factory," Mark said. "Apparently they'd had a hard night."

Jenny and David shared a knowing look.

"We can all go in the same coach," he continued. "Not everyone is going anyway and both young and old always enjoy this excursion."

"I didn't know you did disco dancing, Laura," Jenny interrupted as if she'd been wondering which euphemism to actually use. "How cool is that?"

"It's extra money for what? Showing my tits for about thirty seconds," Laura explained unabashed.

David blushed. He always felt a little uncomfortable at girls using such terms. Surely Jenny wouldn't want to supplement her earnings that way, he assured himself.

The coach drew up. Steven had had the gumption to grab the coach whose air conditioning still worked. They chugged up the hill to meet the ones who had chosen to go. David and Jenny sat in the front. Jenny could do with the practice, Mark had pointed out. Mark and Laura lay across the back seat, bare footed. There was that waft of deodorant again as Tim and Julian got on. Winston still had his cloth cap. The Blackwells asked Steven if he carried a medical kit as they wouldn't have to bring theirs. The family with the little girl carried rubber rings and a lilo. Indeed many of the group had enough touristy diving equipment to make Jacques Cousteau proud! The three girls weren't in evidence and David noticed their curtains were drawn.

"That was quite a scam Danny played with his Italian footballers," Jenny admitted as she counted thirty-one out of forty on the bus.

"No, it's thirty," David advised her. "Don't forget we have the Captain and he's not a tourist. Mind you, he may get off when he realises Theresa doesn't do this one. Yes it was a clever scam and you're about to encounter another."

"Are the Italians coming?" Jenny asked.

I should think anytime now, David reckoned, looking back at the curtains.

"No, they're locals, Jenny. Remember?" he replied.

As the coach headed out of St Julian's, David picked up the mike. "This morning we're going to Ta Qali," he began.

"Great memories," said the Captain, folding the previous day's Daily Telegraph. "My squadron flew from there in the war. Damn fine men I'll tell you."

"Yes, the Captain's right," David continued. "You will see lots of huts which go back to RAF days and in each there is a craft shop with the likes of lace, rugs, carpets, paintings, religious goods and so on, but we're going to the glass factory to see glass being made and then on to Golden Bay."

Half an hour later the coach parked outside the Mdina Glass Factory. Some of the men realised they were also adjacent to Malta's national football stadium and went to have a look. Jenny followed David, looking at all the cheap defect glassware and then marvelled at the glassblowing.

"Gives a blow job a whole new meaning!" Mark grinned, catching them up.

"So what is Danny's scam this time?" Jenny asked picking up a glass sea dragon.

"Well you'll not be surprised to learn he rents one of the huts here and he sells his own lace, glass, paintings and so on, all of which he puts a Malta stamp on but it's bankrupt stock from all over the place. The glass came from some shut-down factory in the Scottish highlands and so on."

They emerged into the bright sunlight, squinted and put their sunspecs back on.

"That ice cream van outside is the one I saw at the quayside at Bugibba isn't it?" Jenny asked. "After the heat of the factory it's a welcome sight."

"It's the same van," Laura confirmed, frantically licking melted ice cream off the back of her hands. "Look closely, Tony's the person selling the ices."

"What's that old town up on the hill?" Jenny asked.

"Mdina, the silent city and once the capital of Malta," David replied.

"And dead boring," Laura pointed out.

"Though it does have a spectacular view," Mark added. "Theresa takes older ones there later in the week."

The tourists were returning from the stadium or emerging from the huts. David couldn't resist a smile. Between Jenny wondering if Mark could be bisexual, and Mark convinced her Mum was a murderer, the spark had, so far, failed to ignite. Mark had always taken the girls David fancied. Anyway he had Laura. The time was surely coming when he should make a move. Faint heart never won fair lady somebody once sang. He remembered his parents playing a scratched Gilbert and Sullivan LP to that effect.

"I showed Winston my hut," the Captain proudly indicated with his walking stick as the group climbed into the coach. "I told him about Faith, Hope and Charity and how hurricanes protected Grand Harbour."

"Don't tell me they were three girls he got off with," said Jenny innocently.

"They were three, in fact, four ancient biplanes called Gloucester Gladiators which initially defended the island," David explained.

"I wouldn't have thought this area had hurricanes," Jenny said incredulously.

"And Typhoons," the Captain added.

"They were aircraft," David enlarged, aware of the young girl's bewilderment.

The coach wended its way along the winding country roads north to Golden Bay. The sky was cloudless and bright blue. A shepherd with a herd of goats delayed the coach at one point.

"You know so much, David," Jenny said supportively.

David settled back in his seat with a smug smile on his face. Life was good.

"Of course, you are much older." Life suddenly got worse!

It wasn't long before they came to the car park overlooking Golden Bay.

"We'll be here till 3 pm," David announced to the party. "Be sure to cover yourselves up once you've had a swim as we don't want anyone getting sun stroke, do we? The toilets are at the back of the beach and that shop on the beach has soft drinks and large filled baguettes."

The group clambered its way, carefully negotiating the old wooden steps down to the sands. Charley and the other young ones were already sunbathing on lilos in front of a rather redundant wind break. David, Jenny and Mark put down towels and began applying suntan lotion. Laura went to the shop with their baguette order. The blue sky and sea merged seamlessly in the distance.

"You'll have noticed," Mark said, "that we don't have all our group with us."

"Usual story," David agreed. "It's Scerri."

"How is it scary?" Jenny asked. "Won't they all be at the St Julian's shops or sunbathing at the hotel pool?"

"No it's Peter Scerri. He's Danny's main competitor. His reps do a spiel at the hotel all about their tours and, of course, they say they'll be 10% or 15 % less than ours and they entice some of our party. It takes a day or two to realise they aren't as good. Peter has been a thorn in Danny's side for many years. They have ice cream wars, their bars, restaurants, boats, nightclubs, karaoke bars, taxis, coaches and so on, all compete. His Reps football team even beat all the other Reps football teams in a summer tournament and big money changes hands. We aren't too bad, as Marco and his water polo pals turn out for us, but I think their Reps include lads who play semi-professional in the winter."

"Can I get a game?" Jenny asked, pushing the peak of her cap over her face.

"Every team does have a couple of girls and if you're as good as Laura, I don't see why not," David agreed.

"I've got the baguettes," said Laura. "Tuna, salmon, chicken, roast beef and some cans of coke," she announced placing them on a towel.

Laura took off her blouse and slacks and lay on the lilo as Mark rubbed some suntan lotion on.

"You should come along to our Reps talk at the hotel tonight," Mark suggested to Jenny "You'll soon see how competitive it is. We've to get folk to Valletta Sunday Market tomorrow and on the Grand Harbour Cruise. Then, on Monday evening we entertain our group at a party and on Thursday, before we get our new group, Danny and Carmen have invited you and David to a meal at their home."

Jenny looked worried. "When you say 'entertain the party' how exactly do you mean?"

"Well," Mark continued, "we can tell jokes, sing, play the guitar and Steven and Tony do folk music and dancing and so on."

"I've never done those things," said Jenny glumly.

"You'll be great," David said, gallantly assuring her. "Just join in the singing. Now, let's get these baguettes unwrapped."

After a short swim, David lay on his towel pretending to have a siesta but couldn't help glancing from time to time at Jenny as she lay beside him in her light blue bikini.

Winston passed by wearing a knotted hankie on his head. "It's better than Scarborough," he said chirpily.

"Yeh, but what about Bridlington?" Jenny countered "We've got a beautiful sandy beach too."

"But not that bright orangey thing in the cloudless sky," David ventured.

"Or palm trees," Laura suggested.

"Let's get our plastic ball out and play some football," Mark volunteered enthusiastically as he rummaged through his holdall. "We need to practice if we are to play Scerri's team in a few weeks."

All four put down slacks and shorts as goal posts and the game began. With Laura and Jenny so scantily clad, a crowd of young Maltese men soon took an interest.

"Can we get a game?" Charley and her pals volunteered as they arrived at the beach.

"You bet!" shouted Mark.

David noticed that Jenny played quite well and twice lobbed Mark in goal to score. The crowd also roared as Charley's top failed to do its job and twice she ended up topless.

"Hey it's illegal in Malta!" Laura laughed.

"Who's caring?" Mark asked. Not the crowd, David gauged.

As Jenny got her hat trick Mark shouted, "That's it! You must be in our team next month. I must tell Danny!"

"Will it be a formal meal at his home?" Jenny asked, putting her skirt back on.

"Just wear a dress," Laura advised her. The Maltese dispersed and David rubbed the cool can on his face and watched the Captain playing with a dog on the sands. The little girl from the coach had made sandcastles and the dog was oblivious of ploughing through them.

"I've put the wife back on the coach," Mr Blackwell announced as he passed by with a beer. "The sun is just too much."

"So, why did you wallies chose Malta?" David whispered in Jenny's direction.

"I wonder if he was allowed his beer when she was with him on the beach," Jenny replied.

With the small group counted, shortly after, the coach moved at some speed down the coast. The Captain got a sing-song of "Ten green bottles" going as they approached St Julian's and the group disembarked. David made a face when he saw the amount of sand on the coach carpet. "Danny will really moan about that" he said, leaning towards Mark on the right.

When David, Jenny, Mark and Laura entered the hotel at 7 pm, in good time for the Reps' talk to all the holidaymakers in the local hotels, Danny's face was as cold as the marble floor in the foyer, only not so welcome!

"I've told you a thousand times you lot, well not you Jenny, obviously, don't let holidaymakers spill half the island's sand on my coach!"

"Sorry," said David as he brushed past into the large conference room. About 150 tourists were already milling about helping themselves to the free snacks, fans whirring above their heads.

"Is it always this well attended?" Jenny asked nervously, her head spinning almost in time with the fans.

"To be honest, yes," David nodded helping himself to a sandwich. "All these vol au vents, sandwiches, sausage rolls and soft drinks all for free do help!"

They took their seats and listened politely to talks by the couriers from JMC, Thomas Cook, Direct Holidays and Sun World. The Reps, in turn, stood up at a lectern in front of eight parallel long tables all well supplied with snacks.

"It's Scerri next," Mark whispered. "Watch him try to undercut us, as usual."

"I thought the other trips sounded expensive," Jenny said optimistically. "Doesn't that give us a chance?"

"True," David acknowledged

"But these companies are catering for older, more affluent, tourists who want to see their cathedrals, churches, architecture, go on long cruises around the island, up in a helicopter or even on a hydrofoil to Sicily," David explained.

"Whereas we get many young ones and families on a budget, who simply want to get to a beach, see the Blue Grotto and Blue Lagoon, go to the market, go on the underwater safari and so on," Laura elaborated.

The tourists applauded, asked a few questions and prepared for Peter Scerri.

"Where are the toilets at Mosta Dome?" Mr Blackwell asked loudly.

"Just outside," Mr Scerri dived in on his way up to the lectern. "On my trips we always tell you such vital information," he added mischievously.

Peter Scerri was a large, bronzed, thin Maltese with jet black hair, a moustache like a spiv, graveyard teeth, and he wore a thin immaculate white suit and black shirt.

"I thought it was John Travolta, only 20 years older!" Jenny suggested "Is he going to sing 'Stayin' Alive'?"

"Doubt it," Laura remarked.

"Maybe he should. He's determined to build up his business by bankrupting ours if he can" Mark said ominously.

David looked around. Everyone seemed to be paying more attention, probably due to the number of posters offering cheap deals Scerri had plastered around every hotel in the town.

"Wake me up when it's over," Danny groaned, taking a seat behind them and deliberately scraping it along the floor to irritate Peter, who had to start again!

"Good evening, Bonju, Bonsoir, Guten Abend, Buenosera, Buenas Noches," he began arrogantly.

"Get on with it," Danny muttered audibly.

"It'll take hours if he translates in 6 languages," Jenny groaned.

"He won't. That's the sum total of his knowledge of languages," David reassured her.

"Our trips are the best value on the island," Peter announced, thumping the lectern to emphasise the point. "It doesn't matter if you want an inexpensive cruise or cheap ice cream, no firm can match us. You don't want to see architecture you want to go to the beach!"

There was a roar of approval from the tourists who had clearly sat through enough culture on a warm evening.

"You don't want churches you want firework displays." Another round of applause followed. "You don't want ancient buses whose air conditioning doesn't work, you want modern coaches."

"Who told him that?" Danny asked, leaning forward.

"You don't want stuffy boring museums you want nightclubs."

"I say, speak for yourself!" Mr Blackwell called out.

Peter Scerri made a face and continued undaunted.

David's attention wandered to Scerri's posters all around the conference room. One glance showed that the prices were all 10% below Danny's.

"We're doomed," he whispered in his best John Laurie impression to Jenny.

She looked at him quizzically then got up to get a sandwich.

Peter finished up to a warm applause and was joined by four of his male reps at the front. "Ask us anything you want and we'll tell you all about our trips serving your individual needs. Sahah, Goodbye, Au Revoir, Arriverderci, Auf Wiedersehen, Adios."

Tourists began to get up to move towards the snacks tables. David strode purposefully up to the lectern, so quickly in fact he stumbled over Mrs Blackwell's walking stick! There was quite a din.

"Good evening." People carried on talking. One or two began to leave the room. "You've heard the rest, now hear the best," David began confidently.

Everyone was chomping on sausage rolls and looking at Peter's posters.

"Because out prices are 10% off."

There was a hush. A large number slowly sat down again. "10% off what exactly?" Peter shouted.

"10% off anything you see on these posters around the room"

"Yes, right!" Peter roared back.

"Let the man speak," said Mr Blackwell.

"We haven't got our posters out yet because we were negotiating the best deals."

Danny sat with his head in his hands. David avoided catching his eye. "But we learned today just how low our prices would be."

"In your two ancient buses? As if!" Peter laughed ominously.

"With free ice cream for every child," David added, warming to his theme.

"A child under 5," Danny added audibly.

"Right, let me tell you all where we go," David announced.

"Bankrupt!" shouted Scerri.

Undaunted he reeled off the tours to the Blue Grotto, Hagar Qim, the Blue Lagoon cruise, Gozo, Mellieha, and Golden Bay beaches, Popeye's village, Valletta Market, the under water safari up at Bugibba and then mentioned Danny's various discounts. As he did so, Peter and his four reps were angrily pulling down their posters from the walls.

"And now, in conclusion," David said, "you can ask our reps anything and they'll serve your needs. Come on up, Jenny and Laura."

Mark had begun to leave his seat but Danny put his hand on his shoulder to restrain him. There was louder applause then than before and he knew the coach would be full tomorrow. He also realised Peter would retaliate.

The tourists dispersed and a panting Danny raced up to the lectern. "What the hell are you doing?" he demanded to know, red faced and flustered "You have just ruined me!"

"I've just made your fortune more like," David smiled. He had seen Danny many times like this before and knew he was a paper tiger. "Your bus will be mobbed tomorrow."

"Well, it had better be," Danny threatened, mopping his forehead with a Malta lace handkerchief. He stared at it. "Must be the wife's" he confessed.

As they moved across to the snack table to plunder a few vol au vents, Peter rushed up, rolls of posters under his arm.

"Think you're clever, Danny?" he asked rhetorically. "You will make yourself bankrupt, then we'll mop up," he threatened.

"Nonsense man, you cannot buck the market, Blair said."

"It was Thatcher," David corrected him quietly.

"Thatcher. I always confuse the great statesmen," Danny added in full flow.

"We can't charge tourists the same sum we pay for our excursions and well you know it," Peter moaned.

He picked up a sandwich and headed off.

"The problem is, he is right," Danny confirmed.

Mark, Jenny and Laura joined them at the table.

"Everyone is booking with us," Mark announced. "What a masterstroke!" he enthused.

"Insanity more like," Danny suggested.

"We'll have both coaches on in the morning and every seat will be taken" Mark added.

"And what will the Scerri man do then?" Danny thought out loud.

"Don't forget you're joining Carmen and me for a meal next Thursday evening, Jenny," Danny said finishing a glass of wine.

"I won't, I am looking forward to it," she enthused. "Now, it's Saturday night. Aren't you young ones out on the town?"

David led Jenny through the tourists who were chatting around the hall. "Right, let's go to the disco," David suggested.

"Great idea," said Jenny. "But I must have a shower and put my face on."

Magic! She's doing it for me, David thought as they walked out of the hotel to be hit by the smell of the sea, vegetation and the familiar sound of the locusts.

"You never know what a hot guy I may meet," Jenny said provocatively.

I wish she wouldn't do that. David bit his lip as they walked along St George's Bay to their apartments.

As they got to the entrance, they saw four females, mutton dressed as lamb, lined up outside with faces caked in make-up, short skirts, high heels, low cut tops which left nothing to the imagination.

"Must be a bus due," Jenny suggested.

"Aye right!" David replied, killing a grin.

An hour later, the couple walked into the 10-pin bowling alley. The sound of Queen and 'Killer Queen' got drowned out by the familiar crash of skittles being toppled. Tony and Steven were both behind the bar.

,"A bacardi and coke and a vodka and coke" David shouted above the racket. "The place is mobbed. Danny will be happy," he smiled.

"I'm not sure. Peter Scerri wants to see him," Tony nodded ominously towards the Maltese playing one of the alleys.

"Why?" David asked, a little anxiety in his voice.

"He wants some sort of deal, I believe," Steven explained, drying some glasses. "I don't think he was too happy at your performance," he added as if as an afterthought.

David ushered Jenny to a seat.

"It's all 1970s retro music," Jenny moaned "It's like being home with my Mum!"

"It's up to the tourists what they put on the juke box," David pointed out, tearing open a packet of peanuts with his teeth.

"You mean people pay for it?" Jenny looked incredulous.

"It's a Danny establishment. Say no more," David smiled. "Danny will be happy tomorrow when he sees two full coaches," he continued. "At least I hope so. He's just a grump!"

"I see that scary Mr Scerri is over there bowling," Jenny said.

"Yeh, apparently he wants some sort of deal with Danny. Having an empty coach tomorrow will concentrate his mind wonderfully."

"He seems to be playing with some venom," Jenny pointed out "He has one strike after another."

"He has his own bowling alley in Bugibba, so he's good," David explained as Danny came in the door.

David pointed out to Danny the Scerri presence. Danny gestured a cut throat sign back.

"Well, we'll soon find out what the deal is," David concluded.

Danny sat down with a long cool Cisk lager. "Carmen's making you a special lasagne, Jenny" he said with a smile "She's looking forward to having you."

So would I, David thought.

"I can't wait," Jenny said diplomatically.

"Both coaches are booked solid tomorrow," Danny carried on. "Remember kids get one ice cream only and they must be under 5."

"Small ices?" David asked.

"Small cones," Danny confirmed.

"I was being sarcastic," David pointed out.

Danny ignored that. "And from my van parked strategically outside Valletta market," he elaborated.

"We'd go to no one else," David assured him. "Another vodka?" he asked Jenny.

As David wandered back up to the bar, he did wonder why the queue parted like the Red Sea. Then he smelt the familiar whiff of Peter Scerri's deodorant.

"Thought you were clever in your speech, did you?" he began rhetorically "Out to impress that girl, were you?"

You're pretty observant, David thought. "I'm sorry, I'm not with you," David said falteringly.

"That's your problem, young man. This is a small town, indeed a small island. Here you are either with me or against me. Get it?"

"Got it!"

"Good." At that moment, Peter let drop a small bowling ball on to David's foot. David gritted his teeth but declined to swear. Shit, he thought.

"Oh sorry, young man," the Maltese said sneeringly.

At the bar Tony dashed to serve him. David forgot his drinks and limped back to Jenny and Danny.

"I wouldn't stand for that," Danny declared pulling out his chair.

"I can barely stand, you're right there." The young man groaned and flopped into his seat.

"Was it an accident?" Jenny asked.

"No way," David replied taking off a sandal and looking at his two blackened toe nails. "It'd be a brave man who would take him and his henchmen on," David added.

"He and his henchmen," Theresa added as she joined them. "I hear we are booked solid tomorrow."

"Two coaches to Valletta," Danny boasted, a glint in his eye.

David kept his eye on Peter at the bar.

"I'll take the older ones around St John's co – cathedral and give them some culture as usual," Theresa volunteered.

"The younger ones will be happy enough in the ice cream parlour," Danny added.

"Yummy!" Jenny enthused.

"Oh God, here he comes," David announced.

Peter Scerri had a whisky in his hand and smiled broadly at Danny.

"I remember I've got something to do," Theresa said unconvincingly and offered up her seat.

"Danny, Danny, my old friend," said Peter, patting both Danny's cheeks like Morecambe greeting Wise. "You and me, we are old mates. Tell me, how far back do we go?"

"Further than I want to admit to," Danny sighed, his face red.

"We are business men together," Peter continued. "We understand each other, we know the market, our tourists, their needs...," he paused, "....our needs."

"To give them a rich experience of the island?" David proffered.

"Don't be stupid, boy. To give Danny and me a rich experience on the island." He clapped his hands and one of his young bronzed lackeys appeared at his side. "Another?"

"Thank you," Danny nodded.

"Can I have sex on the beach?" Jenny asked, surprisingly.

David looked up to heaven.

"I am sure I can arrange that," Scerri replied. "You always have beautiful assistants, sabiha," he smiled at Danny.

"I do my best," Danny acknowledged.

"And I'll have a lager," David interrupted.

Scerri made a face. "Okay you can have one too. How's your foot?"

"It'll be okay," David conceded manfully.

"Right, lets get down to business," Scerri returned to his theme. "Let's forget all this 10% discount and free ice cream crap," he advised. "It'll ruin both of us. It'll ruin you, Danny. You can't just live off the earnings of women in the night."

"What's that?" Jenny asked.

"He has shares in that new Andrew Lloyd Webber London musical," David dived in quickly.

Scerri looked astonished, then continued, "So the answer is simple. We have the same prices for the same tours. You can't say fairer than that. The best man wins, simple as that."

"We don't do exactly the same tours," Danny pointed out. "And you've got your own pleasure boat for the Blue Lagoon trip. If I cut to your prices I'd go to the wall."

"Then stop doing it at all," Scerri suggested, again pinching Danny's cheeks. "There must be another solution," Danny wondered out loud as Scerri's henchman returned with a tray of drinks.

"I do have one," Peter suggested. "Only one of us operates out of this resort."

"The one being you, of course," Danny anticipated.

"One does here with Sliema, the other does Bugibba."

"Bugibba may be popular but it's not half the size," David said.

"And size is important, I did economics at school," Jenny grinned.

Not Biology? David wondered.

"I agree, if we get here," Danny offered.

"I thought you'd take Bugibba being a smaller operation," Peter suggested.

"No way Jose," said Danny bravely, pulling his head back to avoid his cheeks getting pinched a third time.

"Then I know how to settle it."

"Oh not a fight," Danny groaned "I am too old."

"Nothing like that – a football match," Peter beamed.

"We lose every year," Danny reminded him. "£200 you took off me last year."

"But it was a close match," Peter pointed out. "2-1."

"Usual rules?" David asked.

"Yep, 11 of a team, 5 subs, two of your team must be female and no using any professional footballer you've found among your tourists. And whoever wins operates out of Sliema and St Julian's."

"When?" asked Danny.

"Let's say two weeks today."

"Where?"

"At Sliema Wanderers' ground. And let the best man win."

"Or women," Jenny suggested.

Peter took her hand and kissed it "Buenosera signorina," he said. He nodded to his henchman and headed back to the bowling.

"We've never won that bloody match in 5 years," Danny moaned. "And unless Thierry Henry wants a summer job with SAY GO TOURS, I am sunk."

"Don't despair yet, guv," David advised, downing his long glass of cool lager. "Marco and his mates are all fit, Tony, Steven, Mark and I can play, and Jenny and Laura are good for girls."

"Thanks for that," Jenny laughed.

"I nobbled the ref last year. I threatened to tell his wife about the dodgy films he was going to in that club in Valletta and we still lost," Danny confessed.

"For heaven's sake, even I wondered when we got the fourth penalty," David groaned "I thought he was generous."

"And you scored just one," Danny reminded him. "I may as well admit it. I am bankrupt." Danny picked up his glass and forlornly returned to the bar.

"Don't we have a chance?" Jenny asked innocently.

"Can Hartlepool beat Man Utd? Can East Stirling beat Celtic? Can England beat West Indies in a Test match? Oh wait, they have. Forget that one."

"You're saying we don't have a chance?" Jenny inferred.

"That's it in a nutshell," David replied. There was a pause.

"I may have a cunning plan," Jenny beamed tantalisingly.

"Like what?"

"I'll tell you later. Right, can we go back to the apartments as I've a new colour hair dye Laura got me and I want to try it. In fact can you help me?" Jenny asked, getting up.

"You just tell me what to do" David replied, helpfully, taking her hand.

"Will you do most of the commentary in the coach tomorrow?" Jenny asked as they walked along the sand of St George's Bay.

"You want me to talk," David said. Jenny took a bottle out of her handbag. "I want you to dye Meester Bond."

David threw some sand at her as she giggled and ran back to the apartment entrance. As they got to the door, huge new searchlights illuminated the front.

"That's effective," Jenny said, looking for her keys "Now folk outside will know if they are coming or going."

"I am not so sure Danny will be too pleased," David said.

"But if he owns the block, how come he doesn't know? Jenny queried.

"Police regulations," Maria at the reception desk interrupted "You can get some undesirable folk here late at night."

"And that's just Danny," David laughed.

The following morning it was very hot. The blue sky and sea seemed to merge as Mark, Laura and Jenny joined David at the breakfast table.

"Two full coaches! Peter will love this," Mark said, watching Danny's two coaches parking in the St Julian's Hotel car park up the hill.

"It won't last long if our presence in the resort depends on our football ability," Laura declared from behind 19 Magazine.

"Don't despair, mes amis. Just because we've lost every year doesn't mean a thing," David replied encouragingly. "We need a bit of luck."

"And I might score," said Jenny, extricating a jammed slice of bread from the toaster. If only with me, David considered. The fan above them clearly had a fault and was not operating as quickly as usual, so, taking their toast, they all came out of the kitchen, headed for the foyer, and emerged glinting into the entrance area.

"What is that large Scerri ice cream van doing blocking the St Julian's car park?" asked Mark forlornly.

"It appears to be stuck," Jenny confirmed. All four ran along the beach. There was no one in sight, but the bonnet was up and steam was coming out of the engine.

"Sabotage," said David.

"Treachery," said Jenny.

"Damnable," said Mark.

"How much do you reckon the cones are?" Laura inquired. The other three looked at her quizzically, then Theresa appeared.

"It's broken down," she confirmed. "The Scerri driver has apologised."

"Blocking both our coaches in," David confirmed "Where are Tony and Steven?"

"Having a game of pool till it's all sorted out."

It was 8.30 and the first tourists were appearing. Tim and Julian were first on the scene.

"We met that butch ice cream man at the reception desk," Tim announced. "Is he one of your employees?"

"Sadly no," David replied.

"What's wrong?" asked Charley slapping on some sun block.

"Piston broke," Mark replied.

"Aren't we all, love," the blonde replied.

"Did the driver say that?" asked Theresa.

"It's just a joke," Mark admitted.

"I won't stay," said Mr Blackwell. "Wife has a funny tummy this morning."

He headed back into the hotel. At this point the Captain, immaculate in his blue blazer with RAF badge at the left breast and white flannels, came up the hill. "In my day," he grandly said, "you hit it with a walking stick and that would get it going." He did just that.

"Let's see," said Jenny. She clambered into the cab and turned the ignition. The engine spluttered into life first time. "I think we've been conned," she grinned and drove the van away from the entrance.

"Everyone on board!" David shouted and, in the heat, the tourists didn't need any further encouragement to get on the two coaches.

Mark went off to get the two drivers.

"It's an exceeding hot day," Winston said, as he passed Theresa.

"Exceedingly," she corrected him.

"It must be wonderful to be that perfect," Jenny whispered.

"Yes, there are a few of us left," David smiled.

"There's few of us," Theresa interrupted.

"Oops!" David acknowledged.

There was a huge grin on Jenny's face.

She really is a wonderful combination of personality and good looks, David reckoned. He would have to make a move, but when? There was the party for the tourists the following evening and the formal meal at Danny's on Thursday evening. They would both seem opportune moments, but what if she rejected him? How could he continue to work with her then?

"So do you like my dyed hair?" she asked.

"What?"

"My dyed hair, remember."

"I like you as a blonde."

"Oh."

"Oh you know what I mean. You look great with brown hair too. I always stick my flaming foot in it." David grinned.

However he had said she looked great and that had gone down well. He rapidly changed the subject. "So what is your cunning plan with the football match?" he asked. "We'd try anything, heaven knows"

"I am still working on it," she replied tantalisingly, examining a postcard she'd taken out of her handbag.

Late morning Jenny and David were sitting in the outside café in Republic St, the busy main thoroughfare of Valletta opposite the capital's largest ice cream parlour where all the younger ones had congregated.

"I'll get you some pastizzi, a real delicacy," David began authoritatively.

"What are they again? I've had to learn so many Maltese words," asked Jenny, dangling her long legs across the adjacent metal seat.

"Cheese pies, remember, you can't come to Malta and not have a cheese pie."

"Like frogs legs in Paris, Hamburgers in Hamburg, cannabis in Amsterdam," she grinned. "I can't wait for a cold coke. I am roasted," she added.

"Try a local soft drink, Kini."

"I'll stay with a coke, but do tell the waiter to hurry up," Jenny implored, wiping her sunspecs. "Do you think Peter will do any more underhand tactics to try and scupper Danny's travel firm?" Jenny asked, her face brightening up as the waiter appeared with a tray with Cisk lager, coke and 4 pastizzi.

David moved the large cruet, picked up the lager glass, took a sip then rubbed it along his forehead. "Do you mean like torpedo his boat in Grand Harbour? That wouldn't be wise. He'd have to deal with Theresa, definite."

"Definitely," Jenny corrected him. Oh my God, she's got me doing it now. Hey these cheese pies are fabby. What are the plans for the rest of the today?" Jenny asked.

"Once Theresa returns with the culture vultures, we can make a move back to St Julian's. We must rehearse for our show tomorrow evening. Then during the day tomorrow it's the boat trip to the Blue Grotto and we'll see the Stonehenge at Hager Qim, Tuesday is the Mellieha beach and Popeye's Village and Wednesday is a day trip to the sister island of Gozo. You'll see that it is greener and hillier then Malta."

"You can never switch off from being a tour guide, can you?" Jenny commented.

"Oh I'm sorry," David apologised. Idiot, he thought. I am lecturing again. The golden rule of chatting up any female is to get her to talk about herself, he considered.

"So, what's the news of your sister, Sarah?" he inquired.

"Oh it was her who sent the postcard. She was in London. She's wondering where to holiday. I think Cyprus has got her vote."

"Cyprus is Malta with grass," David suggested. "Hey, here come Mark and Laura from the ice cream parlour."

Mark and Laura walked across the main street, arm in arm, avoiding a Karozzin clip-clopping on its way to the SWW museum.

"You know, he does act strangely," Jenny said, thinking out loud.

"How so?"

"He's gay."

"Gay, but so tactile," David hurriedly butted in.

"He's not gay. Tell me he's not gay," Jenny implored, finishing off the dregs of her coke.

Drat, David thought. "He's not gay nowadays."

"He wasn't gay at all, ever," Jenny stressed.

"No." David shamefully hung his head.

Mark and Laura sat down at the table. "Well, I'll be buggered" Mark remarked. "Out in this sunshine my ice cream has melted away."

Jenny avoided David's gaze. She was close to giggling.

"What?" Mark asked.

"Nothing," David answered.

"What can I do at your concert for the tourists?" Jenny asked plaintively as the two coaches headed out of Valletta.

"Don't worry," David said and put a supportive arm around her.

Jenny leaned forward as he did so. That went well, he thought. His heart missed a beat.

"Tony, Steven, Marco and pals do their folk music and dancing. There's a lot of summer songs like 'Agadoo' and 'Macarena' for the families. Mark and I tell jokes, Laura does pop songs. You are good at karaoke, why not accompany her? There's a bar and folk are out to have a good time. You can't go wrong."

Jenny didn't look convinced.

"I am glad we rehearse it," she conceded. She seemed happy leaning back on David's arm but he couldn't decide if Mark's recently acquired status as a heterosexual male made him a rival or not.

"Are Laura and Mark an item?" she asked.

"Definitely," David assured her.

Jenny looked in reflective mood. Theirs was the coach with no air conditioning. Soon he was asleep.

As David walked with Jenny up to the St Julian's hotel, he saw Marco and his water polo pals at the entrance all wearing Maltese folk costumes.

"How handsome Marco looks," Jenny said admiringly, "Don't tell me he's gay."

David didn't answer.

"I am charmed to meet you," the suntanned young man put down a wine flagon, which enhanced the costume, and kissed her hand. "Have you forgiven me for the last time we met?" he asked, a twinkle in his eye.

"But of course!" Jenny beamed. "Do you want to dance with me in the rehearsal?" he asked.

You're chancing your arm, David bit his lip. They all went in. Tony and Steven had cleared all the furniture from the hall. Mark was practising some guitar chords and Laura was quietly singing 'Una Paloma Blanca'. David took some notes out of his pocket.

"Tell me you've got some new jokes since last year and the year before!" Mark demanded. "Maltese drivers don't drive on the left, they drive in the shade. We've all heard them."

"But the tourists haven't."

Everyone took their turn with the remainder acting as the audience. Marco seemed to spin out the folk dancing and he and Jenny kept laughing loudly as he spun her around.

David sat with a glass of bacardi patiently waiting for it to end.

"Marco says he's the best player in our football team," Jenny said as they headed back along the beach to the apartments. They were momentarily blinded by the spotlight at the entrance.

"No women out here tonight," said the Captain as he passed them at the door. "Danny will not be a happy man."

"It's Police regulations," David explained.

"I am not taking it lying down."

"That's not what I've heard," David replied.

The Captain turned, touched his cap to Jenny, and headed up the stairs.

The following morning David and Jenny sat on the wall near the landing at the Blue Grotto. It was roasting.

"What's that little island out there?" asked Jenny, shielding her eyes with her hand.

"Filfla, the RAF used to use it for bombing practice years ago. It's why no one swims out to in, that and the shark."

"Shark?" repeated Jenny nervously.

"Shark," nodded David enjoying her attention. "We never tell the tourists till they're back safely from the caves," he pointed out. "They wouldn't want to get in a boat."

"You've told me."

"You're a holiday rep, you've got to go!"

"I could lose an arm and a leg."

"You've seen Danny's prices then!"

"I meant limbs."

"I know" David laughed. He gave her an impromptu hug.

"That was nice," Jenny beamed.

She said that was nice, that was nice, David's mind raced. Stuff you, Marco and the polo team, and Mark, I've pulled.

"Why are there far fewer folk with us today?" Jenny asked as they carefully picked their feet over fishing nets to the quayside.

"Simple. Peter runs his own boats from here and they undercut Danny. We've only got 14 with us today."

Mr Blackwell joined them.

"Where's your wife today?" David asked politely.

"Up at the café. Tummy trouble," he replied like a man resigned to going through life itemising her many medical ailments.

"She'll see the large photos of the shark there," said David as he clambered into a boat with Charley and her two friends, Mr Blackwell, Winston, Tim and Julian.

"This reminds me of boat trips to the cliffs at Farnborough from Bridlington harbour," Jenny reminisced.

"It's a bit hotter'" David suggested.

The motor putted into action and the boat headed over to the caves. The breeze was welcome. The sea was transparent and the group marvelled at the shoals of fish darting among the rocks. Then there were the usual gasps as the boat entered the cave, the engine was shut off, and the boatman rowed quietly amongst the blue, red, orange and green colours of the rocks.

"This would not be a good time to mention that shark, now would it?" Jenny whispered.

"What was that?" Mr Blackwell asked.

"She said it was dark," David replied and nudged her leg. They all glinted as the boat emerged into the sunlight.

"Is it that Stonehenge next?" Jenny asked.

"After coffees, yes. It's called Hager Qim."

An hour later the 14 stood at the entrance.

"It's a load of old stones," Jenny moaned.

"An historical and archaeological triumph, young lady," was Winston's view.

"It's shut," said David.

"How can a historical monument be shut?" Mr Blackwell asked. "We're standing beside it. We can see it."

"There should be a guide," David explained.

"I've seen something interesting," Winston announced. "There's a Roman lamp. I reckon 2000 years old, stuck to one of the pillars. They must have come here too, fascinating, fascinating."

"Glad you're happy," Charley interrupted. The blonde lay strewn across one of the fallen pillars. "The boat trip was good but this is mega boring."

"Megalithic," Winston corrected her.

"Look, we'll head back to the coach once you've taken photos," David improvised.

"I need a pee," Mrs Blackwell complained.

"I told you to go in the café," her husband reminded her.

"There's a village near here. We can stop," David reassured her.

"I've a sore tummy, I need a pee, I've a bad head, I need a bloody life," Charley mimicked her.

"There's no need for that sort of language" Mr Blackwell reprimanded her.

"I don't use bad words," Charley beamed. "I'm as pure as snow."

"You just drift a bit," one of her friends suggested. The group headed back to the coach. The leather seats burned their bare legs as they sat down.

"I should wear trousers," Jenny groaned putting her hands under her shapely bare thighs.

Don't say that, David muttered under his breath.

"There'll be a delay. We've got a puncture," Tony announced. Then quietly he turned to David, "I thought I saw Peter's car in the car park as I came in. That man is seriously starting to annoy me. If you're wondering where your guide is. Peter's guided tour party is going around now."

"We're heading towards war," said David menacingly, "a war we would not win."

"You're a bit melodramatic," Jenny suggested.

"We'll need to win that football match, that's for sure," David added, "I do hope you have a plan."

"This folk dancing has lasted much longer than usual," Danny remarked as he and David watched the concert at the St Julian's hotel.

The room was crowded. Everyone was tucking into the baking Carmen had provided and were enjoying sweet almond biscuits with their lager.

"Marco just wants to dance with Jenny," David sighed.

"They make a handsome couple," Danny nodded. "Have a vol au vent."

Nothing would console David. He fidgeted nervously with his notes and mouthed his opening gags. After his act, Mark and Laura with Jenny's help would lead the community singing.

"Do you think Peter let down my tyres?" Danny asked.

"He was certainly there," David replied.

"Circumstantial evidence, anyway he can't hijack our cruise to the Blue Lagoon tomorrow. How many are going?"

"We've got 12," David said. "Peter's got his own little steamship and you know he undercuts us every time."

"Well, when you are on stage, tell the tourists that everyone will get 50% off at the shop beside the Blue Lagoon."

"There is no shop at the Blue Lagoon," David reminded him.

"You know, I can hardly hear you for the din," Danny grinned.

"Have you heard the latest Maltese law?" asked David concluding his act. "Exit signs could be on the way out."

The crowd laughed. 2 hours on and with most plastered they'd have laughed at anything. Mark, Laura and Jenny led the singing and David finished off the last of the sandwiches.

"Why the heck did you mention discount on a shop on Comino?" Mark asked.

"I was acting under orders," David pointed out. Danny had long gone. "Hey have you seen Jenny?"

"Probably gone to the toilet," Mark looked around. "She was nervous."

"She's chatting to Marco beside the old palm tree outside," Laura said as she joined them, sausage rolls in both hands. "I see we've got a dozen going tomorrow. Even I didn't know you can shop on Comino," Laura added quizzically.

"You can't," Mark stressed as David dashed outside.

He just caught Marco giving Jenny a goodnight kiss as he held both her hands.

David's heart sank. "Buenosera," Marco waved and drove off on a moped.

David took Jenny's hand, as if to make a point, as they walked down the hill. "Do you like him then?"

"He has a large Suzuki."

"So I've heard."

"He doesn't bring it out much."

"That's not what I've heard!"

"So he came on his moped."

"Why were you holding hands?"

"It's just the culture I'd imagine," Jenny said thoughtfully. "When in Rome........."

David could see the bright lights of the entrance flashing on and off as guests inadvertently activated them.

"It looks like a lighthouse," Jenny remarked. "You can see it for miles around."

"It might suit Danny after all," David thought out loud.

"Marco asked me out for a pizza tomorrow evening," said Jenny after a pause.

"Oh," said David appearing as nonchalant as one can as a dagger pierces the heart. "Where?"

"Pizza Hut in Sliema."

"They call folk Tal Pepe there. I've told you before," David elaborated.

"Meaning?"

"Poseurs."

"He's not, he's cool." The dagger had not only pierced his heart, she'd just twisted it!

"Do you want a soup from the machine?" David offered.

"I'll just call it a night," Jenny replied as the searchlights landed on them. "The Blue Lagoon trip sounds wicked tomorrow."

"Marco takes his different girls there," David fired back.

Jenny looked as if she might respond. Instead she gave a little wave and walked away. Her flip flops made a flapping sound on the cold marble floor. The contest had just begun David realised.

9 am at Sliema sea front and it didn't take long to count 12 tourists on to the bright red Captain Morgan boat. It was a quiet time of day and both Mark and Laura were already chilling out on deck, lying across five seats. A couple of youngsters skateboarded along the pavement which divided the quayside from the yellow and orange gaily painted old buses lined up at their stance.

David perused his clipboard. "All present and correct," he announced.

"It's great going back to the Blue Lagoon," Jenny said, wiping some suntan lotion off the sunspecs it had smeared. They showed their tickets to the deck hands and lay across the seats parallel to Mark and Laura. The latter was already down to a light blue bikini.

"Is there a toilet on board?" Mr Blackwell enquired as he walked by clutching a UK newspaper.

"One deck down, take those steps," Mark said, pointing ahead.

The old man shuffled away.

"Smelly and old" Laura said.

"Mr Blackwell?" Jenny asked.

"The toilet, don't use them unless you have to."

The pleasure boat cast off and the guide began her spiel about Valletta across the creek, Sliema and the opposite Peninsula, Manoel Island.

"I'm going out tonight," Jenny said.

"With David?" Laura asked.

"Nope, Marco."

"Oh," said Laura, displaying some surprise.

"He's a bit of a lad," Mark said.

Thanks for that, David acknowledged with a wink.

"He takes everyone for a pizza."

Even better, keep going, David grinned.

Jenny fell silent and watched some racing yachts moving in the creek. The Mediterranean was as still as a millpond in the hot summer sunshine.

"Are you coming for a drink?" Laura asked and took Jenny up to the bar.

"You fancy her, don't you?" Mark came straight to the point.

"You've noticed then," David smiled. "And who wouldn't, she's funny, sensitive, good looking and bright."

"And daughter of a murderer. Watch it, David. You don't want to wake up one morning dead – oh you know what I mean! Tread carefully. I like her but she does come out with some strange comments. She asked me if I'd always been close to Steven."

David said nothing but watched the crew preparing a large salad lunch for the tourists.

"Have you made a move?"

"Not yet. I was going to, but Marco has stepped in, as usual."

"That young man is not wanting a girl, he wants a harem," Mark suggested.

"So how is it with you and Laura?"

"Could hardly be better. When I watch guys gaping at her as she comes down from the ceiling I feel like saying that bird in the cage is mine!"

"So it'll last?"

"Well, this summer anyway. Then I'll see who the next one is that Danny entices."

"I think the word is recruits."

"You are not Theresa."

"It's still recruits!" he emphasised.

The girls returned with their drinks. "I wonder why we haven't seen Peter's cruise boat today?" Mark asked.

"They've all gone to Popeye's village," Laura explained. "I saw the advert in the hotel."

"But it's a gorgeous day here," Mark emphasised.

Suddenly a lunch steward approached. "Take your places ladies and gentleman. Don't jump overboard after it. There's hundreds of jellyfish here today!"

"He couldn't have arranged that," Jenny said as she queued up and broke some Maltese bread.

"No, but he knew, didn't he?" David sighed.

David sat on the rock where he'd first seen Jenny one week earlier. Across the Blue Lagoon Mark and Laura sat on their towels dabbing suntan lotion on. Winston sat on the sand with a knotted handkerchief on his head. Julian and Tim floated on a blue lilo in the lagoon. The Blackwells had gone to look for a toilet.

"Where's that shop with all the discounts?" Charley asked loudly, cigarette in hand, mobile in the other, flanked by her two mates. "Would you just know it, Tuesday is early closing."

"It's only noon now," Charley stated.

"Siesta," said Jenny. "You know the Maltese customs."

Charley shrugged and headed back along the golden sands, quickly putting her flip-flops back on as the sand burnt the soles of her feet.

"You'll make a holiday rep yet," David congratulated her. "Danny would be proud of you."

Jenny went red. "Tell me, is Marco a bit loose?"

"Not since that meal in Danny's restaurant," David answered quickly.

"You know what I mean. I don't want to end up a notch on his bed post."

"I thought you wanted a pizza of the action," David punned.

"No wonder your jokes got few laughs at our concert," said Jenny.

David kicked some sand in her face. Jenny ran down to the beach, filled up a 7 up can with water and threw it back. David picked her up in his arms.

"Put me down, put me down!" she screamed.

He did, once he was about 15 metres into the lagoon. There was a loud splash. He dashed back to his towel and began to dry himself.

Jenny, her hair bedraggled and with dye coming out, still looked stunning as she ran back to her towel and began to dry herself.

David took his towel and rubbed her back. Then they stopped, their lips came together and they kissed.

"Hey, stop that, you'll frighten the natives!" shouted Charley from a lilo down at the sands.

Jenny lay back on her towel and readjusted her sunspecs. David put his towel across the flat rock and lay beside her. She likes me. She really does like me, he'd concluded.

On the dot of 3 pm, the Captain Morgan raised anchor, hooted and headed out of the lagoon. Laura and Jenny went to the bar. David and Mark, having counted the party of 12, were strewn across their towels on deck at the bow. Radio Malta blared out some Bee Gees music.

"This is bliss," David pointed out.

"Yeh, a load of bliss," Mark smiled pulling his peaked cap over his eyes. "I hear you snogged a member of staff."

"I only kissed Jenny, as well you know." Wish I had snogged her, David thought.

"I'll remember it all when she murders you," Mark grinned.

"You mean die in bed?"

"At your age, probably that too."

David hit him over the head with his rolled up 'Times of Malta'.

The Captain Morgan turned and set course for Sliema.

"Do you know what I like most about her?" David enquired.

"Knockers?" asked Mark.

"What are you talking about?" asked Laura as the two girls returned with a tray of 4 cokes.

"Knockers, they are amazing on Gozo. They're large brass ones, Jenny, and in an island where the crime rate is negligible, you'll see door keys left trustingly in their locks."

"I think they're brass like your neck," Jenny suggested as she ran the cold coke bottle down her arms.

"Did you enjoy your afternoon?" Mark asked rhetorically.

"Oh it was okay," Jenny answered. "Right, I'm going to read my magazine, I don't feel 100%."

You might have said more than okay, David considered.

With all their tourists safely back in their hotel rooms and, having had a pizza carry-out with the other three, David lay on his bed and read up on the itinerary for the day in Gozo. He looked and looked at the page but he knew he wasn't taking it in.

In the next room Jenny would be getting all dolled up for her night out with Marco. He'd rather hoped she might abandon the trip given what she'd been told about him and that kiss; oh that kiss. He went over the moment over and over in his head. Did she see it as a friendly peck from a friend? Could he now go on to the next stage?

The door slammed. That would be her going out to a taxi at the entrance. No, he would not look out. It would just make him jealous all evening. He looked back at the map of Gozo, had a Cisk lager and dozed off.

About 10 pm he came to. Yet again, the lager glass had toppled and he made a face as he stood in the damp patch. He had a quiet smile as he looked out at the entrance below. Four ladies of the night kept standing at the door till someone activated the spot light and then headed back to the shadows. The Captain passed by and he had the same effect.

David put on his sandals and ambled down. He stood at the stone wall looking aimlessly out to sea. Locusts made their distinctive sound in the background. He swatted a mosquito which landed on his cheek. A lone fishing boat sailed past the bay towards St Julian's harbour.

"Only 40 Maltese pounds, meester," came a voice behind him.

"There's no such thing as Maltese pounds," he said without turning around.

"Only 20 Liri," came a different voice, "with extras."

This time he did turn around. A middle-aged female caked in make up and wearing a micro skirt gave a nervous smile.

"Look, just go away," David appealed and walked down to the sand. He stood, hand in pockets, looking up the road.

"Hey meester, only 5 Liri and 2 discount vouchers for Danny's bowling alley."

"I said go away, didn't you hear me? And anyway, when did you give out vouchers?"

"Who's a grump?" came the unexpected reply. It was Laura wearing a cardigan on the cool night air and holding a cup of tomato soup.

"It's hardly surprising," David said. "Jenny's out with Marco. She isn't back yet. It's 10.15 pm for heaven's sake!"

"You aren't her Dad," Laura pointed out.

"God knows what they're doing" David thought out loud.

"And you really care, don't you?"

David gave her a look of acknowledgement.

"She'll be lying on her back in bed at this very moment" Laura said, stirring it.

"Thank you for rubbing it in" David groaned.

"I am not," Laura said triumphantly. "She came to your room at 7.30 pm to say she wasn't going anywhere. We'd called a Doctor for her. She's got minor sunstroke from lying on that deck too long."

"Oh great!.... I mean, how sad. I'll go up and see her."

"She's fast asleep," said Laura.

As they walked back in, the desperate middle-aged lady was heading up the stairs with the Captain.

"Must keep my pecker up!" he shouted to the couple.

Chapter 4

"Where the hell are they?" David asked, talking to himself.
It was 9 am on Wednesday morning. The coach to Gozo was due to have left the St Julian's hotel on the dot as there was a ferry to catch. At 8.45 am his party of 20 had all been on the coach. He'd gone to the hotel toilet. The coach was empty on his return. Tony sat unconcerned on a wall opposite, his feet tapping to his walkman. It was already hot. David's watch strap kept sticking to his wrist.

Suddenly, he saw Jenny emerging from the foyer.

"They're all coming back," she announced triumphantly. "I told them all you don't need a passport for Gozo!"

"And who told them that?" David asked, trying to hide the exasperation in his voice.

"Peter Scerri came on the coach and told them."

David looked up to heaven as the tourists clambered on board.

"He sounded knowledgeable too," Mr Blackwell pointed out helpfully. "Bad business last night. My wife got locked in the toilet."

"Did you seek help?"

"Well I didn't know. I was in the bar," he winked, "She must have been there an hour till I returned!"

"Hey Tony, let's get the show on the road!" David shouted.

The coach headed along the coast road with the young man gazing anxiously at his watch.

"And how do you feel, Jenny?" he asked.

"I'd the shakes last night but I am not bad today. I've got myself covered up. It's pretty uncomfortable though. What are we going to do about Peter?"

"We'll just have to win that football match," David replied with no great optimism in his voice. "We'll discuss it this evening when we're at Danny's villa. I thought you had a cunning plan?"

"I do, believe me," Jenny replied.

The air conditioning was working again and David pointed out Mellieha, Salina and Armier bays as they neared the ferry at Cirkewwa. They made it by the skin of their teeth. As they queued, David dashed round handing out tickets. By mid-morning the car ferry headed north to Gozo.

They were about half way across and Jenny and David were standing, Titanic style, at the bow. "Okay Kate Winslet, don't try jumping off. There are no icebergs here!"

Suddenly, an old grey-haired man in a cap, (a cap always suggests importance on the island), dashed up to David.

"Your young people, they fuq, it not right." Then he repeated it.

Jenny looked alarmed. "I know Charley is outgoing, but she wouldn't – not in broad day light!"

David and Jenny anxiously followed the man past the funnel on the top deck and found Charley and her two pals taking photos and leaning over the rail.

"You shouldn't be here," David pointed out, relieved.

"Sorry mate," Charley apologised and all three headed back down.

"Hold on a minute," said Jenny, tugging at David's arm. "Have I missed something? They clearly weren't doing what I thought, sorry, feared."

"Fuq means the top deck or on top. They shouldn't have been there," he explained. "You see, Malta has many words which sound unfortunate in English like xita is, its raining."

"It's shitty in Yorkshire too, I can assure you."

"And Xaghra," David added.

"Say again," Jenny demanded.

"It's a Gozo village," he explained.

"Thank God for that!" Jenny replied.

"You know, in Titanic, Kate and Leonardo go into a car for a long kiss," David hinted.

"Yeh, but they are locked in, we are almost in Gozo and they were lovers."

As David counted his group, he realised he had again been put in his place.

The party went in the distinctive Gozitan grey and red bus waiting for them in Mgarr to the capital, Victoria, and then roamed around the market.

"We'll stop for coffee," David announced, pointing out a small café. "You'll also get the most amazing honey here."

Soon everyone was having a coffee and they all appeared to have a honey jar by the 'D and C' Company.

Jenny read the label and laughed. "I am getting wise to this. It's Danny and Carmen, isn't it?" she asked.

"Yes, he bought up a local bee-keeper's stock after the poor man got a huge tax demand. He's marked it up by 500%."

"The poor man clearly suffered a sting then," Jenny opined.

"Right, let's take them to the local prehistoric Ggantijja Temple, then lunch at the Cornocopaeia Hotel, we can see the incredible rock formation at the Azure window and end up at Xlendi bay and more coffee."

"Coffee features a lot in your itinerary," Jenny suggested.

"Couldn't do without it actually," David acknowledged. "And I love you honey," he said, his fingers all sticky.

"Is that you talking to a glass jar now?" she asked incredulously.

It was after they'd marvelled at the temple and seen a glass factory that the Captain said loudly, "Look at those large knockers."

Jenny glanced down instinctively while David struggled to keep his face straight.

"He does that every time he comes on this trip," David told Jenny. "It's his party piece."

They were driving through the narrow streets of Victoria again and a number of the tourists took photos of the gaily coloured doors. Jenny picked up the microphone.

"You will note that many Gozitans leave their door key in the lock as there is little crime here."

"Well done," nodded David approvingly.

"And the people of Malta call Victoria, Rabbit."

"It's Rabat," he corrected her quietly.

"Rabat" she said.

"Sounds funnier calling Rabbit!" Charley shouted from the back. "I got a rabbit recently" he added.

"We don't want to know," David said, aware there were youngsters on the bus.

"I do!" the Captain shouted.

"It's a bunny," Charley elaborated.

"That's okay then" David replied, relieved.

"I call it Starsky cos it lives in a hutch!" Charley grinned.

At lunch, the party all had the local Gozo red wine and some on the coach snoozed as they reached the Azure window, the rocky weather-beaten arch above the sea. Some took a walk along it. Jenny, David and some younger ones made a bee line for Danny's ice cream van.

"10c off here!" Steven shouted out. The queue got longer.

"Well, it's Xlendi next, more coffee, then back to the ferry," David told the group.

"What time are we at Danny's?" Jenny asked.

"7.30 for 8 pm. You'll end up with a sore throat. Old Carmen is deaf and gets so confused by evening. Her cooking is great though. That and her money enticed Danny. Ok, her money did. The meals were a bonus!"

At 7.30, Tony drew up in the coach with only David and Jenny on board. David had gone for his cool cotton grey suit and had polished his shoes. Jenny had a long black dress and a Malta cross broach Laura had found in Valletta market. Both had lain strewn across two seats on the journey from St Julian's up to St Paul's bay, where Carmen and her family before her had had a villa for 60 years or so.

"I'll come back at 11 pm. Have a wild time," Tony said sarcastically.

The villa was set apart from the town and across the bay you could see the bright lights of the two new suburbs, the middle class affluence of Qawra and the seaside resort of Bugibba. Two palm trees stood as sentinels in a large unkempt courtyard with lots of weeds. A dog barked menacingly as it leapt at the wrought iron front gate.

"There'll be no meal if we can't get past the Hound of the Baskervilles," Jenny suggested nervously as she rummaged in a shiny black handbag and attended to her make-up.

"He's called Ceremony and he's a friendly mutt," David reassured her.

"Could have fooled me," Jenny replied. "Are we going in then?"

Suddenly a tall formidable figure, immaculately dressed in a full butler's uniform, appeared from nowhere, pressed a remote control and the gates swung open. The dog lay on its back as David stroked its tummy.

"Good evening Mr Bond and ……..?"

"I'm Wearing," Jenny said helpfully.

"Shall I guess, a black dress?"

"No, it's my name."

"Ah, Miss Wearing. Do walk this way."

The butler had a slight limp and Jenny copied it Groucho Marx style as she walked up the path to an entrance supported by two pillars. David made a face to desist.

"Why do you call your dog Ceremony?"

"So I can greet folk, and say 'don't stand on Ceremony'! I'm a big fan of Harry Secombe. It was his joke."

"You never told me Danny had a butler," Jenny whispered in awe. David nodded.

They were in a hall flanked by oil paintings of 16th century knights of St John. A suit of armour, grandfather clock and statue of the Virgin Mary were equally spaced out along the hall on a maroon carpet.

The butler had disappeared but he could be heard calling out, "Your two young guests have arrived."

"Like the carpet," said Jenny. She'd taken off her high heels and stood in her bare feet. David made a face. "I've washed them" she reassured him.

"It's a shag," David suggested.

"Eh?"

"The carpet."

"Oh, I like the Axminster," Jenny said.

"Well I like a ...." David added.

"I've told Danny you're here," the unsmiling butler interrupted. "May I take your jacket, and have you a coat, miss?"

"No, it's so warm here," Jenny answered. "Does Danny have any more staff?" she asked.

"Tessie," said David. "She does."

"She does what?"

"You know, cleans, cooks, makes beds, does dishes. She's a Dyson."

"Well you would. The carpets are bound to get dirty."

"No, I mean her name is Dyson. There's a lot in St Paul's Bay."

"Ah, come in," said Danny who, in an open topped white shirt and jeans seemed staggered his two employees had got all dressed up. He shook their hands left-handedly as he had his usual Havana cigar in the other. "What do you think of the Virgin?" he asked.

David looked aghast.

"The statue," Danny elaborated, seeing the look, flicking some ash into the Virgin's flower vase.

"Lifelike," Jenny suggested.

He led the young couple into the dining room. A large old bay window looked out onto the harbour.

"St Paul is round the corner," Danny said.

"Is he?" Jenny asked incredulously.

"The statue," Danny repeated. "He was shipwrecked here. Who's your Patron Saint, Jenny?"

"Say something," David whispered.

"St Michael," Jenny stammered.

"Patron Saint of?"

"Clothes," Jenny suggested.

"And you David?" "St Francis of S.E.C.C."

"Where?"

"I meant Assissi."

Danny went off to the kitchen puffing his cigar.

"Damn. That's the Scottish Exhibition and Conference Centre," David admitted. "I always confuse them."

At that moment, the butler reappeared.

"An Aperitif?" he asked holding out a tray with glasses of sherry and orange juice to the young man.

"Did he say a pair of teeth?" Jenny whispered.

"It means a drink to start with," David informed her. He took a sherry and Jenny a juice. The butler retired to the kitchen. David and Jenny sat at the table; the girl fidgeted with her napkin holder.

"This is like being with the Addams family or the Munsters," she groaned.

"Oh, don't worry. The evening can only get worse," David admitted, deadpan.

Carmen made an entrance, wearing a long black dress and holding an elegant black fan.

"Snap," said David.

Jenny grinned.

"What?" asked Carmen joining them at the table.

"I like schnapps," said David.

"We only have sherry," Carmen apologised.

"And you brought Ariadne. Some daughter you are, you haven't called in ages."

"I'm Jenny"

"Benny?"

"Jenny." The youngster blushed.

"Well Lenny, I hope you'll like my meal. I've made beetroot soup, Fenek, and Death by Chocolate."

"Not bloody rabbit," Jenny said quietly.

"What, Penny?"

"She says she's a bit crabbit," David explained.

Danny came back into the room, followed by a middle-aged plump woman with a cook's hat and an apron on which the words 'Kitchen closed, cook on strike' were displayed.

"Wish it was if it's rabbit!" Jenny continued.

"This soup is something else, Dyson. Oh I must introduce you to David and Jenny."

Both the young folk shook hands.

"If only it was just tomato," Jenny said.

"Look, love, you must talk louder. Carmen can't hear you," Danny suggested.

David had a go at his soup. Jenny toyed with it.

"Are you leaving a space for the rabbit?" Danny enthused.

Jenny looked thoroughly fed up.

"Where are you from, Penny?" Carmen asked.

"Bridlington in Yorkshire," Jenny replied. "I'm Jenny."

"England?"

"Yes."

"Have you met Ariadne?"

"England's a big place," Danny explained kindly and tapped his wife's hand affectionately.

"Sorry no," Jenny replied.

"Are you Catholic?"

"I am," Jenny said.

"I am devoted to the sacred Heart. What about you?" Carmen went on.

"Her saint is Michael," Danny explained.

"I know folk in Edinburgh who love the sacred Hearts," David said quietly, finishing his soup. No one got the gag. Jenny realised her roll could soak much of it up and put the roll furtively into her pocket.

"How about you, David?" Carmen continued.

"St Francis. He talked to birds."

"That's my sort of saint" Danny concurred.

Tessie came in and to Jenny's ill-concealed joy put out four plates of chicken, chips and side salad.

Danny beamed. "David told us your likes and dislikes. We couldn't resist winding you up! Now, what's your plan for this football match?"

"I am working on it," Jenny replied confidently chewing her chicken leg. "I'll tell you soon."

"It's dyson with death," David implored.

"It sure is," a worried Danny replied.

"No, Dyson has the death with chocolate," David elaborated as Tessie returned to the dining room.

"Do you like the island?" Tessie asked.

"Love it," said Jenny. "The sights, smells, culture, slow pace of life, the beaches, and meeting David!"

David's heart missed a beat. Tessie gave a knowing look, picked up the dishes and returned to the kitchen. The butler returned, lit Danny a cigar, and poured him and David a whisky. Carmen and Jenny had another juice.

"So you like Malta, Benny?"

"Jenny."

"Sorry."

"Yes I love it, Carmen."

"I could never leave" said Carmen.

"Love it too much?" Jenny asked.

"No. Malta's customs seized our passports after a little bit of tax evasion by Danny."

"A fine?" Jenny asked.

"No I'll stick to Juice," Carmen said putting her had over her tumbler.

Danny led David out to the patio and swimming pool. "We must win this blasted match," he repeated.

"How? We cheated last year, remember?" David reminded him.

"If we don't I lose everything. Travel firm, Karaoke, 10-pin, bar, chip shop, nightclub, ice cream sales, cinema, disco amusement arcade, even Carmen." He thought for a moment. "No, maybe it's not all bad eh?"

"You could have them in Bugibba instead, surely?" David ventured.

"It would be a much smaller operation and don't call me Shirley. People will talk! No seriously, I'd have to lay off staff. We'd never recover. We must win that match."

"What if we do lose the game but you simply refuse to abandon your companies in Sliema?"

"That would be courageous," Danny said, puffing on the cigar as both men stood at the pool side.

"Courageous?" David repeated.

"Courageous. Martin, shall we say, has a family in Sicily. I've seen his four young sons with violin cases."

"Danny, they are all members of the Malta Youth Orchestra!" David exclaimed.

Jenny and Carmen joined them. Jenny quietly put the beetroot-coloured roll in a bin in the dark.

"Come and join David at the pool," Danny welcomed them.

"Why are you on the pool?" Carmen asked. "You've got Jenny!"

David felt his face blush even in the dark.

"Thank you for a lovely meal," David changed the subject.

Eventually Tessie appeared wearing a coat. "Thank you young man. Carmen, I must go. I'll see you tomorrow."

"Your taxi awaits," said the Butler as he passed Tessie at the door. "Someone called Tony."

"Who's got a pony?" asked Carmen.

"Never you mind, dear," said Danny. "David and Jenny must leave."

"Why is Lenny peeved?" Carmen asked.

The young couple met Tony at the entrance. David patted Ceremony.

"Just win me that match," Danny implored.

Jenny had stopped to admire the oil paintings in the hall.

"Do you know art?" Danny asked.

"Raphael, Donatello, Michaelangelo, Leonardo," she reeled off. David put his hand over his mouth to stifle a grin.

"Magnificent!" Danny congratulated her.

"Theresa may know her history but she is not so hot on art and I need a courier who can explain and describe the wonderful paintings at St John's Co – Cathedral in Valletta. You will really enhance that day out!"

David and Jenny got into the car. Danny and Carmen waved them off. Ceremony barked.

"Me and my big mouth," Jenny sighed.

David decided to go for it. "You know you were telling Carmen all the reasons you like Malta, and you said meeting me was a highlight."

"I vaguely recall the conversation," Jenny replied tantalisingly.

"Did you mean it?"

"Suppose so. I got fed up answering to Lenny, Penny and Benny for God's sake! You're a nice person, David."

David sank back in the leather upholstered seat. Your pet dog is nice, he reflected. He was always damned by faint praise.

David always enjoyed the Thursday morning lie in. The tourists were all doing last minute shopping in Sliema or were sitting by the pool or had put their suitcases in the luggage room. Mark was taking charge of that so David was still in bed and enjoying an orange juice out of the small fridge. He would be sorry to see the back of the present party but you always got tips on the last day and no doubt there would be some real characters to meet. Once he was washed and shaved, he nipped into the kitchen and met Jenny at the toasting machine.

"What time do we take them back to Luqa airport?" she asked.

"About 6 pm. They've a 2-hour check in," David replied, buttering some toast. "We've got another 36 coming in so we'll have 18 and Mark and Laura 18."

"Maybe we'll have no one wanting to pee at every opportunity," Jenny said optimistically.

"Don't you believe it," David replied authoritatively.

At that moment, a flustered Theresa walked in.

"No school today?" David enquired.

"Sports day, and I am too old. Too old," she repeated. "I could still beat that Head running for a bus. Oh, Jenny, I hear you're to take out cultured tourists around Valletta's paintings. Well done. I get so bored doing that. Once you've seen the beheading of St John 100 times there's not a lot to add."

"Great!" Jenny murmured. "I hear you know a lot about impressionists."

"Only Rory Bremner or Mike Yarwood," David laughed.

"I'll be honest, Theresa," said Jenny blushing "I don't know much about art. I was trying to show off to Danny and I've landed myself in it."

"Surreal," said Theresa sympathetically.

"Yeh, so real," Jenny agreed. "I can't speak Italian either. I just wanted the job so much."

"You're not the first and you certainly won't be the last," the older lady pointed out kindly. "Now I'll give you a toast."

"Cheers!" said Jenny.

"No, I've just buttered this one," Theresa said giving David a glance. Theresa sat down with a coffee. Jenny stood at the window embarrassed.

"Look, I know what I'll do," said Theresa, stirring her cup. "I'll write down some simple notes for you to refer to as you walk round the paintings and you will sound like an expert in no time."

"That's very kind of you," Jenny replied dabbing some suntan lotion on her nose.

"Right, let's go up to the hotel and make our goodbyes," David suggested.

Just before 6 pm, Tony arrived in the coach outside the hotel and he, Mark and David helped put cases into the luggage hold as Jenny and Laura counted their party onto the coach. Charley and her two friends had 'Kiss Me Quick' hats from Bugibba, rubber rings and a lilo under their arms.

"It's been fun," said Charley. "Not as good as Ibiza or Rhodes cos they're wild but it was fun, especially those Italian footballers and Marco's polo team."

David hoped Jenny had heard the remark but she was already on the coach checking seats.

"Thank Theresa for making it all so interesting," said Winston as he put a 5 lm note into David's hand.

"I bet we've forgotten something," said Mr Blackwell resignedly. "We'll be back, you know."

Tim and Julian were last on. Both had yellow cotton trousers and overlarge sunspecs.

"I do hope you'll win that football match. Don't worry if you lose an early goal. You can come from behind," said Julian.

David looked at the notes scrunched up in his hand. About £200 to share out – not bad, he reckoned.

It was already dark as the coach headed off out of St Julian's passing the early disco goers and night clubbers.

"I feel like an experienced courier now," said Jenny checking her new list of tourists.

"Lucky I am here, then," David smiled.

By 9 pm, the group had safely gone and David stood with a welcome cold orange squash, watching his two flights come in. Mark had flopped across four seats. Laura and Jenny, both clutching their clipboards, were looking at the souvenir shop.

"Ah, David!"

David felt a hearty slap on his back and knew immediately it was Peter.

"How's your foot?" he asked.

"Fine, I can still walk," said David sarcastically.

"You'll be okay for the game then."

"I wouldn't miss it for the world."

"You can't win, you know. You fiddled that ref last year and you still couldn't win."

"That's quite an accusation," David pointed out.

"Well I am off to get our new group," said Peter, his voice almost drowned out by the scream of a jet landing. He gave a wave and headed off to arrivals.

"That's our flight," said Jenny as the tannoy boomed out.

"I know you're enthusiastic, but they have to get through customs and luggage reclaim," David reminded her.

Laura and Jenny stood at the carousels and David picked up a 'Times of Malta'.

About ¾ of an hour later David was surrounded by an excited throng of holiday makers. He was surprised to see Jenny nipping into a toilet but no longer wearing her khaki uniform or clutching her clipboard. Most of the new party were heading out to the coaches so he stood outside the WC and waited. When she emerged she wasn't wearing her specs.

"What are you doing?" David asked astonished. "Where's your uniform and clipboard and how can you see?"

Jenny passed him by and picked up a large brown case.

"You aren't meant to carry their luggage, Jenny," he pointed out. "I think you are confusing me with someone else," the stunning blonde said politely. "I am Sarah."

David stopped in his tracks. "But you are Jenny!"

The girl gave a resigned look up to heaven, the sort of look she had clearly given many times before. "I am Jenny's sister. Didn't she say I was coming?"

"No she didn't," said a bemused David, shaking her hand.

My God she's a babe too, David thought.

"You must be Mark. She said he's a looker."

Thanks for that, David grimaced. "I'd better take you to meet Jenny, I suppose," he said and led her out of the Luqa airport exit. They were met by the warm air, the smell of gasoline and the sound of locusts. Jenny was standing beside Tony at the bus.

"Sis!" Sarah shouted and ran towards her, arms outstretched.

"Hi Sarah!" Jenny beamed and the two embraced.

"Sabiha," Tony acknowledged.

"Who's this?" asked Mark as he shut the coaches' luggage hold.

"Sarah, this is Mark. Mark, this is Sarah." David did the introductions.

"I thought you were Jenny," Mark explained, "but I can see you are taller. Gosh, so there are two of you, eh?"

Laura emerged from Steven's coach gazing at her clipboard.

"Why aren't you wearing your specs?" Laura asked.

"Because I am not Jenny, I am Sarah," the girl explained patiently.

"Amazing! Two peas in a pod," said Laura "You might have told us she was coming" she added.

"This could really confuse the holidaymakers, not to mention Danny," Mark said.

"I'm only here for a holiday," Sarah pointed out as she got on the coach and sat opposite David and Jenny. The coach set off on the country road from Luqa to St Julian's.

"Where's your sister actually staying?" David asked.

"Can you never get through a sentence without saying 'actually'?" Jenny grinned. In my room, actually."

"You never said she was coming. I'd have baked a cake."

"Would you really?" Jenny asked clearly surprised.

"It's an expression" David explained.

Jenny picked up the mike. "Good evening, Ladies and Gentlemen. Welcome to Malta. It has been almost 30 degrees today and you can feel it humid even now. We'll take you to your hotel in St Julian's where the hotel staff will direct you to your room. We have a smashing programme for you and we'll tell you about it tomorrow." Jenny put the mike down.

David had been aware of the smell of an expensive perfume but was unsure if it came from Sarah or from behind him. He felt a tap on his shoulder.

"Wotcha mate. I hear there are wild nightclubs, discos, and you can get laid by an Italian footballer!"

"Sounds pretty good," Sarah added to David's right.

He looked around to see another blonde, not unlike Charley, sitting with a dark haired girl behind him.

"Hi I'm Alex," the girl said, lighting up.

"Sorry, no fags Charley - I mean, Alex," David instructed.

"I am not surprised you said Charley. I am her little sister," the girl replied.

You don't look all that little, David thought.

"Pleased to meet you" David said.

This is like being in a scene from Hollyoaks, he reckoned.

"So what do you do, Sarah?" David asked, dying to get acquainted and putting into operation chat up guide rule one, ie, get a girl to talk about her favourite subject, ie, herself!

"I've a temp job in York for a legal firm and I am getting a break from being at Lillieshall."

"But that's a football training camp. Are you typing there or cooking or what?"

"Hey, you never said your friend was so sexist," Sarah complained.

"Well he is older," Jenny explained as the coach entered a tunnel approaching St Julian's.

Sarah took a deep breath. "I am there for sport," she said.

"Hey I am here for sport," Alex chuckled as she peered between the two headrests in front of her.

"Which sport?" David asked.

"Shagging," said Alex provocatively.

"I'm talking to Sarah," David explained.

"It's maybe not as much fun, but it's football."

There was a long pause. The coach was out of the tunnel.

"Did you say what I think you said?" David asked.

"Yes, football."

"You, a girl, play football at England's top training camp?" David was incredulous. "How come? Are you in an amateur team?"

"I am in England's Women's World Cup football team," she added.

"Wow!" said Alex. "You probably score as much as me."

"Excuse me, but are we near a toilet?" an elderly lady asked as she came up to the front seats.

"Don't tell me. You are Mrs Blackwell's sister?" Jenny ventured.

"Who's she?" the old dear asked. "She sounds like a tart."

"No that was Charley," Jenny whispered.

"We'll soon be at the hotel, madam."

"So that is your cunning plan, Jenny," David deduced, full of admiration.

"To find old folk a toilet?" Jenny asked tantalisingly.

"Sarah, you will be in our football match, won't she?"

"Maybes aye, maybes no," Jenny said.

"Thank you Kenny Dalglish," David enthused. "Danny's in for a big surprise."

"And Peter an even bigger one!" Jenny suggested.

"I fancy a bet on the side at 100/1," Tony said above the noise of the old coach.

"Who on earth offered such generous odds?" David asked.

"Danny, of course!" Tony elaborated.

The bus turned into the hotel car park. David sat back in his seat enjoying the moment. He could hardly get the smug expression off his face. Maybe next week's match was not such a lost cause after all. And if Tony was right, and Danny had indeed given up and was offering odds of 100/1 then a fast buck could be made!

It took over an hour for all the group in Mark's coach and David's to be allocated a room. As David and Jenny emerged, Sarah was sitting on the wall outside swinging her shapely long legs and watching a lizard heading towards her.

"All set to see the room you are sharing with me?" Jenny asked.

"Danny will not be happy if he finds out," David warned.

"How can he?" Jenny asked, "He won't be able to differentiate."

At that moment, the Captain came out of the foyer clutching a bottle of bacardi rum. He stopped, looked at Sarah, looked at Jenny, looked back at Sarah, looked at the bottle, and told David, "This stuff is stronger than I thought."

Alex and her pal came out in a multi-coloured top and shorts.

"She'll give any passing chameleon a breakdown," Jenny said. "Where's the guys?" she demanded.

"It's Thursday and everything is shut by now," David pointed out.

"I'm available," said the Captain. "Aren't you Charley?"

"No, I'm Alex."

The Captain put the bottle gently on the ground and headed off, shrugging, back to the apartments. Alex and her pal picked up the bottle.

"Just take it," David suggested.

Alex beamed and headed back in.

Jenny and Sarah walked along the narrow lane to St George's Bay to their room.

"This is so cool, Jenny," Sarah enthused.

"It's pretty warm actually," David said. "Sorry, it's pretty warm full stop."

Sarah got quite a fright when the spot lights were activated as she reached the entrance.

"I installed them," David said proudly.

"Who are the women waiting outside?" she asked.

"The last bus is due," David explained.

"It's 1 am. That's unusual," Sarah decided.

They all got a hot soup at the machine at the entrance and David made his goodnights. This is my best summer yet, he reckoned as he turned the key in his lock.

David's eyes almost popped out of his head as he joined Sarah and Jenny at the breakfast table at 8 am. As he had approached the room, he had heard their chuckling as they admired each other's photos. Both were wearing pink dressing gowns.

"Make sure Danny doesn't know you've been staying in Jenny's room!" David advised as he pressed 6 slices of bread into the toaster.

"He needn't know anything about her," Jenny said. "In fact, if Peter and Danny don't know, then all the better."

"How often have you scored?" David asked.

"I've had my moments," Sarah grinned.

"On the football field?"

"There too."

"How many goals?" David persisted.

"I think you know what he means, don't you, Sis?" Jenny asked.

"I average three in four games," Sarah boasted.

"I am putting my bet on this morning for sure," David confirmed. "Is your Mum still in prison?"

"Yeh, but she escapes at the weekends," Sarah answered.

"Just don't tell Mark," he pleaded.

"Mark who is gay?" Sarah answered.

"Who told you that?"

That's strange. It wasn't me, David thought.

"Jenny did."

David had a quiet smile.

"What are we doing this morning then?" Sarah enquired, crunching on her toast.

"Telling all our tourists about the island and our tours and Danny's discounts, or scams, and then on day one it is up the coast to Bugibba and the under water safari and Mellieha."

"Sounds fun," Sarah said. "I'll get my camera."

Her dressing gown kept flowing open giving the young man an eyeful. "Now I'll go and get changed."

"Must you?" David sighed.

At 9 am, David, Jenny and Sarah walked up to the St Julian's Hotel. Marco was waiting in the car park on his Suzuki.

"I thought I'd catch you here" Marco greeted David. "What are the details for our annual defeat then?"

"Don't be so pessimistic. Why are you so down?"

"Because….," Marco began, giving him a pretend punch in the ribs, "we are crap, we lose every year and we're mainly water polo players."

"Well you haven't seen what Jenny can do yet."

"Well that's true," Marco said ruefully. "Is she well enough to play?"

Sarah was standing out of Marco's line of vision behind a palm tree.

"I'm well enough," Jenny assured him.

"Do you fancy a ride?" Marco asked patting the bike.

"I am off on a tour after our talk," she explained. "Maybe later."

Maybe not at all, David hoped. "Right" he said, "we play Thursday afternoon next week when our party are preparing to leave and they'll want something to watch."

"Where?"

"Tigne Barracks, at the Sliema Wanderers ground."

"Don't we meet to discuss tactics?" Marco asked enthusiastically. "Don't be naive!" David said. "It's made no difference in the past."

Marco put on his helmet and, with a wave to Jenny, headed off as Peter entered the car park in his Range Rover.

"I've decided the odds," Peter said with his head out of the window. "I'll offer 2/5 on we win and 50/1 against you," he said.

"I can get better odds from Danny," David told him. "He says 1/2 you win and 100/1 we do."

"He's betting against his own team?" Peter inferred incredulously. "This match will ruin him. Has he given up?"

"Looks like it," David said convincingly. "We can't compete with you."

Peter mopped his bright red forehead with his handkerchief. He parked the car and headed into the hall. Sarah re-emerged.

"Is that the enemy?" she asked. David nodded. "Who's the Adonis?"

"Marco," Jenny said.

"I'll score with him," Sarah stated.

Oh to be good-looking! David groaned inwardly.

"I liked his bike," Sarah added in a matter-of-fact sort of way.

"You're all wasting your time," Alex interrupted as she bumped into them at the entrance. "I had him last night. He has got a large Suzuki too. I got a ride."

I hope you heard that, Jenny, David considered.

Inside the hall, Peter was giving his talk to the tourists but the truce on the guided tours had held firm. At 10 am, all 36 tourists congregated at Tony's coach for the trip up to Bugibba. A strong smell of suntan lotion wafted down the coach.

David gave Jenny the mike. "It's your turn" he said. "You saw how I did it last week. You'll be great." He moved to the seat beside Sarah leaving Jenny to his left. "Tell me more about playing for England."

"Well, I played for Scarborough, got spotted by Leeds Utd Women's Team and the rest is history," she boasted. "I've got 14 caps and, in my time, we've only lost to Italy but they are really good."

"You must be really fit," David said admiringly. "I do the gym, a bit of judo and so on."

"I can't believe the look on Peter's and Danny's faces when we win," David enthused.

The coach wended its way past the scrubland of the coast road.

"Do we stop soon at a toilet?" the old dear, Mrs King, enquired. Meanwhile, an elderly gent, called Tom Wilkins, a retired lecturer who had been to the island many times kept prompting Jenny with his useful tips about the journey but she looked undermined. Alex was strewn across the back seats and already had her bare feet on the young man's lap opposite.

David smiled. Her target was Tristram and he would have little interest in Alex. According to his register he was training for the priesthood!

The coach parked beside the underwater safari. Steven was in Danny's ice cream van at the entrance to the quayside. "I've no ices, David!" he shouted. "What's wrong?"

"One of Peter's henchmen tampered with the refrigeration," he moaned.

"The truce must be at an end," David sighed.

On a roasting hot, sticky day, everyone naturally made a bee line for Peter's ice cream van a few metres away shortly afterwards.

The Captain Morgan glass-bottomed boat headed off into the bay. Everyone sat with a cool drink as the craft approached St Paul's island.

"St Paul was shipwrecked here in AD 60 when his Roman ship sank in a storm," Mr Wilkins said loudly. "He brought Christianity to the island and later got crucified in Rome."

"So did we, 4-0, last year," Sarah sympathised.

"I wish he wouldn't go on so," Jenny moaned. "The party are paying more attention to him" she added.

They took turns at going down to the glass-bottomed viewing area and marvelled at the wrecks and the fish being fed. Jenny, a bit miffed, stayed on deck and put on more aftersun.

"Jenny has told me why the football match is so important to you all," Sarah pointed out. "But there's only one of me."

"There's Marco and his pals who've played Juventus, Bayern Munich, Barcelona and Man Utd," David said.

"Why do you need me?" Sarah asked quizzically. "Which major club do they play for?"

"Sliema Wanderers"

"Never heard of them. But you said they've played major clubs."

"They have. Sliema keep getting into Round 1 or Round 2 of UEFA and get knocked out, of course, but, in the meantime these young men really have played in the greatest European stadia and they have the club flags to prove it."

David could hear Mr Wilkins voice droning on about fish. He seemed to be an expert about them too. He helped Sarah climb the steps back to the main deck. David led the party to the main Bugibba shopping centre and soon they were all enjoying cheeseburger and chips in Danny's café. Jenny and Sarah joined David in a souvenir shop and Sarah admired the Luzzu ornaments, Maltese lace, floppy hats, flags, Maltese maps, Knights of St John models, etc. David groaned as he heard Tom Wilkins describing the armour to some tourists outside.

"Right let's take them to Popeye's Village and then we can go for a swim at Mellieha," David said as he waved to his group at the café.

An hour later, David, Jenny and Sarah sat in the bright warm sunshine watching actors re-enact scenes from Robin Williams' film.

"This is a film set built in 1981 depicting a Canadian fishing village," Tom said loudly.

"Someone shut him up," Jenny whispered.

"It wasn't much of a film and, for a while the village was derelict, but then the Maltese turned it into a tourist attraction."

"Look," David said to Jenny, "he has given us effectively a day off. Let's get an ice cream and a 7-Up and ignore him."

Jenny volunteered to get them. Sarah sat close to David.

"Do you fancy her?"

"Who?"

"Who do you think? My sis."

"Maybe"

"Do you fancy her, David?" David hesitated. Sarah was such a clone that he'd wondered what his chances were with her if he made no progress with Jenny but, if he was honest, that opportunity would, surely, disappear.

"I like her a lot."

"Do you fancy her?"

"Okay, yes," he conceded reluctantly.

"There, that was quite easy, wasn't it?" Sarah suggested. Jenny returned with the 3 melting ices and welcome cold lemonades.

"You'll never guess what David has just told me," Sarah said tantalisingly.

"What's that then?" Jenny asked, rolling the bottle down her red arm.

Oh no! David squirmed.

"The famous film star was here and so was Brad Pitt when he made Troy," Sarah said giving David a look of triumph at having wound him up so successfully.

"Yes I did know that" Jenny said. "I am a courier."

An hour later, the party were all at Mellieha beach. Jenny and Sarah paddled, Mrs King found the toilet, Alex chatted up a lifeguard and Tom Wilkins told some older tourists about Mellieha 50 years ago. David lay on his towel under the shade of a palm tree and switched on a small transistor radio.

It must be blatantly obvious that I fancy Jenny if Sarah picked up on it so early he contemplated.

Donkeys passed by with little children the rides. Above the bay, a paraglider swept across the beach. There was a strong smell of chips and vinegar as the café was situated directly behind them. The pop record 'Macarena' boomed our and Sarah and Jenny danced back to their towels.

"Don't stay too long in the sun," David cautioned Jenny. "We don't want you getting sunstroke again."

With their belongings now guarded by the two girls, David took off his spectacles and splashed into the sea as he hated walking in gradually when it feels so cold. He did a crawl and a breast stroke. A motor boat swept by in the distance and David enjoyed the resulting waves which carried him along. The water was absolutely clear and he could see the sand and a few fish beneath him.

Mellieha slopes gradually, unlike Golden Bay, and younger children were more in evidence. Now and again youngsters passed by on a lilo. It was a little darker now and time to gather the troops together. He laughed as he got to the water's edge and a little black dog splashed him.

Jenny held out a towel and then rubbed his back and hair. This is the life, he considered.

"What are the plans for this evening?" Sarah asked.

"The young ones will be at the discos and nightclubs, being a Friday. I'll show the older ones where the bingo is on and there's a hotel party for the little kids actually."

"Don't keep saying actually," Jenny demanded.

"Why not? I think it's quite cute," Sarah pointed out. "Hey David who's the old perv who came on to me at the apartment entrance this morning, he told me I'd offered him extras!"

"That's our resident war hero. The Captain," David replied.

"A perv," Sarah repeated. "And what extras were you offering, Jenny?"

"Danny's discounts on ice creams and honey, etc.," Jenny assured her.

"Well, just keep him out of my way," she insisted. "Anyway, what are we doing tonight?"

"Well, we can't have Danny see you, or Peter for that matter. They'll likely be at the 10-pin so we can go into Steven's restaurant and have a chat!"

It was 8 pm when Jenny, Sarah and David entered Danny's empty restaurant where Steven was drying glasses behind the bar. No one was in the dining area. Steven looked fed up.

"What's up?" David enquired. "Why the long face?"

"Are you a little hoarse?" Jenny chuckled.

"Would you stay with the partner whom you thought you loved, if there was evidence they were sleeping around?" Steven asked rhetorically.

"I'm sorry, Steven, I wouldn't." David sympathised.

"Nor will my wife!" Steven explained.

Was that a gag or was he serious? David wondered as he got the tray with 3 lagers and headed to a table.

"Does it matter where we sit?" Sarah asked.

"Hardly" Steven muttered. "Tell me when you want to order. Make the most of it. Either Peter will close this place or the Health Inspectors will."

All three picked up a menu.

"His wife should get him to wear tartan clothes," Jenny suggested. "Why?" David asked.

"It would keep him in check," Sarah interrupted.

"It's a family joke," Jenny pointed out. "When we were kids, Dad sent us to a shop to get tartan paint."

"Okay ravioli for us all?" David ventured.

The girls nodded.

"Then fish and chips and Italian ice cream and coffee?"

"Sounds good," agreed Sarah.

"Ditto," Jenny concurred.

"I don't know why you bother. You always have the same meal," Steven moaned and headed off to the kitchen.

"You know, in films," Sarah said, "Barmen are always drying glasses like Steven was when we came in."

"It's a cliché," David explained. "Like if the goodies in James Bond knock a guard out he always has a uniform the precise size to get dressed in," he added.

"Or aliens in a science fiction film always speak English," Jenny stated.

"As they should," David said firmly. "Or in those black and white war films, whichever pilot has a dog always gets killed, and the dog yelps at the end of the runway," he added.

Just as Steven came in with the meals, Peter entered the restaurant. His hair was covered in grease. His shirt and trousers were black and matched his sunspecs.

"I will own all this next week," he said, provocatively waving his arms expansively. "Maybe the best of your staff can work for me?"

Sarah had dashed to the toilet and Peter looked quizzically at the third plate.

"Yes David, you might well eat 2 meals. You'll need all the strength you can get if you are to avoid complete humiliation on Thursday. And you, Signorina Jenny" - he kissed her hand - "I'd pay you double what skint flint Danny does."

He smiled and headed off into the black limousine parked outside.

"You work for him over my dead body," David stated bravely.

"Yes, you probably would be," Steven agreed.

Sarah returned from the toilet. "Right" she said picking up the cruet, "let's stop being pessimistic. Let's talk tactics."

She put the salt cellar at the edge of the table. "That's Jenny in the first half then me in the second".

The pepper pot, mustard, tomato and HP sauce were still in the middle of the table.

"That's the midfield," she announced.

"Which am I?" David asked.

"You've been as keen as mustard," she suggested, pointing.

"Marco will pepper their goal," Jenny laughed.

"We appear to have no defence," David said.

"That's what Peter argues," Steven helpfully added and dodged a pretend swipe from David.

Steven put 5 sherry glasses and a breakfast cereal footballer at the other end of the table.

"It's a 5-4-1 system," Sarah expertly explained.

"Only the goalie looks human," David pointed out.

"There's no human in their team," Steven reminded him. "It's a bunch of hackers every year. I went home with a broken leg two years ago."

"Whose was it?" Jenny asked.

"Look, stop the banter. This is serious stuff," Sarah interrupted firmly. "It's simple. You all defend like mad and get the ball up to me."

"Milk in this restaurant turns quicker than our defence," Steven said dejectedly.

"We're with you," David said encouragingly. There's only one of you, Sarah, he thought. And if Peter finds out there are two he'll break all our legs!

At that moment, the tomato sauce bottle toppled and smeared the white table cloth.

"That looks a bad one" Steven said. "He'll have to come off."

"If we do lose," Jenny said, adding a note of realism "Wouldn't Peter accept a large cheque instead?"

"Yes, but how would Danny raise it?" David replied. "Without money he couldn't maintain the business in Sliema anyway. Either way he is doomed."

"We must win," Sarah summed up as she finished her ice cream.

"Well Danny won't do it by blackmailing the ref this year," Steven announced.

"How so?" David asked, stirring his coffee.

"Peter has arranged Father Collina from St Mark's church to referee this year and he is a paragon of virtue," Steven said resignedly.

"I think we have to accept we'll be working in Bugibba if we have any work at all after this," Steven said, dejection in his voice.

"We'll see," Sarah said using the salt cellar to slam a peanut into the goal of 2 breadsticks.

"Do we have proper strips for the match?" Jenny asked.

"We certainly do," David said.

"We have the name of our sponsors on the strip," added Steven.

"Who are they?" Jenny asked crunching on a breadstick.

"Howard Duff has the Scottish bar in Mellieha so this year all our tops say proudly, Duff."

"You couldn't make it up," said David nodding his head in disbelief.

"And what do theirs say?" Jenny enquired.

"Scerri," Steven replied. "Their two girl players are pretty scerri." he laughed.

"All their players used to play in the Maltese league and some got trials for Italian Serie C teams. I tell you, we've had it." Steven got up and went back to his kitchen.

"He's right," David confessed. "With only one class player, an unimpeachable ref, I think it would take a miracle," he added. "I wish Danny had never taken this on. By the way, where is he this evening?"

"Oh, you won't see him today," said Steven as he came in with a coffee pot. "He's lost his wife."

"Oh no! Not Carmen?" said David, who was genuinely shocked.

"We only saw her recently," Jenny added.

"Oh no, she's not dead," Steven explained cheerfully filling a cup, "They were in Littlewoods in Sliema and she wandered off."

"Oh not again!" David sympathised.

"He'll find her," Steven said confidently. "She always goes to see the flowers in a park at the end of the creek."

"I wonder if Carmen would bail Danny out if or when we lose the match?" David wondered out loud. "Right, you two," he said, "time to play Ten Pin."

Chapter 5

David sat enjoying a cold chocolate ice cream and a Cisk lager in his favourite outside café in Republic St, Valletta. It was Saturday morning. They had taken their party on the boat trip around Grand Harbour, where the sea breeze had been welcome. As David rested his chin on his hands, he could still smell the salt from the dangling his arms in the water. Now, while the young ones chatted all around him with their cokes and cheese pies, David's thoughts turned to how Jenny was getting on as she took the older contingent around St John's Co Cathedral. Theresa had written extensive notes on the paintings, tapestries, tombs, painted windows, busts and so on and had spent an hour going through it. It was not long before he could see Mark heading down the street threading his way through the groups of sunspec-wearing sleeveless tourists. He was laughing all the way.

"Have you heard a good joke?" David asked, as Mark took a seat and glanced at the menu.

"No, but I've seen one," he replied.

"Go on, what?"

"Jenny." He caught his breath.

"Oh no, what has she done now?"

"Well you know Theresa said to turn left as she entered the art gallery and memorise her notes?"

"Yes."

"Well, she'd memorised them alright, but she took them in on the right side."

"Oh no!" David exclaimed and put his hand to his mouth.

"She did recognise Caravaggio's beheading of St John. That was the good news."

"And the bad?"

"She got everything else wrong!"

"That old lecturer asked her about De Vos, the Flemish painter, and she asserted he was a Dutch footballer who played for Rangers. I think she got all the Grandmaster's graves wrong too. She was asked about religious allegories and she said some saints had been quite ill. She was asked if one art masterpiece was Preti and she said yes! One young tourist asked about the vaults and she said she didn't think a sports day was planned. I could go on."

"No don't," David implored as the waiter replenished the lagers and frowned at Mark's small tip.

At that moment, their 12 tourists appeared at the Café following the red-faced girl. David groaned as he saw Tom Wilkins approaching.

"Thank you, thank you," he puffed, red-faced in the heat.

David was incredulous. "I thought you said the tour was a disaster," he said turning to Mark accusingly.

"Oh, it was, but it was great knockabout stuff," the old lecturer continued. "I've done that stuffy old tour for years and never had a laugh yet. When your guide Sarah said The Dance of Salome was nothing to what Laura could do any Friday night, it just brought the house down. Anyway, the other tourists didn't realise the talk was all back to front," he said patronisingly. He went off to get a drink.

Sarah sat down. "I am so sorry," she apologised.

"Okay, but where's Jenny?" asked David, apprehensively.

There was a long pause.

"I wasn't going to let on" Mark confessed. "She went to see Marco."

David's face fell.

Sarah saw the look. "She means a lot to you, doesn't she?" she asked rhetorically. "Maybe you should tell her."

"Right, let's round up the troops and take them to the souvenir shops. We've got a firework fiesta planned for them tonight too at Naxxar."

"Is that where they make Maltese dentures?" Sarah chuckled.

David headed back down Republic Street holding his "SAY GO TOURS" flag. His mind was on Marco and Jenny. Maybe Sarah was right.

There was a chance to find out at 2 pm as Danny's eleven congregated at the football pitch at Tigne barracks in Sliema. It was roasting hot and there wasn't a cloud in the sky. The strips were varied. David had a Dunfermline one, Jenny a Scarborough one, Mark Leyton Orient, Sarah a Leeds strip. Laura had borrowed a Juventus one. Tony and Steven wore Sliema Wanderers as did Marco and his friends.

As Danny arrived, Sarah hid behind a huge palm tree at the old barracks building. David was concerned Jenny had arrived on the back of Marco's motorbike.

"Right men!" Danny began.

"Excuse me," said Laura.

"Ladies and Gentlemen," Danny corrected himself, "This is our last training session before our match on Thursday."

"It's our only training," David pointed out.

"That's all we'll need," Danny asserted. "After all our years of defeat, the hour of glory has arrived."

"He's delusional," Mark muttered.

"Think of Wallace and the spider in the cave," Danny said.

"Bruce," David corrected him.

"Churchill and Dunkirk," he continued. "Sir Alf Ramsay, and the 1966 World Cup Final."

"Can I bet £100?" David shouted out.

"It's now 5/2 on Peter's lot," Danny said checking his note book.

"For us to win at 100/1," David said confidently.

"Are you mad?" Danny queried.

"What happened to Bruce and Dunkirk?" Laura demanded to know.

"You stupid girl," Danny moaned.

"Yes, David. I'll take your £100."

"Can we start?" Marco asked. "We've a polo match later."

"You'll want to make a splash," Jenny said encouragingly. She turned to David. "If Danny doesn't go, Sarah can't train."

"Leave us to it, Danny," David suggested. "You're a busy man and we must get our coaching done."

"Okay," Danny quickly agreed. "Enjoy your fireworks this evening and remember, if we lose there'll be lay-offs. I am depending on you." He headed off in a BMW puffing on his cigar.

"Okay" Marco said. "My polo chums will play you lot in a 6-a-side and we'll see how we get on."

During the first half Sarah remained out of sight and Jenny played up front with David. Tony went in goal and Steven, Mark and Laura defended. From time to time Marco tripped Jenny up and deliberately fell on top of her. Then he tugged her jersey, conceded a penalty and Jenny scored sending their goalie the wrong way. It wasn't long before Marco and his mates led 3-1, though, as they were far too fit and it was getting hotter.

"Hey can I take my top off?" Laura chuckled.

"Yeah," Marco shouted.

"Come on you slapper, keep focussed," Mark demanded.

Half time came and everyone lay on the pitch having a kini. Everyone wore trainers. Out of Marco's vision, Sarah replaced Jenny. Sarah sat down beside David.

"You still look remarkably fresh," Marco said.

"Just watch," Sarah said.

"Did you enjoy the morning, Jenny?" Marco asked.

"Now what do I say?" she whispered to David. "I mean seeing Sliema's shops."

Thank God for that, David thought. That puts my mind to rest.

"It was wicked," Sarah said. "He really doesn't know," Sarah confirmed quietly as they took their places.

"Can I tell you my favourite position?" Laura asked.

"I think they all know it," Mark sighed.

"I want to play behind the front two," she went on. "I saw it on Match of the Day."

"Just get the ball to Sarah or Jenny," Mark insisted.

The game began. David played a long ball to Sarah who turned and belted it home from 20 yards.

"Fluke!" said Marco.

"Class," said Sarah.

Theresa and the Captain had turned up to watch and a passing dog joined them.

"Play to the crowd," David called out.

Mark hit a speculative lob into the box, the goalie came for it but Sarah got there first and headed it home!

"You are jammy," Marco repeated.

Everyone was getting tired. Sarah went off on a mazy run, beat 3 players and flicked it over the goalie's head. Sarah made a point of running to David and giving him a large kiss.

Marco looked dejected.

"4-3! 4-3! We win!" Laura shouted, hugging Sarah and placing her top over her head and displaying two swinging breasts.

"You are like a different woman," Marco said approvingly. "You seemed to catch your second wind. Maybe we can win after all."

Theresa and the Captain came out to the centre spot and patted the players on the back.

"Marco is inferring we can win," said Laura.

"He's implying," Theresa corrected her.

"In for a penny, in for a pound," Laura added.

"And put your top back on" Theresa demanded.

"You know I fancy that girl," Mark said to David.

Marco and his mates headed back to their bikes and gave Tony and Steven a lift. Once they'd headed off, Jenny came out on to the pitch.

"Oh my God! I can see two of them and I am not even drunk," the Captain groaned.

"I'm going to put £100 on too," Mark announced.

"Yes, but she is one player," David reminded him. "They've a far better team. Okay let's head back to St Julian's."

"I'll call a taxi," said Theresa.

"Tonight you'll enjoy the fireworks," Theresa told Sarah.

"I hear you went shopping," David said to Jenny, ensuring it got confirmed. "Don't do it again, though. Danny would have a fit."

"Sorry," Jenny agreed. "Marco was looking for camouflage trousers but he can never find them!"

David had a shower back at the apartments, looked out a warm jersey and met up with Laura, Mark, Jenny and Sarah in the kitchen.

"I hear a festa is quite an event" Sarah enthused.

"Malta has the 2nd largest firework industry in the world after China," David replied, in courier-mode.

"Isn't it dangerous?" Sarah asked. "There are people killed and injured every year," Mark pointed out. "And I tell you, keep your wits about you tonight because those rockets have to come down somewhere."

"Like on your head!" David added.

By the time the five of them had walked up to the St Julian's hotel, Tony's coach was already packed. The Captain and Theresa were pointing folk to the coach.

"Is there plenty of banging?" Alex enquired.

"I told you to dress warmly," said David eyeing up the young lady with the bare midriff and micro skirt.

As they got on the coach, Tom Wilkins was in full flow all about Malta having 365 churches and each village had its own festa and there was tremendous competition between villages over their firework displays with proper judging.

The coach headed off through the crowds going to the discos and nightclubs. Half an hour later they were at Naxxar.

"See you all at 12," David demanded, "here at the bus stance."

He joined Sarah, Jenny, Mark and Laura who were watching a brass band playing outside the church all gaily lit up with hundreds of light bulbs.

"You'll notice the band do start together but, despite the conductor, they don't necessarily finish together," Mark explained.

"I had noticed," Jenny agreed.

"Why are the flags yellow and white and not just red and white?" Sarah enquired.

"That's the Vatican flag," said Mr Wilkins passing by and chewing some Qubbajt or nougat.

David led the four into the church. It was a spectacular sight with all candles lit and thousands of beautiful scented flowers at the feet of the local saints. A smell of incense was evident.

"Come on," Mark said. "Let's get a good vantage point for the display."

They headed out into the town square, stopping to buy hot dogs and nougat and kwarezimal almond biscuits and coke and then stood on the high steps of a local honey coloured villa. A large crowd congregated.

David could see Alex being chatted up at an ice cream van by 5 Maltese youths and clutching a Maltese flag. A bonfire was lit. Then hundreds of fireworks soared into the night sky and there were whoops of delight from the crowd.

Next there were aerial displays as other fireworks zoomed just above the heads of the crowd and set alight a huge model of the church. The five young people ducked from time to time as rockets came down around them and there was a familiar smell of smoke and gunpowder everywhere.

By 12 and, just beginning to feel cold, they headed back to the coach. David was aware Jenny had not only held his hand all evening but put her head into his chest whenever there were the larger bangs.

"How long do you actually have here, Sarah?" David asked as they boarded the coach.

"I've got an open return on Air Malta," Sarah replied. "And of course I am not paying for my accommodation."

As they walked back to their apartment the bright spotlights came on automatically at the entrance as usual. Sarah, indeed, was startled by it.

"You know," Jenny said thoughtfully, "this is giving me an idea, David. Could you get me a Nativity Angel outfit – you know, wings, halo and so on?"

"It's the sort of thing Theresa would have at the school, but why on earth would you want that?" he asked intrigued.

"I have a second cunning plan," Jenny replied as they entered the foyer and made a bee line for the drinks machine.

As the lights went out, at least 4 females repositioned themselves outside. Then the Captain appeared and they disappeared into the night.

On Sunday morning, about half their tour party came to Valletta market adjacent to the bus station with its famous triton water fountain.

"That is floodlit and pretty spectacular at night," David told Jenny and Sarah as they got off the bus.

"One of the many benefits of their Labour government," said Tom Wilkins provocatively.

"Oh yes and having us all too pally with Gadaffi's lot," Theresa said, taking him on.

David and the youngsters didn't wait to hear the outcome of the political debate.

"Just look at these stalls," Jenny enthused. "Tea towels, car stickers, key rings, Maltese boats and knights in armour, tea trays, snow shakers, flags, towels, football tops ...."

"We can see," Sarah laughed.

"Here's some advice," Mark interrupted. "Tell each stall holder it is your last day on the island and you only have a few Liri left and you'll be surprised how much you can haggle them down!"

"I have another way," David pointed out. "I talk Maltese to them and I always get a discount."

"Well we aren't all as bright as you, clever clogs," Mark suggested.

"Don't go to those stalls over there," David said, pointing out four near Valletta's ramparts.

"Why not?" Jenny asked.

"The produce is, shall we say, only a bit too fresh."

"But isn't that a good thing?" Sarah asked.

"Not when it means a vet could still save it? You see you choose a rabbit and they kill it for you!"

"Oh that's gross," Jenny gasped and held David's hand. This is going so well, David reckoned. He noticed Mark tried to take Sarah's hand but she took it away.

"I've just got the smallest top," Alex said, holding it up against her ample bosom "You must see it."

"I'd like to," Mark enthused.

David got himself a Maltese flag at 50c off.

"You know," Theresa said, "you're only paying what the stall holders really wanted in the first place. You're kidding yourself you get money off."

David was unfazed and showed Jenny some large beach towels.

Was now the moment? "Why don't you and I have a night out?" There he'd said it! He'd summoned up the courage and actually asked her. Unfortunately, he soon realised she hadn't heard him. She was admiring some portable radios and Sony Walkmans which were blasting out the local Gold Coast radio station. Soon, she was rocking about with her hands pressing the ear pieces to her head.

"Did you say something?" she asked "Did you say something about a light had gone out?"

"Hey, here you are," came Laura's familiar voice. You do pick your moments David thought. "I've got an Italian football top and some make up."

"I'm getting a Walkman," Jenny decided.

"Kemmo (how much)?" David asked.

"Just 3 Liri," the man replied.

"Oh I thought it would be less," Jenny cooed.

"Oh senorita, to you 2 Liri 50 cents," he volunteered.

"Done," said Jenny.

"You're using you feminine charms unfairly," David complained, wiping his specs to clear the sweat.

"That's what women do," Laura explained.

"What are we doing for the rest of today?" Jenny asked.

"Back in time for lunch then they have a day of leisure," David replied. "After all, Sundays are quiet in Malta." Shall I ask her again? David wondered.

They were heading back to the coach via the cheese pie stall.

"I found the toilet," Mrs King announced as they reached the stall.

Fortified by a cheese pie and his hands covered in flaky pastry, David tried again. "Jenny, I've something to ask you."

Jenny pulled her sunspecs down her nose and looked at him intently. "Look I apologised for not doing the art gallery," she said. "I'll be there next week," she added.

"No, it's not that. Would you like …….."

"Hey are we heading back today or tomorrow?" Mark shouted from the door.

"Oh come on!" David sighed and they jumped back on.

By 2 pm, Mark, David, Sarah, Jenny and Laura were all back at the little sandy St George's Bay and opposite their apartments. The suntan lotion was applied, everyone had their shades on, the young men had shorts on and the girls wore bikinis. The radio blared across the beach. Little kids queued for pedallos.

Suddenly, Theresa disembarked from a karozzin.

"I've got the stuff you wanted" she said loudly. She was carrying 2 halos, 2 pairs of wings and a white angel's costume. "I got it all from Father Collina but he wants it back in a week and he stressed clearly they must not be used, under any circumstances, for any activity which would bring the church into disrepute. What do you plan to do with it anyway Jenny? It's a mighty peculiar request in the middle of June."

"Yeh do tell us, sis," Sarah encouraged her, holding one of the costumes against her yellow bikini-clad body.

"I can't say yet but I am a Catholic too and it will be worn in a respectful manner."

"I'm glad to hear it," Theresa said, looking red and flustered in the hot summer sun.

"Call us Danny's Angels," Sarah laughed putting the halo on her head.

"I crown you Miss Malta," Laura laughed and put a towel on her back as a cloak and baguette in her hand as a sceptre.

"I want to bring peace to mankind and serve the Third World," Sarah added in role.

"Is that Jupiter?" Laura asked.

"It means poor nations," Theresa said patronisingly.

"Are you close to Father Collina?" David asked.

"Not so close he would endanger his soul by giving you a dodgy penalty," she confirmed.

"Pity!"

"I'll put the clothes in my room," Jenny suggested and headed up the beach.

"If we lose the match, Theresa, do you think Peter would accept money?" David asked.

"I can't see it," Theresa said. "Peter is not a poor man and he would like to see Danny and all his activities, some of which don't forget, are actually legit, out of St Julian's and Sliema."

"Legitimate," Sarah corrected her.

"Don't even think about it, child," Theresa glared. "It would have to be big money and, given Danny's fine for tax evasion, he hasn't got it."

"What about Carmen?"

"Her mind's going," said Jenny as she returned.

"For that reason, Peter could challenge it in court," Theresa said ominously.

"So who do we know with money?" Mark asked.

"Don't look at me," Theresa warned. "Anyway, I am off home to get out of my warm clothes."

"So who do we know?" David wondered out loud.

"No one daft enough to hand over thousands," Mark confirmed.

At that moment the Captain came down the steps, all dapper in his white peaked cap, navy blue jacket, white trousers and walking with a stick.

"Hello, everyone!" he beamed. "A gorgeous hot day, what?"

"They all are," David laughed.

"What were you all taking about?" he asked.

"We may need real money if Danny is not to lose all his business here," David explained.

"What, every business?" the Captain echoed.

"Every." I've caught the old boy's interest, David realised, but has he got money?

"What are you saying man? It seems a rum do."

"If we lose that football match on Thursday, Danny hands over all his local business interests to Peter Scerri and he'd be ruined and we'd lose our jobs."

"Would his business at night at the Apartments stop?"

"Definitely," David answered firmly.

"Would Theresa be laid off?"

"Little doubt"

"That's a bit stiff," he said thoughtfully.

"It's always the weakest who are victims in a war," Mark added helpfully.

"Maybe I need to talk this through with you," the Captain said. "If you lose the match, we can meet at Danny's little restaurant, where Steven works and I'll see what I can do," he volunteered.

And with that he was off along the water's edge.

"Maybe he is our life insurance policy," David ventured.

"Has he really got money?" Mark speculated.

"Well, who else is there?" David groaned.

Laura was making some sandcastles and the others joined her. David put some sun bloc on Jenny's back and Sarah headed off to the beach bar and got some coke.

"Maybe he hasn't got money but has access to some," David added. "We'll soon find out, eh?"

"We certainly have to have a plan B," Mark agreed. "We can hardly expect Sarah to win the match herself."

"And if Danny or Peter ever find out," David butted in "We're all dead meat!"

"She's your friend," Mark smiled "and it's your plan."

"It's her plan or Jenny's to be precise," David corrected him.

A couple of hours later, the five young people headed back into the apartment block. Maria at reception glared as Sarah threw off her sandals on the cold welcoming marble floor and sand flew everywhere.

"Keep them on," Maria commanded. David had a shower and then entered the girls' room to find both Sarah and Jenny in the Angels' outfit complete with halos and wings above their bikinis. They looked stunning.

"Do tell me what your plan is," David implored. "There's no way we can put on a nativity play in the summer."

"I am going to try a little rehearsal tonight," Jenny announced. "And you can watch, David."

"I am all ears," he replied, sitting on the bed. "Just say when."

A mattress lay on the floor, which Sarah used. They admired themselves in the mirror and then Sarah took the outfit off and washed her hair. "I am doing football training with Marco and friends later," she said. "I want to be at full physical fitness"

David looked up and down the bikini-clad girl but said nothing. Outside a karozzin passed by. There was a slight breeze which rattled the Venetian blinds.

"Can I please get changed?" Jenny said modestly. "I'll see you at tea time."

David spent an hour having a siesta, a cold coke and playing Gold Coast radio. From time to time he could hear the girls chuckling in the adjacent room. What could this plan be? he kept wondering.

He was even more intrigued when Marco collected Sarah about 6 pm and Jenny was back wearing the angel's outfit. The couple sped off into the darkness on the Suzuki. "Could I get up on the roof above the foyer entrance?" Jenny asked.

"Yes, there's a ladder round the back," David replied. "Danny uses it for putting a flag up on special days such as Malta's Independence Day or the Queen's birthday or even his own!"

Soon, Jenny had clambered up on the roof. "Switch your mobile on and tell me when the Captain appears," she commanded.

"You're a right bossy boots," David pointed out.

A long hour passed. Jenny lay hidden on the roof.

David sat intrigued on the wall opposite overlooking the small sandy beach.

Suddenly the Captain walked along the narrow street. He got to the entrance and met one of the women of the night outside. He took out his wallet and a note was exchanged.

Instantly the spotlight came on at full power illuminating the entire entrance in a beam of white light.

"Stop Captain, I am a messenger from God!" Jenny shouted.

"My God!" said the Captain. "Are you advertising a nightclub?" he asked helpfully.

Jenny, undaunted, held her arms out. "You must change your ways and repent."

"Repaint what?"

"No, repent"

"Do I get 3 wishes?"

"I am not a Genie I'm an Angel of the Lord."

I think you've been sussed, David feared.

"Can you help me walk without a stick and a limp?" the Captain asked, a note of enthusiasm in his voice.

"You must give up women," Jenny said.

"I'm not gay," the Captain rebuffed her and he sat on the wall near David. "You are pretty fanciable yourself. Are you Charlotte Church? She has the voice of an Angel."

"Do not mock. Were you ever inside church?"

"I'm a bit old for that now," he grinned.

"Look, stop, Jenny!" David implored as he got up and walked across to the entrance.

"Don't be too critical. She was really good, but I knew it was you, Jenny, all along," the Captain added encouragingly. "But what are you young folk up to?" he asked.

Jenny clambered down and joined them. "It was meant to be a rehearsal," Jenny confessed. "But it didn't work," she accepted.

"It might have worked if I didn't know you," the Captain suggested sympathetically. "I haven't seen girls dressed up as Angels since I'd a weekend in Amsterdam," he pointed out.

"I don't want to know," Jenny said.

"Do tell me later," David asked.

The Captain went in and David and Jenny kicked off their shoes and walked barefoot along the sand.

"I love this place and all of you," Jenny said. "I haven't had such fun in ages."

They entered the apartment by a side door. Jenny changed out of the costume and joined David in his room. He cleared his coffee cups and made a drink. As usual, St Julian's vibrated with the sound of the local discos and nightclubs.

"This summer has been the best yet and all because you are here," David remarked. There, he had said it! He took a deep breath.

Suddenly, Jenny leaned across and kissed him, knocking the coffee cup on his bed.

"Don't worry, don't worry," said David mopping it all up.

"For heaven's sake, forget the coffee," Jenny said. Suddenly she cuddled him and David opened his mouth and kissed her. The door opened at that opportune moment and Sarah walked in.

"Has her heart stopped then?" she asked provocatively.

Why did you have to come in at that precise moment? David groaned.

"I was just congratulating Jenny on being an Angel" he explained.

"Oh I can see that," Sarah smiled knowingly. "Did the rehearsal work?" she asked.

"It failed, but only because the Captain recognised her," David explained.

"I'd like to know who your real target is," he added, but neither girl would be drawn on it.

All that night, David couldn't stop thinking about Jenny, the kiss and cuddle. Taking things slowly had clearly borne fruit.

On Monday their party was on board the ferry to Gozo. The sea was a millpond. The sky was clear, blue and cloudless. David couldn't bear to sit on the leather upholstered seats on deck as they burned the back of your legs.

"I've had an adventure," said Alex as she passed by.

"What was that?" David enquired.

"I went up to that top deck to get some photos and an old boy in a white peaked cap said you, you not fuq. Very strange, the Maltese." And with that she was off to the bar. She must have come out of the same mould as Charley, David reckoned. Jenny hung over the deck rail and watched the fish below her. Mark, Sarah and Laura were in the bar. A motor boat passed them as they approached Mgarr Harbour.

"Troy was filmed here," David told her. "Brad Pitt has a small part."

"That's not what I've heard," Jenny retorted.

"Do you know how to tell if your man is well hung?" David asked.

"How?" Jenny asked.

"Put your finger on the gap between his neck and the rope!" David laughed.

Jenny threw a leather cushion at David and then kissed him, a long lingering kiss like the previous evening.

"You know, I never want this summer to end," David said.

"It'll be a shock going back to poor, wet Yorkshire," Jenny agreed.

"Well it's weeks away yet," David reminded her. The ship docked. "Okay, let's get them all up to Victoria and con them into buying honey etc at Danny's café" he said as they headed down the steps and rejoined the party.

"I haven't forgotten," Jenny replied.

An hour later, as the party all browsed round the market, everyone appeared to have a jar of D & C honey.

"We've been busy bees," Laura joked as she caught up with David. Then more seriously she added "You know I might end up working for Peter if Danny has to sell up."

David was shocked and stopped in his tracks. "You wouldn't come to our new base up at Buggibba then?"

"Okay, maybe Danny would keep me on as a courier but I wouldn't get my nightclub dancing or my snooker work, would I?"

"I hadn't thought about it," David conceded. "I feared some of us might end up redundant but I hadn't considered anyone actually working for the enemy."

"That's a bit harsh, Peter is just a businessman," Laura stopped to look at some string baskets. "A pretty unscrupulous one."

"And Danny isn't?" Laura held up her jar of honey. "Exhibit A" she said accusingly.

"Okay, touché," David shrugged.

Laura joined Sarah and Jenny at a tea towel stall and Mark came up. He was already eating honey with his sticky fingers. "Have you heard Laura may leave us?" he asked.

"I'd never considered it," David conceded.

"And if she goes I am going to pull either Sarah or Jenny or both," Mark said convincingly.

"Just keep your hands off Jenny," David demanded.

Mark smiled and headed off to join the girls.

David got himself an ice cream and reflected on the memory that every year Mark or Marco got off with whoever he had fancied. If Mark did not have Laura in tow he would be a threat.

He had another more urgent worry. If Laura was going to join the enemy, what was there to stop her telling Peter about Jenny and Sarah? He was still reflecting on that an hour later at the Cornocopaeia hotel as he drank his Gozo red wine and soaked the coarse local bread with its formidable crust into his soup. A lot of the group were showing off the dainty lace they had bought locally. The meal had been excellent. Tomato soup had been followed by roast beef and Yorkshire pudding and that in turn by Italian ice cream. The local wine gave you a warm glow after one glass. As long as Laura and Jenny were friends there was little danger of a betrayal, he concluded.

His attention was caught by loud laughter from the table where Mark and Sarah were sitting. Jenny nudged David's arm and she nodded to point out the attention her sister was attracting.

"He's been all over her like a rash all day," she confirmed.

David glanced at Laura. She had a face like thunder. Eventually the group headed back out into the warm sunshine. Mr Wilkins was photographed in front of a prickly pear cactus and Miss King delayed the coach as she queued for the toilets. Alex chatted to some washer women opposite. Someone even filmed a donkey doing its business in the street! Everyone eventually got on board and Jenny told the coach load about the Azure window.

As they arrived, a coachload of Germans got there simultaneously.

"Don't mention the war," David joked.

"You've been watching too much Basil Fawlty," Mr Wilkins suggested. "They're all under 40."

The group queued at Danny's ice cream van and then headed off to see the rock formation. Sarah took out a plastic football and began to play keepie-uppie on the rocks. She then slammed a shot off the ice cream van and trapped the ball on the rebound.

"Hey, cut that out!" Steven shouted as he sold his ice creams.

The Germans applauded. "You have real talent" one middle aged man in a German hat and carrying an expensive camera said, admiringly.

"Thank you," Sarah replied as she balanced the ball on the back of her neck.

"She should play in the Scotland team," David grinned.

"Ah, Schottland. No gut, eh? Crap."

"Hey, I wouldn't go that far," David said. "Rangers, Celtic, Larsson, Klaus."

"I know Schottland. Who do you support?"

"Dunfermline"

"They're crap too, I support Bayern."

"Are you Scottish young lady?"

"I am English," Sarah replied firmly.

"I run a German team and our ladies team could do with talent like you. Here's my card" the man said.

"That's kind," Sarah replied. "But I play for a team, England."

"There's no need to joke," the man scolded.

"But I do. The Ladies England Team."

"She does," David confirmed.

David spread out a large towel on the rocks and was surprised when the German promptly sat on it.

"I am Karl Schmidt," he introduced himself and shook David's hand.

"Bond. David Bond," the young man replied. "We're a football team, an amateur one, but a good one, having our summer break."

Sarah and David exchanged knowing glances. "There's something you could do for me to make up for what you've done to my country," said David.

"Ah, the war," Karl replied.

"No, you gave us Berti Vogts as Scotland manager. No, to be serious, we've got an important match on Thursday and I am allowed to have two tourists in it. Can you lend us two?"

The German thought for a moment. "Wolfgang Heinz in midfield and Peter Brandt in defence are pretty good and I can see if they'd play for you. They might enjoy the exercise," Karl added.

"Am I pleased I met you," David acknowledged.

Mark, Laura and Jenny returned and put towels down too.

"Mein Gott! There are two of you, Sarah," Karl gasped.

"Cloning is further advanced in England than Germany," Sarah laughed.

"This game may not be a foregone conclusion after all," David said. "I've a story to tell you three" he added.

Even Karl sat intrigued as David explained that the Germans were an amateur football team and they would lend two players on Thursday to play Peter's team.

"You keep saying they're a scary lot," Karl said quizzically.

"No, his name is Scerri," Mark explained.

"Mind you, I think you were spot on the first time," David acknowledged.

An hour later, David and Jenny were hanging over the side of the Gozo ferry as the ship sailed back to the Maltese port. "Entschuldigen sie mir bitte," came a voice. "I am Heinz."

"Und ich heisse Brandt."

The two bronzed fair-haired young men, both smelling of after shave, introduced themselves.

I wonder if they've splashed it on to impress Jenny, David considered.

"Ve are your players."

"Yes, you are very kind," David said. "We need you."

"Ve are gut ja. Ve often vin," Heinz explained. "Ve haff balls"

"You'll need them," Jenny agreed, stifling a grin with her hand over her mouth.

"I haff many positions," Heinz continued.

Is this a wind-up? David considered. Does this guy know English or not?

David and Jenny smiled politely.

"I expect to get on top. Young lady, do you come?"

"I'll be playing," Jenny said, exchanging a knowing glance with David.

"Ve vill see you on Thursday denn," Heinz added and headed off to the bar.

A breeze was coming up and the two young people clutched their sunspecs lest they fell overboard. Lorries carrying Gozitan onions revved up below deck for a quick getaway.

David began to count his contingent. "I think we should go and see Carmen and learn if she'd bail Danny out if we lose the match," he suggested. "We must have a Plan B and she'd have a reason to help us. The Captain doesn't. Why don't we go and see her this evening? It's Danny's night at his nightclub."

"I'll come," Jenny agreed, "But you do the talking," she stressed.

At 7.30, Tony dropped off Jenny and David at Danny's villa. The butler came out to the gates and Tony took that as his cue to drive off.

"Do you have an appointment, sir?" the butler enquired.

"No, but we would like to see Carmen," David explained.

The butler, dressed immaculately in his black suit, tails, white shirt, and bow tie, said nothing but led the two young people to the entrance hall. They waited and admired the magnificent oil paintings and statues.

Carmen suddenly appeared in her usual black dress and wearing a shawl over her shoulders.

"Ariadne, you are here from London. I knew you'd return!" she exclaimed and gave Jenny a hug.

"We're clearly off to a good start. She's gaga!" David said.

"We haven't got Goya but we do have many other artists," Carmen said proudly.

"What do you think of the Borgs?" Carmen asked.

"I am not much into Star Trek," Jenny said helpfully.

"They're the gentlemen in the oil paintings," he whispered to the young girl.

"They're 16th Century," Carmen added "But you know that, Ariadne. You lived here long enough."

Jenny gave David a look of alarm. The butler led them into the lounge.

"Do have a sherry," Carmen said invitingly. "I am so pleased you have a young man. I thought you were a lesbian," Carmen said

"She wanted to be a Thespian," David quipped.

"Oh my God, you must not give up on Catholicism," Carmen demanded.

"We're getting in deeper," Jenny sighed.

"You don't need fear the grim reaper at your age," Carmen pointed out.

"Yes, I want to marry David and, as your daughter, I need a dowry," Jenny tugged David's arm.

The butler came in with the sherries. "What would you do with a dairy, you've had no interest in farming," Carmen ventured.

"A dowry, money to set us up," Jenny elaborated loudly.

"Of course, of course," Carmen replied. "I can give you shares in all Danny's companies."

"Oh my God, not that," David dived in.

"Don't be so ungracious," Carmen replied sternly.

"We need money," Jenny said. "One day we'll have kids."

"That would be lovely," Carmen agreed. "I'll write you a cheque."

"We'll need 1000 LM."

"20000 LM," David interrupted, "And made out to Peter Scerri," David added.

There was a long pause. Carmen had taken her cheque book out but now put it back in a writing bureau. David and Jenny looked at each other.

"I see it all now. Danny has employed two young people who are working for our main competitor. I must ask you to leave."

"But I am your daughter," Jenny said desperately.

"No, you are a fraud. You are that Penny who was here last week. You can't fool me. Do you think I've lost my skittles?"

"Marbles," David said helpfully.

"Of course not," Jenny said.

"Have we got any more plans?" she asked as they stood in the dark lane and David texted Tony. Drizzle was starting to fall.

Mrs Dyson came out looking for a lift and buttoning up her raincoat. "I heard much of your conversation with the old bat," she said. "We get lots of folk seeing her alone and trying to get money out of her and she always was generous. She rarely turns people down I must say, but there's no way she'd ever give a hand to that crook Scerri. Whatever were you thinking of?"

"We need money to pay Peter. Big money if Danny's football team loses that silly match on Thursday. We all fear for Danny's businesses which are his stupid wager and hence our jobs."

"Thank the Lord you explained that," the housekeeper said with feeling, "We thought you'd joined his lot" she said with contempt. "Anyway there's something else you should know, but you must keep it in strict confidence. Many years ago, Peter was Carmen's lover but he abandoned her with a baby and she has never forgiven him."

"Ariadne!" Jenny exclaimed.

"The same"

"If it had not been for Danny, the shame for Carmen in Catholic Malta 40 years ago would have been horrific."

"Does Danny know?" David ventured.

"Of course," Mrs Dyson replied.

At that moment, both cars arrived.

"Carmen must have been a real slapper," Jenny said as Tony drove them back to St Julian's.

David was deep in thought. Could they win that match or did he have to find someone as an insurance policy and, if so, who?

That Tuesday morning it was already 30 degrees by 9 am when Alex came out of the hotel reception.

"Where are we off to boss?" she smiled at David.

"Ta Qali craft village then a brief look at the old Roman town of Mdina, Malta's former capital, then, a nice 3 hours up at Golden Bay," he reeled off.

"Cool," she said as she tripped over her flip-flops clambering up the steps on the coach. Hot, actually David said under his breath. Jenny was standing in her khaki uniform, sunspecs on, caked in sun bloc and clutching her clipboard at the hotel door. Mark and Laura were doing the same at their coach. Theresa and the Captain were sitting on the car park wall.

"This job comes easy to me now," Jenny said cheerfully.

"Easily. It is an adverb," Theresa corrected her.

Jenny made a face. "Sarah wants to know if she can kick a ball at Ta Qali national football stadium when you are all at the craft village?" she asked.

Tom Wilkins passed by. "I would imagine you would have to get the written authority of the football association," he said authoritatively.

"Or climb a wall!" David said pragmatically.

"I'll take that as a yes," Jenny agreed.

Suddenly Danny appeared from the back of the car park. "Have you got a team to win this match on Thursday?" he asked David. "It's my heart's desire to wipe out Peter's business in Sliema," he stressed.

"We are doing our best, but what if he wipes out yours?" David said resignedly.

"The Germans didn't do it, the Italians didn't bomb us out," Danny said with some emotion.

"You were a toddler," David reminded him.

"They didn't win because of me and people like me," the Captain added. "You all owe me a huge debt."

"My Grandad saved the lives of hundreds in the African desert in the war," Jenny said.

Everyone fell silent, then, "Did he fight with Monty?" the Captain asked.

"I think my Grandad fought with anyone. What regiment was he in, this Monty?"

"Such ignorance," Theresa groaned.

"How did he save lives?" David asked, trying to get the story back on track.

"He accidentally shot dead the regimental cook," Jenny explained, then laughed.

The captain looked up to heaven then got on the bus.

"Are there toilets at this Ta Qali place?" Mrs King asked "And is the glass any good?"

"Don't say she plans to pee into a tumbler," Jenny whispered.

"Yes, madam, there are toilets there," David replied with restraint.

Tony and Steve now revved up.

"I'll get going," Danny said, doffing his hat to Theresa. "Don't forget to guide your tourists to my huts and ice cream van." He didn't seem to notice Sarah getting on, wearing her full England strip.

An hour later Mark, Laura, the Captain and Theresa were in the glass factory but David and Jenny were admiring Sarah hitting shot after shot from the 18-yard line into an empty net at the stadium.

"It's fun to play on grass again," she panted.

David took a turn in goal and still the ball screamed past him into the net.

"This sure is impressive!" he shouted.

Suddenly Sarah took her top off and played on in her bra, shorts and sandals.

"Hey you'll burn," David warned her. Oh never mind, he thought to himself. David was aware that Jenny had a look of annoyance on her face. Next minute she took her top off and similarly played in bra and shorts.

"This has given me an idea about distracting Peter's team," he laughed heartily.

Sarah was aware her arms and back of her neck were getting sore and their tops were soon back on.

"Come on you guys!" came a shout from Mark. "We're all set for Mdina."

"I've not been there before – is it that old town up on the hill?" Jenny asked.

"What do we see?" Sarah added.

"It was once Malta's capital and it is called the silent city."

"Is that because it is quiet?" Jenny asked.

"Could well be," David replied quizzically. "We're going to see the old Roman catacombs carved out of the rock and deep below the surface," he continued. "And then, after cold drinks and ice cream, we're back at Golden Bay."

"Sounds cool," Sarah enthused.

Half an hour later, clambering around the cool catacombs was a relief from the blinding sunshine outside.

"I don't fancy these ancient skeletons much," Alex groaned.

There were indeed scores of them, lying in their tombs.

"Gross!" Jenny agreed.

"How old are they?" Sarah asked.

"The early years of Christianity," Mr Wilkins stated like a walking encyclopaedia.

"That's what I thought," Sarah grinned.

David realised Jenny was holding his hand tightly as they edged along the rocky potholed surface.

"It's a strange smell," David said.

"Probably Mrs King," Jenny ventured.

They all clambered back up to the glaring sunlight.

"There's a chamber of horrors here in Mdina and a remarkable Roman villa but that's for another day," David announced. "We're off to Golden Bay."

"Yippee!" Alex shouted gleefully.

The coaches wended their way past the little farms with their stone walls, waterwheels, people in the fields and, from time to time, the sight of an old Maltese bus being used as a shed.

By the time they arrived at the bay, the heat was oppressive and no one had to be told to cover up. David hated putting on a long-sleeved shirt but his arms would have peeled in half an hour otherwise. They all made a beeline for the stall with the long baguettes and cold cokes. The party were putting up deckchairs and rather redundant windbreakers or lying on towels or lilos.

"This roast beef salad is yummy," Sarah declared.

"Don't get sand in it though," Jenny expertly advised as she lay on a towel beside a delighted David, who'd ensured her towel was parallel. Mark was rubbing suntan lotion into Laura's back.

"I flew over this beach many times in the war," the Captain said as he and Theresa passed with 7-Up and ice creams. "There was nothing here then."

"If Mrs King passes wind again, there'll be nothing here now," Jenny confirmed. "It was unbelievable in the catacombs" she grimaced.

"We all get old," the Captain explained.

"Not Des O'Connor," Jenny countered.

"Or Cliff Richard," David added.

David noticed that Laura was walking disconsolately down to the water's edge and deliberately trod on a sandcastle on her way. He followed her and paddled beside her.

"What's up?" he enquired.

"If you haven't noticed, Mark is all over Sarah."

"Who goes home in about 2 weeks," David reminded her.

"That's as maybe, but there'll just be someone else off the next flight. He doesn't believe in mahogany."

"Monogamy," David corrected her.

"Thank you, Theresa," Laura said pointedly. They veered to the right as two infants splashed each other.

"I see less and less reason not to join Peter," Laura went on.

"And lose all your main friends?" David queried.

"I'd make more."

"Anyway there's no guarantee we'll lose that match."

Laura gave him a look. Sarah, Mark and Jenny ran arm in arm into the clear blue water.

"And if Sarah goes home, I fear you have competition too," Laura said knowingly.

David and Laura looked on as the three youngsters tried to form a pyramid but both girls fell off Mark's shoulders who went under the water and came up gasping for breath. All three splashed David and Laura who instantly retaliated. As they broke up, Mark kissed Sarah on the cheek then they all went back to their towels.

That evening, David was sitting at the skittle alley with Mark and Jenny when the smell of familiar cigar smoke preceded Danny's arrival.

"48 hours till the big match. Are we all set? Why aren't you training? More to the point, why are you all betting £100 that we'll win? I'm not complaining, mind," Danny said, taking off his hat and enjoying his usual whisky.

"Yes we're raring to go," David replied. "We'll go with a fluid diamond formation. I'm up front with Jenny, Tony's in goal with Marco, Steven, Mark and a German in defence. In midfield we've another German, Laura and two of Marco's polo team. All the subs are polo players."

"And yet you are betting £100," Danny reminded him. "Do you have something up your sleeve?"

"Nothing, we can hardly bribe the ref when it's the Parish Priest this time," David pointed out.

"At least there will be no extra time in the heat of the afternoon. Father Collina has mass at 5.30 pm and will dash off at 5 pm. I think that will ensure there'll be a late winning goal."

"But who for?" David moaned.

Peter Scerri had been at the bar but, fortified by a glass of champagne, came across to their table.

"Celebrating prematurely, I see," Danny said bravely.

"Hardly! It's like a sure fire bet in a horse race," Peter said, mopping his brow. "On Thursday night you hand over all your Sliema and St Julian's businesses to me, Danny."

"If I did lose, even though that is an unlikely scenario, how much would I have to pay you instead?" Danny asked nervously.

"We could value your business, I suppose," Peter said thoughtfully. He pulled out a calculator and did a quick computation. "No. I'd rather ruin you, sorry." He scraped his chair and returned to the bar.

Danny headed off disconsolately to the toilet.

"Why not just ignore the bet?" Jenny suggested. "After all, nothing is written down."

"And end up floating down Sliema creek? The whole town knows the match is on," David pointed out.

"And why?" Mark added.

"There must be some way we could influence Father Collina," David wondered out loud.

"Danny already offered to help local orphans," Mark reminded him.

"He's already helping them – he made most of them orphans," David explained.

"A donation to the church?" Jenny suggested.

"Carmen does that already," David said resignedly.

"How about my Angel on the rooftop routine?" Jenny asked.

"It didn't fool the Captain for a minute though," David reminded her. "Though we could try it, I am not clear why God would send an Angel to tell him to throw a football match though!"

"He must have some Achilles heel," Mark speculated.

"Theresa would know" David said, "I'll check her out."

The following day, Jenny and David were assigned to the coach party going to Hagar Qim and them on to the Blue Grotto and Marsalloxx. David couldn't get his mind off the match. Jenny sat beside him doing her commentary. The Captain and Theresa sat to their right.

"You know Father Collina ……..," David began.

"Have done for 30 years," Theresa confirmed.

"Has he got any weaknesses?" David asked.

"Like, will he throw the match if you know of one?" Theresa replied. "He tends to watch too much football. Apart from that he is a pillar of the church."

"Everyone has a skeleton in their cupboard," the Captain ventured.

"Speak for yourself," Theresa suggested.

"Does he gamble on the Maltese lotto?" David asked.

"No," Theresa emphasised.

"Like a drink?" the Captain asked.

"Just football, he adores Totti," Theresa added.

"We've got him. A priest can't like Totti, Theresa," Jenny said victoriously.

"He's a football star, dimwit!" David laughed as the coach pulled up at Malta's Stonehenge.

"I sometimes wonder if Hagar Qim was one of the world's first football stadiums!" Jenny exclaimed.

"Stadia," Theresa murmured.

Jenny took out a plastic football and belted it between the two pillars.

"Put the ball away before the official guide hits you," David commanded.

As the tourists had their tour, David sat on one of the old stones. Jenny sat down with a cold coke. A lizard scampered across the ground.

"I thought we could nobble that Priest," Jenny moaned.

"I think we're back to that Angel on the rooftop routine tonight or tomorrow," David admitted.

"But we knew the captain's weakness, what is Father Collina's?"

"Just make it vague," David suggested and put his arm around her.

"And how do we get the good Priest to come to the apartments at night?" Jenny asked.

"We can say we want to discuss the match," David said.

The party wended its way back to the entrance and the two young people headed back to the coach. The leather seats, already hot in the late morning sun made David and Jenny, in their khaki shorts, put towels underneath their legs.

"I'll get Theresa to phone him and invite him along at 8 pm," David confirmed.

At 7.50 pm, David hid excitedly behind the wall opposite the apartment block. Jenny was up on the roof in her Angel garb. It was pitch dark. The only sound was the waves caressing the shore at St George's bay. On the dot the Priest could be seen walking with a stick along the lane. As he reached the entrance, Jenny put on the spot light on full power and Father Collina was momentarily blinded. Jenny stood up, halo on head, wings on back.

"Father, Father, I can have you walking without a stick," Jenny said in her best haunting voice.

"I can walk without a stick now," the bemused Father replied. "I thought a supernatural being would have known that. I am returning the Captain's cane which he left at Theresa's."

"You must repaint," Jenny said quite flustered.

"Repaint what?" the good Father smiled.

"I meant repent," Jenny corrected herself.

"Struth!" David groaned behind the wall. "Forty days and forty nights for all your sins," Jenny added, warming to her theme.

"That seems harsh," the Priest suggested. Then, "What have I done, dear Angel?"

"You know all your sins," Jenny pointed out.

"Name one."

"I can forgive your sins," Jenny persisted.

"If I throw the match on Thursday, perhaps." Father Collina began to giggle. "Look young lady, or Angel, you are wearing all our Nativity gear we use at the church. I must have a stern word with Theresa."

"Oh don't do that," Jenny asked, taking off her Angel wings. "My grammar will be criticised."

"Does she know your Grandma?"

"No, grammar. She's a teacher of the old school."

"Okay, I'll say nothing. This has been fun but now I've a sick parishioner to go and see and must call in on the Captain." He headed up the stairs still chuckling and Jenny clambered down to the entrance.

"24 hours to go and I think we've had it," David surmised.

Jenny took his hand and walked in the darkness to the wall at the back of St George's bay. The floodlit hotels on both sides were reflected off the still water.

"If or when we lose, we can ask the Captain if he will lend us money," he reassured the girl. Inwardly he wasn't confident at all. Options were running out.

Wednesday morning was hot and sunny like every day which had gone before it. The Maltese didn't share the British obsession of discussing the weather for that reason. Maria at reception, therefore, didn't reply as

David gave her a wave and said, "It's hot." He waited outside for Sarah, Jenny, Mark and Laura.

"We've got a mixed itinerary," Jenny said. "Danny says take them around Mosta Dome, then show them Popeye's village and end up at Mellieha bay."

"We've got the Blue Lagoon cruise," Mark said.

"Lucky you," David replied enviously.

"Would you mind if I went?" Sarah asked.

"No, just you go on and desert us!" Jenny retorted.

Tony and Steven's coaches arrived and they headed up to the St Julian's hotels. Theresa and the Captain were waiting.

"We are coming with you, David," Theresa said grandly. "Architecture beats a beach any day."

"Are you coming too, Captain?" David enquired.

"I suppose so, if the boss commands," he shrugged.

David and Jenny got their clipboards out and the group clambered aboard. At 9 am on the dot the coaches headed out of the town.

Suddenly Danny phoned David's mobile. "Is Jenny with you?" he asked.

"I am here," Jenny confirmed.

"Sorry dear, I am stupid," came the voice. "I thought I saw you get on Mark's coach. It must be old age."

Jenny gave David a look and switched off the mobile.

Half an hour later the coach was parked beside the impressive Mosta Dome. Jenny had gathered all the group in a circle around her and nervously examined Theresa's notes attached to her clipboard.

"This is the most distinctive church on the island," she began.

"You could argue that Ta Qali is now," Mr Wilkins interrupted.

"Not strictly speaking as it is on Gozo," Theresa reminded him confidently.

"It is the third largest unsupported dome in the world," Jenny continued rustling her notes. "The main ones are…," she paused…, "St Peter's in Rome and St Sophia in Constantinople."

"What about the one in Gozo?" Mr Wilkins butted in.

"Oh do shut up!" David muttered under his breath.

"It was built by volunteer labourers from the Parish by gas."

"By gas!" Alex shouted out. "How?"

"By de Vasse, an architect," Mr Wilkins said patronisingly.

"It was completed in 27 years in 1860," Jenny said increasingly flustered.

"Well done," Theresa said encouragingly.

"Don't forget the bomb!" the Captain suggested.

"A bomb pierced the dome but didn't explode and today you can see it defused," Jenny said.

She led the group into the church, reminding the females to cover their heads and arms. Then she rejoined David in the café opposite. David had ordered some pastizzi cheesecakes and mqaret piping hot.

"What are these?" Jenny asked.

"Soft dates in pastry and the aroma comes from the aniseed," David explained as he collected two cold cisk lagers at the bar.

"Grazzi," he said.

"Can I have a date?" Jenny asked. "I need cheering up after the morning I've had. I see Mr Wilkins is taking our group around. I am so fed up."

"Of course you can have a date. You've got 3 on your plate."

"No I mean a date!" she said emphasising the words, "A date, date."

"A date?" David repeated incredulously.

"A date," Jenny replied.

"Magic!" David replied excitedly and choked on the pastry. "Where will I take you?" he asked.

"A restaurant would be nice," Jenny replied.

"Do you know," David said, removing an ashtray to a different table, "I've been wanting to ask you out ever since you arrived," he said, ill concealed relief in his voice. "I thought, indeed feared, Mark or Marco would snap you up first."

"But Mark has Laura and Marco has every girl on the island."

David laughed. She was more aware than he'd anticipated. In his excitement, some cheese pie pastry fell out of his mouth. Jenny wiped his mouth and then she leaned over and kissed him. "There's more where that came from," she promised and winked.

David got two more glasses of lager as Jenny kept an eye on her group coming out of the church. As he sat down again, Jenny looked at him intently and said, "Mum has written and fancies coming out for a week or two. She hasn't had a holiday in 3 years and it would do her a power of good."

"It'll be nice to meet her, but don't put her in your room too, because Maria could report it to Danny and Sarah is there already."

"No, she'll get a hotel room. She's not hard up," Jenny confirmed.

Eventually, the couple could see Tom Wilkins leading the group out of the church, his arms waving expansively.

"Time to get back to the coach," David said.

"Okay. Off to Popeye's village," Jenny agreed looking at her itinerary.

David walked into the Dome and knelt in front of a side altar. "Jenny, have I ever told you about a Maltese boy called Mario who had two girlfriends called Lucia and Maria, and he could never decide which one to marry, so he came here and prayed to God at this very spot."

"And what happened?" Jenny asked.

"He looked up at that beautiful stained glass window and saw those words. Can you read what they say?"

Jenny peered at them in the bright sunlight. "It says 'Ave Maria'" she said.

"And he did!" David grinned.

Jenny thumped the back of his head and headed back to the coach.

David looked back at the altar "Look God, it's about this match tomorrow," he began.

Chapter 6

It took over an hour on Thursday morning for David and Jenny to put up posters around the St Julian's Hotel advertising the match.

"It's 11 am. Isn't it time we got a coffee?" Jenny suggested.

David stood back from the notice board in the Hotel foyer and admired their handiwork. 'Match of the Season' it declared modestly. 'Scerri Monsters V The Maltesers' it announced! Below that, there was one of the trick photos of Danny shaking hands with Pele.

Young Tristram passed by clutching a bible. "Have we time to watch the match before we leave today?" he inquired.

"Easily," David confirmed. We kick off at 3pm as Father Collina has a mass after 5pm," he explained.

"Oh I know him," Tristram said. "I've been attending his morning masses," the young man explained.

"Well, he's refereeing," David stated. "We're going for a coffee. Do you want to join us?"

The young trainee priest followed the couple into the coffee bar behind the reception area and was quick to thank the couriers for such an enjoyable week. As the welcome cappuccinos were poured, Tristram said that he did have one question which he was dying to ask.

"When we had that tour of the paintings in Valletta, that surely wasn't you that day was it?" he nodded at Jenny.

Jenny looked guilty. "It was my sister, Sarah" she confessed.

"She's so like her," David added.

"You can say that again," Tristram acknowledged. "I thought I was hallucinating when I saw two of you on two different coaches at the same time setting off one morning in the Hotel car park."

"And tonight," Jenny beamed, "we plan to do something very naughty."

"Surely not in Malta, this is not Ibiza, Rhodes or Cyprus," Tristram insisted as he fumbled nervously with a sugar cube.

Why did a Priest, like the Police, always make you feel so guilty? David pondered. "No, no Father," he interrupted. "They'll both play as one person in our football match. Sarah is an internationalist at football and will come on fully fit at half time and hopefully win the match for us!"

"The opposition won't know," Jenny elaborated.

"We'll still get crucified," David thought out loud. "Oh, sorry Father, you know what I mean."

"So, you are saying two people will, in fact, be one," Tristram summed up.

"Jesus was three in one," David pointed out.

"Pity we haven't got him too," Jenny laughed.

"I'm surprised Father Collina is ref though," Tristram suggested.

"Why?" David asked.

"He has little vision on his left side."

David paused to take in the enormity of the revelation.

"Theresa never told us that," David gasped.

"How does he get to drive?" Jenny asked.

"This is Malta," David reminded her.

"What worries me," Tristram pointed out, "is that if someone were to go down in the box and everyone shouted penalty, the good Father would regard it as genuine and that wouldn't be sporting."

"Indeed it wouldn't," David winked at Jenny.

"Anyway, I must go and pack my case." Tristram got up and smuggled brown sugar cubes into his pocket.

"That's theft," Jenny said.

"I only took six." Tristram blushed. "No resorting to a dodgy penalty" he demanded.

David waited till he'd left the foyer. "Okay, Jenny, you and Sarah both go down either side of half time and we'll all roar penalty"

"You didn't have to tell me!" she laughed.

As Jenny and David walked along to St George's bay, they could see Danny's coach parked outside. Danny, himself, was standing at the entrance puffing nervously on a large cigar. He gave the couple a wave.

"Only 3 hours to go," he confirmed, needlessly checking his watch. "I've brought you all the same strips," he announced. "Last year you looked like victims from an explosion in a paint factory" he reminded them.

He nipped into the coach and pulled out a pile of Inter Milan tops.

"Why have you chosen these?" David asked.

"Father Collina hates AC Milan," Danny beamed. "And Peter's lot have got their strips."

"That was rather naive of Peter," said David quizzically. "It's not like Peter not to have done his research."

"He got amazing discount on strip hire at my sports shop," Danny laughed at his little coup.

David was about to carry them into the apartments when a taxi arrived and the two strapping blond Germans emerged.

"We are Wolfgang und Peter. Midfielder und Defender," Wolfgang introduced themselves. "Morgen Sarah"

"I am Jenny," the girl blushed and shook hands.

"But on Gozo we saw your pair."

"Grief!" Danny muttered. "What did you show them Jenny?"

"Nothing Danny, nothing at all"

"I am pleased to meet you in the new spirit of European co-operation and partnership against our common foe."

"France?" Peter asked.

"No the Scerri lot," Danny explained. "Oh I liked your posters, David" Danny smiled. "See you at 3 pm. Victory will be ours – or you lot are dead." He got back into the coach and headed off.

"Don't ever mention Sarah," David warned the two young Germans. "Now let's go in and have a coffee," he added.

Mark and Laura were already in the kitchen making toast as they entered.

"Oh great! Real strips!" Laura shouted excitedly.

"Where's Sarah?" David asked.

"Already practising at the pitch with Marco and the polo players."

"Let's get these strips on and join them," David said measuring up a top. "And remember, Jenny, you can't be on the pitch whenever your sister is."

"Come on Jenny, let's get changed in my room," Laura beckoned. "Where's my strip?"

The Germans helpfully chose one for her.

"We both like to give you what you are needing, young Fraulein," said Wolfgang who clicked his heels.

"I bet you would" Jenny scowled.

At 2pm the group arrived at the ground in Steven's coach. Scerri's lot were doing all manner of fitness routines on one side of the pitch. They all looked tall, athletic and fit. Jenny waved at Sarah who got on the coach and lay down already red faced and puffed. David could see Theresa, the Captain, Mrs King, Tom Wilkins, Tristram and Alex in the crowd of about 200 at the touchline.

"David, a word of advice," the Captain said, waving his stick at the sky. "That bright sun will blind folk on the far side including the ref. Use it to your advantage."

"Thanks for that," David nodded and ran out to the centre circle.

He was Gary Lineker playing in front of a 100,000 crowd and TV audience of 1 billion in the World Cup Final. There was thunderous applause. He alone led this team to the Final and now he alone could win the Jules Rimet Trophy against mighty Brazil.

"Hey, where are our Germans?" Jenny shouted.

He was about to say they'd been knocked out in the semi-final when he saw Peter and Wolfgang chatting up Alex at the side of the pitch.

"Tell them to get on the field of play!" he commanded.

Wolfgang gave Alex a kiss and ran on.

David ran around the pitch in front of the 100,000 strong adoring crowd and fired a couple of shots into the net.

"Want a drink?" Theresa shouted, "I've brought all our team some energy drinks."

As David gulped down a bottle, he saw Peter Scerri arrive in his Jaguar. His team trooped off and stood around him for final instructions.

"Where's our great leader?" David asked.

"He's seeing the Police about some Italian football strips which fell off the back of a lorry," Theresa smiled, knowingly. "What's our team then?

"It's Tony in goal, Peter the German, Mark and Laura in defence. Wolfgang, Marco, Steven and 2 more Polo players in midfield. Jenny upfront with me, only later it will be Sarah," David rhymed off.

"I think you are short of a man," the Captain interrupted. "Alex and Peter have gone off in a taxi!"

"Damnation!" David roared.

"Can I play?" Tristram asked.

"Get stripped in the coach," David said in exasperation.

The 100,000 crowd was getting noisier in expectation as the hour approached. The manager made a last minute tactical substitution as a key player had a calf problem or at least he had problems with a little cow. A scream came from the bus. David had forgotten Sarah was on it.

"Get out you perv!" came a shout.

"I am sorry, madam." Tristram ran out red-faced clutching his gear.

Suddenly, Danny arrived in his BMW. "Who are our subs?" he roared.

"Theresa and the Captain," David laughed.

"Where are they really?"

"The German had something which came up and some of the Polo players had a match that clashed," he explained. Danny put down a rug and shook his head resignedly. He looked a broken man.

At that moment, Father Collina arrived in a taxi all dressed in full ref's gear and wearing headphones.

"Are you in contact with your linesman with your earpiece?" Danny asked naively.

"No, I am listening to the BBC World Service," he replied. "There's a talk on the impact of John Paul's papacy and I didn't want to miss it. I can referee as well."

"He'll be wearing his underpants over his trousers like Superman next!" Danny whispered to David.

Suddenly, Jenny ran up to David and tugged his arm. "Are there any last minute instructions?" she asked.

"The ref's partially sighted in his left eye, will be blinded by the sun on his right, and he won't be able to hear a damn thing, he hates AC Milan and we've a young Priest in our team. Things look good, I'd say."

As Jenny walked away disconsolately, Marco looked anxious.

"David, they've got Cruncher Mintoff at centre back. Ten years he played in SERIE B till he got banned for dirty play. You and Jenny, watch out. He's a killer. Beside him they've Scerri's bodyguard Chopper Catignani. He's done time for GBH."

"Okay, Okay, let's get started!" Father Collina shouted grabbing the ball.

Jenny and David walked up to the centre circle. Lineker prepared for kick off. For the millions back home he knew he had to have the game of his life. Father Collina threw a 50 cent piece into the air.

"Heads," David called.

"Tails," Jenny said.

"Heads it is," Father Collina agreed picking up the coin. "What do you want to do?"

"Kick off," David decided. "We need to avoid an early goal" he told Jenny.

Cruncher Mintoff, who hadn't called, looked decidedly perplexed, shrugged and walked back to his position at the heart of defence. A stunning black-haired, tall, bronzed Maltese girl lined up with another similar but smaller, as strikers.

"Hey, they are real lookers!" Mark shouted approvingly.

"Yes, Da Luca. Lucy Da Luca and this is Carmella!" she shouted back. "So you're right."

"Are you any good?" Mark enquired.

"At?" she retorted.

"Football"

"Oh that. Yes!"

"Stop talking to them!" Marco cried out. "They are sirens."

"You mean fog horns?" Laura asked.

"No, the Greek babes who smashed you on the rocks!"

"Look, Danny's business and our jobs will be on the rocks if we don't get started and win this," David implored.

"Is your team any good?" Carmella asked, grinning.

"Some say I am no use," Laura groaned, "I have my knockers."

"That's true" Mark agreed.

"Can we start?" Father Collina implored. "Who are my linesmen?"

"I'll do it," the Captain volunteered.

"Me too!" Theresa shouted.

"This is turning into an old age pensioners outing," Mark suggested.

"Yeh, but they are on our side," David winked.

"If I score, I'll give you a good time," Lucy said.

"You can forget that," Jenny said firmly, her foot on the ball on the centre circle.

Father Collina blew and David kicked off. The 100,000 crowd and huge worldwide audience watched intently as David ran down the wing and, as Cruncher dived in, kicked the ball in front of him only for a dog to get it and run off towards a large bush. The 2 sets of players flew after it and extricated it along with a totally embarrassed German and Alex!

"It's a throw to Scerri's team," the Priest announced.

Cruncher threw the ball to Lucy, she sidestepped Tristram then Mark, then Laura in defence before tapping it past Tony into the net.

Lucy was smothered in her team mates and Mark kissed her on the way back, to Laura's horror.

"The linesman's flag is up!" David shouted desperately.

The 100,000 crowd and the dog were still. Father Collina dashed across to the Captain, who'd attached Theresa's hanky to his walking cane.

"What could he, possibly, see wrong with that goal?" Jenny asked David.

"Beats me, but it was on the good Father's left hand side, his blind side!"

Danny stood on the touchline behind the Captain, hands over his eyes. There was a long discussion before the Priest gave the goal.

David nipped across to the Captain. "Did my best, old boy" he shrugged. "I said we hadn't checked the pressure of the ball prior to the game beginning."

"It's okay," David sympathised.

The game was up and running again. The defence was under siege with Tristram, Mark and Laura barely hanging on in the onslaught. David knew that Jenny and he couldn't get past Cruncher and Chopper. At every dead ball situation Mark chatted up Lucy and Carmella.

Then, suddenly, Marco lobbed the ball high from the midfield towards Jenny in the box. Cruncher barely made contact as she turned on a sixpence but the blonde went down, pole-axed. Up went Theresa's flag.

"Penalty, Penalty!" Danny roared from behind her.

Father Colina strode purposefully across the pitch. He consulted Theresa, then pointed to the spot.

"Shameful!" Peter Scerri roared from the touchline.

David picked up the ball. Could he equalise in the World Cup Final?

"Miss it and I'll show you a good time later," Lucy offered quietly.

David's mind was focused. He slammed the ball bottom right.

"Goal!" the 100,000 fans roared.

The captain clapped till he saw Scerri's glare!

"You're the loser," Lucy scowled.

"You're a dead man," Cruncher said ominously.

Jenny hugged David as they ran back to the centre.

"Come on team!" roared Danny.

"Can we get Tristram off and German Peter on?" Mark implored. "He's crap."

"Wait a few minutes," David suggested as Scerri's team regained control. Tristram was being repeatedly dispossessed by the De Luca girls and the midfield had joined the defence to try to hold on. Father Collina, puffing badly, wasn't keeping up with play and now and again Lucy would handle the ball as she weaved her way through David's defence. Jenny would soon copy her as she tried to take the ball up the other end and give her team a respite.

On one occasion, David watched in disbelief as Jenny took on all Scerri's defence, mesmerised as Laura had lifted her top, but the Scerri goalie saved it. Then it was back to the siege.

On the half hour mark, Lucy took the ball off Tristram, did a one-two with her friend and slammed the ball past Tony. Now David took him off and on came Peter. It made no difference.

On the half-time whistle the German tugged Lucy's arm, the old Priest saw it, and Lucy scored from the spot.

"We must get one back before half time," David commanded.

He went on a breath-taking, lung-bursting, sinew-snapping run doing one-twos with Jenny until they reached the edge of the box. On came the friendly dog. It is debatable whether Jenny fell over Cruncher's leg or the dog but everyone heard the familiar 'crack' as Jenny fell on the pitch.

Oh my God! thought David. Is she alright?

The ref made the sign of the cross. Mark and David helped her, limping, over to the coach.

"Her ankle looks broken," Theresa surmised.

The whistle blew for half-time. As Danny came in to check how she was, Sarah hid behind a seat.

"How can we bring Sarah on fully fit now?" Mark asked. "No one's going to believe it."

"The Priest would," David pondered.

"Better get her to the hospital" Danny declared.

Theresa was already on her mobile phone. David dashed out to Father Collina having an orange in the centre circle.

"Could you say a prayer for Jenny, Father?"

"Of course, my son. I hope your girl is alright."

By the time the team came out again, Theresa had driven Jenny away.

"You can bring Tristram back on," the ref said kindly. "I can't see it'll make much difference and Mr Scerri has kindly agreed."

The 100,000 crowd was subdued, shocked that Beckham had been carted off. The top Doctors in Spain would have to examine the extent of the damage. Now the whole nation looked to him and him alone, Gary Lineker, to retrieve the situation. It would not be easy. It was extremely hot and David was a lonely figure on the half way mark.

"Hey, your player just pinched my bum!" Lucy roared, pointing at Mark.

"I didn't see it," the ref conceded.

"And my flag isn't up!" the Captain shouted.

"I need a second linesman" the ref moaned.

"I'll do it!" Danny volunteered.

"No way!" said Scerri menacingly.

"I'll do it" Alex offered.

"Have you ever done it before?" Father Collina asked, taking off his earpiece.

"No."

"Not much point then." The game continued.

Lucy went off on another mazy run, beat Tristram, Mark and Marco, then as she was about to pull the trigger, Marco pulled her shorts down.

"Perv!" she roared then, "Oh it's you Marco!"

Father Collina pulled out a red card.

"Off, off!" roared Scerri.

"No, don't send him off," Lucy begged. "It was unintentional."

"He pulled your shorts down," the ref protested.

"Consult your linesman," David suggested, aware the Captain had his cane aloft.

Father Collina ambled across. David went with him.

"It can only be a penalty and a red card," Scerri muttered.

"Well?" Father Collina asked.

"Lucy touched the ball as she entered the box so I gave a free kick before the incident."

"I didn't blow my whistle," Father Collina reminded him. "He pulled her shorts down."

"But did he?" Laura challenged.

"My shorts often come down unintentionally.

"That's not what I've heard!" Mark laughed, then saw the Priest's face. "Sorry!"

"Okay the penalty stands, but Marco stays on."

"Thanks," Lucy said. "Now I'll finish you off."

The 100,000 crowd fell silent. Could Tony save the goal from Ronaldo and save the day? At 4-1 it'd be all over. Lucy took a run and hit a screamer into the top left hand postage stamp corner.

"I am finished," said Danny and sank to his knees.

The Captain began to raise his flag.

"Don't even think about it," Father Collina warned sternly.

David stood, hands on hips, resigned to defeat.

"Cream always rises to the top," said Scerri. "Lets go to your bar, sorry my bar, Danny, and discuss terms for the handover."

Danny and Scerri drove off.

There were 15 minutes left.

"Look, let's stop the clock on the clock tower at the Primary school over there" Mark suggested.

"And what good would that do?" David asked.

"It'd give us more time," he pointed out.

"And lose more goals?" David said fearfully.

"We haff to go now," Wolfgang said. "Peter und I haff our hotel meal at 5 pm."

"You never mentioned it before" David reminded him.

"Ve did not know your team vas crap," Wolfgang elaborated.

"Go on," David said resignedly. "It doesn't matter much now anyway."

Suddenly, Sarah emerged from the coach. The 100,000 crowd roared as Wayne Rooney warmed up; if that was the term in a temperature of 35 degrees!

"My prayers worked, I see," said the Good Father devoutly.

Sarah came on, took a pass from David and played, keepie-uppie, lobbed Chopper and hit a powerful 25 yard shot into the bottom left hand corner.

The crowd went crazy. Everyone ran to hug her and pat her.

"Mark, go put that clock back!" David roared. "Only make sure no one notices you. This game isn't finished yet."

"Jenny! Jenny!" the crowd roared, including the Captain!

"Pity your name isn't Springer," David laughed heartily. "How long do we have ref?"

"Over 10 minutes yet," the Priest answered.

They ran back to the centre circle. Sarah winked slyly. Within minutes she'd dispossessed Cruncher and was off on another run. She fired a 20 yard screamer but this time it was saved. Up in the clock tower, Mark had put the hands 5 minutes back.

Theresa returned and David signalled that Sarah was on and to give nothing away. Marco ran through the midfield and passed to David who hit the ball immediately to Sarah. She nutmegged Cruncher, drew the keeper and lobbed the ball into the net. Again she was mobbed.

Five minutes to go according to the clock tower.

"Mobie Danny," David hailed Theresa.

The problem was that with only 9 players left, Scerri's lot realised they could pass their way to the final whistle. Lucy got the ball and took it for a walk to the corner flag.

Up went the Captain's flag. "Obstruction" he shouted.

"Overruled!" the ref shouted back.

This is like Perry Mason, David grinned. "What news of Jenny?" he asked Theresa as he reached the touchline.

"It's not a bad break, just a chip."

"Maybe Father Collina's prayers weren't in vain!" Tristram remarked pointedly.

Marco got the ball off Carmella, pinched her bum and blasted the ball up to Sarah on the half way line. She hit the ball past 2 defenders and ran, beat the goalie, and tapped it the 15 yards into the net, turning to claim the goal.

Suddenly, the dog ran on and diverted it onto a post.

The goalie, Sarah and Cruncher all ran towards the stationary ball. The Priest glanced at his watch. Sarah got to the ball first, got a foot to it, the ball hit one post, then the other and trickled over the line, 4-4.

Scerri's lot weren't happy that both linesmen joined in the celebration!

As the celebration continued, the whistle went and the game continued. Lucy took the ball from her sister, went on a mazy run and whipped the ball past Tony. It had all been in vain.

The final whistle went and Scerri arrived in time to dance a jig as Lucy was carried shoulder high from the field.

"I'm so, so sorry," Sarah sympathised keeping out of Scerri's sight.

David sank to his knees. Father Collina dashed off in the taxi which had brought Danny. He saw Scerri dancing and got back in with the Father.

"We did all we could," Mark reassured David.

"Well, we cheated every way we could," the Captain nodded. "Damn good show I would say. Like the time 4 Italian planes took on my pal Alf and me over Grand Harbour ...."

"Not now," David sighed.

"Lucy was too good. And her sister," Laura analysed.

"We had Sarah," David added.

"We'd 9 men for part of the game," Mark reminded them as he lay on the parched grass.

"5-4 was a great result," Theresa agreed. "Don't put yourselves down."

"Can we protest about the match in some way?" the Captain speculated.

"Like the dodgy linesmanship?" David managed a grin.

"Point taken." The Captain looked down.

"Danny's business will be ruined," David reiterated. "Look, let's get changed and head back to the apartments."

Peter Scerri was passing some cold bottles of sparking wine around his team and poured a bottle over Lucy's head as she was carried in triumph on Cruncher's back.

David's lot made no comment and boarded the coach. I must check how Jenny is, David remembered, taking out his mobile.

It was early evening when David and Mark reached the casualty department at St Luke's Hospital. Jenny was already plastered around her right ankle and had been given a stick.

"Peter Scerri came to check how I was with Cruncher, then Danny called in, so I know how well you did," she began.

"I'll arrange a taxi back" David offered, getting out his mobile.

"Danny's very down," Jenny continued as they walked past visitors out to the entrance hall.

"Well that's the Sliema business gone," said Mark unnecessarily.

"Unless we arrange some money," David pointed out.

"Or we put the wind up Peter Scerri with our Angel on the roof routine," Jenny reminded the two young men.

"Look it's already failed twice," David said.

"But there's one big difference," she added determinedly. "Neither knows about Sarah's existence and Peter's seen me limping about in a plaster. He'll not understand how anyone could heal so quickly without it being a miracle. He is religious isn't he?"

"That's true," David accepted as she opened the taxi door.

"Well let's go for it. I'll see Sarah and we'll get it all planned. Get Scerri along to the apartments one night soon when it's dark and Sarah can do the routine."

"Well go ahead if you want," David agreed, "but I want to have a meal with the Captain as he keeps hinting he has money."

"Peter Scerri would want a lot," Mark said resignedly.

"And who's to say he hasn't got it?" David asked. "Right, here's the plan. We'll get the Captain along to Danny's restaurant tomorrow evening and you get Sarah to do the Angel bit. Now we must go up to Luqa with our tourists and get our new group."

The taxi stopped at the apartments. Sarah and Laura were waiting.

"We've got a plan," Jenny announced firmly as she hobbled out.

"It'd better be good," Laura said.

"Bet it involves me," Sarah grinned. "Your plans always do. Even in our school days we used to get off with truancy as Teachers couldn't differentiate between us. Oh and I've got news for you, Jenny. Our Mum has escaped from Durham. She's planning to come here for a fortnight."

"Oh my God!" said Mark putting his hand over his mouth. David stifled a quiet smile.

At 10 pm the young couriers had waved their "Goodbyes". Mrs King almost missed her plane as she didn't hear the tannoy announcement in the toilet. Tom Wilkins had told David all about Luqa airport in the 1960s and 1970s interminably. Tristram had given them all a blessing and apologised for any lack of ability whatsoever in the football field. Alex had snogged Marco to death until Mark disentangled them!

As the flights came in, Jenny and Sarah's Mum was about the first off. She hugged the two girls and spied Mark having a cold orangeade at the carousel.

"I could murder you for that cool drink in this heat," she laughed.

Mark choked on it and handed it to her. "You can have it, here you can have it," he spluttered.

Their Mum looked bemused. "Very strange," she said as David, Laura and a hobbling Jenny looked out for their new group.

Mark returned from the toilet and composed himself. "What are your plans for Malta then?" he asked politely.

"I'll lie low for a bit," she said.

"Well you would," Mark added. "What attracted you here? No extradition?"

"Climate and seeing my daughters." She whispered, "Strange boy," to David.

"Here they all come!" Laura exclaimed and held up her 'SAY GO TOURS' clipboard.

"Hope that babe's one of ours," Mark said enthusiastically watching a blonde heading towards them.

"I'm Donna, I work in Comet," the young lady announced and shook hands with David.

"They're two of Santa's reindeer," Laura whispered till David nudged her.

"I'm here looking for Cupid."

"My God, Laura's right," Mark laughed.

"Is she a vixen though?" Jenny asked as the girl looked back for her friends.

"If those German players come up and say 'Donner und Blizen' that will be the set," David grinned.

"Where's the toilet?" an old Lady asked.

"Yes where?" an equally old friend enquired.

"Show Hinge and Bracket where they are, Laura," David commanded.

Laura guided them along, then asked, "Who's Hinge and Bracket?"

"I forgot to say, I am Winnie," Jenny and Sarah's Mum suddenly interrupted.

"Do you travel alone?" David asked.

"I used to travel with my hubby but I ended up wanting to strangle him," Winnie added.

Mark had definitely gone white!

"And talking of strangling folk, just tell me who injured my dear Jenny and he won't have a life!"

David headed out with the Couriers and the new party in tow.

"You don't think Winnie could murder Scerri, do you?" Mark asked.

"Don't be ludicrous," David put him down.

The coach was full. Jenny glared at David for casting his eyes over Donna and her two equally blonde, long-legged, short-skirted companions.

"These are Caz and Tracey, my friends from home," she announced loudly to all. "We call ourselves the three musketeers. It's ironic really."

"How so"? David enquired.

"Caz does fencing."

"As a sport?" Jenny asked.

"No, at the local garden centre!" Donna replied.

The coach headed off to St Julian's.

"Welcome to Malta everyone" Jenny began, clipboard on lap. "It was 34 degrees today so get a drink once you are in your rooms."

"We like sex on the beach," Donna said. Bet you do, David thought.

David was preparing to take the party to Bugibba on the Friday morning when he saw the Captain walking beside St George's Bay to get his Daily Telegraph.

"Captain," he hailed him. "Would you join me for a meal at Danny's Restaurant this evening? I want to ask you about your war stories to incorporate them in to my guided tours."

The Captain looked startled at first. "Damn decent of you, old man, although by the time the pudding is served, we'll be on to how to raise the dosh to save Danny's business, what!"

"You're very astute," David conceded, shielding his eyes with the Times of Malta.

"I do have ideas. We can discuss them later," he added encouragingly as he headed off.

"What is Bugibba like?" Donna asked as she got on the bus.

"Is it wicked?" Caz asked.

"It's great. You'll like it," David confirmed.

"Cool!" Tracey agreed.

The smell of suntan lotion was over powering.

"I don't have to tell you Binge and Hackett are in the toilet," Laura laughed.

"Hinge and Brackett," David corrected her.

"Thank you, Theresa," Laura said provocatively.

"Of course, in my day it was all St Paul's Bay," said an old gent as he began to board. "Oh I'm Wanker Thomson." The old man with a handlebar moustache offered his hand. David shook it.

"Yes, Wanker Thomson, I was in the RAF here in the War."

"You must meet the Captain. We've a friend who was in the RAF in the War here."

"Jolly good show. That will be a real treat for later!" He boarded almost falling over Donna's lilo.

"Did he say what I think he said?" Jenny asked incredulously.

"It must have meant something different in the 1940s," Mark offered.

"Or he flew solo a lot," Laura grinned. "Oh here come the two old dears."

"Are you the courier, young man?" the taller of the two asked. "I want to discuss our plumbing."

"We carry a medical box and stop at toilets," David pointed out helpfully.

"No" the smaller one interrupted. "Our flush doesn't...."

"What?"

"Flush!"

"I'll attend to it," David promised. He held out his arm as they clambered up the steps.

"Don't we have any gays this time?" Laura asked.

"Don't think so, and that's not very politically correct," said David. "But what have we here?"

A family of four overweight Glaswegians, parents, boy about 14, and girl about 5 had appeared. The man and boy wore Rangers scarves in the stifling heat over a Rangers top.

"Get a life!" David muttered.

"Couldnae get a bloody Irn Bru," the boy moaned.

"Oh dinnae fach Jimmy," said the Mum. "We'll try up in that Bugger ba."

"Hey, that's what I once called it!" Jenny sympathised.

"Irn Bru?" asked the Mum.

"Bugibba," Jenny said, politely stifling a grin.

"Hope there's nae Celtic fans on our coach," the man declared loudly.

The little girl accidentally smeared some ice cream on David's shorts but he retained his fixed airline stewardess type smile!

"Why on earth have they chosen a Catholic island?" David asked quietly.

"Cos, they're bloody thick," Mark suggested.

"What would they say if they knew I supported the Pars?" David added.

They got on too. All four couriers sat in the front and Jenny put her plastered foot into the aisle.

"Sarah's taking Mum around Sliema shops," she said as David tried to wipe his shorts clean.

"What is your Captain's name?" Mr Thomson asked.

"Dunno, we all call him Captain," Mark confessed.

"I was a Squadron Leader. I flew out of Ta Qali and Kalifrana," he explained. Do you know them?"

"We see Ta Qali a lot," David said. "It's got the craft village and football stadium. The Captain was in one of the huts."

"Gosh!" said Mr Thomson. "If he's Group Captain Wilkins, he had so many scores. He was famous!"

"Planes shot down?" Jenny asked.

"That too. No, women he bedded in Valletta. He'll be a different man in old age."

"Not entirely!" David disagreed.

"They shot him down twice but he always came back for more."

"He's got a bullet in his leg even now," David told him.

"I feared he'd end the War legless," Mr Thomson added.

"He's not that different then," said Mark. He saw the old man's glare and looked away.

"Look" said David, "I am meeting him in a restaurant this evening. Why not join us for a meal? It would be fascinating to hear your stories," David enthused.

The coach turned into Bugibba.

"This is the under-water safari," Jenny announced on the microphone.

Danny's ice cream van was already in position as they got off.

"Are the ice creams free for kids?" the Glaswegian man asked.

"Sorry, that offer was last week," Jenny replied.

"You are awful!" David poked her. "But Danny will love you!"

It was an uneventful day, first on the boat at Bugibba and later at Popeye's village. This was going to be an important evening David knew full well as he deliberately washed and shaved in cold water on such a humid, sticky evening. It seemed the Captain could offer some help and he should be in a good mood when he met Mr Thomson. Danny had left him a bottle of his best scotch and that would enhance the ambience. There was also the hope that Sarah, as an Angel on the roof, could scare Scerri witless if all else failed. He splashed some aftershave and put on a black sleeveless shirt and white cotton trousers.

"Eat your heart out, Brad Pitt," he told the mirror.

"Have you got someone in there?" Jenny asked as she banged the door. She and Sarah came in both dressed as Angels with Winnie in tow.

"I'd a great time at the shops!" she exclaimed opening a designer shopping bag. "Everything is a lot cheaper than the best London shops. I've got some tops, a necklace, make-up and lace hankies. I've just sent my Mother a long text telling her all I've got."

Mark came in and smiled when he saw the girls all made up.

"Winnie's just made a killing," David began.

"I'd rather not know," Mark said quietly. "If I know I'll be questioned about it."

"I am just saying I've been on the mobie. The sentence was too long."

Mark went red and left hurriedly.

"I was going to add that I was out of credit," a bemused Winnie added.

David smiled broadly. "Okay girls. Jenny, are you coming with me to the restaurant? And Sarah, good luck with Scerri."

"It means taking off all my Angel gear," Jenny moaned.

"It's pitch dark," David reminded her. "Just keep it on. No one will see you and, in any case, I am late."

David took her hand and led her out.

Winnie noticed approvingly.

Jenny limped, self consciously along the coastal path and tried to keep up. There was a sound of locusts and pedalloes knocking against the wooden quayside.

The Captain was already sitting alone in Danny's restaurant, and eyed up Jenny as she hopped down the steps.

"You are a vision, my dear" he said, his eyes glinting.

Steven pulled out the chairs. "Will I serve that good whisky later as we try to loosen his tongue?" Steven asked quietly.

"Yes, he has a great friend coming later, not that he knows it yet, and he'll probably agree to anything by then. At least I am hoping so," David said not too confidently.

David picked up the menu. He and Jenny chose the Tagliettella, chicken and chips, Italian ice cream washed down by a Marsovin wine. David smiled when the Captain ordered fish and chips. He always chose that.

Through courses one and two, the three made small talk about the weather, the tours, and the Captain's War memories.

By the time the Captain was pouring chocolate sauce over his ice cream and over his tie, David cut to the chase. "As you know, we're all concerned at Danny's packing up here in Sliema and St Julian's and having to move up to Bugibba, a much smaller resort. Some of us could lose our jobs and, in any case, it would probably ruin Danny."

"Just how much money do you think Scerri would accept to buy him off?" the Captain asked, taking a fag out of his silver metallic cigarette case then pouring another wine.

"We guess about £150,000, maybe a bit less."

The Captain looked thoughtful. "I've got about £10,000 in all but it's for my old age."

"We'd never take any of it then," Jenny butted in reassuringly.

"But can you think of any way of raising the money, and quickly?" David asked, biting on an ice cream wafer.

"He could sell part of his business here, e.g. his apartment block or nightclub and raise that sum," the Captain pointed out.

"But that would only leave the restaurant and 10-pin bowling and tours. You'd be back where you started. No, we must raise cash and keep the businesses going."

The captain refilled his glass. "Give me a few days to think," he said.

"Now I've got a surprise for you," David smiled. "In the War do you remember Squadron Leader Thomson?"

"Wanker?"

"Got it in one," said Jenny, adjusting her halo.

"Can't stand the man, he'd more kills than me. Good-looking chap, too good-looking," the Captain reflected. "I was engaged to a Maltese girl called Stella, a lovely little filly, early 20s, and he snatched her from me. They married, moved to Southern England and I believe he made his money art dealing. I could have killed the man. How do you young people know about him?"

There was a desperately long pause. The only sound was the fan whirring above their heads.

The door opened. The couple hadn't had time to answer. It was Wanker Thomson.

"Oh my God!" said the Captain.

He gulped down the wine and beckoned Steven for another bottle.

"Get that whisky now," David demanded.

"Group Captain Wilco Wilkins. I don't believe it!" Wanker said enthusiastically.

He jumped down the steps two at a time and embraced the Captain.

"We really must go," Jenny reminded David, tugging his arm. "We've a spiritual experience to watch at the apartments and we don't want to miss it, do we?"

David watched the Captain's facial expression intently. Steven opened the bottle flamboyantly.

"An excellent year!" Wanker announced as he examined the label through half rimmed specs.

David and Jenny headed out in time for Sarah to tell them on the mobile that Scerri had appeared.

The couple ran down the street and dashed behind the sea wall. Peter was standing in pitch darkness, pacing up and down, hands behind his back. Suddenly, the beam of light picked out Sarah on the roof top complete with wings and halo.

"Oh my God! Who are you? What are you?" Peter stammered and sank to his knees averting his gaze.

"My God, you were both spot on! It's working a treat this time," David conceded.

"Get down or he'll see us," Jenny said firmly putting her hand on his head and pushing him down.

"What do you want, oh divine being?" Peter asked, as flustered as David had ever seen him.

"I am Jenny's Guardian Angel!" Sarah shouted back.

"Can we talk in Maltese?" Peter asked.

"Oh no, that's done it!" David groaned.

"Angels speak in the language of the person we're assigned to," Sarah replied confidently.

"Not to mention the Yorkshire dialect," Jenny sniggered.

This time it was David's chance to remind her to pipe down.

"What do you want me to do?" Scerri asked almost fearfully. "I could build a shrine to the Virgin."

"That would be nice," Sarah answered thoughtfully.

"Yeh, and you are no virgin!" Jenny whispered.

"I am here to remind you how you treated my sis ……., my assignee today, Jenny. Watch!" Sarah picked up a football and played keepie up with it.

"You are an Angel indeed," said Scerri, still on his knees. "I thought at first, you were Jenny. Father Collina told me she'd dressed up as an Angel, but I know how injured she was, she couldn't do that, not in that plaster. Can you forgive me my sins?"

"There is one thing you must do and you know it. There is someone you have wronged, isn't there?"

"I didn't mean to sleep with Laura, that young girl led me on ……."

Jenny and David shared a glance.

"You slept with Laura!" Sarah exclaimed.

"You are an infinite spirit. Didn't you know?" Scerri said incredulously.

"I am not her Guardian Angel. It's a different department," Sarah quickly explained.

"I don't believe it," Jenny whispered.

"No wonder she talked of working for him," David added.

"My eyes are starting to hurt looking into that beam," Jenny pointed out looking down at her flip-flops.

"There is someone else you have wronged," Sarah continued. "A dear old friend and now your rival"

"Danny?"

"The same! You must call off your feud."

"I don't supply his food. I'd nothing to do with the food poisoning at his restaurant."

"I said feud."

"Sorry! Look, Danny is a twisted, conniving crook and we won that football match fair and square."

"Didn't you puncture his tyres or block the car park entrance or change prices knowing you would ruin him or get Cruncher to injure Jenny or ...."

"Okay, okay," Scerri put his hand up.

"It's your immortal soul, Peter. Don't ruin Danny, be his friend again. After all, the man brought up your daughter as his own."

Scerri looked crestfallen. "Dear Angel. I will do as you say. You clearly know my awful secret. I will erect a statue to you outside these apartments and they'll call it the Angel of the South. And pilgrims will come from miles around and pay to pray here and buy small statues of you at discount prices."

"Stop, stop!" said Sarah. "They must come here for free if they so wish," she said emphatically.

"But we'll need a miracle to attract them here," Scerri went on.

Suddenly the beam of light disappeared and Sarah vanished into the night.

"I must see Father Collina," Scerri said out loud and headed off up the lane to St Julian's at some speed.

Jenny and David walked up the steps to meet Sarah and congratulate her.

Suddenly, David's mobile ring tone sounded. It was a frantic sounding Steven. "David get back here now! The Captain had a verbal bust-up with Wanker and, well, he's collapsed!"

David, Jenny and Sarah, both still dressed as Angels, ran along the lane and back to Danny's restaurant. They found Steven and Wanker leaning over the Captain who was lying under the table and looking a strange colour.

"Oh my God, he's dead!" Jenny cried and put her hand to her mouth.

"Is he?" Sarah asked.

"I am sure he's gone, and this is just what Danny doesn't need," Steven went on unnecessarily.

"How old was that fish this time?" David demanded to know.

"Only a few days," Steven stammered. "Okay, only a week or two" he corrected himself.

"And the whisky seemed a bit off," Wanker suggested.

"And he took some tablets during the meal" Steven diagnosed.

"Look, we'll get him back to the apartments," David decided. "It'll look better if he died in his bed."

"Many thought he would, given the company he kept at night," Steven smiled nervously.

"Do you have a stretcher?" Sarah asked helpfully.

"All the time, in our kitchen, we've never been without one!" Steven replied sarcastically.

"Look, we can carry him," David said. "It's pitch dark. No one will see us."

Jenny and Sarah got him by his arms and legs and carried him out into the street and down to the lane which led to the apartments. Only one person was approaching them in the darkness.

"Oh my God, it's Scerri!" Jenny groaned.

"Peter Scerri took one look at the two Angels walking along with the Captain. "Oh my God! Oh my God!" he screamed, clutching his chest.

"The Captain is dead. The Angels have come for him," David announced.

But Scerri was running scared out of his skin towards St Julian's and didn't hear.

The trio had just reached the apartment entrance when there was a groan in the darkness.

"Was that you?" Sarah and Jenny both asked in Stereo.

It was the Captain.

"He's not dead!" shouted David utterly relieved. "I'll get him some cold water." David headed into the foyer.

By the time he came out, the Captain was sitting up on the steps outside.

"What happened old boy?" he asked. "Did I faint? I thought my antihistamine tablets were too strong."

"Can I see the packet?" David asked.

One glance confirmed what he'd expected. They were not to be taken with alcohol.

"I never told you how we could help Danny," he apologised.

"You won't need to," David boasted. "Peter Scerri will not force Danny to sell up" he explained.

"How did you manage that feat?" the Captain asked incredulously, "And why are you two dressed as Angels again?"

"Scerri required some spiritual guidance," Sarah laughed. "Come on let's get you up to your room."

The Ladies of the Night scowled. The Captain clearly wouldn't offer business tonight.

Chapter 7

As David headed along the corridor, the following morning, he realised he had never actually been in the Captain's room. Certainly he had passed it many times as it was near the launderette and small store and, with a Sunday pullout magazine print of a Hurricane on the door, there was no doubting whose it was. Now, however, he wanted to know what the Doctor had said and what had transpired with Wanker the night before.

He banged the door twice. The Captain, a dapper dresser, already had on his blue blazer, white flannels and peaked cap and was putting on his sunspecs.

"In you come, old boy," he said, pulling the Venetian blinds and opening the bedroom window. SWW photos of planes and aircrew adorned the walls like a student bedroom and there were a good few of a dashing Group Captain 60 years earlier.

The Captain looked pleased that David took an interest. "Happy days" he sighed, and beckoned David to sit on the bed.

"You suffered terrible losses, almost starved to death, endured a worse blitz than London, lived in daily fear of death and lost many comrades," David reeled off. "You've told me many times."

"But they were happy too," the Captain suggested. "We were young, we lived life on the edge, there was excitement, women, we were heroes, a disciplined force who knew what they were fighting for; and I loved flying."

"By the seat of your pants sometimes, you've told me," David reminded him.

"There were many times over Grand Harbour I was outnumbered by the Italians and I thought my number was up but I survived. Some of my old friends didn't," he paused reflectively. "Unfortunately, Wanker

194

did. And he had more kills than me. And he took the one girl I loved, Stella," he concluded with feeling.

"I am so sorry I introduced him to you," David confessed.

There was a long pause.

"You weren't to know." The Captain acknowledged the apology with a wave of the hand. "Look at me now," he went on, glancing at his shaving mirror. "Old, decrepit, forgotten, alone."

"You are not alone," David interrupted. "You have all of us, and Theresa."

"I was a hero then." He continued his train of thought. "And yet I almost died a pathetic old man, under a table in a Maltese restaurant like Oliver Reed."

"I am glad you've got Venetian blinds," David said.

"Eh?" The Captain was bemused.

"It could have been curtains!"

The Captain smiled. David had tried to lighten the mood.

"What did the Quack say?"

"Dr Zermatt said I was an old fool. Too much drink on a hot day and I'd been warned about the tablets."

"Was it really upsetting to meet old Mr Thomson?" David asked as he watched a cockroach head out from the whb beside the bed.

"No, not really. I just would have liked some warning. He told me about two of my air crew who are still alive, so it wasn't all bad."

"And Stella?"

"Long gone"

"Died?"

"Met someone else!"

"Did she return to Malta?"

"He doesn't know. It was all a long time ago."

Suddenly, there was a knock at the door. It was Jenny.

"David," she said, looking flustered, "I went up to Father Collina's first thing this morning to return all the Angel equipment, before we go on today's tour, and he wants to see you, me and what he called my other half."

"Who's that?"

"Sarah, of course, he's not stupid, David. Peter Scerri will have told him all about the Angel, his plans for a statue, and hopes for a miracle, as he would have to run the idea past the Parish Priest, a Priest who knows we borrowed all the Xmas nativity costumes," she added pointedly.

"Good luck, old boy," the Captain laughed, a twinkle in his eye.

"I've told him we'll call after our siesta. Sarah and I will back you in all you say." She smiled and gave him a peck on the cheek.

"How's the ankle?" the Captain asked.

"Sore after carrying you home yesterday evening," she admitted.

Saturday, as usual, was only the half day tour into Valletta. David and Jenny took the tourists around the Co Cathedral, SWW museum and medieval armoury. Laura and Mark took a group on the Grand Harbour boat cruise and on to the ice cream parlour. Winnie and Sarah toured the shops. David, standing beside Faith, the SWW Gloucester Gladiator, kept going through in his mind what he could say to the good Father.

Suddenly Wanker broke his train of thought. "It's so nostalgic seeing that old plane again," he said, taking a photo. "Faith, Hope and Charity had done their stuff by the time I got here with my hurricane squadron. Seeing it here brings it all back."

"How did you get on with the Captain before he collapsed?" David asked, cutting to the chase.

"He didn't say a lot, I recall. I reminisced about the war, he knocked back the whisky, swore a lot when I mentioned Stella, and then collapsed. Then you lot turned up. I say, those Angelic gals were a picture. Next time I collapse, please call them!"

"Jenny and Sarah," David said.

"Were they at some sort of dressing-up party?"

"In a way," David confirmed.

"Would you get that fat boy out of the Cockpit of Faith," came an angry voice from the museum guide.

"Jimmy, get oot of the plane," his Mum demanded.

"I'm stuck, Maw!" he roared back unconvincingly.

"I'll help," Jenny offered, putting down her clipboard.

"Would you touch my joystick?" the boy asked.

"In your dreams!" Jenny glared and dragged him out by the arms. She grimaced as she forgot about her ankle.

"Your Paw will skelp you if you dae anything else on the holiday!" the Mum scolded him.

The boy was unconcerned, shrugged and moved on to the rifle section.

"Why didn't they go on the boat trip?" Jenny moaned as she joined Wanker and David.

"The Dad and girl did."

"Then he's probably sunk the boat by now," David suggested. He gave her a hug and they walked outside and looked across Grand Harbour from the battlements. Some dahaisas were converging on a newly arrived ocean liner. They put on their sunspecs and chose an ice cream and cold coke at the kiosk. They were delayed meeting up at the coach as Hinge and Brackett could not find a toilet.

As they walked back to Valletta bus station, David could see Mark revelling in the company of Caz, Tracey and Donna. The fat Glaswegian and daughter had their feet in the cool water of Triton fountain. Laura had a face like fizz and was eating a cheese pie. She kissed Mark to make a point and smeared his face in pastry. Mark gave David a knowing look as he passed the girls.

"Time for bed, Zebedee!" he whispered in David's ear.

"Laura would kill you," David reminded him.

"He's trying it on," Jenny remarked.

"What?" Laura asked.

"Look, the Triton fountain," said David quickly. "The water's on!"

Laura did not look convinced.

Another person who was not easily going to be convinced was Father Collina.

The bells of St Mark's chimed 3 pm as David, Jenny and Sarah walked along the seafront to Father Collina's residence. The dusty lane got narrower, it was pot-holed in places, and a donkey and cart carrying melons struggled to make much progress along it.

"Juicy ripe melons?" the owner shouted optimistically.

"Is he looking at me?" Jenny laughed.

"I am not looking forward to this interview," Sarah confessed opening the rusted creaking wrought iron gate.

David read the notice on the door. "Oh he's a Canon."

"He won't fire it at us?" Jenny asked.

"No, it means he's the town's senior Priest. Let's go in."

They rang the bell and they were surprised to be met by an apron clad Mrs Dyson. "Saturday work" she explained without prompting, duster in hand. "Are you here to see the Holy Father?"

"You don't call him that?" David said incredulously.

"You never know when he'll pope up," the housekeeper chuckled at her own joke. "I'll lead you to his waiting room."

The three entered an austere office. There was a desk and four cheap metal chairs. A fan was on above their heads. There was a filing cabinet on which sat a photo frame and a picture of Father Collina with the Pope.

"That's impressive," Sarah gasped, picking it up.

"It's one of the trick photos from Danny's restaurant" David explained knowingly. "Look carefully. John Paul II is clutching Danny's dodgy menu in his left hand."

"What's that smell?" Jenny asked.

"Father Collina's incense," David suggested.

"We weren't that bad," Jenny pointed out.

"I said incense not incensed," David reminded her.

"It could be candles," Sarah reckoned.

The door opened, Father Collina came in, shook their hands and sat down. He got down to business.

"I want to talk to you about a miracle," he began. "An Angel has been seen in my Parish. My Parish," he repeated for effect. "It's every Priest's dream to have such a visit. What do you know of Lourdes?"

"I am not into Test cricket," Jenny said helpfully.

"No Lourdes or Fatima?"

The three young ones looked blank.

"All visitations which are followed by miracles lead to pilgrims and conversions and financial stability for a Parish, not to mention fame and quick promotion for the Priest." He looked up to the ceiling as if seeking divine inspiration. "A miracle is a truly wonderful thing" he continued looking at the three young people for a reaction. "It can change lives."

"It has certainly done wonders for Danny's business and our jobs," David agreed, butting in.

"How so?"

"If it had not been for Scerri's change of attitude, Danny was to lose his business due to our defeat in the match."

"I didn't know that." The Priest shook his head and paused. "What I do know is that Peter, a devout man all his life, believes he saw an Angel, he wants to erect a statue down at the apartments, and it has changed his life. All we need is a miracle."

"What sort?" David enthused.

"Something truly amazing which man could not explain such as Malta wins the skiing at the Olympics."

"But Malta is good at skiing," David pointed out.

"Down hill snow skiing?" Father Collina elaborated. "Or someone seemingly crippled and in plaster, returns to a football match, runs around and scores goals!"

"You know, don't you," Sarah said ruefully.

"Of course, of course, my child. Did Danny put you all up to it?"

"He doesn't know a thing about it and that's the truth," David admitted honestly.

"I trust you will all be at confession. I will deal with you three severely," he warned. "Peter Scerri almost died when he saw Angels carrying the supposedly dead Captain to the apartments. Didn't you think about his weak heart? You really should apologise. Now, I have a sermon to write. Let's say no more about it."

The Priest got up, scraping his chair, blessed all three and they headed back along to the apartments.

"Once Scerri knows, we're back to square one," David said, kicking a stone along the lane. "Danny loses the business and Scerri probably kills us and, even if he doesn't, we end up at Bugibba if we even have a job at all."

"I've another fear," Sarah reminded him. "Scerri thinks the Captain is dead. What if he sees him?"

"Oh no!" David exclaimed. "Scerri is usually at the 10-pin on Saturdays and the Captain often calls in. We must get to him first."

Back in the kitchen and, over some toast with the rapidly melting butter dripping down their chins, the three told Mark, Laura and Winnie all that had happened.

"I'd have loved to see Scerri's face when he saw the Angels," Mark enthused.

"He obviously fell for it hook, line and sinker," Jenny added. "He began to tell us some astonishing confidences we'd never have believed." She caught Laura's gaze. "I must go to the toilet" she blushed.

"Like what?" Mark asked, intrigued.

"How he's been screwing Danny," David said.

"And not just Danny," Jenny said tantalisingly.

"He sounds a fierce bloke," Winnie summed up. "I'd kill him if he wrecked your jobs."

Mark looked aghast. "Don't take him on," Mark warned. "His Chopper is fearsome."

"Can you rephrase that?" Winnie advised, "Or are you saying attitudes could harden?"

"Chopper was one of the tough defenders we faced in that match. He acts as a bodyguard for Scerri."

"He almost broke my toe deliberately," David elaborated.

"But he doesn't know Winnie's record. All that time in prison," Mark pointed out. Winnie looked bemused.

At that moment, David could see the Captain heading to the entrance. There was worse. Scerri's car had just driven up. Scerri pulled down his window and looked in utter amazement at the old man.

"Oh grief" David muttered under his breath.

Scerri looked utterly flustered as he drove off at speed!

"He'll build his statue now, whatever Father Collina tells him," David assured them. "And even if he doesn't. I know one young lady who's got Scerri's ear."

"Amongst other body parts," Jenny insisted.

As Jenny and David entered the bowling alley that evening, both looked around nervously for Scerri or the Captain. Neither was in evidence. The hall was mobbed. Pop music blared out and there was the familiar crash of a strike. David found a seat for Jenny then ordered at the bar.

Danny stood, three empty whisky glasses in front of him, with a broad smile on his face. "There has been a miracle" he announced.

"Tell Father Collina, he wants one," David suggested.

"I prayed Scerri would change his mind and he has. He doesn't want my businesses here any more. He's talking of going into a monastery."

"Good grief!" David exclaimed as he led Danny to his table. "What was the miracle that so changed his life?" David asked as they joined Jenny.

"In a blinding flash he actually saw Jenny's Guardian Angel – yes, you," he nodded at the girl, "Don't be alarmed though my dear!"

Jenny wasn't. "If only I'd known," Jenny said, drinking her vodka and orange.

"So why has he given up on the idea of taking your businesses?" David asked innocently.

"He has mended his ways and found God. I wish it would happen to me," Danny added thinking out loud. The young couple looked at each other. Danny threw back his head. "I am a happy man. It's incredible to think God would intervene on my behalf," he said modestly. He got up and returned to the bar.

"It's time to discuss our night out," David said eating his peanuts. "St Julian's has real international cuisine and I want to treat you."

"You mean McDonald's?" she grinned. "Well it is American."

"No, I mean French, Italian, Chinese ....," David reeled off.

"German"

"German?"

"Why not?" said Jenny. "You said I could choose and Peter and Wolfgang talked about the Bier Garten and their steins of lager and steaks and sausages."

"That's wurst," David pointed out.

"What's worst?"

"I mean German sausage. I can speak German, you know," David was enjoying showing off.

"When can we go?" Jenny asked excitedly.

"Let's get changed and go now," David enthused.

"Okay, let's go for it," Jenny agreed.

As she got up he kissed her, grabbed her hand and they ran along the seafront in the dark. There was the usual smell of vegetation and palm trees. The sound of locusts competed with car horns.

They quickly changed in the apartments, chatted to Winnie and Sarah sitting on the sea wall, and headed back to the German restaurant. As they approached, they could hear a German oompah band playing within.

"Just perfick," David beamed. "They only play here once a month and I'd forgotten they were on."

They stopped at the door and David's face fell when he saw the menu was in Gothic script and, worse, he couldn't translate any of it! As they entered, some of the guests were wearing lederhosen and hats with feathers in, Bavarian style. Everyone had the large bier steins and were tucking into steak, chicken or sausage.

"Gosh, look at the yummy black forest gateau!" Jenny shrieked with delight as they passed a dessert trolley.

A waiter beckoned them to a table for two and put a flower in the vase beside the cruet.

"Will you choose a wine?" the waiter asked.

David knew how to ask for a sweet white table wine but still couldn't fathom out the menu.

"Do you want me to help?" the waiter asked as David smelt then tasted the wine.

"You are a real connoisseur," Jenny said admiringly.

There was no going back now. "We'll both have spiegelei" he announced.

"Really," said the clearly surprised waiter.

What the hell, have I ordered, he wondered. It had one major criterion in its favour, at least. It was the cheapest thing on the menu. 15 minutes later, the waiter returned. He flamboyantly lifted the metal lid off both plates and unveiled, one fried egg each! The guests at the next table smiled knowingly.

"I couldn't read the Gothic script," he confessed. "Can we both have steak and chips?" he asked.

"Don't worry" Jenny said kindly. "I am having so much fun."

Jenny was wearing her light blue short skirt, yellow top with bare midriff and rubbed her leg under the table against David's. This has never happened in my life, he thought, trying hard not to drop his soup spoon in his excitement.

By the time the steaks had been served, Jenny had moved her foot up to his lap. She had had a lot to drink and giggled at all David's best jokes. There was no doubt they would have to finish with the black forest gateau and coffee. The band got louder, the room began to spin and David felt very warm.

"The bill, sir," the waiter said, interrupting the mood.

David opened it in trepidation. He could afford the 12 lm but he wouldn't be able to buy food for the next 3 days!

The young couple walked along the beach and stood at the pedaloes, looking out across the bay. The lights from the two hotels reflected off the surface.

Suddenly Jenny opened her mouth and they French kissed. David never wanted the moment to end!

"I suppose I'd better walk you back to your room or your Mum will start to worry."

"Why not walk me back to your room and make her worry all night?" Jenny responded mischievously.

They walked back to the room, their pace quickening. David fumbled for his key then found there were no lights. "That damn fuse has gone again" he groaned.

"Who cares?" Jenny replied. "Lock the door!"

When David woke the following morning, as usual to the sound of pealing bells, he did wonder, at first, why he was lying on the floor. Then he remembered: Jenny had a snore to waken the dead! She was lying with the light blue duvet wrapped around her. Bra, pants, sandals, top and skirt were strewn all over the floor.

"Hey, show a leg," he said. "We're taking our lot to Valletta market at 9 am."

Jenny got up, bleary-eyed, still wrapped in the duvet and walked along to the shower.

As they eventually entered the kitchen, Winnie, Sarah, Laura and Mark all exchanged knowing looks.

"German restaurant good, I take it?" Winnie said.

"I loved the afters," David stammered.

"He means the gateau," Jenny explained.

"Of course," Sarah smiled.

Winnie sat down beside David as the coach headed through Sliema that Sunday morning. "I've not had much of a chance to speak to you yet" she said, cleaning her sunspecs, "but you clearly mean a lot to Jenny."

"She means a lot to me," David confirmed.

She and Sarah to their right were deep in conversation. "At least you don't act strangely towards me like that other boy, Mark."

"I can explain that," David confessed, looking around to check he was still near the back of the coach with Laura. "He thinks you are a murderer."

"A what?"

"A murderer."

There was a long pause.

"I take it he was told I was in prison."

"You've guessed. I must say that we planted the idea in his head just as I implied to Jenny he was gay."

"But why?"

"I was so determined to date your daughter. I told you she means so much to me."

That went down well, David knew, as he saw Winnie's smile. "What do you do apart from the prison?"

"I keep my mind active," Winnie replied, taking note of the major Sliema shops they were passing. "I do a creative writing course. It's indescribable! Hey can I see this painting Jenny told me about in Valletta, the one that scared her so?"

"The man with good or bad angels at his death bed?"

"That's it. You know," Winnie continued. "It's only a year since my own Father died. His last wish was to have all his family around him. I thought he would have wanted more oxygen."

There was a pause. Jenny leaned over, "Mum's joking, David."

David laughed as he wanted to do in the first place.

"How do you want to die?" Winnie asked.

"Like my Grandad, quietly in his sleep," David said. "Not screaming like his passengers."

Both Winnie and Jenny laughed. "Okay. You've got me back" she conceded.

The coach entered Valletta bus station and everyone got a cheese pie, coke or ice cream before they headed off to their favourite market stalls. David knew he couldn't buy anything and was glad when Winnie offered an Italian tutti frutti.

"What did you do before you became a courier here?" she asked.

"I was a student at Stirling. You get the cream of Scotland's students there."

"How were you there then?" Winnie smiled mischievously.

"You always get one clot in cream," David replied. That was one he had used before.

David had just started to chat to Wanker about buying models of Faith, Hope and Charity when there was a screech of deliberate brakes and Peter Scerri got out of a BMW flanked by Cruncher and Chopper in black suits and matching sunspecs.

"Get in, I want to see you," he demanded.

"I'm rather busy," David protested in vain.

"Get in or you too will see your Guardian Angel," he insisted.

David shrugged and sat nervously in the back seat of the leather upholstered limousine.

"The Captain isn't dead at all, is he?" Scerri stated menacingly.

"He just looks it," David ventured in a brave attempt to lighten the mood.

It failed. "Father Collina says Jenny has a twin sister and she is fit."

"You can say that again," David agreed.

"Fit, she isn't injured," he elaborated unnecessarily.

"Yes that was Sarah."

"And you borrowed Xmas nativity Angel outfits."

"Yes, guilty."

"You tried to con me. You tried to make a fool out of me."

Chopper and Cruncher glared and scrunched their knuckles in a threatening manner.

"Look, we were trying to protect Danny and his businesses."

"And your jobs?"

"That too"

"But I offered you a position with me. Laura said she'd try several."

"So I've heard," David replied.

"Oh yes, I admitted to that too!" groaned Scerri. He paused. "Right, we must come to a deal. Either, Danny forfeits his businesses in Sliema and St Julian's within 2 weeks, or makes good an equivalent. It's up to you. Get it?"

"Got it."

"Good!"

Wanker was standing with an ice cream as David emerged from the limousine blinking in the bright sunlight. "How the hell does Danny raise about £100,000 in 2 weeks?" he wondered out loud.

"Is that the forfeit for your football match?" asked Wanker.

"Yes, ridiculous, isn't it? I must tell Sarah, Jenny and the rest that Scerri has sussed us. Then I must break it to Danny that there was no miracle."

"You know," Wanker said. "£100,000 sounds a lot, yet I dealt with that on a daily basis for even an ordinary painting. It depends what you are used to."

David had a long think as he walked up to the rest of the party. "Is Theresa back from the Cathedral?" he asked.

"Yes," Mark said, "She's getting her Sunday paper."

David dashed off to the news stand. "Skuzi, Theresa" he began, "You know Danny's paintings at Carmen's villa in St Paul's Bay?"

"Of course," she confirmed.

"What do you reckon they are worth?"

"If they were original 16th Century paintings of the Knights of St John and the siege of Malta, they'd be around £1 million each."

"Gosh! And are they?"

"No, they are late 19th Century, I believe."

"And worth?"

"Maybe £4000 or £5000 each. Why do you ask?"

"I thought I'd find a solution for Danny's forfeit but, even if he sold all his paintings, that wouldn't raise enough." He paused. "Not unless an acknowledged Art expert put the idea into Scerri's head that Danny had an old master worth a fortune," he reflected.

"And where do we find an Art expert?" Theresa asked.

"Wanker of course"

"Mark knows nothing about Art."

"I meant Wanker Thomson, the old RAF gent."

"Oh, him. The Captain can't stand him."

"It doesn't matter. Here's a new way to raise the money." David tugged Theresa's arm and led her through the throng to meet the old man who was choosing a key ring. "May I introduce Theresa Thinn?" he said formally.

"Enchanted, my dear," Wanker added.

"We have a plan," David began. "And it involves you."

"I am not standing on a roof dressed as an Angel in a beam of light," he protested.

"We want you to tell Scerri that Danny has some master piece like Canaletto and doesn't know."

"Wouldn't Danny know his own paintings?" Wanker asked incredulously.

"He doesn't even know his cornettos and he sells ice cream," Theresa assured him.

"I'll tell Laura, Mark, Jenny, Sarah and Winnie we have a new cunning plan," David said enthusiastically.

It was a relaxed David who sat at the front of the coach tapping his clipboard as Tony played Una Paloma Blanca on the bus intercom.

"I saw that painting. It was really scary," Winnie agreed.

"It's been there for years, apparently. The shop will never sell it," David explained. "It's the main talking point for tourists, as you've proved."

"I'll be good for a week after seeing that," Winnie confessed.

Sunday meant the rest of the day was free and the next aim would be to hook Scerri without him becoming suspicious he was being led into a trap.

The way to do it was, surely, to convince Danny that he truly had a masterpiece. What was needed was to get Wanker invited up to Carmen's villa.

David made a mental note to phone later on.

"And don't you let on to Scerri," David said quietly to Laura as they got off at St Julian's. David phoned late afternoon and told Danny that an Art expert would like to view Carmen's paintings. Danny jumped at the idea and sent his limousine down at 6 pm to collect Wanker. David and Jenny accompanied him.

Half an hour later, Tony pulled up outside Carmen's villa. It was pitch dark and the dog snarled behind the metal gate.

"Don't be alarmed," David reassured Wanker. "The Butler will let us in."

Minutes later, the Butler did just that. He held on to Ceremony and ushered the three into the hall.

"Well there are your paintings," David said, waving his arm expansively.

Wanker stood up close and took out a magnifying glass.

"Good evening," Carmen greeted them, entering with a tray of sherry glasses.

"Mr Thomson has spent years in the Louvre," David said.

"I've spent a lot of time in the loo, too. What was wrong?" Carmen asked sympathetically.

But Wanker was busy examining a painting. Carmen handed out the Sherries.

"Welcome, welcome," Danny said as he entered the room in his dressing gown and strangely, his hat having had a shower. "I hear I may have a Van Dyke."

"Like in Mary Poppins?" Jenny asked.

Wanker looked up to heaven.

"He means a famous Dutch painter," David explained.

"I was hoping you might have a Caravaggio," Wanker said.

"No, just a sherry. Carmen didn't have time to make a meal," Danny explained helpfully. "I'll leave you to it."

Danny and Carmen went back to the lounge to watch TV.

"Look David. These are late 19th century copies of 13th and 16th century paintings," Wanker said, disappointment permeating his voice.

"Are they worthless?"

"The frames are good but the paintings may fetch a few hundred. I'd hoped for a bust or a poussin."

"Laura has a bust and a ……," Jenny responded.

"Don't go there," David implored. "Go on, Wanker."

"Well, he could have had a Rubens."

"Ribena?" Jenny interrupted.

"A Rubens or an Algardi bust, a De Vos tapestry."

"But they haven't" David groaned. "We must convince Danny that he has a masterpiece or he'll never be able to sell the story convincingly to Scerri."

"Then that is what we will do," Wanker conspired. "Call him back in."

"Well, spill the beans," Danny said excitedly.

"You have a Rossini," Wanker said authoritatively.

"Is that good?"

"It certainly is," Wanker said. "Here you have a picture of Grand Master Tigne telling Prince William the great news that the Knights of St John have won the siege against the Turks."

"Wonderful," Danny beamed. "What's it called?"

"It's Rossini's Tell William, making overtures. It'll fetch £100,000, enough to pay off Peter Scerri."

"Just brilliant!" Danny sighed with relief. "Thank you so much Mr Thomson," he said gratefully.

Carmen reappeared with the butler carrying more sherries.

"The paintings do look good," Jenny added.

"We've just been framed," Carmen stated.

Wanker looked anxious.

"I can see that," David agreed.

"Let's have a toast," Danny recommended. "To my businesses in Sliema and St Julian's."

They raised their glasses and Wanker turned away to kill his grin.

"I'll go make your toast," Carmen volunteered.

David couldn't wait to tell the rest of the gang the news on his return. They dropped Wanker off at his hotel then David and Jenny looked for the rest in the lounge at the apartments. Winnie, Sarah and Laura were reading shop catalogues and were lying, flip flops off, across three chairs each.

"We've got Danny convinced that he has got a masterpiece thanks to Wanker. Now we need a little bird," said David.

Laura looked up.

"It's an expression, Laura; to slip to Scerri that Danny has a master piece he doesn't know the value of."

"I know a little bit about art," Winnie said. "What is the painting?"

"It's a Rossini," Jenny volunteered. "Tell William."

"It's a Rossini," Winnie grinned.

"Yes," said David, "but it's worth £500. Danny believes it to be worth £100,000 or more. And so will Scerri. Do you know a lot about art?"

"She's had paintings displayed," Jenny proudly pointed out.

"She should have had more in galleries," Sarah elaborated.

Mark entered the lounge and threw off his sandals. "What are you all talking about?"

"Sarah and Jenny feel I should have been hung."

"Not in this day and age," Mark reassured her.

"And why ever not?" Jenny asked. "Not good enough I suppose?" she added.

"I didn't mean that," Mark said, flustered, and went over to the coffee pot making a retreat.

"We'll get Wanker to talk to Scerri, he'll demand the painting as the equivalent of the forfeit and we all live happily ever after."

"He's not short of money," Mark pointed out. "He's even supplying his homemade meals to the monastery at Rabat."

"I heard they had a case of syphilis there a few months ago," Laura added.

"No it was champagne," Mark pointed out.

"When Scerri hears Danny has a Rossini it could be music to his ears," said Winnie, thinking out loud.

"Right, there's no time like the present," David said, getting up. "I'll take Danny's car up to the 10 pin and introduce Wanker to Scerri."

He headed outside with Jenny. Tony was sitting on the wall overlooking the bay.

"Can I borrow the car?" David asked. "It's a long way for Jenny to limp after all." He got the keys but groaned when he realised it was an automatic. "I'll be in the wrong gear" he said as they drove slowly along the road to St Julian's.

"You look okay to me!" said Jenny and hugged him.

The skittle alley was as busy as ever that Sunday evening. As Jenny and David entered, they could see Wanker chatting at a table to Theresa. Scerri, with his two bodyguards, was at the bar. David ordered a cold lager and a vodka and coke and smiled nervously at Scerri.

"It hasn't taken us two weeks to meet your demands. We've an offer you cannot refuse," David began optimistically.

"And what would that be?" Scerri replied.

"You see that old guy over there with Theresa? He is an art dealer."

"This doesn't interest me so far, but do go on," Scerri demanded.

"You know Danny and Carmen have their oil paintings of the siege of Malta?"

"Of course," Scerri replied, chewing on a peanut.

"Well, one of them is a genuine old master."

Scerri put down his glass. "Are you being serious?"

"Yes, I can prove it. Or that man with Theresa will."

"If you are stitching me up again, David, I'll unleash Chopper and Cruncher."

"Come with me," David said. David led Scerri with the two bodyguards and Jenny in tow and they joined Theresa and Wanker. David made the introductions.

"Let's do this proper," Peter said.

"Properly. It's an adverb," Theresa pointed out.

"Properly." Scerri corrected himself. "What are your credentials, Mr Thomson?"

"The Tate, Louvre, Lowry gallery, you name it, I've been there."

"And what has Danny got exactly?"

"A hernia, I'd imagine," Theresa suggested, "if he's taken a painting off that wall."

"A Rossini," said Wanker.

"A Rossini," Scerri echoed. "Is that good?"

"It's the Tell William. Everyone believed it had been lost."

"What is it worth?"

"A huge sum, not including my commission for tipping you off."

"And does Danny know?"

"Not it's full worth," Wanker confirmed.

"If you tell Danny you'd accept it as the forfeit everyone would be happy," David elaborated.

"This sounds rather underhand," Theresa interrupted convincingly.

David and Jenny exchanged looks.

"I'll take it," Scerri announced. "I'll send Chopper round with a van tomorrow."

Scerri shook hands with David.

"All's well that ends well," David agreed.

The following day, Jenny was booked in at St Luke's Hospital outpatients so it was Sarah, wearing Jenny's khaki uniform, who accompanied David on their early morning coach to Gozo. Theresa accompanied Mark and Laura as they planned to take in the shrine of Ta Pinu church in Gozo with its remarkable architecture and Stations of the Cross. Unusually, the Captain clambered on board David's coach and asked if he could have a chat. David was glad to learn Tony had fixed the air conditioning. The morning was roasting as Tony headed north up the winding coast road past its succession of barren rocky beaches and scrubland.

"You haven't joined us because Caz, Tracey and Donna are on our trip?" David asked with a smile.

"Hardly old boy, they are a bit young for me," the Captain replied. "I've my idea to raise money to save Danny."

"We may be okay there. Scerri looks likely to accept one of his paintings this morning as the forfeit."

"And how did you manage that?" the Captain asked incredulously. He noticed Wanker on his right with a smug smile on his face. "Don't tell me. An art expert told him one of the paintings was worth a lot. What a scream!"

"No, that one's in Norway," Wanker pointed out.

"But Theresa says they are crap."

"Scerri has gone with Thumper to get it this very morning," Sarah confirmed.

"Chopper," David corrected her. "I hope you know what you are doing" the Captain insisted.

"I'd like to hear your plan even so," David confirmed.

"I'll tell you over lunch," he replied.

"Hey I trust we dinnae see any Pape churches on this trip!" the fat Glaswegian shouted down the coach.

"We won't threaten you with any culture," David muttered under his breath.

"I cannae see a vulture!" little Jimmy shouted back.

David sat looking at a jar of D and C honey as he sat in Danny's café in Victoria Gozo. The Captain was ordering drinks at the bar. Wanker was fiddling with the menu.

"Lend us 2 Liri," he beckoned to David as he returned with the lagers.

David checked his pockets nervously.

"I'll get it" said Wanker.

"Right I'll tell you my suggestion," the Captain began. "There could be gold bars somewhere on the island."

"Gosh you've immediately got my interest!" David gasped.

"I've heard this story," Wanker sighed.

"Just before the war, Italy hoped to take Malta without a fight. Some members of the British Cabinet also believed Malta should be surrendered to avoid loss of life. Well, anyway, there was a rumour that an Italian fighter flew here with gold bars to encourage Malta to capitulate."

"And what happened?" asked David.

"It got hit over Valletta and came down somewhere over St Paul's Bay. If we could find it, we might have the gold bars."

"But I wonder who shot him down?" said David.

"Find that Pilot and he would know."

"It was 60 years ago" said Wanker. "It was one of many rumours at the time and all wreckage was picked up immediately and bodies buried. Malta is a small island".

The Captain looked crestfallen.

"Don't be dismayed," David sympathised. "We can't dig up all of St Paul's Bay" he pointed out. "In any case, if the plane was ever there, it would be under the concrete of the Qwara and Bugibba resorts by now. I wouldn't worry. By now Scerri will have his painting and Danny's businesses will be safe."

David walked out to the bus.

Sarah had bought a fan at the market and she waved it in front of his face.

"That's welcome" David said.

Gozo was always a full day's trip and it was 5.30 pm with the sun going down when David and Sarah walked along the lane back to the apartments. Danny's car was outside. Sarah entered the building by the back door.

"David, David, my worries are over," Danny beamed, spilling his whisky as he dashed out of the bar. "Scerri took my Rossini so that's it. But I've told him no more stupid football matches for high stakes. We'll simply compete as businessmen and may the best man win. I am so grateful to you for introducing me to Mr Thomson. Come in and have a drink."

David was glad to accept a long cold Frisk lager and sat down in the lounge.

"Now I've a great idea, David. Scerri told me all about the apparition, you remember? Jenny's Guardian Angel? Well, he agrees I should pay for an expensive statue opposite the apartments overlooking the bay or even on the roof and then Pilgrims will come from all over to pray here.

"You would need a miracle," David reminded him.

"That would surely come," Danny added. "I only wish the Angel had appeared to me. Of course, I'm not the sinner Peter Scerri undoubtedly is. Anyway, I must get back to Carmen and get a new picture to cover the gap on the wall."

Danny doffed his hat and headed out.

David watched nervously in case the beam of light came on which would have explained the miracle but it was not yet dark enough to be activated.

Jenny and Winnie entered the lounge.

"I've never been plastered so long," Jenny moaned.

"What, have you been drinking, like?" David asked innocently.

"In case you have forgotten, we've been at St Luke's in a 2-hour queue while you were sunning yourself in Gozo," Jenny complained.

"Why are you still in plaster?" David asked, showing concern.

"It'll be another week or two yet. It was a bad break. It's itching like mad too. Thank heavens for knitting needles."

David explained that Danny had got the painting accepted by Scerri. By the time he finished, Mark and Laura came in with Sarah and he had to repeat the story. Mark got the drinks in and some bags of crisps.

"I'm not sure Danny should give up the annual match though," Sarah suggested.

"And get hammered every year?" Mark reminded her.

"We could play other sports," Laura wondered.

"Such as?" Mark enquired.

"We could race them at boating and celebrate by dipping our cox in the water," David chuckled till he caught Winnie's glance.

"How about Laura, Sarah and me row as a coxless trio?" Jenny asked.

"How about a tug of war?" was Mark's suggestion. "We'd win by going backwards."

"There's always yingling," David pointed out.

"Is that legal?" Mark retorted.

"I could offer cricket and show people my googlies," David added.

"I could play beach volley ball and get my tits out," Laura interrupted.

"You don't really understand subtle innuendo, do you?" Mark sighed.

It was after their evening meal that David decided to ask Jenny the question which had been gnawing at him all day.

"Have you actually moved in?" He held his breath.

"Do you want me to?" Jenny asked, putting a shawl over her shoulders as it had got cooler.

"Of course"

"So I can pass wind, pick my nose, shave my legs, squeeze your toothpaste tube in the middle, leave a ring in the bath, play Bohemian Rhapsody at full blast on my ghetto blaster, get back to eating garlic, leave make-up on your pillow, wear your slippers, leave toe nails on the rug, eat up your chocolate, leave my bra and pants inside your bedding, use up your mobile credit, snore loudly ……."

"You do snore loudly," David interrupted. "Why are you making the experience sound awful?"

"And can I take out my false teeth ……"

"Look, just stop," David implored. "Anyway, you haven't got false teeth!" he added as an afterthought.

"It'll be lovely," Jenny confirmed.

She stopped and they cuddled, leaning against the sea wall.

"Of course, there is one sad thing," Jenny said.

"What's that?"

"I go home early September," Jenny reminded him. "And now you have taken my virginity."

"Did I?"

"No."

That would have been nice, David thought. "Look, we'll talk about our plan later. For the moment, just move all your belongings in. It'll give your Mum and Sarah more space anyway."

The couple walked hand in hand along the lane till they stood outside the apartments and on came the familiar beam of light.

"We really should let Danny have his miracle, you know," David said reflectively.

"Meeting you was my little miracle," Jenny confirmed romantically.

"What's the choice of tour this morning?" asked the Captain as he caught up with Jenny, David, Laura and Winnie walking along to the St Julian's Hotel. The clock on St Mark's tower pealed nine times.

"Mark and Laura, along with Theresa, are taking folk to Mosta Dome, then up to Golden Bay and we're doing the Under Water Safari at Bugibba followed by Mellieha beach," David said perusing his clipboard.

"Look at Mark," Laura groaned. "He's all over the three musketeers like a rash."

Mark was standing at the door of the coach chatting up Caz, Donna and Tracey, all three of whom had short skirts and low tops on. He was grinning from ear to ear like the cat who'd got the cream.

"The three musketeers are all set," Mark said cheerily.

"Three zombies, more like," Caz corrected him.

"What time did you all roll back in last night?" David asked.

"About 3 am, I think," Donna said.

"I've lost the will to live," Tracey added. "That Gemini night club is something else."

They got on board David's bus.

"I knew they'd not be on mine," Mark groaned.

The Glaswegian family appeared. "We're going to the beach" the fat Father announced. "I'd go to Mosta Dome if it wiz Presbyterian, ye ken, but it isnae."

David said nothing. Theresa looked up to Heaven and tutted.

"What's wrong with your puss?" the fat man challenged her. "Waiting for a plastic surgeon?"

"In this heat he'd melt," David quickly interrupted to reduce the tension.

Theresa backed off. 40 years of dealing with petulant kids had prepared her well.

"We've got Hinge and Brackett," Mark confirmed looking at his clipboard.

"And me," said Wanker as he dashed up, checking his watch. "Mosta Dome and Theresa, what a combination," he said provocatively.

"I'll be watching you, you old letch," the Captain threatened and hopped on.

"I'm just glad the three musketeers are with you," Laura said quietly to David. "Mark will be less distracted." She shrugged and jumped on board.

David checked Danny was nowhere to be seen and Sarah appeared from behind a large cactus.

"That's us. Let's go!" David shouted to Tony.

As they headed up the coast, David sat and read the 'Times of Malta'.

"Now that's interesting," he said out loud. "Some archaeologists have found some Roman coins dating from the time St Paul was in the bay named after him."

"You and your history," Jenny replied, speaking to the tourists with her mike.

"You don't understand," he continued. "They've got a metal detector and a mechanical digger."

"So?"

"So, what do we need to find those gold bars?"

"But we were told that plane would have been uplifted at the time," Jenny reminded him. "Anyway, we don't know where it came down."

"But I know someone who would: Carmen."

"How old would Carmen have been?" Jenny asked.

"About 7 or 8. Even as a little child, she could hardly have forgotten such an event," David added excitedly. "I must go and see her."

David knew that he could safely leave the party for one hour when they were enjoying the Under Water Safari. Carmen's villa was only about ten minutes walk away. He strode along the Bugibba sea front, stopped for an ice cream, watched a dog swimming at the quayside, and soon reached the metal gates.

"Danny's not in," said Mrs Dyson who'd arrived off the coastal bus at the same time.

"I'd like to see Carmen, please."

Mrs Dyson ushered him into the hall. The wall looked so bare where the Rossini had been displayed. Carmen came in holding a flower vase.

"This vase is cheap rubbish. Danny got me it at Ta Qali. What do you know about pottery, David?"

"I've read a famous book about it: 'Of Meissen Men'!" He laughed at his own joke.

Carmen looked blank.

"Carmen, can I ask you about a plane?"

"It's all cleared up. I got indigestion tablets."

"A plane, not a pain," said David patiently.

"What plane?"

"An Italian fighter which came down when you were a child."

A look of horror appeared on Carmen's old wrinkled face. "Yes I remember. It was awful."

"You do remember?"

"So sad, it was so sad."

"But they were your Enemy. The Captain has told me what they did to Malta."

"My little friend Ariadne and I saw it come down. We cheered. Then, in the morning, we went out to the field and saw the charred remains of the pilot. There were photographs in the cockpit of his wife and child, a prayer book, ID papers and so on. It was a terrible scene.

We put all his belongings in a little case and swore we'd return it after the war but we never did. I still feel guilty about it."

"Where's the case?"

"Their base was Sicily, I believe."

"The case!"

"Oh, I've kept it in a drawer upstairs all these years."

David's chest was pounding with excitement. Carmen went upstairs. He could hear her rummaging around. Then she emerged empty-handed.

"What was I to find again?" she asked.

"The Italian case," David repeated patiently.

There were more sounds of rummaging. Then, this time, she appeared with a small battered brown case. She opened it slowly and pulled out the photos, ID papers, map and prayer book. Something was wrapped in an old oily cloth. It was long and hard.

David unwrapped it excitedly. It was an old rusted torch!

David realised instantly that the torch was unusually heavy by today's standards but Carmen was watching him intently so he replaced it in the case.

"You definitely never found anything else?" he asked.

"No," Carmen recalled. "Ariadne and I looked around the plane in case there were more belongings but the RAF turned up in a lorry and took it all away. His belongings were to be our secret, you see."

"Very commendable," David agreed.

"So then I found something long and hard," said David, two hours later as he lay on Mellieha beach with Jenny, Sarah and Winnie.

"Your boyfriend does boast a lot," Sarah laughed.

"And it was just a rusty torch," David completed his story. "Mind you, I am not too concerned. Scerri has his oil painting and he is happy. Danny kept his business and will rake in money from his statue and miracle in due course."

"He hasn't had a miracle yet," Sarah reminded him.

"Well, we'll give him one," David insisted.

"This has been a fun holiday," Winnie reflected, "But Sarah and I must start to pack our cases tomorrow. I've got to get back to work and Sarah has her England training."

A banana motor boat had stopped where the sea met the sand and Winnie and Sarah joined most of their party paying for the next circuit. Jenny put needles down her plaster and scratched happily. "I'll just watch the entertainment tonight" she reminded David, "When you do the dancing and singing and, your awful jokes. I can hardly dance in plaster."

"Well no chatting up Marco," he implored.

"If we're to do our Guardian Angel miracle with Sarah," Jenny said thoughtfully, "it will have to be tomorrow evening. Sarah's away on Thursday."

"Okay, we'll think of a pretext to get Danny along," David said.

"And what if Father Collina tells him?"

"Danny would give a large proportion of any money to St Mark's so Father Collina may not complain," came David's optimistic reply.

The banana motor boat returned and the party got together for the coach back.

"We need another miracle tomorrow," David told Sarah.

"Well you'd better tell me where to get a halo and wings and white robes," Sarah reminded him. "We took all the stuff back," she reminded him.

The fat Glaswegian had a Rangers top on over his orange shorts and had a rubber ring round his ample tummy. His head was red with sunburn.

"Why didn't you cover up?" David asked kindly, aware of his obvious discomfort.

"Whit, his face?" his wife laughed.

"I didnae think it'd be so sair," the fat man replied.

"I'll get you some calamine lotion," Jenny offered.

"Naw if it's green," the fat man demanded.

"It's pink," Jenny assured him.

"Will ye rub it on tae, lassie?"

"No thanks," Jenny declined.

As usual the St Julian's Hotel hall was crowded for the entertainment evening. David told his awful jokes, Tony and Steven took part in the folk music and dancing, Mark, Laura and David got Sarah to join in the community singing, Marco as usual, turned up with his polo playing pals and made a bee line for Caz, Tracey and Donna who, soon after, were seen heading across the road to a nightclub opposite. The Captain and Theresa beckoned Wanker to their table. Hinge and Bracket seemed to go to the toilet between every song. The Glaswegian family kept shouting out that their choice of song was 'The Orange Sash'.

David pretended he didn't hear. Later he joined Winnie, Jenny, Sarah, Laura and Mark at the table with his favourite vol au vents.

"I'll be sad to leave on Thursday," Winnie admitted. "It was great to escape but now I must return."

"It's admirable to give yourself up," Mark said sympathetically.

"After being in a room with Sarah and Jenny, it'll be like solitary confinement," she added, ignoring Mark's comment.

"Will you be met by folk from the prison?" Mark added.

"Yes, two friends."

"You regard the wardens as your friends then? That's good."

"Mark, look, there's something you should know," Winnie finally blurted out, "I didn't murder anyone."

"I understand," Mark said graciously. "You're in denial."

"I have not been in denial since I fell off a cruise boat at Luxor," Winnie quickly replied.

Mark looked blank.

"I'm sorry mate," David intervened, "Winnie is not a murderer, Mark. It was a wind-up. She's a prison warden in Durham!"

There was a long pause. Only the sound of the folk dancing at the end of the room broke the silence.

"You mean I could have asked Jenny out?"

"Thanks a bunch," said Laura who got up dramatically and walked out to the entrance.

"Yeh, that wasn't very nice at all," Jenny said as she went out and gave her a hug.

"Are you saying you were put off dating Jenny because you thought I was in prison?" Winnie asked rhetorically.

"I am sorry," a contrite Mark shrugged. "I am due you an apology."

"Right, you've got a great highlight to your hols tomorrow," David said, lightening the mood. "It's the cruise to the Blue Lagoon, Comino. Where I met Jenny," David sighed.

"Yeh, Laura and I are meant to go too," Mark interrupted.

"If she's still talking to you," Sarah added.

"We mustn't forget to get Danny along to the apartments tomorrow and get your Angel outfit arranged, Sarah," David reminded her.

"And let's hope Scerri never speaks to anyone who either knows music or art," Winnie pointed out.

"Look, I'll make it up to you all by forgoing the cruise tomorrow and I'll go into the Theatrical outfitters in Valletta and get the Angel stuff," Mark said.

"Done!" David readily agreed. "It'll make Danny's day having a visitation and Scerri may come to regret not building a statue and inviting all the pilgrims."

"My one regret," said Sarah taking out a cigarette, "is that I won't be able to see my own statue."

"You'll just have to return to the island," David suggested.

Jenny and Laura came back in and sat down. It was clear that Laura had been crying.

"Come on love, let's go for a Big Mac," Mark said encouragingly.

David watched the couple heading to the door. Laura looked so disconsolate. That was a worry if she was so close to Scerri.

Chapter 8

"Will Mark have an easy time getting the Angel costumes?" Jenny asked as their party all sat in neat rows under cover at the stern of the Captain Morgan cruise boat in Sliema Harbour.

David was rubbing suntan lotion on his red raw nose. "It's easy. There's a theatrical outfitters in Republic Street and we use it for our occasional fancy dress parties," he explained. "I've dressed up as Dracula, Superman, Santa Claus and Batman over the years."

"Sounds cool," Jenny said. "So no problem getting Angel stuff?"

"What, on a Catholic island?" he reassured her.

Winnie appeared with a tray of coffee in paper cups as the red little steamship upped anchor and began to edge its way serenely through all the yachts. Jenny grimaced as she got suntan lotion on her sunspecs.

Laura read a female mag. "I see we've got everyone today" she said.

"Even the Captain and Theresa," David added.

"Have you brought your camera, Ash?" Jenny asked.

"Who's Ash?" David queried.

"It's me," Sarah replied. "It's my nickname."

"Why?"

"Cos at school I used to smoke, even though I play football."

"She's an idiot," Jenny suggested.

"Do you have a nickname?" David asked.

"At school I got called Duff Jen, as folk felt I exaggerated stories. Once, I said my form Teacher in Drama was a lesbian. In fact she had said a Thespian. It's a mistake anyone could make!" Jenny defended herself.

"Who else has a nickname?" David asked.

"Oh, I was always Winnie the Pooh; so predictable," her Mum groaned. "How about you, David?"

"Folk in my flat called me DHL because every summer I came here and did courier work."

"That's quite original," Laura said. "I was called Oddie."

There was a pause. No one really wanted to ask.

"Okay, I'll bite the bullet, Laura," David said graciously, "Why Oddie?"

"He was a like a bird watcher or something."

"I don't get the link," Jenny admitted. "They weren't saying you were odd?"

"No," Laura smiled. "I was always getting my tits out."

David put his hand over his mouth. Both Sarah and Jenny grinned. Winnie rummaged nervously in her handbag.

"Hey, can I play this gemme?" came a voice from behind them. It was the fat Glaswegian. "I've got a nickname."

"By all means tell us," Winnie said politely.

"I'm Billy King," he began.

"You couldn't make this up," David whispered to Jenny.

"Well, I worked behind the bar at a Ranger's loyal pub in Larkhall and they called me a Hun at the till."

David grinned. No one else laughed.

"Ach, you Sassenachs!" he shrugged and stomped off to the bar.

The boat was now at the entrance to the harbour and David enjoyed the welcome breeze.

"I used to live there as a child," he said, pointing out the seafront to Jenny. "That block of flats there. In those days Tigne Creek had a squadron of grey battle class destroyers which I used to watch entering or leaving the harbour. Sometimes American warships joined them. You could also see large aircraft carriers passing the creek to go to Grand Harbour."

Jenny listened politely but did not add to the conversation, a sure sign she was bored. David decided to stop. He didn't want to reinforce the fact he was all of 30.

"We didn't ask Wanker how he got his nickname," she said, changing the subject.

"The Captain says he flew solo a lot. Actually, he must have been a brave man. Later in the war he flew over German lines in Italy and North Africa and photographed German troops and tanks. That meant he had a large camera where his cannon should have been. He was unarmed."

"Wow!" said Jenny. "That's like, amazing."

"Talking of a Cannon, will Father Collina play ball with us when Danny puts up that statue?"

"It'll be fun tonight when Danny has his apparition, eh?" Jenny beamed in anticipation.

The day at the Blue Lagoon was uneventful. Everyone enjoyed their meal on the Captain Morgan boat, washed down by a Marsovin wine. Folk swam, had a siesta and got a tan lying wherever they could find a flat piece of rock, not easy when so many are jagged. The drinks and ice cream boats did a good trade.

As the boat tied up back at Sliema, Mark was waiting at the jetty, a large brown parcel under his arm. "Hi Angel!" he shouted at Sarah as she disembarked. "Get it?"

"Got it."

"Good," Sarah replied.

At 8 pm Sarah was ready on the roof. Jenny and David hid behind the sea wall.

When Danny did walk along the lane, David groaned when he saw Billy King and his wife ambling along behind him.

"Oh well, we've no choice, let's go for it," David said.

He signalled and on came the beam of light. Danny looked as stunned as a rabbit in a car's headlights.

"My God!" he gasped and sank nervously to his knees. Sarah appeared in all her regalia.

"Oh hell, she's got a wand!" Jenny gulped. "She's a bloody fairy, not an Angel!"

"I've been sent by God," Sarah began loudly.

David was as intent watching the reaction of Billy and his wife. They had stopped in their tracks and were peering gobsmacked up at the roof.

"What do you wish of me, dear Angel?" Danny asked, gathering his thoughts.

"You must repent, Danny. You have done some terrible things."

"I confess, I confess." Danny knelt and looked genuinely contrite. The Kings sat down on the lane still looking up in awe.

"I wish she'd dispose of the wand," David said.

"What were the worst sins?" Sarah asked.

"There are so many," Danny murmured.

"Let's start with money," Sarah suggested.

"Yes, tax evasion," Danny readily agreed. "But I have sent my tax return."

"It reads like a fairytale," Sarah said with an inspired guess.

"Grim." Danny acknowledged.

"That too. And sins of the flesh?"

"There was only one night with Laura," he conceded.

"My God, she's insatiable!" Jenny gasped.

"And exploitation?" Sarah continued.

"I look after my employees well," Danny said more assertively.

"Jenny is in plaster. Have you given her any compensation?" Sarah asked.

"Hey, well done, Sis," Jenny whispered behind the wall.

"Conning your tour parties with dodgy deals."

"Can you specify?" Danny asked bravely.

"Honey."

"I'm sorry, but please don't be so familiar," he asked. "Oh D and C Honey, I do apologise."

"Manoeuvring folk towards your ice cream van, an expensive boat at the Blue Grotto, discount vouchers for non-existent shops, need I go on? I know everything."

"There's no need," Danny acknowledged.

"Hey pal, I couldnae find your shops," Billy interrupted.

"Judas Iscariot," said Sarah, "I've yet to deal with you, Billy."

"I havenae got a cairry ooot," Billy stumbled.

"On your knees!" Sarah demanded.

Billy and his wife did so without a murmur.

"You have sneered all through your holiday at anything to do with churches, have you not?"

"Suppose so," Billy stammered.

"And you sing anti-Catholic songs at your matches."

"I know, I know," Billy murmured.

"And you told your wife, Daphne, you'd diet and drink less and did you?"

"Nope"

"Och naw," said Daphne. "Ye tellt me ye were oan slimming foods tae."

"Ach, I know, but I tak them a'," Billy confessed. "I'm sorry doll!"

"You must all change your ways from today or suffer the consequences," Sarah warned.

"I'll build a statue," Danny offered.

"I'll get him to support Celtic!" Daphne volunteered.

"There's one miracle," Danny suggested.

The beam of light faded and Sarah hid behind the roof wall.

David and Jenny emerged from the behind the sea wall.

"Could ye naw hae suggested Partick Thistle?" Billy demanded. "My life is ruined."

The Kings headed forlornly back up the lane. He threw his Rangers scarf melodramatically on the ground but Daphne picked it up and put it round his neck with a consoling hug.

"Did you see it, did you see it?" Danny exclaimed getting to his feet.

"What?" David asked.

"The Angel. It was your Guardian Angel, Jenny. Oh, I must have a quiet chat to you about some compensation for ending up in plaster. All I need now is a miracle."

Danny excitedly got into his car and turned for St Julian's. Sarah, having taken off the Angel's wings and halo, came down to the entrance.

"What's with the wand, Sis?" Jenny asked.

"Look, I forgot. I just put on what Mark had got," she explained.

"Good thing he didn't give you a Batgirl outfit then," Jenny pointed out.

"Now there's a fantasy!" David gasped before dodging Jenny's playful slap.

It was Thursday morning, when David was relaxing painting Danny's boat on the sands at St George's bay, with Gold Coast radio blaring away, a 7-Up bottle cooling at the water's edge, and Jenny lying on the sand prodding knitting needles inside her plaster cast, that, ominously, Scerri's car pulled up.

He got out flanked by Chopper and Cruncher all in black even down to the sunspecs. "I want to see you, young man!" he began with a glare.

"How can I help?" David asked politely.

"You can get Danny to drive along and pick up his ridiculous painting," he demanded. "Do you take me for a fool?"

"Goodness, no," David blurted out.

"My young children play in the Sliema Youth Orchestra and they told me about Rossini."

"I see," David sympathised.

"Is there anything Danny can do to make up?" Jenny asked.

"How's about a percentage of the money he makes from pilgrims coming to see the statue?" David asked.

Scerri was about to answer when Father Collina appeared at the sea wall like the Angel of Death in his black cape.

"I want to make it absolutely clear there will be no statue, no pilgrims, and no miracle" he declared emphatically. "I thought I made myself clear. I've told Danny about Sarah. Now, let that be an end to it."

He headed off along the sands, the sea water filling his deep foot prints.

"The money within seven days or Danny closes his businesses here," Scerri repeated menacingly. "Do not disappoint me!"

He and his two bodyguards got into their limo, slammed the doors and drove off.

"Well that's it." David shrugged. "All we can do is tell Danny that we tried," he added.

"And it was a good try," Jenny emphasised. "Look, everyone is doing last minute shopping in Sliema. Let's have some retail therapy," she suggested.

Half an hour later, they were on the gaily yellow- and orange-coloured bus heading to the bus stance overlooking Sliema Creek.

They passed Hinge and Bracket coming out of the public toilet.

"Marvellous week," one of them said. "Do thank Theresa for her commentaries."

They hadn't walked much further along the seafront when they passed the Glaswegian family all wearing Celtic tops.

"I haven't got the heart to tell him!" David said.

They entered Marks and Spencer and met Donna looking at leather goods.

"What a wicked week!" she exclaimed. "Almost as good as Ibiza and the Monday night with Marco was something else!"

It was while Jenny was trying out some fans that Caz passed them by. "What did you like best?" he asked politely.

"The Blue Lagoon cruise," she replied, "and Tuesday night with Marco."

David ushered Jenny over to look at lace hankies and met Tracey.

"Have you had a good time?" Jenny enquired.

"I enjoyed the day in Gozo," she replied instantly.

"And?" David prompted.

"And what?" Tracey asked.

"Your night with Marco"

"Oh my God, how did you know?" she stammered.

"He was free on Wednesday," David laughed.

Tracey had gone beetroot red and headed off to the toilet. Jenny chose a fan and they walked out into the street.

"At least now I know I was right not to get involved with Marco," Jenny agreed.

David nodded wisely.

"It would just have been some mindblowing torrid sex night after night and then some, leaving me exhausted. He would have seen me as a piece of meat with that gorgeous six pack and great biceps and suntanned complexion," she gasped.

David tried to interrupt.

"Treating me gently and being responsive to my needs."

"Okay, okay, I get the gist!" David insisted.

Jenny was winding him up by breathing more deeply.

Father Collina passed, glared, and moved on down the street without speaking.

"Just our luck," David groaned.

As they passed Littlewoods, Sarah and Winnie came out with a bag of new clothes each.

"We're all packed for tonight's flight," Winnie confirmed. "We just had to get some last minute things at these cheap prices."

"We saw the Captain, Wanker and Theresa in Tony's bar next door."

"All our plans for Danny got scuppered. Scerri realised the painting was pretty worthless and Father Collina will not allow the statue," David pointed out.

"So my Oscar-winning performance was all for nothing," Sarah moaned, trying on some new sunspecs.

"Sorry," Jenny sympathised.

They ambled next door into Tony's bar and ordered 2 cool Frisk lagers.

"Can we join you?" Jenny asked politely.

"It's may," Theresa pointed.

"No, late July," Jenny answered quizzically.

"*May* we join you?" Theresa elaborated.

"Of course!" said Jenny.

"I heard about the painting," Wanker began, "We did try."

"I know," David agreed. "We've got a week to think up another wheeze."

"Do let me know," said Wanker, "I've enjoyed meeting up with you all and catching up with the Captain."

"Maybe we should dig up that plane," the Captain persisted.

"Even if it is there, it is under thousands of tons of concrete," David reminded him.

David looked around the bar. On the walls were hanging stirring pictures of SWW naval convoys and aircraft gallantly reaching the beleaguered island.

"I can see why you chose this bar," David said, chewing open a bag of peanuts. "I wonder what our latest group of tourists will be like?"

It would only be a few hours till they found out.

At 8 pm, Jenny made an emotional 'goodbye' to her Mum and Sarah. The latter handed over her shrapnel of loose change to her sister before going to the departure lounge. Caz, Tracey and Donna all used up their film photographing Marco in his Customs Officer uniform. At different times, and different parts of the airport, David saw Marco snog each of them in turn. Normally he would have felt envious but now he was holding Jenny's hand and waving 'Goodbye' to the party. Wanker shook hands with the Captain. The Glaswegian family, still wearing Celtic tops, trudged forlornly to passport control clearly wondering what fate would befall them back in Glasgow. Hinge and Brackett left the couriers some sweets and then they were all gone and thoughts turned to the latest group who would be arriving.

Laura and Jenny held their 'SAY GO' notice boards aloft till their arms ached. Soon a new group were milling around them, and Mark and David feverishly ticked off names.

"I still can't believe you had me convinced Winnie was a murderer," he said over the din of the carousel.

David just smiled. "Bags I get the babes," Mark called out as three young females approached already wearing Malta tops.

"We were here last year," explained the smallest of the three.

"I don't quite remember," Mark apologised. "And I think I would have," he added gallantly.

"I'm Leanne," the girl said. "And they are Carol and Lesley." She pointed at the other two as they struggled with large cases.

"No we were with the Scerri lot," Carol, the blonde of the trio, replied.

"I can't wait to see the Blue Lagoon," Lesley said.

"Gozo," said Leanne.

"Blue Grotto," added Carol.

"Why didn't you stay with Scerri Travel?" David asked.

"He showed me his chopper," Leanne said. "I didn't want to date a hardman like that."

"I did wonder what you meant for a moment there," David conceded.

"Hey, who's that gorg guy?" Lesley shouted excitedly as Marco passed by resplendent in his uniform.

"Imagine being attracted to Scerri's chopper," Mark echoed.

Laura said nothing.

The three girls went off to chat to Marco.

A distinguished looking gentleman with grey hair, half rimmed spectacles, a paper under his arm and struggling with his case shook hands with David. "Prof Gilchrist," he said.

"Pleased to meet you," David replied scanning his list. "From York I see."

"Yes I have a chair."

"Where?" asked Mark looking around.

"It means a Professor in a specialist field," he explained with all the resignation of someone who had answered the same question many times. "World War 2 archaeology," he elaborated.

"Do you have digs?" David asked enthusiastically.

"No I've got a St Julian's Hotel," he replied. "Archaeological ones"

"Where abouts?"

"Somewhere called St Paul's. Some colleagues looking for Roman artefacts have located a World War 2 fighter," The Prof added.

David almost froze on the spot. He tried hard not to make any facial expression of interest or recognition. "I'll see you at the coach" he said.

Mark was surrounded by families and was trying with Laura to keep all the little kids nearby.

"I'm sorry I can't help anyone with a case," Jenny said. "This plaster is so restricting."

"You'll have it off next week," Mark kindly pointed out.

"Oh it hasn't stopped that. Oh I see what you mean," she laughed. "Could that be our Italian plane?" Jenny asked excitedly.

"The Captain never mentioned any other plane ever coming down there," David replied. "I'll sound out the Prof tomorrow."

David noticed a young man standing quietly by himself looking all around. He stuck out like a sore thumb given he was wearing a pinstripe suit when everyone else had short sleeves and shorts on. "I am David Bond, Say Go."

"Go," the young man politely replied.

"No, Say Go Tours."

"Oh, I'm Andrew, pleased to meet you. I am with you. I've travelled alone. My Mum said at 25 I'd to strike out and essentially get a life. I hope to meet a girl."

"Someone you know on the Island?" David asked.

"No I just want to meet a girl. I am 25," he stressed. "And I've seen all these late night Sky programmes about what goes on in these places. You know Aya Napa and Falkirk."

"Faliraki. Look, you may find Malta a bit tame though," David counselled.

"Have you ever been abroad before?" Mark asked.

"I've hardly ever been out of Cambridgeshire actually," he said. "Wisbech."

"Is the beach nice?" Mark asked.

"No it's just a town. There's no beach," he pointed out.

David counted with Laura and then shouted, "We're all here. Out to the coaches everyone."

He had to delay as Marco was already snogging Leanne beside a billboard advertising safe sex. He gave Marco a look. Marco did make some comment but it was drowned out by a plane landing.

"Do you have many cases?" David asked Andrew to make small talk.

"Just my large blue one," he said.

"Legal ones," David explained.

"Criminal Defence mainly," he replied.

"I've been called to the bar," Laura added.

"Really?" Andrew replied.

"Many times" Mark explained.

"You could show me your briefs," Andrew said, tongue in cheek.

"Hey, watch it mate!" Mark warned.

The coach headed out into the dark countryside. The small children very soon fell asleep. David's eyes burned with tiredness.

"Marco says he'll show me everything," Leanne said, sitting behind Jenny and David.

"I don't doubt it," David replied politely.

"I am fascinated at what you may dig up Prof," David said as he walked down the aisle of the coach.

"It'll be painstaking," the Prof said. "After all, it's been in the soil more than 60 years and we don't want it all disintegrating. And there could be human remains and we'd have to contact the appropriate authorities."

"Do tell me more in due course," David asked.

David peered out of the back of the coach and saw Marco following on his scooter. You are a fast worker, he thought.

"Are you trying to tell me there is no Plan B?" Danny, red and flustered, asked at the breakfast table in the apartments the following morning.

David, Mark, Laura and Jenny all looked at their feet.

"Look," David said "we did try to win at the football, we tried the dodgy painting, we even attempted divine intervention."

"Don't get me on to that topic," Danny moaned. "I believed it. I really did."

"Sorry," Jenny apologised, pouring herself a coffee.

"Trying to fob Scerri and me with the same Angelic miracle was like sleeping with the Enemy. And don't say it, Laura!"

Laura turned red.

"We do have one more plan," David finally piped up. "We believe they have found an Italian fighter aircraft near St Paul's bay and ………."

"It contains gold bars," Danny completed the sentence. He sat down and fanned his face with his hat.

"You know?" David asked.

"The whole of Malta knows that myth."

"What is a myth?" Laura asked.

"An effeminate moth," Mark laughed.

"It means a legend, dopey."

"Don't call me Dopey!" Laura demanded.

"It means it's a good story but it simply isn't true," Danny concluded.

"I sometimes wake up feeling dopey," Mark chuckled trying to lighten the mood.

"Well, I believe we should go up to St Paul's one night in the dark and take a look," David suggested.

"That's entirely up to you but we need to come up with something much more realistic. Now this morning I want you, Laura, to accompany David. Jenny, you've got your St Luke's Out-Patients. Mark, you take the culture vultures up to Valletta with Theresa, please."

As David counted his party on to the coach, he was aware that Laura was noticeably subdued.

"He was only joking about you being dopey. You know," he comforted her.

"Yeh, but it's all the time," Laura protested. "Mark's always into innuendo and it gets embarrassing. The other night, he took me out to the German restaurant, as Jenny had raved about your evening. Well, I asked what was the difference between medium and rare and he said three inches!"

David stifled a smile but made a mental note of the gag. "He's just a macho guy" he pointed out.

"I know that," Laura conceded, "ever since he jogged home from his vasectomy."

"And he's conceited," David added.

"Oh yeh, when he has an orgasm, he calls out his own name!"

"I've mixed feelings about Mark," David reflected.

"What's a mixed feeling?"

"When you see your Mother-in-law backing over a cliff in your car."

Laura laughed. "I think he prefers his golf to me," she continued. "He'll look for a golf club but can't find my G spot."

"He must love your sense of humour," David suggested.

"Yes, but I am not dopey, as he suggests, though I do pay more attention to my looks then my mind."

"Why?"

"Cos men may be stupid but they aren't blind."

"Hey, I saw a blind man at the local nudist beach."

"How?" Laura asked.

"It wasn't hard!"

There was a long pause. The three girls sitting behind them began to laugh.

"Well, that's our routine for the next entertainment evening perfected again," David said.

"Yes, but I began seriously about Mark, David," Laura reiterated. "Everyone sees me as being funny and lighthearted and a bit dizzy but I have a serious side too."

"I know you do," David sympathised and put his arm round her.

"I'd like him to talk about future plans or even about getting engaged."

"I didn't know that," David said in surprise. "Why don't you initiate the discussion?"

"I hint at it now and again but Mark comes from a rich respectable family, few people know that, and let's be honest, how would he sell me to them? I am a courier who adds to her pay packet by doing a late night strip in a night club."

"I didn't put Mark down as a snob," David said.

"No, but his Parents sound as if they are," Laura moaned.

Tony had driven into a traffic jam in Bugibba. Nothing moved but everyone paarped their horn, regardless.

"Isn't that Marco on his scooter behind us?" Laura asked.

David peered at the coach wing mirror. "Looks like it. And I think I know the attraction too." He grinned, glancing at the three girls behind him.

"Have you seen the Prof today?" Laura asked as Tony nipped down a side street and managed to get to the quayside in time to catch the Under Water Safari.

"No he's gone on the cultural Valletta trip. I believe he'll be at the dig on Monday."

"If there are gold bars, they'll surely be long gone," Laura pondered.

"I doubt if they are there but we must find some way of putting that money together for Scerri," David repeated. "Don't you have any influence at all, Laura?"

Laura didn't reply.

"Okay folks, back on the coach please at 1 pm after you've all had a snack. I'll show you which ice cream van and Café to go to."

"That'll be Danny's," Leanne inferred. "We were here last year and got directed towards Peter Scerri's. Oh look, here's Marco. What a coincidence."

Marco helped her off the coach and Carol and Lesley gave each other a knowing look. Laura and David waited till everyone got off the bus and Tony had gone to get some fags.

"Look, David, I only spent one night with him. Anyway he was impudent."

"It's impotent," David corrected her.

"Well, he's that as well but he was rude and cheeky."

They walked along the quayside and sat on the top deck of the glass-bottomed boat.

"I hate to be intrusive, Laura, but did you really spend a night with Danny?"

The engines came on and the boat edged out into St Paul's bay by sending some ducks scurrying to safety.

"I feared I was going to be sacked. Look David, I've never told you this but I send money home to my Mum as she's too unwell to work. I cannot afford to have my money stop. Believe me it wasn't pleasant."

David bought a couple of drinks off the passing steward and smiled as he watched Marco and Leanne snogging at the stern. Carol saw his grin.

"You can't take her anywhere!" she complained. "Same last year, in Cyprus the year before, and Tenerife the year before that."

"She's just having a good time," David confirmed.

"We're meant to be seeing an old wreck!" Lesley pointed out.

"You can stare at David," Laura volunteered.

David was relieved the atmosphere had temporarily lifted. "Look, Laura, would you like me to have a word with Mark?" he suggested.

"I don't know." She paused to reflect. "If you do, don't make it too apparent I prompted you."

"Hey, it's our turn to see the fish being fed!" Lesley exclaimed.

Everyone took their turn at heading backwards down the steps. Leanne and Marco continued to snog.

"Come on before he swallows you up!" Carol suggested.

It was a very enjoyable morning. Leanne, Carol and Lesley joined David and Laura in Danny's café and enjoyed a cheese and tomato pizza and a glass of wine. Marco headed back to Luqa airport.

"Do you have any parties?" Leanne asked.

"We've a weekly party with songs, dancing and a great comedy routine," David outlined.

"He means his awful double act with me," Laura elaborated.

"Yeh, I heard your routine on the coach. It was really funny," Leanne said.

"Like Morecambe and Wise, Cannon and Ball or Little and Large?" David suggested.

"Who are they?" Lesley asked.

"Yeh, just how old are you?" Laura grinned.

David shut up. He didn't enjoy being leg-pulled about his age.

A waiter served ice creams. A text came in.

"Jenny's got her plaster off," David announced to Laura.

"Do you ever do fancy dress?" Leanne asked. "Mr Scerri did that last year. I love dressing up!"

"We can if you want," Laura offered. "How about it for next Monday, David?"

"No problem," David replied as he turned to his cappuccino. "I'll nip into Republic St and get some hired stuff on Danny's account for the couriers."

He could see the party heading back towards Tony's coach in Bugibba square and many were standing under a palm tree to get some shade, much as folk at home dash to a bus shelter in the rain.

"Is it the beach now?" Carol enthused.

"A lovely long sandy one called Mellieha," David replied. "And we can all speed around the bay on the banana motor boat."

There wasn't a cloud in the sky and David was glad Tony had the air conditioning on at full blast. As they drove out of St Paul's Bay, David could see the archaeological dig fenced off near the water and just outwith the town. A few students appeared to be using spoons and toothbrushes to remove the earth. Above them, there were arc lights which must floodlight the area at night. There was no obvious sign of a plane or trench where one would have been.

"Penny for your thoughts?" Laura interrupted his train of thought.

"I think we should come up here late tonight and see what we can find," he said.

"Won't it all be guarded?" Laura asked as the dig disappeared from view.

"Maybe, but I can't see any security," David remarked. "We'll see what Mark and Jenny reckon."

"I reckon we should take a look, you're right" Mark concurred, as they sat in the small restaurant having their evening meal. Steven had served up egg, chips and beans.

"It's funny," said Jenny. "I've had my joint in a case and you want to case the joint."

"That's like that plumber we'd here last week," Steven butted in. "He changed our drains and drained our change."

"We didn't ask you!" Jenny laughed. "At least I don't need needles to itch anymore."

"You're clever with words. Maybe you should work for an advertising agency," David suggested.

"I do competitions but I never have much success," she said. "I always admire folk who think up slogans like it Asda be Asda, or partners in grime. Anyway, I'll have my ice cream and wafer now as I've a one snack mind."

"You see, there you go again," David pointed out. "You don't even know you are doing it."

"Look can we get back to the plot?" Mark suggested. "Let's get some warm clothing on and get the bus up to St Paul's Bay."

"And then what?" Jenny asked. "Do we all sit on the bus clutching a spade? It would be rather conspicuous."

"You've a point there," David agreed. "We're going to have to think this through."

"We could bluff it," Mark suggested. "We could just walk in, say, on Sunday afternoon after we get back from Valletta market, and say we are archaeological students and have come to help."

"They'd ask for ID or ask us some difficult questions," Laura said. "I'm not good at hard questions. I am not good at easy questions," she reflected.

"I have an idea. Steven has his trick photography. Get him to take a photo of me with Prof Gilchrist and have some archaeological scene in the background," David outlined.

"What, like a pyramid?" Mark asked.

"He's a specialist in the SWW. It would have to be a war background and I know the very man. I'll nip along to the Captain's room and get back to you."

"We'll just drink up our coffees then while we wait," Jenny agreed.

David headed along the lane towards the apartments. The evening was still. Only the sound of water lapping against the pedaloes and the distant sound of locusts rent the air. It was pleasant when an evening became cool as it got dark. The lights of the hotels reflected off the dark unwelcoming sea.

As David approached the apartments he saw Theresa heading out of the lounge bar. "Is the Captain in?" he enquired.

"He's in his room playing Mozart."

"Is he winning?" David asked.

"I've heard that one," Theresa moaned, "You must get some new gags. Oh, and your name is mud with Father Collina with all your Angelic appearances and talk of miracles. I didn't borrow all that angel equipment from him for you to do that, you know," she scolded. "Anyway, how are your plans coming along to raise the money to save Danny?"

"We'll dig something up" David answered. "Right, I must get a drink and see the Captain."

242

Theresa headed off into the night.

Suddenly, David was momentarily blinded by a shaft of light which almost knocked him off his feet. He looked instinctively up at the roof and could make out a female all in white but with no halo or wings.

"David, David, I bring you a celestial message. I'm Ariadne."

"Harry who?"

"Ariadne. I will guide you to your destiny."

"Great stuff" said David intrigued as to who this was. "Where are your halo and wings?"

"I am not an Angel. I am a spirit of the dead."

"Can I make a wish?"

"Do not mock me, human. You would not want to see me when I get angry."

"Do you go green?" David asked.

"I will ignore your impertinence. I have a message. Be guided by the light."

"What does it mean?"

"I repeat, you can be guided by the light."

"Can you tell me the Malta National Lottery numbers this weekend?"

The beam of light disappeared. David looked all around but there was no one about. The only sound was the sea lapping against the shore. Now who was that? He wondered.

He headed up to the stairs to the Captain's room and found him in his dressing gown doing mock conducting of an orchestra. David waited patiently for him to turn down the music.

"Do you want a whisky?" the Captain asked.

"Not for me thanks. You won't believe this but someone tried to do the same apparition gag that we did to you but I didn't fall for it."

"Someone getting revenge, eh? Now what can I do for you?"

"Can I borrow one of your SWW photos of you standing in front of your hurricane at Ta Qali?"

"No problem at all," the Captain said pulling one off the wall and removing the blue tack. "But why?"

"We need to get into that dig at St Paul's and we want to convince the archaeologists that we're qualified to be there."

"Do tell me how you get on," the Captain insisted.

"Right, I must get back to the restaurant. Bye."

"Yes I can use that photo" Steven confirmed. "Just get a photo of you and Prof Gilchrist when you go to the Blue Grotto tomorrow and I'll superimpose both of you in front of the aircraft."

Mark joined David at the bar and got a round in. "You were longer than expected" Mark pointed out.

David glanced at his watch. It was 10 pm. He held it up to his ear. "I don't understand" he said, his eyebrows knitted in puzzlement. "I left at 6 pm. I saw the Captain and I spoke to that nut on the roof. That didn't take 4 hours, surely."

"What nut on the roof?" Mark asked opening a bag of crisps.

"Oh some middle aged female was doing the beam of light and Angel routine. Probably a friend of Scerri taking revenge."

There was a long pause. Across the floor, Laura and Jenny were giggling at a joke and Steven could be heard chopping meat in the kitchen.

"David, there couldn't be a beam of light," Mark said slowly and deliberately.

"How do you mean?" David asked intrigued.

"The bulb was taken out earlier today."

"So, someone renewed it. Don't give me the willies," David demanded.

"There wasn't a new bulb to put in, David. Anyway, you do all our electrical work."

David had put his hand in his mouth. He must have gone white, as Jenny saw his expression.

"What's wrong, David? You look like you've seen a ghost."

"Maybe he has," Mark grinned.

They took their seats beside Laura.

"You know, it was strange looking back on it," David recalled.

"How?" Mark asked.

"She didn't have wings or a halo."

"Who didn't?" asked Laura who had, up till now, been out of the loop.

"The ghost," said Mark.

Laura looked all set to make one of her usual flippant remarks, but seeing David's expression, thought the better of it.

"What was the ghost called?" Mark asked.

"Ariadne," David remembered.

"That name rings a bell," Jenny said.

"Carmen and Danny's daughter," David said. "I hope she is okay."

"What did she say? This is exciting!" Laura enthused.

"Maybe you'll marry someone handsome," Jenny laughed.

"Well that rules out Mark," Laura said pointedly.

"It's not a joke, Jenny," David insisted. "She had a message."

"Like the Royal Mail?" Jenny grinned undaunted.

"We must be guided by the light."

"She probably meant to get that bulb fixed," Jenny suggested. "Only a gay ghost can give you the willies."

David suffered the leg pull and then repeated, "This was for real. What could the message mean? Jenny, you are really good with words," David said.

"The light can mean many things," Jenny thought out loud. "It could be the light we need at the archaeological dig."

"What about God?" David asked.

"Hey, you don't mess around," Mark said. "You go straight to the top."

"I still think it's a Scerri hoax," Laura emphasised.

"Let's go to that Dig soon and we'll soon find out," David insisted. "Steven, can we have our bill?"

The four couriers came back to the same topic as they bobbed about in the motor boat at the Blue Grotto. It was rare for them to be together, but each boatman gave a running commentary as he rowed under the caves and pointed out the myriad of colours among the rocks. The water was turquoise and you could watch the fish darting around the boat.

"As I see it," David began, "We either go at night, and try to get over the fence and avoid security guards and dogs and arc lights or we go Sunday afternoon with false ID and our fake photo."

"I say tonight," Mark decided.

"If we're caught we can still bluff it out with our ID."

"There's a far simpler possibility," Laura said brainstorming. "No one will be there on a Sunday afternoon. Let's take our ID and just walk in."

"I'll go for that," Jenny declared.

The boatman had waited patiently. "Can I point out the colours?" he interrupted.

"Look mate, we'll give you a tip, but we've seen them many times," Mark pointed out.

"Should I tell Father Collina that he's had his miracle?" David returned to his theme.

"Why not? It sounds convincing to me," Mark agreed.

"He won't believe it for a minute," Jenny counselled them. "Not after our track record of halos, wings and wands."

"I wouldn't either," Laura said. "It will be Scerri's lot having a laugh at our expense."

"What if we learn that Ariadne is dead?" David asked seriously.

"I agree that would change everything," Laura admitted.

"We'll have to find out in a subtle way," Jenny pointed out. "We can't go to Danny and ask is Ariadne dead?"

As they got back to the inlet they disembarked and they saw Prof Gilchrist in a large straw hat carefully picking his way among and lobster pots back up to the café.

"When do you go to the Dig?" David asked.

"I'll go Monday," he replied. "No one works there at the weekend, of course."

"Right," said David. "Oh, can I have a photo taken beside you?"

"Of course, old chap." He readily acceded to the request.

After cokes and almond biscuits at the café, and then horrifying the party by pointing out the photo of a shark caught a few miles from the Blue Grotto, the party headed off to Hagar Qim Stonehenge.

When they returned to the St Julian's hotel, David noticed Danny's BMW in the car park. "Now we'll learn if there was a miracle or not," David concluded.

"I tell you, it was a Scerri wind up," Laura insisted.

"Cynic!" Mark said as they all trooped into reception.

"Hi guys, join me in a cappuccino!" Danny offered.

"He doesn't seem too down," Laura suggested.

They all sat round a coffee table as Danny summoned a waiter.

"Can I ask you something?" David began.

"Of course" Danny replied.

"How is Ariadne?" Four pairs of eyes watched his expression attentively.

"Well, we're all sad she was taken from us."

David looked serious. "We didn't know," he uttered, wondering how to choose his words.

"Of course, you did," Danny retorted. "She went to London"

"Oh that, oh that's okay then."

"David, what are you on about? You're talking in riddles." Danny looked quizzical.

"Look, it's okay now to tell you," Mark butted in. "We feared Ariadne had died. You see, you won't believe this but ...."

"The Ariadne who died yesterday was Carmen's childhood friend, Ariadne."

There was a long, long pause. Mark, David, Jenny and Laura all exchanged anxious glances.

"How?" David asked sympathetically.

"She was roaming around the archaeological dig in the dark at St Paul's bay and for some strange reason she was knocked down by a mechanical digger. She fell into a trench and was only found this morning. Ironically they had to dig her up in order to bury her."

"Oh my God! I am starting to believe you, David!" Laura exclaimed.

"Believe what?" Danny enquired again.

"I think you've got your miracle," David stated. "At the time poor Ariadne died she was talking to me!"

"But if you saw her lying in the trench, why didn't you dig her out, man?"

"No, he saw her as a ghost in a beam of light," Mark explained, "On the roof of your St George's apartments."

"Good God!" Danny murmured. "I must tell Father Collina. We'll build a statue and pilgrims will come from all over the world and I'll issue tickets, souvenirs, holy pictures, prayer books, rosary beads etc."

"She had a message too," David added. "We must be guided by the light."

"What did it mean?" Danny asked.

"We don't know but I was being blinded by a beam of light at the time and there was no bulb in the searchlight yesterday evening."

"I am off to see the Priest right now," Danny said. He finished his coffee, doffed his hat to the girls and headed off into the sunlight.

That evening, David decided he would have a quiet word with Mark. Jenny was at the nightclub and was helping Laura at the snooker tables. Mark was at the karaoke bar and, as he entered, David realised that Mark was all over Carol and Lesley. Marco was chatting up Leanne in a corner and, although early in the evening, they'd all had a fair bit to drink. Carol and Lesley moved off to look at the choice of music and David got himself a lager and nuts.

"You know, Mark," he began, "You have a really attractive, loyal, funny girlfriend, yet you are always chatting up others!"

"What has Jenny said? I deny it all," he replied pre-empting what David could be about to accuse him of.

"I know you haven't chatted Jenny up," David said, having a mouthful of lager. "Hey you haven't, have you?"

"No," Mark emphasised.

Mark stopped to serve Marco two coconut rums.

"Look at you. You were all over Lesley and Carol. How do you reckon Laura feels?"

"Pretty good usually"

"No, I mean emotionally," David unnecessarily elaborated. "Do you see yourself as God's gift to women?" he asked rhetorically.

"That's me!" Marco laughed as he returned to Leanne.

"I wouldn't say that," Mark insisted, "But in St Julian's, I am probably in the top one eh!"

"Are you aware that Laura would like you to be committed?"

"What, to a mental home?"

"I mean engaged," David said. "I am being serious, Mark."

"Yes, you sure are," said Mark, who had clearly misjudged the mood.

At that moment, Carol and Lesley began to sing, 'It's not unusual'. Young Andrew, the lawyer, walked in nervously and asked for a coke.

"On the pull?" Mark asked.

"Well I fancy those two," he said pointing to the two girls.

"Who doesn't?" Mark agreed.

"There you go again," David emphasised. "Folk would give their right arm for a girlfriend like Laura, Mark. Do think about it, don't lose her. Give her a ring."

"Oh yes, do phone her," Andrew agreed. "What's a 20p call?"

"He means get engaged," Mark explained. "And why am I telling you anyway?"

The two girls returned to their drinks. Andrew went up to them. "Do you come here often?" he asked. He got no response.

Mark watched sympathetically. "Ask them, if you said they had a beautiful body, would you hold it against me?"

"In you dreams," Lesley said with a face.

Andrew went red with acute embarrassment and headed out of the bar.

Mark drank up the lawyer's coke. "Do you reckon he has ever had a girlfriend?" Mark asked.

David didn't want to admit Jenny was really his first one too.

On the Saturday, as the party toured Valletta, and most were on the Grand Harbour cruise on a sweltering day, David walked along to the theatrical outfitters in Republic Street. In the window there were Dracula, Batman and Superman outfits on display.

"Bonju," said an elderly lady behind the counter.

The shop was long and narrow with lots of costumes on hangers, much like a dry cleaners.

"Do you want Superman, as usual, David, or the Angel outfits?"

"I want something different," David said. "SAY GO TOURS are planning a fancy dress party next week."

"Well, we've Dracula or the skeleton, or a 1930s gangster or Aladdin or Catwoman, or a cowboy or Robin Hood in the latest intake."

David had a brief perusal and then chose Catwoman and Calamity Jane outfits for Jenny and Laura and the skeleton and Aladdin for Mark and himself. He noticed all the costumes had security tags.

"We'd to get them as youngsters nip and steal our stuff," the Lady explained.

"I didn't know Valletta had any crime," David said.

"I'd show you the crime figures from last week's Times," she offered, "but someone nicked them off my counter."

"Oh wow! I like the skeleton outfit," Mark whooped as David met the party back on the coach. "I'll try it on the moment we get back."

"We're all debating what to wear at the party," Leanne, sitting behind them, stated.

"In that Catwoman outfit, folk will think I'm a haemophiliac," Laura said.

"Nymphomaniac, you silly girl," Theresa groaned.

Laura bent across Mark to whisper to David, "I never understand why that old school ma'am never has any patience. I thought you told me she helps out with special needs kids."

"Look," David replied, "she once had one who was only 4 feet tall and she didn't even ridicule him. It wasn't big and it wasn't clever!"

"You could use that one in your joke routine," Jenny suggested.

"It's not too politically correct," David conceded.

"How's about we just wear bikinis and go as strippers?" Carol asked.

"Oh do," Mark agreed, till he saw Laura's look.

"Hey, I could go as a lawyer!" Andrew shouted from further down the coach.

"Don't tell us you've come here with a wig and gown," Mark despaired.

"Oh. I forgot!" he blushed.

"Surely the whole point is to be something different?" Prof Gilchrist pointed out.

"That's why Laura can't be a nymphomaniac," Mark laughed. Laura gave him a slap.

"It's why Danny couldn't be a cowboy too," David smiled.

The coach was approaching Sliema and yellow and orange buses were in front of the coach in the usual Saturday traffic jam.

"In the old days," David said on the mike, "Buses were all different colours going to different destinations eg, Sliema was a dark green but once the island became literate they all had the same colour."

"You are full of facts," Leanne said admiringly.

"Do you know half of all Maltese 15-year-olds drink alcohol?" he continued.

"Yeh, this is my sort of island," Leanne agreed. "Do we pass where Marco plays Polo soon?" she enquired.

A few minutes later, where Sliema meets St Julian's, they did. Marco was leaning against a light blue scooter and chatting up a blonde in a red bikini.

"Some you win, some you lose," David nodded knowingly.

Leanne went red and flicked through the pages of her magazine in a desperate bid to look nonchalant.

"Right, before you go," David announced on the mike, "I've got a room and bar booked for our Fancy Dress party on Monday evening at 7.30 pm and there will be a prize for best dress."

"Or undress," Mark said quietly.

As the four couriers walked along the sea front towards the Apartments, a text came in.

"Father Collina wants to see me" David said predictably.

He had his meal first then, with Mark in tow, he walked along to St Mark's. As they were ushered in to his office, Father Collina was already sitting behind his desk making animal figures out of candle wax.

"I am missing an AC Milan match in Serie A on TV to see you two," he groaned. "It's time we brought this nonsense to a halt though, we all had a laugh with your Angel routine and I know your intentions were good, but a fine lady has died, dear old Ariadne, and you will cause upset to her family and friends by carrying on. I'm asking you, no, telling you, to stop it now. You have got Danny convinced you had a vision."

David kept waiting for a chance to butt in.

"At least he believes me then?" David sought reassurance.

"I advised him to act rationally but he's gone to see Peter Scerri with a business plan, and Scerri will accept if Danny makes the sort of cash he's talking about. However, we must consider Ethics."

"An English county?" Mark interrupted.

"It means doing the right thing," David pointed out.

"Father," David said, composing himself, "I saw Ariadne. There were no wings, haloes, wands or whatever. I have no reason for lying. I was quick to admit our previous scam."

"Pork luncheon meat?" asked Mark.

"A con" David elaborated.

"You'd every reason," Father Collina looked serious. "You're trying to save Danny's bacon."

"There, we're back to pork luncheon meat."

"Shut up!" the Priest and David said in unison.

Father Collina picked up a bible theatrically. "Put your hand on this, David, and swear you really saw a vision."

David picked it up in his left hand and held up his right. "I swear I saw the vision."

"You would not put your immortal soul in danger," the old Priest admitted. "I must have time to think."

The two young men realised the interview was over, shook hands and left. As they walked down the hall to the entrance, they heard him switching on the match.

"Tomorrow we must go to that Dig," Mark demanded, "Whatever the answer is, it is there."

"I agree," David replied. They walked deep in thought along the lane. "Did you think more about Laura and you?" David asked.

"I'm thinking about popping the question," Mark conceded.

"My advice did you good," David inferred proudly.

"Yeh, that and the fact she is 8 weeks pregnant," Mark admitted.

"How did that happen?" David asked incredulously.

Mark gave him a knowing look. "I'll tell you one day," he grinned.

"Laura's pregnant!" Jenny exclaimed as she woke on Sunday morning.

"How do you know? I haven't told you yet," David replied, as he felt for his watch on the bedside cabinet. "Did Mark or Laura tell you?"

"You left your diary open," Jenny confessed. "I'm sorry, I glanced at it."

"You shouldn't be reading it," David said, chucking a pillow at her. "I have all my innermost thoughts there."

"Like what you'd like to do to Holly Valance?"

"I never wrote that, did I?" he blushed.

"No, I'm just winding you up."

"Yes she's pregnant. I always thought it could happen after what he gave her on her birthday," David enlarged.

"A ring?" Laura suggested innocently.

"Chlamydia," he said.

"Will they get engaged now?" she asked putting on a bra.

"He's hinting strongly," David said.

"Great, a party!" Jenny exclaimed.

The bells of St Mark's rang out summoning the locals to morning mass.

"Turning to more pressing matters, I am getting fake ID from Steven to enter that dig this afternoon once we're back from Valletta market, and I'll get trowels there. We'll find out how reliable Ariadne's message was."

He opened the Venetian blinds momentarily dazzling the girl as she frantically looked for her clip-up sunspecs. "Let's wait till it gets a bit dark" she suggested. "Maybe no one will notice."

"I've asked Steven to give me some cheap champagne from his cellar at the restaurant," David said, "Just in case we're right about Mark. Okay, time for breakfast!"

Mark and Laura were already making, and indeed burning, toast as they came in, grabbed an orange juice, made a coffee, and got a continental roll and D and C honey.

"David keeps moaning about me infringing his privacy," Jenny told them licking honey off her fingers.

"Did he really say that?" Mark asked incredulously.

"No, I read it in his diary," she confessed.

"Well are we going to that dig later today?" Laura asked.

"Not till you've got my laundry done, wench," Mark demanded.

"Don't call her wench!" Jenny insisted. "Not till we're married at least," Laura said.

Mark made no reaction.

Jenny and David exchanged a look.

Having spent Sunday morning at Valletta market, David nipped into Steven's restaurant and picked up a bottle of Asti Spumanti. Steven also gave him fake ID for all four as archaeological students at the University of Valletta and the photo of David taken with Professor Gilchrist.

At 4 pm, David, who was never the most patient individual, waited for Mark to get his laundry completed or, to be more precise, Laura to get it out of the Apartment launderette. Jenny sat in the kitchen with him reading a Saturday magazine which she'd got a day late as usual, in the capital.

"How much longer will they be?" he groaned.

"She's doing all his washing," Jenny explained.

Suddenly, the two of them heard an excited shriek which came from the vicinity of the beach.

"He couldn't have, could he?" David wondered.

"Get that champagne now!" Jenny commanded.

David rummaged in the fridge then, dashed down to the sands.

The Captain was patting Mark on the back, a not inconsiderable feat given his inability to balance on the sand at the best of times. He toppled and fell over like a skittle. Mark dusted him down and picked him up.

"He's done it, he's actually done it!" Laura shouted as David and Jenny ran down the steps.

"About 8 weeks ago, I reckon," Jenny said quietly.

"Are you, are you ....?" David gasped.

254

"Yes, we're engaged" Mark confirmed.

David opened the bottle and Mark got showered in the champagne.

"Oops!" David apologised.

"Who cares?" Mark beamed. "It's the happiest day of my life!"

"Is it really?" Laura asked, taking her turn at the bottle and thrusting her head back, while looking for confirmation.

"What were his actual words?" Jenny wanted to know.

"You're what, I asked?" said Mark.

Jenny and David, embarrassed, said nothing.

"She's pregnant," Mark announced.

"Yes, congratulations," said David, a bit uncomfortably.

He shook her hand. Jenny kissed her and embraced her warmly. I should have done that, David thought. Mark was absolutely drenched and gestured that they should return to the apartments. The Captain was quick to finish off the bottle.

"Mark, you've nothing else to put on, dear," Laura said as they entered the kitchen. "It's all in the washing machine, remember."

"Oh no!" Mark said, and flopped onto a chair.

"Have you nothing at all?" David asked. "I feel badly now about showering you in champers."

"You have got one thing," Laura said.

"I'm not wearing my winter overcoat in this sticky heat," Mark was quick to respond.

"You have the skeleton costume for our fancy dress party," she reminded him.

"I can hardly wear that on a bus or at the dig," he groaned.

"You've no choice mate," David dived in. "We must get going. There's only one bus once an hour."

So reluctantly, Mark stood at the St Julian's bus stop in this skeleton outfit, his eyes peering through the skull and desperately covering himself in his coat. Eventually, the bus arrived and all four got on with a small trowel each.

"Are you going to bury him?" the conductor laughed.

Half an hour later, as St Paul's bay, it was already dark.

"We've got a long walk," David said as they got off the bus, "There's no bus up to that part of the town."

At that moment, a tourist horse and cab came trotting along.

"Manna from Heaven!" Mark cried.

"Stop him!" David hailed him and they all got into the cab.

"The dig, please," Mark said. The old ruddy-faced horseman said nothing, looked with incredulity at Mark, shrugged, and headed off.

"Do you think he understood?" David asked, anything but convinced.

Suddenly, the old man began a commentary. "There is St Paul's island. He was shipwrecked here in AD60."

"We know," said David. "Do you know where the dig is?"

"There's St Paul's church," the man continued.

"We know. Do you know where the dig is?"

He didn't reply. "That is Bugibba. A nice seaside resort, you can go in a glass-bottomed boat."

"We know!" said Laura, exasperated.

"Hey, I don't think he can understand" Jenny suggested. "Look he's reading from a sheet of commentary notes."

"Do you know where the dig is?" David persisted.

"Quwra is a more affluent resort," he went on.

"Look, let's get off," David suggested.

"5 Liri," the man declared.

"He, at least, knows the money is due," David said, rummaging in his pocket.

They walked through the quiet streets. A youngster passing by carrying a kitten saw Mark and threw herself into a doorway. Then they were there. They came to a tall fence and a sign 'University of Valletta, St Paul's Dig, and Keep out' all displayed.

"Is it electrified?" Laura asked.

"Look, it's not the Great Escape!" David laughed.

"What's that?" Jenny asked.

"An old War film," he sighed. He hated giving away his age. It was quiet. Too quiet, David reckoned. There was no light, no apparent guard.

"We could scale the fence," Mark offered.

"Or open this little gate," Laura said gleefully. The door opened and in they trooped. David handed out the towels.

"Now what cap'n?" Jenny asked.

"Well, I'm taking off this coat for a start," Mark confirmed, throwing it to the ground.

They walked about the dig. They could see skeletons in six open graves. Some pottery and coins lay on wooden shelves all tagged.

"That's gross," said Laura peering into a grave.

Mark jumped into a vacant one and lay down.

"That's not funny" Laura said.

At that moment, they could see someone walking towards them. There was nowhere to hide. Then a dog appeared.

"We're done for," said David. "It must be a guard."

"What are you three doing here?" came a familiar voice. It was Danny.

"We're all going to a party and got lost," Laura volunteered.

"Why are you here?" David enquired.

"I wanted to see where Ariadne fell and leave a few flowers especially after your vision."

At that precise moment, the dog, Ceremony, must have smelled Mark and barked at him. Mark emerged from the grave. Danny took one look, screamed, "Oh my good God!" and ran desperately down the street with the dog scampering after him.

"I'll explain later," Mark volunteered.

"We're meant to be guided by the light but the lights haven't come on," David said disappointedly. "And I don't see any plane either."

"Why don't I switch a light on?" Laura asked.

"I was waiting for you to work that out," Mark patronised her.

Laura switched a button at the base of the floodlight and the digging area all became illuminated.

"It's all Roman stuff," David confirmed. "There's nothing from World War two unless Italian pilots flew here with swords and shields."

"The expedition has ended in failure," Jenny summed up.

"Can we get discount on four trowels?" David wondered.

"I hate to say I told you so but I still think the ghost was a Scerri creation. We've all been had," Laura declared.

"Speak for yourself!" Jenny laughed.

"The ghost was so precise," David kept repeating. "We were to be guided by the light."

"We could take our trowels and start digging," Laura offered kindly.

"And how long would it take to unearth an entire fighter aircraft?" David asked rhetorically.

"Yes I see the flaws in the proposal too," Mark laughed.

"And before you ask, I am not attempting to drive a mechanical digger," Jenny ensured.

"Okay, let's head back to the bus stance," David said with a resigned shrug. "Mark, please put your coat back on!"

"Call me a dipstick," Laura continued, "but I'm afraid I never believed this story from the start."

"Sceptic," David corrected her.

"No, I think dipstick was right the first time," Mark laughed.

David felt quite dejected as they began the walk back.

"Don't be too down," Jenny sympathised, giving him a hug. "Maybe we've interpreted the message wrong."

At that moment, the horse and carriage reappeared. All four jumped on.

"The bus stance!" Mark shouted.

"On your left is St Paul's church. It is 250 years old," the horseman began.

"Here we go again," Jenny sighed.

"So we think we interpreted it wrong," Jenny repeated as they sat in the Apartment lounge with the Captain and Theresa later that evening.

"Interpreted it wrongly," Theresa put her right.

"I'm still a cynic," said Laura.

"Sceptic," David repeated.

"Well, I don't believe it anyway," Laura reiterated, a little exasperated.

"I wouldn't worry about Danny," Theresa reassured them. "He'll build his statue, make a fortune from pilgrims and give the proceeds to Peter Scerri."

"Do you believe my story?"

"I'd believe it more if you could unravel the message," Theresa said. "Be guided by the light" she repeated to herself.

At that moment, Prof Gilchrist appeared at the bar.

"The very man," David said, leaving his seat. "I'm sorry to bother you Prof, but did they definitely find a fighter aircraft up at that dig?"

The Prof ordered a couple of lagers and looked disappointed. "I've learned they only found fragments of a wing and the area has been thoroughly searched. They've moved it to the SWW museum in Valletta and I'll go and see it tomorrow but, frankly, it is rather disappointing," he said, disconsolately.

"Have you got a ring yet?" Theresa was asking Laura.

"I hope Mark will give me one," she replied.

"I think he already did," Jenny whispered to David but he was lost in thought. Ariadne had given him a message. He just had to decipher it. All he had to go on was a wing and a prayer!

Chapter 9

"We must make this fancy dress party this evening our engagement party as well," Laura suggested as the Gozo ferry headed back serenely towards Malta late Monday afternoon. David, Mark, Jenny and Laura were all sitting in the bar with their usual supply of D and C honey and some Gozitan red wine.

"You two need to go into a Sliema jewellers and get a ring," David pointed out.

"And not a cheap one" Jenny emphasised.

"Thanks for that," Mark groaned.

"Will you two go back and live near Mark's family or yours?" Jenny asked Laura.

"We could stay here in the winter," Mark offered.

"Why don't you, Jenny?" David watched intently for her reaction.

"I'm going back to Yorkshire at the end of August," she replied emphatically.

David felt as if a dagger had been pressed into his chest. Mark and Laura looked surprised too.

"The party will be wicked tonight," Leanne declared as she passed with Lesley and Carol in tow.

David felt relieved at the change of topic. "What are you all going as?" he asked.

"I've a blue dress and red towel and so I thought I'd be Supergirl," Leanne announced.

"I'll wear a bikini and be Jordan," Carol volunteered.

"I'll look forward to that one," Mark agreed mischievously.

"And you Lesley?" Jenny asked.

"I've got a cowboy hat and mask and will be the Lone Ranger."

"The last time I saw a loan arranger, I got turned down," Laura said.

"It's a cowboy outfit," Mark explained.

"I think that bank was," Laura admitted.

Andrew was standing looking out of a porthole, leaning on one foot then the other. Jenny realised he felt out of things.

"Are you coming tonight then?" she asked cheerfully.

"Oh yes, I'll say."

"And what will you be?" Laura asked. "A nerd," she whispered.

"Carol is being Jordan," Leanne added.

"Can you be a whole country?" he asked innocently.

Everyone exchanged looks.

"I want to be cool, you see," he explained needlessly.

"You could be Chile then!" Mark suggested.

"No it's too warm here," Laura contradicted.

"I could be Ben In, Martin Ique or Dan Mark or Sam Oa," Andrew said, showing off.

"They're all rather contrived, wouldn't you say?" David pointed out. "Anyway how would you dress?"

"I'll think up something," he said, rather embarrassed at having failed to get a laugh and headed out to the deck.

The ship was approaching the harbour and David could see Tony's coach waiting at the quayside. He was disconsolate as he kept going over in his mind Jenny's abrupt comment about returning to Yorkshire.

As they all stood behind Gozo onion lorries belching their exhausts and waiting to disembark, Laura patted David on the back. "Penny for them?" she queried.

"I wonder if I would have any chance if I popped the question?" he asked.

"Gosh that's a bit sudden, isn't?" Laura gasped. "It must be catching."

"If she goes back to Yorkshire, I'll probably lose her," he explained. "And I can't have that."

The lorries moved and everyone headed along the quayside.

"Would I have a chance, Laura?"

"I just don't know," Laura replied diplomatically.

By early evening, as all four got out of their khaki uniforms and began putting on their fancy dress, David had cheered up considerably.

Jenny put on the cow girl outfit and Laura was Cat Woman. Mark, as the skeleton, laughed when he saw David as Aladdin. "One chicken flied lice!" he ordered.

"Ha Ha!" David groaned. "You are so predictable."

When they came out to the foyer, Theresa was waiting in a gown and mortar board. Her heels on the marble floor resonated like gunshots.

Then the Captain appeared resplendent in his RAF uniform. "I can still get into it after 60 years," he said proudly.

"You must have looked a fine figure of a man," Theresa said admiringly.

"Thank you," the Captain replied, looking unusually embarrassed. "I was decorated, you know," he added proudly.

"So was my Mum," Laura said.

"In a War?"

"No her bungalow."

Theresa looked up to Heaven as they all headed out to the lane past the trees which stood as sentinels in the dark, and walked along the beach to the St Julian's Hotel.

David, as Aladdin, shuffled along, Chinese panto style.

"It was a woman who had bound feet," Theresa explained to him patronisingly.

As they arrived, Leanne was waiting as Supergirl, the blue top tucked in her red pants, and Carol as Jordon and Lesley as the Lone Ranger. Mark clearly couldn't take his eyes off Carol. Laura headed off to the bar looking disconsolate. The Professor arrived back from the dig dressed in a khaki shirt and shorts, not unlike the SAY GO TOURS uniform.

"What have you come as?" David asked.

"One of our Tour guides?" Jenny suggested.

"No, just an archaeologist," the Prof apologised, rather wrongfooted.

Suddenly, everyone's attention was drawn to what appeared to be a Pantomime Dame who had so much padding she could hardly negotiate the glass entrance door.

"My God, it's Andrew!" David exclaimed with no little admiration.

"What are you?" Mark asked.

"An ugly sister," he replied proudly.

"Never a truer word!" Jenny whispered.

"Hey, are we going to get judged?" Leanne asked impatiently.

"I'll gladly do it," Prof Gilchrist offered.

At that moment, Marco arrived.

"You are superb as a Customs Officer," Leanne cooed.

"He is one," David pointed out.

By now, a large crowd had gathered and, indeed, some of Peter Scerri's tourists were among them. Mark had taken over as DJ and 'Agadoo', 'Una Paloma Blanca' and 'Macarena' were soon blasting out in the increasingly hot and sweaty room. David and the two girls kept an eye on the hotel staff putting out sausage rolls, vol-au-vents and sandwiches.

It was an hour later, that Danny arrived looking for all the world like Arthur Daley even down to the hat. He was accompanied by Carmen dressed all in black in memory of her friend, Ariadne, and with a Maltese cross chain dangling round her neck.

"Is that the iron cross for valour?" Jenny whispered in David's ear.

"What valour?" David asked.

"Being married to Danny for years," she suggested mischievously.

Danny organised his whisky and Carmen's sherry then came across with a broad smile.

"You look happy," David confirmed.

"My worries are all over," Danny explained. "Peter Scerri will take a 50/50 cut in my profit from my pilgrims coming to the statue, so we're all happy."

"That's kind," David said.

"Well I am kind too," Danny declared. "I've told Father Collina I will give my share to the local orphans."

"That's true philanthropy," Jenny agreed.

"More like paternity," David whispered.

"You all look great all dressed up," Danny said graciously, lighting a cigar.

The Captain and Theresa came across with a plate of sandwiches and chatted to Carmen.

"Did you hear Danny's a philanthropist?" Jenny asked Laura.

"Surely not after one whisky," Laura replied quizzically.

A lot of the tourists were now dancing and the atmosphere was enhanced by disco lights which flickered in time with the music. Moths turned to dancers in the spotlights.

"Who will the statue actually be of?" David asked.

"Ariadne, of course," Danny confirmed. "Her family are all delighted.

"That's lovely," David replied. "Though I am still not clear what my message was."

His attention was caught by Carol, aka Jordan, in the flimsiest bikini trying to resist the advances of an ugly sister. Leanne was in a corner snogging Marco. David tapped Jenny on the shoulder and led her out to the dance floor. The music of Girls Aloud, Natasha Bedingfield and Atomic Kitten blared out though the older contingent appealed to Mark to Play Queen, Abba, Wings or Bee Gees and, at one embarrassing moment, Danny asked loudly if Mark would play Bing Crosby.

"Must you return to Yorks?" David mouthed above the din, returning to his theme which was gnawing at him.

"Who looks a dork?" she shouted back.

"Bridlington."

She heard that okay but did not respond. She just gave David a long, loving kiss.

After a number of dances, David danced with Laura, Mark with Jenny.

Then it was time for the judging. The lights were put on and Mark handed the Prof the mike.

"1, 2, 3, and now, Ladies and Gentlemen, I will announce the results in reverse order" he began, tapping the microphone professionally.

"You must have a chance. You are a superb Aladdin," Jenny hugged him.

"Do you take laundry?" Danny laughed.

"If I was judging and I'd three prizes, I'd give Carol one," Mark said predictably.

Laura let go his hand and scowled.

"In third place the Captain as a Second World War pilot."

There was thunderous applause.

"But I am, was, a SWW pilot," the Captain protested till he looked down and saw the small bottle of whisky which Danny had donated as the prize.

"In second place ......" - there was a pause as the Prof milked the tension -"the ugly sister."

Andrew excitedly went up to the record decks where Mark handed him a bottle of Marsovin wine. He attempted to kiss Carol on the way but she turned away.

"And now ....," again the Prof paused.

"I reckon it's you!" Jenny nudged David confidently.

"Ladies and Gentlemen!"

"Get on with it!" Theresa shouted impatiently.

"The winner is ...." He paused again.

The room was now so hushed, you could hear the two fans struggling in the heat above their heads.

"The wicked witch!"

Everyone looked around.

"What wicked witch?" David asked incredulously. "I know the room is crowded but I didn't see that one."

He suddenly realised that Danny was leading Carmen out of the hall sobbing.

"Oh my sainted Aunt! He means Carmen," David groaned aghast. He waved frantically at the Prof but he didn't see David in the crowd.

Mark, however, had realised there was a commotion and whispered in the Prof's ear.

"Ladies and Gentlemen, I have a correction to make."

Again there was hush.

"The winner of the Fancy Dress is ………"

"Get on with it!" Theresa shouted from the back.

"Carol as Jordan."

"Where's her dresh?" Theresa, who'd clearly had about four sherries too many, roared again.

There was considerable applause from the males. Andrew tried again to kiss her as she passed and failed. Mark did kiss her and gave her a bottle of champagne.

"We're okay tonight!" Leanne declared triumphantly.

"Let's get going to the nightclub," Lesley suggested and the three girls left with Marco in tow.

David headed out to the car park with Jenny. "You might have won if you'd had a magic lamp," Jenny consoled him.

They met Carmen and Danny at their car. Carmen was drying her eyes.

"They are so sorry for the misunderstanding," David stressed.

"I know, I know," Danny said reassuringly. "It was just an unfortunate mistake."

"Shurely shome mistake," echoed Theresa as she joined them, "Meester Bond" she added in David's direction. Then she sat, a crumpled heap, on the tarmac.

"Why did they call me best witch?" Carmen moaned.

David was relieved she had even misheard the insult.

"I'll take you home, dear," Danny insisted and ushered her into the car.

Mark and Laura came out with the Captain and Professor and the latter apologised too.

"How the hell could you make Carol the winner, Mark, you moron?" Laura asked.

"I was thinking on my feet," Mark explained.

"I can't think on my feet," Theresa added in a gallant effort to get back up.

"She'll have quite a hangover in the morning," the Captain expertly pointed out. He gallantly picked her up and offered to take her home.

The Prof went back into his hotel and Danny drove off.

"Oh well, tomorrow is Ta Qali, Mosta, then up to Golden Bay," David reminded them.

"This Catwoman outfit is too warm. I can't wait to get out of my clothes," Laura said tantalisingly. "But you can sleep on the floor, Mark!"

"Are you too warm too?" David asked Jenny optimistically.

If the truth be told, David didn't want to take off the Aladdin costume. "I must get Steven to photograph me in it before I return it to the shop," he declared as he stood in front of his bedroom mirror.

Jenny was already out of her costume and reading a letter from home. "Did you say something?" she asked, kicking off her sandals and throwing sand all over the carpet.

"I am the genie of the lamp. Which three wishes do you want?"

"You can't be the Genie and Aladdin," she pointed out dismissively. "Don't you know your pantos?"

"I haven't got a magic lamp for you to rub," David replied putting on the electric kettle.

"I know what you asked me to rub last night and you said that was magic!" she reminded him.

"Okay, okay, you will go to the ball," David laughed.

"Wrong pantomime again," she passed him sugar cubes for the coffee.

"Ah, seeds to plant a beanstalk," he said, putting them in the mugs.

"Stop, stop," she insisted putting her hand over his mouth.

David picked up a Malta fan and waved it in front of his face. "Okay, what wishes do you want?" he repeated.

"Laura to get engaged," she replied immediately. "Scerri to have a meal in Danny's restaurant thereby endangering his life ...."

"You are entitled to a third," David reminded her.

"Every wish I make from now on to come true."

"That is cheating," he pointed out.

The coffee was ready and, finally, he got out of his costume and took off the false droopy moustache.

"Letter from home?" he asked.

"Yes, home," Jenny replied.

Not only did she not elaborate but she blushed.

David did not want to press her. They finished their coffees.

David switched the light out and unbuttoned Jenny's bra and pulled the duvet over her.

"Oh my God, I've got it!" he suddenly shouted.

"Got what? Don't stop now!" she implored in the dark.

"The message. Be guided by the light."

"You've always managed in the dark so far," she groaned.

"New lamps for old," he said, sitting up in bed.

"You haven't got a lamp."

"But I must get one," David stressed. "And I know exactly who's got the old one I need too."

"Is that it? Can we get back to what we'd started?" Jenny asked.

"I wish you'd moan more when we're doing it," David asserted.

"Okay, I hate Theresa pulling me up for grammatical errors, Danny's wages are crap and Scerri ruins our fun."

"I don't mean like that," David pointed out.

"Just put your hand here," Jenny replied, "and shut up!"

David woke to the sound of the shower across the hall. The duvet was strewn across the floor and he could see Jenny's letter jammed down the side of the bed. He pulled it out and realised immediately it wasn't Winnie's or Sarah's handwriting. He could see the E Yorkshire postmark and put it back.

Aware that Jenny was reading his diary, he decided to write in it that he too was thinking of getting engaged. By the time he had written it for the previous day, Jenny was back in the room drying her hair.

"Do tell me what the message meant," she asked as she opened the Venetian blinds.

"At Ta Qali craft village today we must get an oil lamp and this evening we will take it up to Carmen's."

"I'm not with you but I'll go along with it," Jenny concurred. "Do you think Mark and Laura will last?" she asked.

"I'd like to think so," David said, putting on his khaki uniform. "But he has a wandering eye and his parents, who've quite an influence over him, are unlikely to readily accept Laura."

"I don't see why not," Jenny said indignantly. "She is funny, attractive and has a lovely personality. Oh, and a baby."

"Yeh, and how did that happen?" David asked. He could see Jenny preparing to come out with the obvious funny reply and put his hand up to her mouth. "I keep wondering if she has tried to trap him."

"Well, if he gets a ring he must surely mean it" Jenny stressed.

All the way up to Ta Qali in the coach he kept going through in his mind whether he should pop the question and, if so, when, where and indeed, how? He was a fair bit older and maybe she would not want to be tied down.

Prof Gilchrist had gone back to the SWW museum in Valletta but the rest of the party were all on the coach. Jenny kept up an informed running commentary to his left.

"I'm glad you three aren't wearing too much," he said in the general direction of Carol, Leanne and Lesley who were sitting behind them.

"You what!" a startled Carol replied.

"I mean the huts which have the glass blowing are really hot," he rapidly explained.

"And I'll take you to Luigi's café," he said to Jenny. "There, among the bric-a-brac and jumble we will find an oil lamp. Will you want to see the football stadium?" he asked Andrew.

"Goodness, no," the Lawyer replied indignantly. "Foul working class sport."

"Sorry I asked," David sighed.

The coach pulled up at the glass-making hut and about half of the party went straight there and as many to Steven in Danny's ice cream van. David steered Jenny to Luigi's cavern.

"Gosh, it's like a church jumble sale!" Jenny gasped as she entered.

"It was an RAF dormitory 60 years ago according to the Captain," David explained, "but today Luigi has all his junk here."

"Do I hear my name being said in vain?" came a voice behind an enormous Indian elephant on the counter. "Bonjourno signorina, come esta?" he kissed Jenny's hand.

Luigi had jet black greasy hair, a determined shadowy jaw in need of a shave. He was wearing a light blue shirt, white cotton trousers, was suntanned, and had a broad smile with a twinkle in his eye. Now 45, he was probably a very handsome man about 20 years earlier. "What do you mean 'his junk'? That's defamation."

"It's only defamation if untrue," said Andrew expertly, who'd come in behind them.

"Thank you," David smiled.

"You have me there," Luigi admitted. "I think the technical term is junk. Now how can I help you?" His eyes suddenly intent.

"I need an oil lamp, the clearer and newer the better."

"I'll check my lighting dept," Luigi said helpfully.

He led them to the back of the hut and Jenny clearly believed they were being taken to a different building. Instead 'the lighting dept' was in fact a shelf along the wall with light bulbs, torches, a candelabra no less, candles and so on.

"Ah here you are: one oil lamp."

"How much?" David asked.

"Let's say 5 Liri," Luigi suggested optimistically.

"2 Liri," David replied emphatically.

"You take the food out of my kids' mouths," Luigi protested.

"You've no kids," David asserted.

"Ok 2 Liri 50 cents," Luigi finally agreed. "Grazzi talli zortna, thanks for coming", he beamed with the look of a man who clearly thought he had the better deal.

They headed out into the dazzling sunlight.

"Now we're all set for tonight" David confirmed.

That evening Jenny, and David, again dressed as Aladdin, got dropped off by Tony outside Carmen's villa. It was getting dark and the couple were amazed to find at least 6 young students weeding Danny's overgrown, untidy courtyard.

"The Chinese meals have arrived!" one shouted out.

"No, no, I am not doing deliveries," he stressed. "What are you all doing here?"

"That is confidential," another replied.

David took out his photo of him with Prof Gilchrist. "You can tell me. I've been on digs."

"In China?"

"No, here in Malta."

"Okay, I suppose it is okay to tell you," the student conceded, handing it back. "The owner was digging here in the courtyard and found some Roman coins and pottery identical to our dig down by the harbour."

"That's truly remarkable," David replied with a grin.

"Identical?" Jenny echoed.

"Yes, and we've never found any Roman stuff up here. Hardly surprising as it was a dense inhospitable forest 2000 years ago," the student continued.

"Well, jolly good luck!" David beamed. "you will need it," he muttered under his breath!

The butler opened the door.

"What a scam!" David admitted.

"May I help?" the butler asked.

"Can I see Carmen, please?"

The butler beckoned them into the wooden-panelled hall impressively lined with old leather books, which echoed with its emptiness. There was still a gap on the wall where the Rossini had been.

Carmen arrived drying her hands on a tea towel. "How can I help you, David?"

"I'm hoping you can you give me a light," he said, raising his voice.

"I don't smoke."

"I'll elaborate. Here I have a new lamp, what can you give me for it?"

Carmen took if off him and looked at it closely, "About 2 liri."

"I mean another light."

"David, are you delivering Chinese meals? Doesn't Danny pay you enough?"

"I am doing new lamps for old like in a Panto."

Carmen headed off and returned with an old desk light.

"I was thinking more in terms of a torch. Have you an old torch?" She headed off again.

"Why on earth do you want that?" Jenny asked.

"Wait and see. I have a theory."

After much loud rummaging upstairs, she returned again. "Is this any use?"

She was holding the Old Italian rusted torch. "It doesn't work you know. I've had it for years, it's useless."

David swapped the two.

"I'm surprised you want the old thing," she admitted.

"That's what folk say to Danny," David whispered to Jenny. "I must dash" he said. He didn't want Carmen to change her mind. "Thank you so much."

Jenny and David flopped in the back seat of Tony's car. David felt really smug.

"What is this all about?" Jenny asked intrigued.

"I don't even have to look inside the torch," he smirked.

"You mean...?"

"Yes, there will be a gold bar."

Jenny playfully dragged it off him, they both took turns to unscrew it and out came something wrapped in an old rag. They dragged it off and there in their hands was one shiny gold bar.

"Oh my God!" Jenny shrieked.

"No hanky panky in the back seat," Tony demanded, misinterpreting the euphoria.

"I've got something long and hard in my hands," Jenny told him.

"And it's pure gold!" David elaborated.

"I'm sure I don't want to know," Tony confirmed.

"It really is a gold bar!" David exclaimed. "We're saved. The church will agree it was a miracle. Danny can pay for his statue, pay off Peter and, more importantly, we all stay in a job."

"Amen to that," Tony agreed.

"I hope Danny appreciates all we've done," Jenny stated. "It strikes me that we're the ones who've bent over backwards to save him."

"Laura certainly has!" David agreed. "We must tell Father Collina we have a miracle too. We solved the ghost's riddle and followed the light."

And now I need another miracle, David reckoned.

If he was going to pop the question, the cruise to Comino and the Blue Lagoon was, surely, the best time. It was the highlight of the week's tours, a day of relaxation when the Captain Morgan crew did the commentary and all they had to do, really, was not lose anyone.

As he counted everyone on board at the quayside at Sliema Creek he could see Marco passing by on his scooter and hailed him. Marco, in his customs official uniform, was clearly driving to work.

"I need your expert advice," David began, buttering him up.

"Okay it is this," Marco replied unprompted. "Don't date more than one girl at the same time, never have a threesome and use Durex on every conceivable occasion."

"Have you quite finished?" David butted in. "I have a Gold bar."

"Well keep it in a fridge. It will melt in this weather, my friend. Is it for Jenny?"

"No I have a real Gold bar. A Gold bar," he repeated. "Capisce?"

He went on to explain the story, always mindful that the crew were preparing to cast off.

"Look, I must stop you there," Marco said suddenly, looking more serious. "I mean you'd be stopped if you try to smuggle it out of the country. You cannot sell it either. It is treasure trove. You do not own it."

"But it will help the church orphans and help Danny," David said desperately.

"Danny will be all right provided Father Collina endorses him," Marco assured him. "He's away to get a statue from Luigi's cave and has already put details of the ghost on the internet because I found it last night."

"I thought he was getting a statue of Ariadne," David protested.

"Luigi had some spare statues at about 10%, the cost of getting a sculptor to do one. Ask yourself which Danny would choose. But in the mean time, hand the gold over, David!"

A despondent David rejoined Jenny, Mark and Laura on the seats at the stern of the ship. The red-hulled craft headed out of the creek and he watched Marco zig-zagging through a traffic jam along the seafront.

"The ghost must have wanted you to have the Gold bar," Mark said reassuringly.

"Well, that's what I believed," David readily agreed. "Marco is right though. Our jobs are safe. Danny will make a fortune from the pilgrims, and Scerri is off our backs."

Jenny was hardly paying attention. She had another letter from home and was giving it her full attention.

"I'd suggest you offer it to Peter Scerri," Laura said. "You won't have to ask what happens to it and you'll get a fortune."

David went up to the bar and got two lagers and two cokes. Andrew was trying to chat up Leanne, Carol and Lesley but clearly failing. Prof Gilchrist looked thoroughly fed up as he read a day-old paper.

David had thought of popping the question at the Blue Lagoon, but Jenny seemed distracted. Maybe he would leave it for now, he concluded.

He glanced at the back page. 'Rangers fan found nearly strangled by a Celtic jersey in Larkhall!' a headline read.

"Oh it couldn't be!" he groaned.

Once the Captain Morgan anchored at the Blue Lagoon, the crew served the usual buffet meal.

David chose chicken legs, egg, tomato, lettuce, chips and coleslaw along with Maltese crusted bread. He found himself choosing his glass of wine with Andrew.

"Can I tax your legal mind?" he asked flatteringly.

"Fire away," he replied pleasantly.

"If you dig up an historical item of real monetary value, does it belong to the State?"

"Back home it would, and I can't see here being any different. Why? What have you found?"

"Oh, just Roman coins," David lied and rejoined the other couriers.

Prof Gilchrist was reading a paperback as he ate lunch. "Do you like Kipling?" he asked.

"I've never kipled," Laura replied.

"As I see it, there is no choice but to hand it over to the police," David returned to his theme.

"It's a great pity. We'd be mega rich," Mark pointed out.

"Did you ask Jenny that question you were going to ask?" Laura asked provocatively.

"And what question was that, then?" Jenny butted in.

"I forgot to ask her to take our costumes back tomorrow," David replied quickly and threw Laura a glance.

"I'll come with you," Laura offered. "We are going anyway to choose a ring."

"Are we?" Mark asked with no great enthusiasm.

"You can help me choose," Laura said pointedly to Jenny.

Some of the tourists were jumping straight into the lagoon after lunch rather than clambering along some jagged rocks to the beach. A roar went up as Leanne jumped in and her bikini top fell off in an almighty splash. Two crew members dived in to help her hide her embarrassment!

David and Jenny walked hand in hand along the rocks where they had met only a few weeks earlier. As usual, the boats selling ice cream and drinks were both moored in the lagoon. As they carefully picked their way along the jagged rocks, they stopped to look at the different rock pools full of crabs and fish.

The main beach area was already mobbed. David could see Mark and Laura floating on the lilo past the Captain Morgan. Leanne, Carol and Lesley were splashing each other and simultaneously annoying everyone around them. Prof Gilchrist had got himself a cool lager to enhance his reading enjoyment. Andrew looked a forlorn figure sitting alone on one of the rocks. He'd put on a snorkel and flippers.

"They've landed!" Jenny laughed. She lay down on a flat piece of rock and David rubbed on the sun bloc. He left some 7-Ups cooling at the water's edge where the blue sea frothed to the shore, and then took off his khaki uniform As usual, he was already wearing his swimming trunks. Jenny again was reading her letter from home.

"Can I ask you something?" he asked.

"Fire away," Jenny replied, putting the letter back in the envelope.

"You didn't seem very keen to stay here once the season ends. I thought you loved it here." What he actually meant was he thought she loved him here.

"I do"

"But not enough to stay," he pointed out.

"I could come back at the end of May next year."

"But that's a long time without me."

"You could come to Yorkshire."

"Oh yes. Cold, frost, snow, sleet, wind"

"You wouldn't have to go out in it, much. Anyway what enjoyment do you get painting boats?"

"I was hoping you would stay," David repeated seriously. "I love you."

There was a long pause. A shout went up from Mark and Laura as someone toppled their lilo.

"I love you too," Jenny responded, unprompted.

David wondered if now was the moment to ask.

"But there is someone else." No, it wasn't the moment to ask even if he could detect her ill concealed grin.

"Who?"

"Gerry"

"Gerry who?"

"You don't know him. A young policeman I got off with while watching one of Sarah's matches a year ago."

"Where's he live?"

"Letsby Avenue"

"Is he in the police now?"

"He's doing a summer job painting motorway lanes. It's well paid. He's going to university and hopes to do politics."

"What are his views?"

"Middle of the road," she replied. "It's his letter I was reading."

"Oh," David said, hardly able to conceal his concern.

"The problem is he's not that reliable. He's always changing jobs. He was a booking agent for Virgin but it didn't last long either."

"Why not?"

"Virgin trains rarely go all the way."

"So what's Gerry saying in his letter?"

"He says it's been so long."

"He shouldn't boast."

"He's been watching old films about Steve Irwin in Queensland and wondered about emigrating."

"Do you like men with large crocs?"

Jenny had to turn away. She was clearly about to get a fit of the giggles.

"There isn't a Gerry, is there?" David inferred.

"There is a Geri and this is their letter," she said holding it up, "but she's my female cousin."

"Thank heavens for that!" David gulped, "I thought you were winding me up."

He paused. In for a penny, in for a pound, he decided. The mood was right. He rubbed more sun bloc on her back and sat at right angles so their eyes could not meet.

"I want to ask you a serious question," he emphasised.

"About what?"

"Engagement, what do you think?"

That's not how I meant to phrase it, he groaned inwardly. Mark and Laura gave a wave as they came out of the water and towelled themselves down a few metres away.

"Okay. I'll be serious. Is this in confidence?"

"Well of course," David replied, rather surprised.

"I think a couple has to be compatible, have the same interests, be roughly the same age, they should talk about career and baby desires, be about the same intelligence, want to be in the same place, be sufficiently mature, and so on."

"You've really thought it out," David replied with no little admiration. "So what do you think?" he asked. This is it, he knew. He was still subconsciously putting far too much cream on her back.

"Well, I've my doubts, if I am being honest."

David's heart sank.

"Mark has eyes for too many females and doesn't look set to settle down and would his family accept Laura? I don't deny that Laura loves him. That's blatantly obvious to all of us. Anyway I'll go with her and choose the ring and keep my concerns to myself."

David moved around and sat directly in front of her, his sunspecs hiding his expression to some extent. He took a deep breath.

"I meant you and me," he said. There. He had said it! He could feel his heart miss a beat.

"You and me go and choose their ring?"

"No Jenny, you and me choose OUR ring." He swallowed hard.

There was a desperately long pause. Jenny looked stunned.

"Hey, it's time we headed back to the boat," Laura said, kicking some sand at David.

"Come on, uniforms back on," Mark demanded.

"Yes!" Jenny suddenly exclaimed. "Yes, yes!"

"Yes?" David echoed in a mixture of surprise and relief.

They began jumping up and down arm in arm.

"Going back isn't usually so exciting," Mark said in puzzlement.

"We're engaged!" Jenny shrieked.

"Oh my God!" Laura shouted as she and Mark joined in what had become a veritable rugby scrum.

"I've read this sentence four times," Prof Gilchrist said, reluctantly putting down his book. "What's all the excitement?"

"I am engaged, I am engaged!" Jenny could only shout breathlessly.

As the Captain Morgan steamed back to Sliema, all four couriers lay on their towels sunbathing in the mid-afternoon sunshine.

David had never felt so happy. He had already texted home to friends and family as had Jenny. At five minute intervals, happy texts were being returned. A steward came round with a choice of baguettes.

"If Laura and I stay on the island outwith the season, we'll have no real money," Jenny pointed out.

"We're all forgetting we have the gold bar," Mark reminded them.

David shook his head and was going to reply it would be illegal to sell it, but Laura cut him short with a smile and a half-raised hand.

"And your God led us to it. Obviously it was a miracle," she stressed with more than a little scepticism in her voice.

"We can get it out of the island by bribing Marco at customs," Jenny added.

"He'd never agree to an illegal act," David stressed. "He'd lose his job."

"I suggest we see Peter Scerri. He has contacts and we could pay him commission and not even miss it," Laura suggested.

There was a silence only broken by the Captain Morgan tour guide pointing out they were passing St Paul's Bay.

"Let's sleep on it," Mark advised.

"Tomorrow is Thursday and we'll have all the fun of choosing our rings," Jenny said.

"And think what sort of ring we could afford with money from the gold bar," Laura reminded them mischievously.

David chose the baguettes and took a walk along to the side of the ship. The four of them stood on the verge of a fortune but how could that Ghost's message, if it were indeed a ghost, have led them to an immoral act?

The ship turned into Sliema creek and thoughts of the gold bar evaporated as they reverted to their duty of returning their party to the hotels.

The following morning, the gorgeous sunshine penetrated the very stones of Valletta as the two happy couples headed along Republic St to

Winski, the Polish Jewellers. Out on the pavements, as usual, small clusters of Maltese sat eating cheese pies with their morning coffee.

As they passed the café hedonists, David and Jenny realised that the jewellers was situated beside that bookshop and that painting! David didn't want to look at it but he knew he would. He knew Jenny would too. They stared at the main picture in the front window.

"It is so lovely, so wonderful," Jenny confirmed.

"Yes," David replied, deep in thought.

Jenny gripped his hand tightly. Mark and Laura were at the ice cream parlour across the street choosing tutti frutti ice creams. "I can't look at that other horrible one in the side window," she stressed.

"Nor can I," David confirmed. "And that has made my mind up. We turn that gold bar over to the authorities."

They all went into the Jewellers in a narrow, cool, dark little shop where the dapper Mr Winski was standing grandly in his suit behind a counter, a watch maker's eyeglass on his face.

"Jean dobreh. How can I help today?" he asked politely.

"We're all engaged," Laura blurted out excitedly. "We'd like to see your rings."

"What sort of price range?" the Pole asked diplomatically.

"Under 200 liri," Mark insisted. "£400," he explained to Jenny.

Mr Winski returned with a tray with 25 rings, five in groups of five.

"Oh wow!" Laura exclaimed. "I want the cluster one!"

"I love the solitaire," Jenny said, trying it on.

"They're 180 LM and 190 LM," Mr Winski checked needlessly.

The girls' attention turned to some trays behind a glass cabinet.

"What do they cost?" Laura enquired.

"They start at 1000 liri," Mr Winski said.

"Do you deal in pure gold?" Mark asked.

"Don't," David said sternly.

"I am not sure I understand," Mr Winski said quizzically.

"If I had an item of pure gold, could we sell it to you?"

"Well, yes," Mr Winski said. "It's a most unusual request. No teeth though!" he emphasised.

"I'll get back to you," Mark concluded, mindful of David's expression.

As the coach drove off that evening with the latest tour party to be deposited at Luqa airport, David was aware his excitement at being engaged had been diluted by his concern that Mark might tell Mr Winski about the gold bar and, if he didn't, Laura could inform Peter Scerri.

As usual, the group handed the couriers generous tips as they got off at the coach park. Leanne, Carol and Lesley admired the two engagement rings. Mark kissed all three goodbye. David commiserated with the Professor that there hadn't been an intact Italian fighter aircraft. Andrew stood alone in the baggage queue.

"I wonder what characters we'll get this time," David said out loud.

He didn't have long to wait. The first character at the carousel was an enormous Scotsman with a beer belly.

"I am a pal of Billy King. Call me Gregor," he said.

"They didn't really try to strangle him?" David asked concerned.

"Naw, he got plastered. He wiz lying pissed outside the Rangers pub on Friday night but he was too heavy to lift."

"So what happened?" David asked.

"We took off the Celtic top and dressed him in female clothing. It was less embarrassing."

Gregor headed off to the coach with an ancient blue suitcase which had clearly accompanied him to Rangers UEFA Cup ties.

"We've got an American!" Mark announced.

"I am Hank from Buffalo," a man about 50 with a large hat, sunspecs, loud red shirt and large cigar, introduced himself. "Do you know Buffalo?" he asked.

"The animal?" David suggested.

"It's a City near Canada. I'm touring the Med'. I'm a writer."

"Pleased to meet you," David said honestly, well aware Americans paid the most generous tips.

Jenny was standing marking off names on her clipboard. "Getting engaged to you means I can't marry any of the England players Sarah has introduced me to," she moaned, still glancing furtively at her ring.

"Would you want to"?

"Well they get on top early on and tend to come second," she explained.

"We're Catherine and Ashlie," said two young, dark-haired, long-legged females who'd seen Laura holding up her 'SAY GO TOURS' sign.

"Have you a list of all the hot spots?"

"I'll see what I can do," Laura replied helpfully.

"Okay, time to head out to the coaches!" Mark shouted above the din of a loudspeaker announcement and a plane landing.

"Have you met Sacha?" Mark asked. David saw the look on Jenny's and Laura's faces. Sacha was French, 25 or so, suntanned, handsome, had a white open shirt and light blue trousers.

"Bonsoir Mesdemoiselles," he said and kissed the girls' hands romantically.

Give me strength, David thought. "This is my fiancée" he muttered defensively.

8 am the following morning, David was disentangling toast from the jammed toaster in the apartment kitchen. Outside the sea shimmered with the promise of a hot day.

"You have to put six slices in at one go," he explained, patiently again, to Jenny who was making the coffee, "or it doesn't bounce up."

"And then it catches fire," Laura added defiantly as she ate her FTIRA crispy roll.

A large lorry pulled up outside with a loud squeal of brakes and they could hear a small crowd gathering.

Sacha appeared unannounced in the kitchen.

"I am sorry but these rooms are for staff only" Mark explained.

"J'ai faim," he explained.

"He has a wife," Mark translated helpfully.

"I think you'll find he is hungry," said Theresa, who'd appeared behind him. "He has paid for accommodation but not meals. I'm a Francophile."

"She'd better not say that publicly," Laura whispered. "Folk will stone her house!"

"What's happening outside?" Mark asked, quickly changing the subject and craning his neck to peer out of the window.

"Luigi's cavern lorry has brought a choice of three statues. You couldn't make it up," Theresa groaned.

"Eet iez an errection formidable," Sacha suggested.

"They are not erected yet and they can't be," Theresa demanded.

"Are they all of Ariadne?" Jenny asked naively.

"Are you kidding?" Theresa replied. "It's one of Danny's scams."

They all headed out blinking into the glaring sun, the pavement radiating the day's heat and their flip-flops feeling fit to melt.

Danny had arrived in his BMW. The Captain was chatting to Luigi.

"So which one do you want?" Luigi asked. They're all at huge discount. I am crippling myself offering these," he said, not entirely convincingly.

David looked up. One was of, seemingly, a girl, in full armour wielding a sword. The second was of a man in medieval clothes pointing into the distance and, apparently poking the eye out of the third, a plump elderly regal woman.

"A child of ten could tell you who they are of," Theresa said patronisingly.

"Fetch me a child of ten," David whispered to Jenny.

"The man pointing is Christopher Columbus."

"We could use that one and have it pointing at St Paul's Bay appropriately," Danny said, optimistically.

"Ariadne didn't have a moustache, you silly man," Theresa moaned.

"How about the girl in armour?" Luigi suggested.

"It's Joan of Arc," Theresa added.

"Clothed in the armour of righteousness," Danny thought out loud, rubbing his chin.

"Hey it's the Queen Mum!" Jenny suddenly realised.

"It would be disrespectful," Theresa insisted.

"Okay, we go for Joan of Arc and, once funds come in, I guarantee I'll get a real statue of Ariadne sculpted. Now I've a plaque to show you all! It was made specially in memory of Ariadne," he stressed.

Everyone got into a huddle around Danny in eager anticipation.

He took it, wrapped in a towel, from the footwell, and flamboyantly unveiled it. David looked in complete incredulity.

"Ariadne 1934 – 2004," it read. "Goon, but not forgotten."

He could see the look of horror on the Captain and Theresa's faces. They were about to make the obvious comment when Danny opened his back door and a frail old grey-haired gentleman in a black suit with respectful black tie had to be helped out.

"I just know this will be her husband," David confessed to Jenny. "The nightmare just gets worse."

The old man held up his hands but not in horror. A broad smile lit up his face and he chuckled heartily. "My Ariadne, she loved the Goons. All those evenings we sat in the 1950s listening to the BBC World service – however did you know, Danny? I am a happy, happy man."

He stumbled back into the back seat and Danny drove him off.

"Don't tell me that's our miracle!" Laura demanded.

"Time for our trip to Mellieha and Bugibba," David said, bewildered.

"Can I have some toast?" Sacha asked.

"Would you object if I nipped into Valletta with Laura to get my ring enlarged?" Jenny asked, "It's too tight."

"Not at all," David agreed. "I've done this trip umpteen times and Mark and Theresa will be there too."

Luigi began to pull the Joan of Arc statue down from the truck.

As David lay on the Mellieha beach, watching the youngsters on the banana boat, Hank and Gregor joined him.

"That statue is awesome, man," the American gushed. "And I hear there's talk of a miracle. Your courier pal, Mark, told me."

"Sadly our miracles have been as useful as a 3-pin plug in Malta. Useless," David said.

"Or as useless as Celtic in Europe," Gregor suggested.

"Until our local Priest gives us a nod of approval, we're at a bit of a loss," David explained.

"I'll still put it in my book about the Med," the American kindly offered. "What do you write about?" David asked.

"I review American autobiographies usually. I've just read Clinton. I thought Monica Lewinsky would get a whole chapter, but he only gave her five inches."

"I think Monica was badly misunderstood," David conjectured.

"How do you mean?" asked Hank.

"I think she was simply deaf. When she entered the Oval Office, Clinton had said sack my cook."

"That's a clever gag. I'll use that one," Hank smiled.

"I've got one!" Gregor butted in. "How is Martin O'Neill different from a jet engine? A jet engine eventually stops whining."

Their brief joke telling session suddenly ceased, as Ashlie came down the steps at the back of the beach, red faced and breathless. "I've lost Cath!" she exclaimed.

"Where was she last?" David asked calmly. "She can't have gone far."

"We went to walk around those cactus gardens across the road from the beach and it was like a maze. I've called for her but no luck."

"I'll go and look," David offered.

"I'll stay on the sidewalk in case she returns," Hank volunteered.

Mark was on the banana boat, so David left a text.

Ashlie, Gregor and David set off through the gardens between the palms, red hibiscus, spiky agaves and spiky burgainvillea, and took different paths along the honey-coloured paving stones.

David had only looked for five minutes or so when he saw a dark-haired stunner in a light blue skirt and low cut matching top staring at a prickly pear. He went up behind her, quietly put his hands across her eyes and said "Guess who?"

"Well hello big boy," came the reply.

He knew the voice instantly. It was Carmella, she of the Scerri football team. "I didn't know you cared. Do you like my new courier's uniform?"

"Very impressive, Carmella, but I'm trying to find a girl."

"You shouldn't have a problem," she said flatteringly. "I offered an arrangement in that football match and you turned it down and hey, you lost anyway remember?"

David tried to mouth "Yes" but she continued.

"Anyway, you are the very person. I'd like to meet with you at Peter's disco this evening and I will offer a deal that will end all the animosity between Peter's business and Danny's."

David began to mull over what could be getting offered when she suddenly put a hand behind his head and kissed him on the lips. He knew he was mad to respond but Carmella was a bronzed stunner and a solid wave of the smell of her perfume had now wafted over him. He was turned on and she felt it. She opened her mouth, he responded on automatic pilot.

"I've found Cath!" Ashlie shouted as they came along the path.

Carmella and David disengaged.

"I don't want to cast nasturtiums but were you really trying?" Ashlie asked.

"Oh yes, he was," Carmella assured her.

"I thought Carmella was you," David explained to Cath.

"So you stopped and snogged her," Cath said incredulously.

"I'll see you later. I'll text you," Carmella said seductively. "That was only the first course," she explained tantalisingly.

David sat, rather subdued, in the coach heading back to St Julian's. He had only been engaged for a day and he had already betrayed Jenny. In all his years in Malta, such an opportunity had never arisen. Carmella was very fanciable but he had always felt she was out of his league.

"I've had to pay for a snack of Imqaret fried pastries with date, then Granita Ice cream for Sacha," Theresa said, grudgingly sitting down beside him. "He seems to have very little money for his holiday," she said, concern in her voice.

But David's mind was elsewhere. Carmella had asked to see him later and offered peace between the two companies. It didn't take long to convince himself it was his duty, surely, to meet her and hear what she had to say.

Theresa headed off to rejoin the Captain. Mark replaced her in the front seat.

"Cath and Ashlie have told me, in strictest confidence mind, you were snogging some female in the Mellieha gardens."

"That's all I need!" David groaned putting his head in his hands.

"But they told me in confidence," Mark repeated.

"They were meant to tell no one," David insisted. "If they've told you, who else have they told?"

"Och I willnae let oan," Gregor said reassuringly behind him.

"Gee, you have my silence, man," said Hank.

"Mais oui, moi aussi," Sacha joined him diagonally opposite.

"This is some sort of hellish nightmare," David concluded.

"Who was it?" Mark asked.

"Carmella"

"Lucky you" said Mark admiringly.

"Ditto. Ding dong!" the Captain echoed.

"Dotty," Theresa opined.

Even when the coach returned, and Mark and David caught up with Laura and Jenny, sitting on the wall staring at the Joan of Arc statue, and Jenny excitedly showed off her ring, he couldn't take his mind off seeing Carmella again. He had to buy her silence and find out what the deal was Scerri offered. He would ask Mark to accompany him and he could not be led astray however hot she was. His mind was made up.

They took a bus along to Scerri's nightclub on Sliema seafront at 8 pm. Laura was working on the snooker tables and Jenny was content to anticipate phone calls from Winnie and Sarah.

"I'm going to be happier when I've told my olds I've got engaged," Mark admitted. "I'm an only child and they always fear I'll not return" he explained. "They always say that they will let go, but parents never do. Who was it who said that at a Xmas dinner table you are the child you once were?"

"That's very profound," David said, glancing at his watch and not wanting to get distracted.

"They see me as their future, not in the genetic sense, but in an emotional one too. My Dad, in particular, sees me as his main friend."

"And won't they accept Laura?"

Mark gave him a knowing look. "A Church of England Minister will really take to a nightclub stripper."

"One with a heart of gold though," David reminded him.

"And talking of gold, let's get Scerri on side. He could sell the damn thing."

"Let's see what Carmella has to say first," David insisted. He still felt distinctly uncomfortable about it.

They got out of the ancient bus outside Scerri's nightclub near the Sliema suburb of Ta Xbiex, not far from various western embassies. A large crowd of young people queued patiently in a long crocodile which meandered around the block in the darkness and down to the yachting marina.

At the doors stood, ominously, Chopper and Cruncher, looking as menacing as ever. David was filled with dread but was determined that no facial expression would betray that emotion.

As they approached, David was relieved to see Carmella looking stunning in a fashionable yellow low cut top, light blue skirt and bare midriff, waiting for him in the Gallerija or balcony above. She gave him a friendly wave. "I'm coming down," she mouthed. As they reached the door, the two bouncers parted like the Red Sea. They were in! They were met by a wall of sound and a heaving mass of youngsters all engaged in the serious business of getting off with someone. The 'Ketchup Song' was blaring out.

"I'll just go and get a drink. Just look at these babes!" Mark enthused.

Carmella took David's hand.

"You don't need Mark. We've things to discuss. You can give me something I need!"

She led him up to the bar. It was mobbed but she clicked her fingers and, impressively a steward immediately attended to her. David chose his usual bacardi and coke, Carmella had one of those drinks with a dainty pink umbrella in it.

To David's utter amazement, Gregor, looking the worse for wear, passed by, conspicuous by his age, and open-necked shirt with a ludicrous medallion. "Lead us tae ra burdzz," he announced in passing.

"Come to my room," Carmella said seductively and David was led out of the dance area, up a narrow winding marble stair to a room which was clearly hers as there was a name plate with 'Carmella' on the door. They went into a cosy, warm, little bedroom lit up by a pink light bulb. A large teddy sat on a single bed. Along the walls were photos of Carmella with Leonardo di Caprio, David Beckham, Robbie Williams, Ryan Giggs and Brad Pitt.

"You've been to Steven's photographic lab, I see," David smiled knowingly as he sat on the bed beside her.

"You guessed," she replied kicking off her sandals. "I did see Brad though."

"Really?"

"When he filmed 'Troy' he had a small part."

"So I hear."

The room had a wardrobe, desk and light, chest of drawers and a WHB. His eyes were becoming adjusted to the light. The desk top seemed to have every perfume and deodorant. The room smelt like a brothel but he didn't point that out. She poured a glass of marsovin but didn't take one herself. "I'm on duty," she explained.

"Now," said Carmella, unbuttoning David's shirt. "Do you know what I want, David? Can you guess?"

"You want to make wild passionate love, full of torrid lust, to kiss me all over and leave me panting and crying out for more," he guessed.

"No," she replied firmly. "But you have something long and hard which I do want and it's been hidden too long, hasn't it, David?"

His shirt was now off and their lips touched. He could feel his heart racing as it had earlier to his shame at Mellieha gardens. He felt a bit drowsy too but it wasn't so late. "It's a treasure and it's not for you."

"That's a bit boastful, David. I am surprised at you."

"I want everyone to enjoy it."

"David, what are we discussing?" she asked perplexed.

"You know I've got the gold bar, don't you?"

Carmella smiled. "Laura told us. Anyway, Peter can place it for you and give you a generous cut 10%."

"I am not discussing it." He paused. "Anyway 20% at least. No, no." he felt himself nodding off. That bed looked so welcoming. "I must return it!"

"No matter," said Carmella. "No hard feelings. Bring your girlfriend to the Dragonorara Casino tomorrow evening and you will be Peter's guest."

At 11 pm David woke up. The room was empty. His head throbbed to the beat of the disco below. He dashed down the stairs two at a time and ran out of the club to the bus stop. He was lucky. Marco was passing on his scooter and drove him back to the apartments. He still felt groggy. Had Carmella slipped something in his drink?

The following day, Jenny and David took his group with Theresa into Valletta. As the group had their Grand Harbour cruise or toured the Co-Cathedral, Jenny and David made a bee line for their favourite café al fresco. They had the usual cappuccinos and pastizzis. He still felt drowsy, though.

They watched tourists relishing being splashed by cold water at the Triton fountain, at the island's main bus terminus, with its fish-tailed figures bearing aloft a shallow bowl which sent the water cascading down.

"Do I have to dress for the casino?" Jenny asked excitedly, throwing a piece of cheese and pastry towards a flock of pigeons.

"I'd imagine so. It should be a great night even if we are Scerri's guests."

It should be, he reflected. Presumably Carmella was not going to spill the beans about that kiss, or would she? Was he walking into a trap?

"Can I have a - how do you say? - a cheese pie," came a familiar French voice.

Jenny rummaged in her purse and called to a waiter to serve Sacha. David could see her admiring his physique. So I can still look in the window even if I don't go in, he decided.

Suddenly they could hear Theresa's educated voice telling the party that the flat roofs and domes of Valletta were a reminder of the Arabic influence. "I've had them at the Upper Baracca Gardens and showed the men the statues of former prime ministers and the women the kerbed flower beds," she recounted. Theresa was always blissfully unaware of her politically incorrect sexist attitudes. Some Ghanejja, folk singers, entertained us too and showed us a Miltkja, country dance. There was a fleet-fingered accordian player and the guitarist's fingers flew as they plucked their strings," she enthused. "they're really enjoying themselves though some almost keeled over in the heat and we were glad to get into the cool of the cathedral."

The American scraped a metal chair along the paving stones. "Gee, the Cathedral was awesome!" Hank shouted as he sat opposite. "We've nothing like it in Buffalo."

"Too many Pape statues!" Gregor moaned, as he passed by with a cold lager. "There was some excitement too. The Police were there taking statements."

"Why?" David asked.

"Some statues were stolen a day or two ago."

It's got to be a coincidence, David hoped, as Jenny gave him a knowing look.

Chapter 10

At the age of 30, you don't easily get excited about anything, but David walked along to the casino in eager anticipation. At night it was always floodlit and he could see it jutting out across the bay from St Julian's, like Atlantis emerging from the sea. Now Jenny and he were outside, weaving their way among the Mercedes, BMWs and Jags. He felt uncomfortable in the pinstriped suit, white shirt and bow tie which the Captain had kindly lent him. The Captain was a good six inches smaller and David was well aware his trousers were at half mast. They appreciated the slight breeze which made the red and white Maltese flags and blue EU flag flutter slightly.

Carmella was standing at the entrance in a similar business-like pinstripe wearing a broad smile. "Do come in. Good evening. You must be Jenny," she gushed, offering her hand. "I am Carmella."

Jenny shook hands without great enthusiasm and followed David in.

As they walked past the gaming tables, past people playing roulette and card games, David was aware that Jenny seemed rather subdued. With the women wearing mainly evening gowns, she rather stood out in a yellow top and skirt.

Carmella ordered the drinks. "We often get celebs here," she boasted. "We've had Sir Alex Ferguson and Man Utd, Brad Pitt, Robin Williams and even Jermaine Defoe."

"The author of Robinson Crusoe?"

"A footballer, Jenny," David corrected her.

"We recently had Vladimir Putin. He's an asthmatic, you know. We called him Vlad the inhaler," Carmella added her clearly well-worn joke. "Now I am going to give you your chips."

"We've just eaten," Jenny pointed out.

"To play the games," Carmella patiently explained. "Faites vos jeux!" rang out at the roulette wheels.

"Finish your drink Jenny. David, can you come outside with me?"

David followed her, intrigued, out to a cactus garden at the side of the casino. Clutching his bacardi, the ice cubes clanging in the glass, he suddenly realised they were not alone. His heart pounded. Surely it couldn't be Chopper or Cruncher? It was Sacha. David tried hard not to show his relief.

"Bonsoir Monsieur. Eet eez a plaisir to meet you encore," he said.

"Sacha came to the island to be a trainee croupier," Carmella explained.

"What did you do in France?" David asked.

"I worked in wines, monsieur, but it was, how you say, ennuyant."

"Boring?" David ventured.

"The people, they say, Sacha distil theez and Sacha distil that, so I pack eet een and venez here." With that, Sacha smiled and headed back to the entrance.

"He's so gorgeous," Carmella cooed.

Thanks for that, David kept to himself.

Carmella rummaged in her pocket and pulled out a photo. "David, you are a nice person and I am sorry about this." She put it in his hand.

David looked at it aghast. It showed Carmella and himself lying on the bed in her room the previous evening. "Oh my God, you've trapped me!" he groaned. "Anyone can see it is a staged photo," he said, more in hope than expectation.

"I've not trapped you," she insisted. "Yes, it's one of Steven's trick photos but I wanted to see you alone to warn you."

"Warn me about what?" he asked incredulously.

"Peter will threaten to show the photo to Jenny unless you do a deal on that gold bar. He'll give you a fortune, you realise that, don't you?"

"So why have you tipped me off?"

"To warn your fiancée about the photo, then it will lessen its impact and I'll back you up."

"Was I drugged yesterday evening?" he asked.

"Not by me," Carmella assured him, "but you did fall off very easily despite my charms," she smiled. "Good luck, David!"

She looked at his trousers. "Has someone died?" she asked.

David and Carmella headed back to the gaming tables and he was surprised to see Mrs Dyson in charge of the roulette wheel.

"Your Saturday evening job?" he asked rhetorically.

"You've got it in one" she confirmed.

Jenny appeared to have cheered up considerably. "I've got five chips," she explained. "That kind Peter Scerri gave me them."

"I'll tell you a story before we play," David insisted and led her near the bar. At first Jenny looked horrified but David pointed out Steven's familiar photographic studio mark on the back of the photo.

Then Carmella returned. "I am glad you are reasonable, Jenny. Peter wants that gold bar. Be careful. He will stop at nothing." With that she went back to Sacha's card table.

"How do we play this?" Jenny asked.

"Put a chip on red or black," David suggested. She put one on black.

"Noir," said Mrs Dyson.

"You've won!" David beamed as she got two chips back. "I'll put these two on red," Jenny smiled.

"Rouge," said Mrs Dyson.

"You've won another two," David confirmed.

"I'll put five on," Jenny decided. "Black"

"C'est noir," Mrs Dyson said.

"That's another five!" Jenny shrieked as they were placed in front of her.

They had another couple of drinks and Jenny kept playing with her now thirteen chips. "Do you realise we've got 130 Liri here?" she asked.

"Are you having a lot of fun?" Peter Scerri asked in passing.

"Lots," Jenny gushed. "I've thirteen chips."

"Good for you," Peter replied, an ominous smile on his face.

"I keep waiting for him to produce that photo," David said, "but thanks to Carmella he is wasting his time."

"Why don't we finish our drinks and put ten chips on at one go and have a bit of fun?" Jenny suggested. "After all we got them free."

"Let's go," David concurred. "Put them all on if you want. It's a bit of fun!"

Jenny and David approached Mrs Dyson.

"All on – ehm – red, no black," Jenny hesitated.

"I need to know," Mrs Dyson insisted.

"Okay, red," Jenny said.

"I think black," David said.

"Okay, black," Jenny agreed.

"Faites vos jeux!" Mrs Dyson shouted. "Rouge."

"Oh flip!" said David. "I'm sorry."

"Shurely shome mishtake, Meester Bond," Jenny said sympathetically.

"Look, I'll lend you ten more," Peter Scerri insisted, appearing from nowhere.

"That's really kind," Jenny accepted.

"Hey, that's 100 Liri!" David reminded her.

"Look. If it doesn't work out, we'll go home," Jenny pointed out. "It's all been a bit of fun. I know when to stop. If we lose we'll pay Peter 50 Liri each."

David was happy at that and they headed back to the roulette wheel.

"Okay. Which colour?" David asked.

"Ehm, red," said Jenny. "It must be red!"

"Faites vos jeux!" Mrs Dyson cried.

The wheel turned and turned. The ball seemed to bounce around interminably.

"Noir!" Mrs Dyson shouted.

"Oh God!" David exclaimed.

"How are you getting on?" Carmella asked with Sacha in tow.

"We're going home," David said. "We've just lost 100 flipping Liri!"

"Rather more, I should say," Mrs Dyson interrupted authoritatively.

"Which chips did you use?" Carmella asked anxiously.

Jenny pointed out the black ones.

"Oh no!" Carmella put her hand to her mouth. "David, that's 100,000 Liri. Who gave you them? Oh, don't tell me. Peter?"

David stood motionless in horror. Jenny had lost all colour in her face.

"Do you wish to settle up now?" Peter asked, as he returned, whisky in hand. "I take cash, cheque, credit card .... or a gold bar! I'll give you 24 hours," he said pointedly.

"You can't blackmail me," David insisted. "I've told Jenny about the photo of Carmella and me."

"The naked one in each other's arms?" he asked rhetorically.

Jenny turned, tears welling up in her eyes and ran out of the casino. David ran after her. "It's rubbish, it's rubbish! You know it is. Ask Carmella!" he kept shouting after her, but to no avail.

As she reached the bay opposite the apartments, she turned. "Cath and Ashlie told me, in confidence, about you and Carmella. I suppose you didn't kiss her in Mellieha gardens either?"

David stood dumbfounded.

"You can't answer, can you?"

With that, Jenny, tears streaming down her face, took off her engagement ring and threw it in the darkness on to the anonymous sands below. "I will pack up my things and leave on next Thursday's flight!" she screamed. "It's over David!"

David just stood numb. The bells of St Mark's chimed 11. He leaned against the wall and looked at the black water lapping against the dark sands. He'd had what? 48 hours of happiness? Now he had lost Jenny, would have to sell the gold bar or end up heavily in debt. He headed back disconsolately along to his room on automatic pilot.

Jenny was pushing all her clothes into her suitcase. "If I've forgotten anything you can send it to me, in, well, wherever I am."

She headed off down the corridor, a pair of tights hanging out of her case. David lay on the bed, turned out the bed headlight, took a swig from his can of coke, and dozed off.

David gazed at the plaque at the foot of the statue. "Gone but not forgotten – Jenny" he said to no one in particular.

This girl had exploded into his life and now she had gone. He walked across the road to the sea wall. And where amongst all that sand was that beautiful ring? What a complete and utter idiot he had been. As Mark and Laura came out of the front door, Danny arrived in his BMW.

"Why on earth has Jenny phoned to resign?" he asked incredulously as he got out. "Where is she?"

"In my room," Laura replied to David's surprise.

"I ended up on the Captain's floor," Mark explained.

Suddenly, Jenny appeared with a sullen face. She pointedly avoided all eye contact with David and sat at the feet of the statue.

Before anyone could speak, a police car appeared. Immediately Danny looked anxious. An elderly policeman got out clutching a clipboard which made him look important.

"I am Constable Borg" he said. "You get more Borgs in Malta than on Star Trek," Mark pointed out.

"We have more constables that an art gallery but I must move on," he replied. "I am part of a major investigation" he said importantly. "I am looking for stolen statues. Have you seen one, Danny?"

"Ours is legit," Danny assured him. "I have all the papers."

Jenny, trying to look detached from the conversation, leaned back on Joan of Arc's sword, which promptly fell off.

"Oh no! It looks as if she's giving a v-sign," David groaned.

There was a brief encouraging flicker of a smile on Jenny's face, then it was gone as quickly as it had come.

"Excuse me Danny. You didn't have your lights on," the Policeman said, suddenly going off at a tangent.

Danny stared in disbelief. "It is 8.45 am, in broad daylight, officer."

"Oh I am sorry, Danny. I've been on nights. I keep forgetting! Well, if anyone sees a statue of the Queen Mother and Christopher Columbus, do report it to me," he reaffirmed.

PC Borg got into his car and drove off with his headlights on.

"Right you lot," Danny said, "get your group off to Valletta market and I'll have a long chat with my favourite courier."

David looked at Jenny but she made a face. With heavy heart he walked along the sands with Mark and Laura looking at his feet as he went.

"When we come back we'll have a look for your ring," Laura assured him. "And we'll have to discuss how you raise 100,000 Liri by tonight."

"Jenny explained to you then" David inferred.

"There's only one way" Mark confirmed. David shrugged in resignation.

"We'd all be loaded" Laura reminded him.

David simply wasn't in the mood to take the mike and do a commentary, so he gave it to Mark sitting with Laura to his left and then stared vacantly out across St George's Bay. Laura counted everyone including the Captain and Theresa on and the coach headed off.

"I've got a text from Carmella," Laura said suddenly. "She must have been at a Star Trek convention!"

"Let's see," David asked, intrigued, as the mobile was thrust under his nose.

"Look" Laura said, "It reads 'SPOK TO JEN ABOUT HER SCOTTIE. ALL GR8. SPNT NIT WITH SACH.'"

Mark looked too. "She's saying she's cleared things up with Jenny. Thank God, and Sacha has scored. He told me he was getting his chips not his oats," Mark laughed.

David cheered up no end. He hadn't fancied telling his family the engagement had collapsed after 48 hours! The coach sped on through Sliema and towards Valletta.

"You know, you've such a lot to learn about women," Mark stressed. "Look at Laura and Jenny. If you wrote a book about them you'd have to call it Clash of The Tantrums, for heaven's sake."

"I must admit I do not fully understand the species. Look at Cath and Ashlie. You ask them to keep a secret and they tell every single person in confidence," David confirmed.

Laura made a face.

"They have different brains," Mark explained. He paused as the bus bounced over a pot hole.

"How so?" David asked.

"Look, if I was to have lunch with Steven and I asked him where he got the meat, he'd say logically Feruggia the butcher's. If I asked my dear Laura at lunch where she'd got her meat she would reply, 'Why what's wrong with it!'"

"Yeh, I suppose that's true," Laura nodded.

"Have you ever seen a woman run for a bus or throw a ball in a park?" Mark asked, warming to his theme.

"Point made," David agreed.

"Look, we'll go to the florists in Valletta market and choose some flowers and patch things up with her. Any girl likes to be pampered and making up can be a lot of fun," Laura said, presumably with experience.

Tony drove the coach into Valletta bus station and everyone made a move to get off.

"I'm off to the Co-Cathedral as Father Collina is helping at a sung mass," Theresa announced.

"I'll look around the market with you," the Captain said, folding up his Telegraph and Times of Malta."

"I widnae mind gettin' a cheap fitba' strip," Gregor pointed out.

"Where are the souvenirs?" Cath and Ashlie asked.

"At least we won't have to spend our hard-earned cash on Sacha," Laura reminded Mark and David.

David walked along the stalls with the Captain.

"Have you seen today's paper?" the Captain asked. "There's talk of a power cut tonight."

"We'd better get some candles or a new torch," David suggested.

"What else is in the paper?" Laura asked politely.

"Malta may spend £120 million on new Hawk trainers," the Captain read out loud.

"That's a hell of a price for footwear these days," Laura commented.

"If you had a brain you'd be dangerous," Mark pointed out, as he caught them up. "I've actually got a couple of torches. Could you carry them, love?"

"What did your last slave die of?" Laura asked.

"Answering back!" Mark replied, handing her a bag.

David noticed that a group of Indians were standing around a souvenir stall. "I've never seen Indians in Malta," David said.

"I haven't seen any cowboys either. Oh, I see what you mean," Laura said.

"They work in those electronic firms at Birkikara," Mark told them.

Not one seemed to be enjoying these Maltese cheese pies and one or two had even put then in a litter bin.

"The Injuns cannae take it, Captain," Gregor said as he passed by in an Inter Milan top.

"Oh another text from Carmella!" Laura announced excitedly.

"Let me see it here!" David demanded almost impolitely in his urgency. "Jen hippy. Nose we wernt in nud. GR8! GSOH. Sach good cok."

"Jen's a hippy," Laura deciphered.

"And Sacha's got a good …….." Mark began.

"She has hit the wrong letter to spell happy and Sacha is a good cook. More importantly she loves me again," David said. His heart leapt in his chest. "Can I text back on your mobile, Laura?"

"Damn, I'm out of cred!" Laura said.

"We can nip along to Republic Street and get some," Mark suggested. "The tourists will be in the market another hour yet."

"I'll just get the flowers bought," Laura reminded them.

As they headed through the grand fortified entrance into Republic St, thronged with the locals, many in their Sunday best heading to or from mass, Mark had an unpleasant reminder for David.

"So what is your plan about raising 100,000 Liri?"

"I am still waiting for that miracle. Something will turn up."

"You've had your miracle," Mark declared. "A gold bar, for heaven's sake. How big a miracle do you need?"

"The ghost could not have asked us to engage in an immoral act," David assured him.

They broke off as David nipped into a sweet shop and came out with Laura's mobile topped up.

"Can I send her a text?" he implored.

"Of course," Laura smiled.

He tapped out, 'I luv u. BTW. We'll not fall out again k. LOL David xx'.

The reply soon came back. 'I luv u 2. Cum soon. Jen'.

"Come on, I'll treat you to a meal," David suddenly insisted magnanimously as he led them to his favourite café.

They sat down and a frazzled looking waitress approached.

"A Marsovin red wine and we'll see the menu, please."

"Do you really believe you saw a ghost?" Laura returned to the subject, kicking off her flip-flops. "Call me a Coptic but I don't really believe in them."

"A sceptic," David said. "What do you think, Mark? Do you think I am seeing things?"

"I know you genuinely believe you saw one, but as I am not on the militant wing of the Anglican Church, I really don't know, sorry."

"How do you explain the message and the gold bar then?" David demanded to know.

"Hey, here comes Father Collina and he has a carburettor on his head," Laura interrupted.

"A biretta!" Mark corrected her. "Come and sit down."

David waved as the good Father, with Theresa in tow, slowed to have a look at the menu.

"They do a lovely quiche here," Theresa declared, pointing to a trolley in the corner.

"Do join us," said David. "We're about to order."

The waitress returned to the table.

"What is your name, child?" Father Collina asked kindly.

"Lorraine," she replied.

"I will have a quiche Lorraine, Lorraine."

"And we'll all have a quiche Lorraine, Lorraine, Lorraine and chips too," Laura said.

The waitress wrote in her book, shrugged and headed back to the kitchen.

"Would you like to say, Grace?" Father Collina asked.

"Grace," replied Laura helpfully.

"It's a prayer," Theresa groaned. She looked down at the table and closed her eyes. "Bless us, oh Lord, and these thy gifts which we are about to receive from your bounty, through Christ, our Lord, amen!"

Lorraine returned to the table with the quiches.

"And I'd like bread and butter pudding," Father Collina insisted.

The waitress looked uneasy. "We don't have it on the menu, Father."

"Well, you did when I came here with the Bishop," he reminded her.

"I'll see what I can do." The young lady blushed and headed off to the kitchen.

"Father," said Mark, "Collina is an Italian name. Did you come from Italy?"

"I did"

"Why?" Mark persisted.

"I came here to forget."

"To forget what?" Laura asked.

"I've forgotten," Father Collina replied and blew on his hankie. "Now Laura, my child, I've something to say to you. I have detected, shall we say, a little bulge. Good news, I would suggest. Am I right?"

"Yes Father," She blushed.

"Then I would like to marry you."

Laura almost choked on her quiche and looked aghast.

"It's alright," Theresa assured her. "He has married so many young women."

"But," she spluttered, "You are a Priest and so old. Anyway I love Mark. I am sorry."

Theresa looked in disbelief. "He means to officiate at the wedding, you stupid girl," Theresa explained.

"Oh. That's okay then," Laura said in relief.

"Now I have something to say to you all before there is any animosity between Danny's lot and Peter's lot and, above all, any more talk of miracles" Father Collina said. "I spoke to the Bishop today and he is not happy about talk of a ghost, that statue or miracles. We live in a rational age. The church demands strict tests."

"Would they send a papal bull?" Mark asked.

"How could we feed it?" Laura asked.

"I'm not getting sidetracked," Collina continued determinedly. "I want to see all of you at the apartments at say 8 pm and we'll bring the whole matter to an end."

"Cool" said Laura. "It'll be like the end of an Agatha Christie film when Poirot calls everyone together, solves the clues, and points to the guilty party."

"Then, it is all arranged," the Priest smiled. "Now, am I getting that pudding or not?"

David could not wait to get back to the apartments to see Jenny. He sat with the flowers on his lap all the way back and kept glancing at Laura's mobile in anticipation of any further texts. Eventually, having dropped off the party at the St Julian's Hotel, and accepted without challenge Hank's view that if Malta had hot dogs and a McDonalds it constituted civilisation, he moved at speed along the lane towards the apartments.

As he reached the seawall, he was surprised to see Carmella on her hands and knees peering at the sand. He leapt down the steps and smiled broadly. Apparently Sacha was further up the beach with a child's bucket and spade. Sacha nodded that he was aware David had arrived. Carmella gave him a very distinctive look, the sort of knowing look which is unambiguous. She picked herself up and dusted the sand off her denim blue shorts. She looked stunning and the smell of suntan lotion and deodorant would have knocked you dead at twenty paces.

"Are you looking for the ring?" he asked.

"Of course, David, it's the least I could do."

"And Sacha?"

"I could not explain what I was doing but he has made a sandcastle and moat. David, I saw Jenny after I texted her. She is alright. We've been hours looking for the ring. Even Danny helped. Jenny's only gone to the toilet. Wait a moment and she'll be back. As for me, I reckon Scerri is bound to sack me now. I'm meant to be the courier on a trip to Mosta and I am here," she said resignedly.

Suddenly, the searchlight at the entrance came on, as it did ludicrously even in the day time. Jenny hesitated. She looked as though she'd been crying. David recognised instantly that she had her khaki jacket and shorts on so the threat of resignation had clearly been rescinded. She saw the flowers and ran towards David pinning him to the sea wall.

"I love you. I am so sorry," she gushed.

With Carmella behind Jenny she gave him a glance, the sort of glance that gives everything away, that if circumstances had been different ....

"How wonderful life is when you're in my world," David said and gave her the flowers.

"Was I your first love?" Jenny asked.

"Music was my first love and it will be my last," David replied, frantically trying to think of another relevant song title.

"If I could turn back time," Jenny laughed.

"The Hot dogs go on," David sang.

"Eh?"

"From Titanic. The only sea lion which ever made number one in the charts."

Jenny still looked blank.

"Sealion Dion, get it?"

Jenny sniffed the flowers. "Carmella told me everything. How they may have doped your drink. The fake photo and the scam with the casino chips. I was wrong to doubt you. I'm still worried about Peter's demand for that huge sum though."

"You needn't be," David assured her, walking her back to the apartments. "We saw Father Collina in Valletta and he has called everyone together this evening. He says he will settle it. Right, let's get some tomato soups from the machine. We'll be back in a moment to help with the search!" he shouted back to Carmella.

By the time they returned to the sands, Mark and Laura had joined them.

"This is going to be hopeless, you know," Mark said pessimistically. A few metres away, a group of youngsters were playing with a football and churning up the sand. "And there's the evidence" he continued.

"It's only fair I should pay for the ring," Jenny said, downcast.

"We haven't given up yet," David reassured her.

Two hours of searching later in the blinding hot sun of an August afternoon, and with their skin peeling, he was nothing like as confident. They had now covered a large area and Sacha was helping if not actually knowing what the search was for. No one knew the French for ring.

"I had plans this evening," Jenny said.

"Like what?" David asked.

"The World Origami Championships are on TV. It's paper view!"

Everyone groaned and continued running sand through their fingers.

Suddenly a scooter could be heard. It was Marco, clearly on duty in his uniform.

"Bonju!" he shouted as he headed down to the sands. "Tell me you haven't lost the gold bar."

"Hardly," David replied. "We're trying to find an engagement ring."

"How can I help?"

"Can we all go and sit in your kitchen?" he asked mysteriously. All six trooped along, intrigued, and Laura put the kettle on."

"I'll come straight to the point. I want you to hand over the gold bar before anyone tries to sell it and gets in terrible trouble."

"You know all about getting folk into trouble," Carmella reminded him.

"Let's keep to the point," he said firmly.

Mark, Laura and Jenny said nothing so David went up to his bedroom. He removed it from the old rusty torch and returned to the kitchen. Laura had the coffees out on his return.

"Should we shut the Venetian blinds in case folk see it?" Jenny asked.

"There's no need," Marco said, picking it up and then throwing it in the air and catching it. "It's not a gold bar!"

"What do you mean?" David asked incredulously.

"Yes, explain yourself," Mark demanded.

"Didn't you ever weigh it?" Marco asked. "It is not heavy enough."

Everyone looked at everyone else.

"I don't understand" David said, crestfallen. "So much for my miracle."

"Or your ghost," Laura reminded him.

"Or message," Mark added.

"So what is it?" Jenny asked.

"It's a clever Italian SWW cigarette case made from part of a shell and it resembles a gold bar – clever, eh?"

"So, why would Carmen have put it in a torch as a youngster?" David asked.

"Her family came into money suddenly," Marco explained. "Her parents did find a gold bar, and when she and Ariadne found this they probably concluded that they too had an investment for the future. When they got older they'll have realised it was worthless. She must have had a smile when you were so determined to con her out of it, David."

"Well, I hope Father Collina has a real solution this evening," Jenny said, "because there's little point Danny having pilgrims coming to his statue anymore."

"I still believe I saw something that night," David repeated, aware all support in the room had evaporated.

"Okay, let's help you look for your ring," Marco said cheerfully.

"I'll put out our candles and torches in the kitchen," Mark said. "We've got that power cut later on, remember."

"The ladies of the night won't be complaining though!" Marco laughed.

Two more hours of searching turned up nothing, and all four couriers felt tired, sticky and distinctly fed up as they sat in the kitchen having bacon rolls before the electricity went off. Marco and Carmella promised to return later and Scerri had agreed to turn up. The Captain and Theresa had been spotted in the lounge bar so they were on the premises. By the time they were washing the dishes, they all smiled when they saw the Captain waving his stick to activate the entrance lights and then dashing to the sands to have a look for the ring, before the light expired again. Mark got some candlesticks from Theresa, and Laura arranged some Gozitan red wine and almond biscuits.

At 8 pm on the dot, all power was lost.

As the four couriers sat at the table waiting for everyone to arrive, Mark articulated what everyone was clearly thinking. "This is awfully like a séance!" he suggested.

"I can't see my flowers but I can smell them," Jenny said holding David's hand in the dark.

Mark instinctively reached for Laura's too.

"I'm scared of the dark" Laura admitted.

"But you don't believe in ghosts," David reminded her.

"Yeh, but it's eerie," Laura explained.

Someone could be heard approaching the door.

"Could this be Father Collina?" Mark asked.

The door creaked open. Both Mark and David shone their torches at the face.

It was the Captain. "I am willing to keep looking for your ring when the beach is quiet" he offered.

"Have you another torch?"

"Yeh, in my room," Mark replied. "It's on the bedside cabinet. Our door is open."

As he headed off, Theresa came in and poured herself some red wine.

Laura looked out of the window. "I can see Marco parking his scooter," she announced.

Peter Scerri came in with Carmella in tow. David couldn't really see her but he recognised that perfume instantly. He was suddenly aware that Father Collina had taken the chair opposite. The room was getting crowded.

"I hope the electricity will come on again soon or everything in our freezer will melt," Laura, said returning to her seat.

"Are we all here?" the Priest asked in a croaking voice which suggested laryngitis. That sung mass had obviously been a strain. His face was lit up by the flickering candles.

"We haven't got Danny" Theresa said, some surprise in her voice.

"This room is so dark, you wouldn't know," Mark laughed.

"Just phone him," Laura offered. "Here's my mobile."

"I've never actually used one," the old Priest replied. "How do I speak into it?"

Laura dialled the number and held it up for him.

"Is anyone there?" the Priest asked.

Suddenly, the door thumped loudly twice. David jumped in his seat.

"Oh my God!" Laura shrieked, "He's brought back the dead!"

"Don't talk utter rot," Theresa commanded.

"One knock for yes, two for no," Mark chuckled.

The door creaked open.

"It's Ariadne," Theresa announced.

"It's Ariadne, oh my God, David was right, it's the ghost!" Laura was hysterical and began to sob.

David and Mark shone their torches in the newcomer's face.

Instinctively, the stranger blinked and turned away.

"I was wrong to disbelieve you!" Laura shouted, holding her hands over her eyes.

David wanted to interrupt to point out this person was nothing like the apparition he'd witnessed on the roof but there was no stopping Laura whose performance was met in stunned silence by her audience.

"Father I confess everything. The night I spent with Scerri to try and get a job, telling Danny I'd years of experience as a courier, getting pregnant to trap Mark, the hot torrid nights with Marco, jamming the toaster in the mornings deliberately hoping we'd get a new one, muttering under my breath about Theresa's condescending attitude and getting that Des O'Connor CD from my Mum and enjoying it. It's horrible, horrible!" she splurted.

"She enjoyed a Des O'Connor record? That's gross!" Mark groaned.

"I'm shocked," Father Collina added.

"I thought she had better taste" David suggested.

"Gosh, she knows the word 'condescending'" Theresa said in awe.

"The nights were that good?" Marco repeated.

David was aware that a wind was getting up and the Venetian blinds rattled. There was a peal of thunder in the distance. It was as atmospheric as it was unusual in mid-August and it made the candles flicker.

Father Collina switched on the kettle. "Ariadne is Danny's daughter," he pointed out.

David could see that Laura's reaction had clearly unnerved Ariadne.

"Yes, I am. I've never had such a reaction in my life," the young woman said.

"Best get some sweet tea," Theresa suggested as she and Laura came back in and took their seats.

"You haven't seen a ghost. It's only Danny's daughter," Mark repeated.

"I am so sorry," Laura apologised. "The atmosphere got to me. There's something creepy here in the dark!"

David was pondering why the door was creaking so much. It, more than anything, had, as Laura said, made it feel creepy. Mind you, he had never sat quietly in the dark in the kitchen before. He wondered if Mark was making it creak with his feet.

The tea was ready and David got up and peered out of the window. He could just make out the Captain scouring the sands with the torch. There was an awkward silence in the room. David could smell Carmella's gorgeous perfume as it competed with the smell of the candles. He could make out Collina's scrawny hands accentuated in the candlelight.

"I have brought you all together as I have something to say to you all," Father Collina said rather theatrically. "Ariadne, you can represent your Dad and tell him later what I've said. Laura, are you alright?"

"I am, Father," Laura said sipping her cup of tea.

"But just not that mentally stable," Ariadne whispered.

"Don't be cruel," Theresa uncharacteristically retorted.

"Can we continue?" the Father said exasperated. "I must be somewhere else soon."

At this time of night, David wondered.

"For years I have watched the competition between Danny and you, Peter, and I have felt impotent."

"I'd a boyfriend like that once," Laura said helpfully. "He took matters into his own hands."

"Sh!" demanded Theresa impatiently.

"But now I must intervene. If Danny decides to have a statue outside his own apartments giving a V sign and with a ridiculous plaque in front, that is up to him. And if you, Peter, want to share the costs or takings, fine, but what I will not have, is any more talk of a miracle!" he emphasised.

"The orphans will miss out," Scerri protested. He had been so quiet, David had wondered if he'd dozed off!

"That's as maybe," Collina retorted having clearly considered the downside.

A candle went out and Jenny rummaged in a kitchen drawer for matches.

"Look" Collina went on, "You all know full well what a miracle is. You all know how the bomb came through the roof at Mosta Dome during a mass and didn't explode. You have all seen the abandoned crutches at Ta Pinu, evidence that believers can walk unaided after years of disability and suffering. Frankly, I want no more talk of Angels, wings, halos, beams of light, secret messages and – heaven help me – a magic wand!"

There was a pause. Collina seemed to shut his eyes for a moment of contemplation.

"Now, I have something to say to each of you individually" he croaked. "Theresa, you are a lovely woman."

"Thank you," came the surprised voice in the corner.

"But, where do you think you go wrong?"

There was a stunned silence. "I suppose I am patronising. It means I talk down to folk."

"There. That wasn't difficult," Collina said. "And you have started the ball rolling. Who'll go next?"

"I've done mine," Laura reminded everyone.

"Accepted," Mark acknowledged on her behalf.

Again there was silence. Thunder claps continued some distance away.

"You've had so many scams, Peter, may I focus on one? When the Bishop came to the casino and you told him the chips were worth thousands"

"I am sorry" Peter said glumly.

"And so you will withdraw your similar claim against David?"

"I suppose so," came the reluctant reply.

David heaved an audible sigh of relief. Indeed it blew out one of the candles. Jenny got the matches out again.

"And will you stop trying to ruin Danny's businesses by devious means?"

"If he does too, I will shake on it."

"He's not trying to ruin his own businesses, you stupid man; oh I am sorry," Theresa apologised realising her promise moments earlier.

Again there was a pause. A fishing boat could be heard passing St George's Bay outside.

"Okay, I've sold stuff for profit we confiscated at customs," Marco volunteered. "That's how I got my scooter. I am so ashamed, Father."

"And the Gold bar?" the Priest prompted him.

David sat bolt upright. "It was a Gold bar! You cheat!" he exclaimed leaping to his feet dramatically.

"Let him speak," Theresa commanded. "Sit down!"

"I'd planned to sell it on to Peter Scerri and get the commission."

David heard Scerri groaning in the darkness.

"But now you will hand it to the Authorities," Father Collina encouraged him.

"Yes," he replied quietly.

"And you, David?"

As the tension grew, David had been rehearsing in his mind what to say, but he was hardly going to confess he had always fancied Carmella.

"Yes, I was involved in the miracle scam," he conceded.

"And so was I," Mark added.

"And I did the Sarah substitution at the football match," Jenny dived in.

"I fancied Carmella and hoped my gold bar commission would allow me to treat her luxuriously," Marco pointed out.

"Yeh I fancied her too," Mark said.

Laura groaned. David stayed quiet.

"And so did someone else," Collina prompted again.

How does Collina know all this? David wondered.

"Eet was moi," Sacha interrupted.

David was relieved. He'd started to feel sweaty as he grew more anxious.

"I'd forgotten you were there," David admitted.

"And I, how you say, did things terrible" Sacha went on. "At the wine factory I had piss."

"You found peace," Collina tried to translate.

"Non, monsieur, I did piss in ze wine."

"Gross!" Carmella gasped.

"Yuck!" Jenny added.

"And you now, Carmella?" Collina singled her out.

"I carried out Peter's awful scams and now I am sacked. I bedded a number of people in my room. I am sorry. Now there will be none, I promise."

"You will be a nun?" Collina misheard.

"No I meant there will be no more. I've found happiness in Sach."

"Does she mean the sack?" David speculated.

Again, the unusually muffled bell of St Mark's rang out and thunder cracked. Father Collina seemed startled.

"I must go," Collina said, suddenly pushing his seat back and standing up. "Remember the importance of forgiveness, let today be a starting point, and, above all, only ever talk of a miracle if you genuinely witness one. There would be a sign you could not miss."

"I'm sorry my Dad hasn't made it," Ariadne apologised. "This session would have done him good."

They watched him disappear into the darkness, then Jenny refilled the wine glasses.

"Father Collina had his own little miracle in Valletta today" Theresa said, sniffing the wine professionally.

"What was that?" David asked.

"He has managed to buy that painting which frightens all the tourists of the man on the death bed with the two pictures of good and bad Angels approaching, and he'll put it up as a backdrop to St Mark's high altar.

"Oops!" said Laura as she spilled her wine in the pitch dark.

"I am sorry I said you were mental. That was so rude of me," Ariadne conceded.

"I accept your apology. It happens all the time," Laura smiled graciously. "I just feel so stupid now. But something wasn't right this evening. I just know it."

"You are certainly persistent, I'll give you that," Mark said, giving her a hug.

"Look, you can have your job back, Carmella," Scerri finally conceded. He gulped down his wine and they prepared to leave. He looked at the glass. "It's not poisoned then! Sorry, old ways die hard, eh?"

"Look, I feel so bad," Marco sighed. "I was driven by greed. I'll make it up to you." He put on his crash helmet and headed out, following Sacha who had taken a bottle of wine with him.

"You know, all that's happened this evening is incredulous," Laura said.

"Incredible," Theresa corrected her.

"Oh sorry, there I go again," she apologised. "What ever it was, I tell you something wasn't quite right" Laura continued determinedly.

"You know what I've been wondering all evening?" David chipped in, "How could Father Collina have known about the gold bar, and why did we get that lecture on forgiveness?"

"Haven't you worked it out yet?" Theresa said, finishing her wine. "His Father was the pilot of that Italian Fighter."

"And the forgiveness he alluded to?" David added.

"It was the Captain who shot him down. It can't have been at all easy to forgive. Once he became a priest in his Rome seminary, he was posted to Malta and eventually met up with the Captain. It is a small island after all."

"I still wish my Dad had been here," Ariadne returned to her theme. "But some old friend died in St Luke's hospital this afternoon and he was away to pay his respects. I'd better get back."

Suddenly, a great shout came up from the beach.

"I've found it!" The Captain was racing, if that was the word, back towards the steps at the sea wall.

"Oh my God, he has too!" Jenny cried as she gleefully took if from him and put it on using the beam of the torch.

"I've been out here for four hours in these peculiar weather conditions," the Captain declared, rubbing his hands. "I need a whisky! I don't know why it has been so cold and that breeze has fairly got up."

"I can't thank you enough," Jenny repeated, putting it on her finger and admiring it.

"Come and see!" David shouted to Mark and Laura to join them. Jenny was almost dancing for joy. "I'll gladly buy you a drink, Captain" David offered. "I've some questions to ask you too about the war."

They headed back to the entrance and suddenly all the lights came on. A huge cheer rang round the building.

"Well, I won't need this now," the Captain said, handing David the torch. As Mark, Laura and Jenny took their seats at the bar Steven reminded them there were no ice cubes as David got a round in.

Suddenly he stared in utter disbelief at the torch. "Who gave you this?" he asked as he held up the rusted Italian silver one.

The Captain looked quizzical. "Don't you remember, Mark told me to go up to his room and take it out of the bedside cabinet."

"Captain, it's mine!" David gasped. He felt a chill run up the back of his spine. He felt his chest tighten.

"Oh I apologise, old boy," the Captain said picking up his whisky and acknowledging Theresa entering the lounge. He was totally oblivious to what David was telling him. "I must have simply chosen the wrong room. It had a strong beam though."

"Captain it doesn't have a bloody battery in it." David would normally have felt embarrassed at his resorting to an expletive but the hairs on the back of the neck had stood on end. His heart had leapt in his chest. He unscrewed the top then shook it to reinforce the point.

"Captain, our gold bar was all that was contained in this torch." He picked up his lager, left the speechless old man, and rushed across to his three young companions.

"You are not going to believe what I am about to tell you" he said loudly, interrupting their conversation.

"It had better be good because we're all discussing how creepy our evening has been," Laura complained. "I won't be able to sleep alone in my bed tonight."

"Suits me," Mark replied with a twinkle in his eye.

David beckoned the Captain to join them and as he elaborated on the story, Mark, Laura and Jenny sat in open-mouthed silence. No one even began their drink.

"You know I am finally beginning to understand that ghostly message," David confirmed.

"And what Father Collina told us about a miracle being verified," Mark added.

"It's well creepy," Laura said unnecessarily.

The Captain had a double whisky in one go and then rejoined Theresa to tell it all again at the bar.

"You know what has troubled me all night," Jenny said thoughtfully. "How did Father Collina put on that kettle during the power cut to give Laura and Ariadne sweetened tea?"

Before they could answer, a flustered Danny entered the lounge bar, white-faced, with his daughter in tow. Ariadne looked as if she'd been crying.

"Whatever is wrong?" the Captain asked.

"And why couldn't you join us this evening?" Theresa added.

As they spoke, Danny signalled for a brandy, and gulped it down. Then he got another. "I told Ariadne to tell you, there was this sad bereavement" he spluttered. "I'd to pay my respects."

"Anyone I know?" Theresa asked.

"Father Collina!" Danny said and paused for theatrical effect. "He died this afternoon."

David put his hand to his mouth.

"This afternoon? Are you sure, Danny?" David asked, that chill up his spine returning.

"Of course I am sure, man. I was there, for heaven's sake. I was at the Bishop's Palace in Valletta and the Bishop, Father Collina, Mrs Dyson, the Bishop's housekeeper and I were playing a game of charades. Well Father Collina had a massive heart attack but we thought it was a superb mime!"

"That's shocking," David concurred. "That woman has too many part-time jobs at her age."

Danny looked perplexed. "Anyway, that's why I want you all to explain to me why you are holding a séance in my kitchen and, according to my daughter, bringing the tormented soul back. I have to say, I am surprised at you, Theresa."

But Theresa had not only taken a swig of Danny's brandy, she had flopped in her armchair and now kept repeating, "I do not believe it," like some demented Victor Meldrew! Then she picked up the Captain's whisky and drank it in one go too.

"It really happened," David said. "I don't understand it, but it did happen. All of us were there Ariadne was there. Ask her."

"I don't actually know him, remember?" Ariadne said, "But I accept everyone called him by that name and he responded to it."

"Ask Peter Scerri, Carmella, Marco, Sacha," Mark reeled off the names to reinforce the point. "There was no lack of witnesses."

"Then we have our miracle," Danny said, collapsing into an armchair.

"Captain, didn't you see Father Collina leaving the apartments half an hour ago?" David asked, looking for confirmation.

"Well of course not. How could I have done? We all heard what Danny said," the Captain replied sadly.

Outside the thunder cracked and the flags bent in the near gale which had intensified. The rain spat against the windows.

"And what was the point of the evening? Why would Father Collina want to see you all before he took his leave?" Danny enquired.

"Forgiveness," Laura replied. "To err is human, to forgive, bovine," she explained.

"Stupid cow," Theresa retorted. "Sorry I'm being rude. I'm pissed," she quickly added.

"I'll say my goodnights," the Captain said, touching his peaked cap.

Outside the peal of bells stopped. It suddenly got warmer, thunder ceased and the gale evaporated.

"I'll get you home, Theresa," said Danny gallantly. He and Ariadne helped her staggering out to the entrance.

"The funeral will be in two days," Danny announced.

"We'll all be there," David confirmed.

The four young couriers sat down and Steven refilled their drinks.

"So the funeral is in two days but there's one thing worrying me," Jenny said.

"What is it?" Laura asked.

"It's a service for dead folk."

"No, what is worrying you?" Laura persisted.

"I have to look at that awful picture again."

"They'll only display the nice version, I am sure," David predicted. "And if we're never to see the flip side, we must all stop our scams," he chuckled.

"Done!" they all agreed and held their hands together above the centre of the table.

"That reminds me," said Mark. "My olds are coming out for a week mainly to meet my fiancé. Hey, Jenny, could you pretend you are Laura?"

Laura threw a beer mat at him and poked out her tongue.

"And on that note, let's call it a night," Jenny suggested.

David finished his glass and they walked hand in hand for comfort through the entrance and then slowly along the sands enjoying a breath of fresh air. Then they sat for a while on Danny's upturned rowing boat.

"Will you stay on once this season is over?" he asked nervously.

"Of course," Jenny replied without hesitation. "There is no way I would ever miss all this excitement and return to rainy Bridlington. Our jobs are assured and I am getting the hang of this courier lark! I just wonder what we have all witnessed tonight. It was so spooky, David."

"I still find it hard to believe even now," David confessed. "Though Danny confirmed that Collina died this afternoon and we all saw him. Hey, I hope you haven't got paint on my khaki uniform shorts. Danny will have a fit."

"I see you kept the torch in your pocket," Jenny pointed out.

"No I didn't," he grinned.

As they walked back, they activated the flood lights and a figure could be seen stumbling on the roof.

"Don't tell me it's a Ghost!" Jenny gasped.

"No," said Danny appearing from behind the statue, "Theresa is as drunk as a skunk. We drove up to St Mark's to view that painting and the coffin and she saw something which forced her back to the bar and more brandies."

"But it's a happy painting," David protested. "What could possibly have made her flip?"

"One of the Angels in the picture was holding a magic wand," Danny replied. "It was most peculiar."

David and Jenny gave each other a knowing look, grinned and headed back to their room.

"Collina promised a sign that would convince us," David said, "and he has surely done that."

"Yes, well, I've got far more pressing things on my mind," Jenny interrupted. "How do I convince Mark's parents I am Laura?"

"I thought the scams had to stop," David reminded her.

Jenny gave a cheeky look and switched the bedroom light out. "Oh it's not the torch is it!" she whooped.

Lightning Source UK Ltd.
Milton Keynes UK
02 October 2010

160707UK00001B/5/P